QUANTUM GIRL THEORY

QUANTUM GIRL THEORY

A NOVEL

ERIN KATE RYAN

RANDOM HOUSE
NEW YORK

Published in the United States by Random House, an imprint and division of Penguin Random House LLC, New York.

Random House and the House colophon are registered trademarks of Penguin Random House LLC.

Hardback ISBN 9780593133439
Ebook ISBN 9780593133446

Printed in the United States of America on acid-free paper

randomhousebooks.com

2 4 6 8 9 7 5 3 1

First Edition

Book design by Susan Turner

QUANTUM GIRL THEORY

ION EVENING BANNER

BENNINGTON, VERMONT, TUESDAY, DECEMBER 3, 1946

PRICE THREE CENTS

Soviet Russia. It Is Absolutely Impossible That Mr. Molotov Can Know So Many Things Wrong as Mr. Stalin

Missing Student

Paula Welden Missing Since Sunday From College Campus; Search Is Made Over Wide Area

Girl's Father Arrives Here From His Stamford Home

When Last Seen Missing Student Was Wearing Red Parka, Blue Jeans and Thick-Soled Sneakers

---

SDAY, DECEMBER 4, 1946

s Friends Will Do That More Effectively and That It Will Humiliate Him as Effec...

$500 Reward Offered For Information Leading To Location Of Missing Paula Welden; Halt Intensive Hunt On Trail

Keeping Close Contact

(Ottman, Times-Union)
W. Archibald Welden, father of the missing Bennington College sophomore, Pauli, converses on the Banner office phone with authorities in an effort to locate some tangible clue to follow.

Father of Paula Welden Checking on All Leads

Mother of Missing Girl Under Doctor's Care in Stamford Home; Father Maintains Self Control

(By Pete Stevenson)

W. Archibald Welden, father of Paula Welden, who has been missing five days from Bennington College, has caused wonder among those connected directly with the search.

For five days while search parties combed the Long Trail district and the authorities trackd down a multitude of clues from all over New England, Mr. Welden has never at any time lost control of himself.

Mrs. Welden, who is confined to her bed by her doctor in Stamford, is kept posted on latest developments by Mr. Welden who telephones to his home every evening. Mr. Welden on Thursday said that he knew his wife would feel a great deal better when he gave her the news that their daughter was not ... each on Glastenbury mountain.

During daylight, when searchers were combing the Long Trail, the father spent a good deal of time with them and at the same time he kept in touch with search headquarters at Bennington College, so that he might offer any information

Resumes Classes

(Ottman Times-Union)
Miss Elizabeth Johnson of Steamboat Springs, Colorado, roommate of missing Paula Welden at Bennington College, who has been lending her every aid to the ...

(Continued on Page Four)

Father Plans to Contact FBI for Advice and Aid

Conference at College Following Search Concludes Missing Girl Not in Long Trail Area; Nationwide Radio Appeal for Help Considered by W. Archibald Welden

(By Pete Stevenson)

A $500 reward has been offered to anyone providing information which will lead to the location of Paula Welden, Bennington College student missing since last Sunday. This information was made public at 10 o'clock this morning by State's Atty. William Travers Jerome, who said the money had been posted by a friend of the Welden family in Stamford, but he would not disclose the name.

At a press conference last night, College President Lewis Webster Jones stated that the extensive two-day combing of the Long Trail district was now concluded and that the authorities were of the belief the missing girl was not in the area bounded by Glastenbury and Bald mountains. He stated that searchers had done all they could to locate the girl in the region, if she was still there. W. Archibald Welden, the father, said that he was satisfied the search had been well conducted and that no stone had been left unturned. He expressed gratitude to the concentrated efforts made by all those who had conducted the hunt.

At the conclusion of the conference Mr. Jones stated that the next steps to be taken probably would include a nationwide radio appeal by the missing girl's father which is hoped will reach the girl herself, or will be heard by someone who has seen her or who might be with her.

Mr. Welden this morning said he was going to Albany this afternoon to ask advice of the Federal Bureau of Investigation as to what steps they would advise should now be taken. He thought that, though they cannot take up the case themselves because it does not come under their jurisdiction, they might be able to put him on to some organization which might conduct an investigation. With the FBI's experience, he felt, they would give good advice.

Although the widespread search of the Long Trail and surrounding territory had been concluded, Sheriff W. Clyde Peck this morning said that he was going back to the area and that a bus load of Norwich University students from Northfield would arrive here today and would join him.

Step - by - Step With Clues to Missing Girl

(By Pete Stevenson)

Paula Welden told her roommate, Elizabeth Johnson, in Dewey House dormitory on Sunday that she was going for a hike. She was next seen about 2:30 o'clock Sunday afternoon by two College friends who passed her in their car as she walked down the front drive toward highway 67-A. She was next seen by Danny Fager at the College gas station. Mr. Fager reported that she came out through the College gate and turned to her right, walking into some small woods to the top of a knoll. She then turned around and came down the knoll onto the road and headed in the direction of Bennington.

Louis Knapp, Bennington contractor, was the next person who saw her. At about three o'clock she signalled him as he drove toward Bennington on the North Bennington flats and he picked her up. He remembered that she slipped on the rushing board, as she got into his pickup truck and he told her she had better watch her step. They did not converse until they reached Bennington and he then asked her where she wanted to be dropped off. She told him she wanted to get to Route 9 which leads east from Bennington and goes to Brattleboro, 40 miles distant. He said that he was going east, that highway because he lived that way. She said that was fine. She then told him she was making for the Long Trail. Arriving at Mr. Knapp's house, she got out of the truck and he saw her start up the highway in the direction of the entrance to the Long Trail, three miles away.

Mr. Knapp states that he was positive that the girl's identity because of spending a considerable time between the North Bennington flats and his home with the girl. He definitely identified her.

A woman who lives near the Woodford Hollow road that branches from that highway and leads to the Trail said she saw a girl answering to the description walking on the highway and signalling passing cars for a lift.

Next person to report to the authorities was Ernie Whitman, Banner building night watchman who, with three friends, was coming

(Continued on Page Four)

R. N. Thompson, manager of the Vermont Transit bus office in Burlington, assured the Banner this morning that he would contact all the bus drivers who were driving out of Bennington at 2:25 Sunday afternoon in an effort to find out if Miss Welden had boarded any of these buses.

Authorities at Williams College when notified of the missing college student have offered volunteers to look for her in case Miss Welden did not board a bus.

The whereabouts of Paula Welden, 18, Bennington College sophomore and daughter of Mr. and Mrs. W. Archibald Welden of Stamford, Conn., who has been missing from the college campus since Sunday afternoon when she was last seen by students in Dewey hall dormitory, where she resides, remained unknown at noon today.

With the arrival of the girl's father, industrial designer for the Revere Copper and Brass Company of Stamford, authorities here with the aid of college officials and the entire student body joined in an extensive search of the surrounding area. Earlier in the afternoon on Sunday, she had told her roommate, Elizabeth Johnson, that she might take a hike before she pursued her studies.

Apparently when she left the college, she was wearing a red parka, blue jeans and thick soled sneakers, but was not clothed to withstand the freezing temperatures of the past 48 hours.

State's Attorney William Travers Jerome, jr was called to the college Monday noontime by Mrs. Mary Garrett, director of admissions, after the girl had failed to report to classes that morning. Miss Welden did not go to her home in Stamford for the Thanksgiving holidays. It was learned this morning, but stayed at the college.

No reason for her sudden disappearance has been forthcoming although no stone has been left unturned in the investigation. Miss Welden had once mentioned that she would like to visit the Everett out on Mt. Anthony and so a few from the college accompanied by

(Continued on Page Four)

BULLETIN

If Paula Welden, 18-year-old college sophomore, missing from Bennington College since last Sunday, comes to Times Square newspaper stand to purchase her home town paper, the Stamford, Conn. Advocate, Johnny Fowler is on the lookout. It was learned at the Banner office this noontime.

Johnny in his long years of duty and handling of papers from all

Mrs. Jones Delivers

QUANTUM GIRL THEORY

Bennington College, Bennington, Vermont, 1946

On December 1, 1946, Paula Jean Welden put on a bright-red parka, left her dorm for a hike on the Long Trail, and vanished into the thin mountain air of the trailhead.

On December 1, 1946, Paula Jean Welden put on a bright-red parka, left her dorm for a hike on the Long Trail, and was kidnapped by a man with a long maroon car and a history of violence against women.

On December 1, 1946, Paula Jean Welden put on a bright-red parka and left her dorm to take a cab to the bus station, where she set off for Montreal and the impossible idea of being a brand-new girl.

On December 1, 1946, Paula Jean Welden put on a bright-red parka and left her dorm to meet her unkind boyfriend, who carted her to Fall River, blew through her cash, then ditched her for a moment in a diner, where she leaned over the counter and whispered to the waitress how had it come to this.

On December 1, 1946, Paula Jean Welden put on a bright-red

parka, left her dorm, and was quietly institutionalized by a mortified family who'd rather pretend she was dead than admit to her troubled mind.

On December 1, 1946, Paula Jean Welden put on a bright-red parka, left her dorm, and met her botany teacher; after a quarrel over their relationship, he bludgeoned her in a damp clearing deep in the early winter woods.

On December 1, 1946, Paula Jean Welden put on a bright-red parka and ran away to join the circus, where she turned handstands on the backs of galloping horses and learned to tame fire by swallowing it.

Quantum Girl Theory: Once she is gone, a missing girl becomes everything that everyone thinks she might be; our theories create her fate. She's a runaway, she's a maniac, she is bones shrouded in red cloth beneath an evergreen tree. She is a double, triple, quadruple exposure of any lifetime anyone could dream.

On December 1, 1946, Paula Jean Welden put on a bright-red parka, left her dorm, and began to exist by disappearing.

And on December 2, the sun rose high and light hit the spot where the missing girl ought to have been.

The National Guard climbed mountains in search, as did her father, the Boy Scouts, a wily private eye.

Clairvoyants dreamt of her, calling the newspapers to report their visions: ice picks, black cars, an all-consuming fire.

The detective gathered facts: the eldest of four sisters, father a Scotsman (*whispers:* mother a drunk). She preferred to be called Paul, but the Bennington girls rarely called her anything at all. Quiet, studious. Unremarkable.

The hole she left somehow bigger than the space she once filled.

Quantum Girl Theory: A missing girl, by virtue of having endless possible lives, is more real than a non-missing girl, who gets only one life, at most.

Newsmen flooded the rural Vermont town, wingtips sinking into mud. Spectators, readers of the mystery, postured as heroes—they stopped lovely blondes in New York and Charleston; they rounded up white girls in Miami and Spokane. Holding up smudged newspaper snapshots, squinting with suspicion and spite. Gripping the elbows of strangers on opposite coasts, competing to capture the hefty reward, to capture the true Paula Jean—to tell the story's true end.

On December 1, 1946, Paula Jean Welden put on a bright-red parka and shattered into innumerable futures. One life could never be enough.

Quantum Girl Theory: A missing girl's potential life stamps a new world into being. All her paths are possible—they are happening all at once, and in symphony.

Across the nation, newspapers recorded every sighting, writing into existence Paula Jean as a starlet, Paula Jean as a housewife, Paula Jean as a hollow-faced nurse. A misfit, a mistress, a victim, a crime.

At a stained and round dining table, imagine infinite Paula Jeans: aged and cherub-faced, scarred and broken and barely touched. Each looks at the others—a sister, a self. Lives lived and half-lived, lives thrown away, redeemed, or lost.

She is legion.

She reaches across the table and takes her own hand.

nty as
mmit-
to the
lative

nittees
e this
to be

named

Clairvoyant's Tip Leads Father of Paula Welden to Parka Frozen in Walloomsac

Garment Hacked from Ice Not That of Missing College Student, Says W. Archibald Welden

A red, hooded parka was found by W. Archibald Welden late Monday afternoon one half mile from the entrance gate of Bennington College. Following directions given him by a prominent New York clairvoyant, Paula Welden's father came upon the garment sheathed in ice, frozen to a concrete sluiceway on the Walloomsac river. For a few minutes, as he chopped away the ice, it looked as if the 45-day-old mystery had been solved. When Paula left Bennington College December 1 she was wearing a red, hooded parka.

Discovery of the parka came about after a series of almost unbelievable coincidents. Last week, at the suggestion of a friend, Mr. Welden went to New York and visited the clairvoyant. She was not the first psychic he had visited. Two days after his daughter vanished

(Continued on Page Four)

She's 'Not My Daughter', Mrs. Welden Says, After Talk Over Telephone

Mother of Paula of Bennington College Talks With Girl Located in South Carolina

Finding a person closely answering the description of Paula Welden, missing Bennington College student, created an intense interest today in the year-old mystery, but the "bubble" burst when Mrs. W. Archibald Welden, mother of the girl, reported that a girl in Charleston, S. C., Sunday was definitely "not her daughter." This was based on a telephone conversation with the girl who was held by South Carolina state police.

More than unusual significance was attached to the latest story as the girl picked up in the south had registered at a tourist camp under the name of "Mary Welden" and also "Mary Garrett." The latter name is that of the former registrar of the college who is now Mary Garrett Woodburn, director of records and student personnel. The coincidence of the use of the latter name still puzzles local authorities.

Contact with Vermont authorities was made Sunday night with State Detective Almo Franzoni by telegram. State's Attorney James S. Holden was in touch with Mr. Franzoni this morning and asked for a more thorough check by telephone but word had not been received here by press time. An endeavor was made to contact Mr. Welden at his home in Stamford, Conn., but he was on his way to Rome, N. Y., where he is employed by the Rome Manufacturing Company, a branch of the Revere Copper and Brass Company with headquarters in Stamford.

Despite the collapse of the latest attempted identification, Mrs. Wel-

den informed the Associated Press that both she and her husband are confident that Paula is still alive.

No inquiry was received at the college.

SPELLS FOR SINNERS, PART ONE

BLADEN COUNTY, NORTH CAROLINA, 1961

Mary missed her connection in Fayetteville and, still marked from the creases in the bus seat and stinking of diesel, sweet-talked her way into the pickup truck of a lanky Dublin kid headed home for supper. The boy moved to scooch his little brother out of the cab to make room. Mary patted her palm on the open window and leaned against the door to keep the younger boy from opening it.

"I like the fresh air," she said, and tossed her twine-tied valise into the empty truck bed. She dug through her pocketbook for a scarf. "I will take a hand up, though."

The pickup was newish, still shiny under the bus depot street lamp. Mary settled herself atop her case and tied the scarf over her wilting French pleat. She used a folded REWARD poster to clean the road grime from beneath her nails, then ate a mealy apple from her pocketbook, the last of her travel food. She threw the apple core into a field of great black crows and swiveled the band of her watch—5:46. The boy was a conscientious driver and took her the whole way to the Starkings' house in Elizabethtown. After he hoisted her down from the back, Mary offered to write a note to his ma to help explain his tardiness for dinner, to which he aw-shucks'ed and that's-mighty-nice-but-no-thank-you-ma'am'ed. She waited for the truck to turn the corner before she approached the Starkings' door.

Mary would normally have figured a way to take a room in town, to brush her teeth before landing on the doorstep of the family of a missing child. With her ancient broken bag, she looked the part of traveling salesman, a closer cut than she cared for. Mary slid the valise behind the grayed porch swing. A layer of lace and the reflection from the setting sun blocked her view into the front window. She caught movement, though, the brush of a skirt hem. Mary rang the doorbell.

She let up on the bell at the creak of advancing footsteps. Her hand was in her cardigan pocket, gripping the rolled REWARD poster. An unease was building in her gut. The door cracked open.

It was so black inside the house that at first Mary couldn't see who had answered the door. Her eyes at last found a lined and sunbrowned face wearing a neutral expression. The man, white, dressed in a rolled-sleeve work shirt, opened the door a bit wider, filling the gap with his chest. He was chewing, Mary realized, and he didn't offer a greeting.

"Mr. Starking?" She spoke clearly, not trying to hide her New England accent. "I'm Mary Garrett. I'm hoping I can help you find your daughter." She reached out her hand to shake his, and the man slowly returned the gesture. His palm was a deep brown in the creases, not dirty but stained, and he smelled of meat and melted butter.

"You down from Raleigh?" he said through his mouthful, hand still on hers. Mary could hear the scrape of fork on plate inside the house, a woman clearing her throat.

"No, sir. I was traveling in Baltimore and I read about your girl. I have experience with these cases, and I'd like to be of assistance in looking for Polly." The REWARD poster, pulled down from a bus shelter in Richmond, noted a seven-thousand-dollar reward. Enough to set her right for three full years.

Starking held her hand still and finally swallowed his mouthful. "What kind of assistance is that?"

"I have a deep women's intuition, Mr. Starking, and dozens of families have found my services quite valuable. With time to acquaint myself with Polly, I'll be able to provide a great deal of insight to the case. Bring Polly home safe." Mary no longer needed to think as she ran through her customary speech and focused instead on the tension in Mr. Starking's jaw, fluttering like moth wings.

Starking stepped forward, crowding Mary on the porch. She minced back and pulled her hand free from his.

"You telling me you're a lady detective or that you're a clairvoyant?" he asked, so tall above Mary's head that she settled her gaze on his Adam's apple. The evening's stubble was poking forth from his ruddy skin, sharp black hairs that would burn with hard contact, that could rub soft cheeks and necks raw from the friction of it.

"I wouldn't put it in those terms, Mr. Starking." But if he paid her, she'd let him call her whatever he wanted.

"My grandmama was clairvoyant," he said over her, and palmed at his neck. "She had a real gift—burdened her tremendously. Angel at her back, she called it."

Mary waited, hand over wrist, clasped at her waist. She shifted back to give herself more room from the man, swiveled her watch with pointy fingers.

"You can help find our Paul?" Starking's gruffness gave way to a pleading tone.

The name hit Mary like an electric shock, a hard pinch on the bridge of her nose. A wash of warmth crept down her arms. Of course some other girl might have that name, *her* name, the name she'd shed fifteen years earlier when she became Mary Garrett. Mary tried to reason away her body's reaction before she blew her chance here, but she couldn't stop feeling the clench of resentment, of having something ripped from her. An arm thrown across her shoulder, heads tilted toward each other, a sigh of *oh, my Paul,* a swallowed sob.

"What's that, Gurnie?" A woman's voice called from inside the house, weak and impatient at the same time. The woman herself appeared in the open door, fingers smudging an empty water glass. Medium height, moderately plump, flushed pink skin, nondescript but for the grief that Mary felt swirling around her. Her housedress was stained along the skirt, and Mary suddenly saw the tumble of the gravy boat as the woman's fingers lost feeling when she noticed she had set a place for her daughter at the dinner table. A flickering newsreel behind Mary's eyelids, the vision lasted less than a second, but it gave her the beat she needed to recover.

"Mrs. Starking, ma'am," Mary began, extending her hand. "I—"

The man, Gurnie, held out his hand to keep the woman behind him. "You seen my Paul?" he asked, leaning toward Mary. "You get dreams? Visions? You see her?" His voice deepened as he bent, until he nearly swallowed the final word. His demeanor, more expressive now than when he'd opened the door, was still controlled.

My Paul. The sour smell of his dinner turned Mary's stomach. "No, sir, not yet. I'll need some time with you, that's why I'm here—" Mary stopped as she heard the woman draw a breath.

"What's this?" the woman asked, twisting her hands on that water glass, looking mostly at the man. "There's news?"

"Bernice, Mrs. . . . Garrett, was it?" He looked back for confirmation. "Says she's got the Sight and might could find our girl." His voice broke on the word *girl,* and he straightened and leaned back to the chipped clapboard siding. "My brother—"

"Lord, not this story, Gurnie," Bernice said. She tugged at his shirtsleeve. "God knows I don't have it in me for this right now." A plea in her tone shortcut to the whole of their relationship—Gurnie with the wild hairs, Bernice with her deep desire for calm, for happiness in measured teacups. Bernice won most of the time. Mary didn't need a vision to see that.

The text from the REWARD poster nearly a poem to Mary now, so many times she had read it: *Polly Starking, last seen six days back in camp shirt and dungarees, riding a horse from the family farm out past Jones Lake. Horse found, girl missing.* The overexposed photo: soft smile breaking a wide face, a short dark pixie cut, white browline glasses tipped up and to the right of the yearbook's photographer. Exposing a tender neck, still pliant and plump as unkneaded bread dough. While worrying at the poster in Fayetteville, Mary had gotten a flickering vision—the horse, swampy and flustered, wandering the trail alone—that she'd followed all the way to this barely-there town. She was unlikely to get anything more without a visitation to the girl's room, an interview with her parents, a chance to shut out the other noise and focus her mind on Polly. At least half the time, the parents offered up the missing girl's bed for the duration; at others, she was happy to accept a nest of blankets in the parlor. But she'd been without success the past few months, and her savings had dwindled to less than eight dollars.

Nauseated and road-weary, Mary needed time to ingratiate herself; she needed the offer of hospitality to be their own idea. Otherwise, they would expect too much too soon.

"I don't mean to impose on your time so late in the evening," Mary said, voice smooth as glass. What a distance there was, between her ragged insides and her measured demeanor. "Why don't I make an appointment to come back tomorrow a little before lunch? I can telephone, if you'd like. I'll just be staying at the motor inn over"—she took a stab—"near the bank."

"You mean Safe Lodge, then," Gurnie said. He glanced over at Bernice and back at Mary. "I can't have you off on your own, now, nice lady like you. Ain't safe. Not now, not since . . ." and he didn't finish.

And in the end, he declined to call a taxicab for her (it was after six, he said, and Sigsbee had likely already begun his evening drink) and insisted upon taking her himself. As he went back in to grab the keys to his truck, Mary slid her valise down to the curb. The truck, green with white lettering: *Starking Bros. est. 1956.* Mary studied the back of Gurnie's truck, overfilled with sinister-looking farm equipment—thrasher, reaper, tunneler, slicer. There was no avoiding that front seat.

Gurnie gave her a hand up, and as he walked around to the driver's side, Mary installed her valise upright on the bench seat between them, a wall of tweed and twine. She smiled across the top at Gurnie and kept her hand cupped over the door's lock the whole ride. She would have preferred the taxi with the drunken driver, even if she was nearing broke.

"You have a business?" Mary said. She prized silence over chit-chat, but she hadn't learned a damn thing back at the house. The waves of fear and loss coming at her from both Gurnie and Bernice did nothing to exonerate them in Mary's mind. Villains had fears like anyone else.

"Mmph," Gurnie grunted. "With my brother, Clarence. We share the company, the truck, the heartache."

Gurnie interrupted himself to point out the direction of Polly's high school. Mary nodded and adjusted her case.

"Hogs," Gurnie said.

"Hogs," Mary said, matching his matter-of-fact tone.

"What we farm," Gurnie said. "Four miles or so out of town."

They crunched into the lot of the Safe Lodge. Weak neon from the motel sign blued the whole front seat and dash, as though they were sitting side by side at a drive-in movie. Gurnie started to move awkwardly, to clear his throat. Was he about to offer her money for a room? Would she take it? She might just take it. It was less wounding to accept a reward than a handout, but her back was still wretched from two nights on a depot bench and then another on a bus seat.

Yet whatever brewed inside Gurnie never made it out of him. Instead, he coughed into a handkerchief and said, "I do hope you have a dream about my Paul tonight, ma'am. I suspect Bernice might soften to the idea, too. Though anything I could ferry back to her with me tonight would be of great assistance." His hands rested on the bottom curve of the steering wheel; to Mary, fingers like his, long and thin, always looked ready to press on the soft spot of some girl's throat.

"Anything at all that I could pass on," he said.

Because Gurnie was expecting her to, and because she wasn't ready to explain to him how it all worked and how often it didn't, Mary closed her eyes and leaned her head back against the seat, her left elbow propped on the top of the valise. Fatigue washed over her. The start of each of these searches was never an occasion of hope but of grief. Exhaustion layered over mourning. Even Mary's salesman's attitude couldn't barter that truth away.

And then Mary let out a sigh and her chest sank back into hearing this man say *Paul* again and again, what used to be the quiet name whispered to her in the dark, the teasing name offered as a thumb pinched hard at her cheek, pretending to press her a new dimple. Mary had to fight the squeeze of her shoulders each time, a breath of recognition. Of being recognized. The boundary that marked the edge of Mary's self was already worn smooth by years of visions and other girls' pain, and here was a new girl with her own name. Her old name. Mary hadn't been called Paul since the last day of her old life, since that dry winter evening she had said to a stranger in a Studebaker, *You can call me Paul.*

Paul's no kind of name for such a pretty girl, the stranger had said, white cigar smoke seeping from his lips as he spoke.

Gurnie cleared his throat again and Mary heard not him but the gunning engine of that 1945 Studebaker, the fabric-on-fabric movement of someone shifting in the driver's seat. Her throat muscles clenched: The image on the inside of her eyelids was not a newsreel but a worn loop of memory. Mary opened her eyes, stared at a spot on the motor-inn roof until her vision no longer shadowed at the edges.

Then she said, "Polly was wearing blue jeans and a sort of work shirt. She was on horseback." She barely rephrased it from that RE-WARD poster, but already Gurnie was nodding. She wasn't attaching herself to Gurnie, of course—too many fathers were murderers—

but her own deception tasted bitter on her tongue. How easily she lied just to save her own skin. Not even to save it; to avoid her own discomfort.

Mary wouldn't be fooled into seeing herself as honorable, yet she could choose to be decent.

"That's so, yes, that's right," Gurnie said, nearly smiling, running his hands along the steering wheel. "What else?"

Mary shook her head and put her hand on her valise handle. "Nothing, I'm afraid. I'm awfully exhausted, Mr. Starking. A good night's sleep and some time with your family and Polly's things, as I said." She alighted from the truck's cab. "Good night."

"Good enough," Gurnie said. He flicked two fingers up from the steering wheel in farewell and rolled back onto the street, threshers and reapers clanking.

A listless ceiling fan barely stirred the stale lobby air. No one manned the high tile counter. Mary scouted a table for recent newspapers and dug lightly through the wastebasket. She looked up when a short white man, early fifties and in shirtsleeves, leaned across her chest to put out a cigarette in a foil ashtray.

"What you on the hunt for there, sugar?" he said, and reached down to snag her case. He carried it around the back of the desk and made a show of paging through the register. "Kitchenette? Honeymoon suite? Or is the mister here, awaiting your arrival?"

Mary smoothed the newspapers under her arm, tidied her skirt, and stood up straight. She wore a tin wedding band so that she could avoid just this type of interaction and yet—she palmed the ring into her pocket—needs must.

"Are you the proprietor?" she asked.

The motor of a Hoover next door blurred Mary into wakefulness, and she squinted at the television on the dresser, where an image skipped between bands of static. Beside her, the sleeping innkeeper radiated heat. In the drab green of the drape-darkened room, Mary's skin shone purple. The Hoover motor whirred to silent, and the ticking of

Mary's watch swelled to fill the quiet. She pulled it from the night-stand and fastened it on.

Mary squinted at the television. Polly Starking was on the screen, not the image from the REWARD poster but a candid shot, Polly in a prom dress, plopped in a folding chair, knees splayed and toes tipped to the sky. Cheek cupped in her hand, some piece of jewelry on her neck catching the glare of the camera's flash. Mary found her own reflection on the curved glass of the screen, too, and she watched them both, herself and Polly, like an old double exposure. Polly's image shimmied on the screen and Mary's scalp prickled.

At the sound of a door closing nearby, Mary glanced to her left and back again.

The television screen now shone like graphite, blank and not at all on.

Mary flicked on the light and pulled the newspapers from the bedside table onto her lap. After three years at this, she might have been able to write the articles herself. Whether in sleepy towns or anonymous cities, the refrains were always the same: where had the missing girl been seen, how broken were her parents at her disap-pearance, why must a good family suffer such a loss. The gossipy revelations would come a few weeks later, that the girl was secretly fast, secretly sneaking out to swim after dark, secretly not whom they all had supposed her to be.

Mary envisioned the missing girls as paper dolls cut from news-paper, lined up hand to hand, each disappearance filling exactly the same predetermined shape. She becomes she becomes she.

Polly Starking's school photo filled the upper-right quadrant of the county paper's front page. Sheriff's officials had conducted inter-views with her classmates at East Bladen High School, had spoken with her parents and the uncle who found the horse returning on its own to the stables. The mayor's wife had hand-delivered a chess pie to the distraught Mrs. Starking. The stables, the article read, were only two miles from Jones Lake, the Black recreational facility across the Cape Fear River. Certain Black youth had been known, it was pointedly noted, to roughhouse nearby. Any information should be forwarded directly to the county sheriff, Rusty Maynard.

Mary's well-worn fortune cards were in her pocketbook on the bedside table, and she slipped them onto her lap. Beneath the nubbly coverlet, she spread her knees into an altar. She laid out the cards, leaving her fingertips lightly resting on each, hoping for a vibration or flicker of that old newsreel. But the cards were muddled, as though they too were still waking up. The knight of cups, turning up again and again. Mary could see passive movement, maybe Polly's body transported? Nothing that would stick. Mary reached for her notebook.

The innkeeper rolled and resituated, collapsing the cards into a mess on her lap. Mary moved the deck back to the nightstand, and her eyesight flickered as a few of the cards tipped into the space between the table and side of the mattress. A knock hit the motel room door, bringing with it a flash of a moving image: the man beside her, red-faced and smelling of brown booze, shirt front open, reaching roughly to grope at the waist of a Black woman in uniform. Mary snapped her fingers to pull herself out of the unbidden vision. Distractions abounded. The innkeeper shifted again.

"A moment, please!" Mary called out. She coughed on the words, knocking the rest of her cards to the carpet. Mary reached for her dress, the fabric making staticky clicks in the dark. She trained her eyes on a shoddy van Gogh reproduction above the bed, a faceless pink girl toeing at the edge of a forest. When the second knock hit the door, Mary was snapping her stockings over the faded vaccination scar on her thigh. She called the maid in.

But why in the world did Mary invite the woman into this room rather than turning her away? To scare away her own shame, perhaps, but more likely to avoid demurring in any way, to avoid the maid's idea of Mary as loose or low. Mary's stockings were mended ten times over, her cardigan worn thin at the elbows, her wedding band pulled from a church lost and found. From time to time, when money was short, she allowed men like the one in her bed to put their hands on her. She was frequently humbled, but she would be seen as respectable. Unbothered.

The door opened.

The Black maid wasn't jaded enough to hide her surprise or spiteful delight at finding her employer, extremely hirsute and naked, in this bed, his small lambskin penis draped across the crease of his hip. Mary kept her face smooth even as she recognized the woman in uniform from her vision of the innkeeper's groping hands.

"I need coffee and some breakfast," Mary said before the maid could recover. "I'm on foot."

"That'll be Tom Hunt's," the maid said, eyes still on the man. "Down that way." She gestured with her head, her hands holding the doorknob and the Hoover handle.

"What's your name?" Mary was agitated by hunger and the intrusive reminder that she couldn't control her visions in any practical way. The flashes of Sight came as they liked, doing the bidding of some unseen master that sure as hell wasn't Mary.

"I'm Martha, ma'am." The maid, in the straight-piped lines of her uniform, the permanent-pressed collar, and the sewn-on name tag (*Housekeeping,* in red thread script), looked far more respectable than did Mary herself.

Mary straightened the waistline of her dress. From everything she'd read in the papers, the dynamics between the races here were secret and tied to customs she couldn't hope to understand. She'd followed the "Negro sit-downs" in this state from her perches in Maryland and Pennsylvania; they seemed to her unlikely to succeed.

In the fourteen hours Mary had been in Elizabethtown, she couldn't say she'd seen an appreciable difference from her last dip into the South, looking for a missing thirteen-year-old in Nashville in 1959. Last night, the block-lettered WHITES ONLY signs on the businesses she and Gurnie passed no longer shocked her as they had the first time. Until her first trip down two years ago, Mary had never thought about her own race—even though in her youth, her mother would raise a cocktail and sneer, "Free, white, and twenty-one!" on her way to draining the glass.

"All right, then, Martha," Mary said. "I appreciate it. I'll be leaving my case here for the morning, but I trust you can clean around it."

"Yes, ma'am," Martha said.

From the diner, where she couldn't afford to waste money on breakfast no matter what she'd blustered at the maid, Mary telephoned the Starkings several times, but no one answered. Between attempts, she smoked cigarettes out of the pack that she'd pinched from the innkeeper. The diner counter was fully taken up on either side of her, and she kept her elbows close and her movements contained as she sipped down to the dregs of her coffee, flipped the cup upside down on the saucer, spun it one direction then the next, and palmed it upright.

Mary pulled out her notebook, dark with the script from three correspondence courses in divination and inner sight. The pages were pliant and oiled from years and the frequent glide of her fingertips. Anyone could learn divination, or so the course book said, but Mary knew full well that it was empty ritual; without the Sight, uncontrolled and unyielding to her will, she would have nothing to offer. Even the Sight's appearance in her life five years ago had been unbidden, dropping on her like revenge for past deeds, just as she'd nearly built a boring little life for herself, living in a rented room and standing day after day behind a department-store counter.

A white waitress with a cloudy-day expression floated past, snapping the ticket onto the counter. Mary avoided her eyes.

The damp coffee grounds in her mug organized themselves into a girl, leaping, diving, flying toward the rim. Mary copied the images in the margins of a crowded notebook page, nicked several packets of saltines from the bowl on the counter, and moved as though headed back to the WHITES ONLY telephone booth. Instead, she tucked everything under her arm and ducked out of the diner without leaving a nickel for her coffee.

The walk to the Starking house took about twenty minutes. She watched her step in the ditches alongside the sparse residential roads. Her skin dampened beneath her sweater; North Carolina's February might be mild, but it was muggy and grim.

In yesterday's golden hour, the Starking house had swelled and sparkled. Romantic, set against shading evergreens with branches that started two stories up. But in the gray light of the late morning, the house sat dim and deflated, siding coming apart at the seams, the asphalt cover of the porch warped and settled away from the building, exposing rotting wood and a deep trench of brown pine needles.

Bernice Starking answered the door after the third bell ring. Her movements were glacial; even the suctioning of the door from the frame took so long to break that Mary thought her ears had popped.

Bernice grimaced against the filtered daylight, her expression pained as her eyes flicked with recognition. "You're that lady," she said. "The one who dropped in like coal last night."

"Still hoping I may be of some help," Mary said. "Mr. Starking thought I should come by." But Bernice had already turned back. The door hung wide.

After years at this, Mary knew it was best to take every opening. She stepped inside.

Since she began this queer mission, this endlessly sorrowful search for missing girls, Mary had been turned away from a dozen doorsteps, had had the phone put down in her ear over and again. Of the homes she had slipped inside, though, all were like this one, whether dressed in fine rugs or blackened grout. They closed around her, airless, existing outside time. Family members slumped against hard-lined furniture as though spectators to some invisible event. It made Mary want to shriek like a vengeful witch, to throw open curtains and upend portrait-laden tables. *Move!* she would have shouted. *Fuck!* she would have shouted, just for the thrill of the word, of their grimaces of distaste. Their shock was abandonment. The family members may not have made these girls go missing, but their refusal to seek, their inability to find them, was a betrayal. Too often no one could be roused to help Mary look. These families didn't deserve their girls, not before and not once they had gone.

But that's why she was here. Of all the things she might have done with the Sight, it was always missing girls. They were not to her merely cautionary tales. She had lived their lives. She remembered each and every one of them.

But she also needed a place to sleep. She needed to be paid.

Above the Starkings' fireplace, a series of department-store photographs of Polly and her parents. Polly's round face elongating over years, her wide-spaced front teeth settling into a mildly crooked smile. Mary often looked at these photos of missing girls and wondered whether one could tell from the photographs that they would go missing, wondered what evidence she had left on her own parents' walls, in her high school yearbook.

Mary seated herself on the upright settee, beside Bernice. Legs crossed at the ankles, pocketbook on lap, handkerchief tucked in her cuff, she waited for Bernice to offer coffee, to gesture at the biscuits on the table. Bernice wore a smart skirt, dark gray and pleated, but moved her body like an afterthought, a heavy and sagging thing she dragged behind. Her despair would have been palpable to anyone, but Mary had to exert effort to keep it from flattening her: She took on others' pain the way a boxer might take punches. As tough as Mary might try to make herself, pain like Bernice's was a knockout.

"Mr. Starking has returned to the farm?" Mary asked.

"Had to," Bernice said.

The article in the paper had filled in Gurnie's sparse account: He owned a hog farm on the other side of the Cape Fear River, a joint venture with his brother, Clarence. *The amiable Starking boys,* the paper had called them.

"How long have those two had that farm?" Mary asked.

"Not long," Bernice said.

There would be no invitation to biscuits.

The room, like Bernice, was dressed in a pretense toward being finer than it was. The tabletop: plaster painted as veined marble. Beautifully executed seams on cheap fabrics, Bernice's pride and desire for gentility wound into each faultless hand stitch. Now her grief coated every surface like a powder. Mary could have reached out to run her fingertips through it.

"How you going to tell me all this works, then?" Bernice's voice cracked on the words.

Mary knew there was no answer that would satisfy her. People like Bernice were always looking for the rules of things and wouldn't accept that some things simply defied order. Mary's intuition was chaos and confusion most of the time—unending visions and sounds and knowledge flooding Mary's mind. The pain of every person she passed hovering in the air like a cloud. She had never learned to control the Sight; she'd merely found methods for protecting herself from being eclipsed. Putting herself to work seeking a missing girl—trying to focus on one story of loss to make the others recede—was as much about protecting herself as saving them.

More.

Yet she resented having to prove herself again and again.

Mary opened the clasp of her pocketbook and removed her cards. "It will demand patience of us both and offer back frustration," she said. "But wouldn't you agree that Polly deserves every possible effort?" Cloaking her agitation and resentment with gentle movements, Mary shuffled the deck of fortune cards, soft and faded gold at the edges. She didn't notice Bernice move until her hand, red and hot, draped over Mary's.

"Sheriff said we shouldn't pay you mind at all," she said. It sounded to Mary like *uh-tall*. Pay you mind uh-tall. Mary hated how aware of herself she was in this town, of her Northern speech patterns and her white skin and her failures.

"Rusty's seen plenty of your type," Bernice said, "and he says you'll only bring heartache and disappear when you fail us." Bernice dropped her head to her shoulder.

Mary placed her hand over Bernice's stubby fingers, her ripped and ragged nail beds. Mary had watched hands like this before, hands that could meticulously parcel rat poison into stews, that could toss boiling water at a daughter who was garnering too much attention from the wrong kind of man. Bernice's despair made her unpredictable, unsafe.

"Can I make you a cup of coffee?" Mary asked. She stood before Bernice either nodded or didn't. Six steps across the living room, Mary felt her stomach rumble. She remembered reading of the mayor's wife's chess pie. Behind her, she heard Bernice say, "How many these girls you've found alive?"

A vision bore down and in. Mary reached for something to hold, whisked her fingernails against the doorframe as a newsreel overlaid the hallway, coming in at first like a double exposure, until Mary closed her eyes. She could feel grit on the bottoms of Polly's bare feet as she made her way into the kitchen for breakfast. She could hear the slap of Polly's pink and yellow soles on the kitchen linoleum and feel the press of the wooden chair seat into the knobby part of Polly's knees as she surveyed her plate of eggs. *The yolks are wobbling,* Polly said in a whine. Bernice, standing at the stove, turned and delivered a swift slap across Polly's face.

You'll eat what was made for you, miss, Bernice said.

The ache of that memory hovered in the hallway like a ghost, and Mary had wandered right into it.

"Five," Mary called back to Bernice, still feeling the sharp shock of the slap, keeping her voice pitched low. Five girls that Mary had found alive.

"And how many times you collect a reward?" Bernice was now at the threshold, hands worrying at a handkerchief.

Mary took in air through flared nostrils, drying the back of her throat and tongue. The air tasted of soil and salt. "Eleven."

She could see Bernice doing the math. Six dead girls.

The noise from Bernice's throat was a click, the tick of a wristwatch.

Mary could still name them all, the girls she had found too late. Beryl Meager, Genette Brace, Betty Jefferson, Agnes Alvarado, Ayelet Fischl, Rosamunde Shake. Taking rewards for dead girls was something she did because she needed to. She would give herself over to this wretched quest, but she would be compensated. It was fair, it had to be fair, when she counted up the hours of toil, the travel, the fevered nights she spent with these girls, their terrors blossoming whole inside her, appearing like a drop of blood in water: of choking; of cigarette burns; of fathers' crooked smiles; of leaving the house, the motel room, the depressed, creaking bed at night.

Ayelet had been training to become a dental assistant and got motion sickness on the subway. When the landlord noticed she was gone, he found that all the lightbulbs in her apartment had been unscrewed but left in their sockets, except for the one bulb missing from her bedside lamp. Sliver-thin white glass was embedded in Ayelet's cheek when she was found, rolled into a rug in the basement of a neighboring building.

Mary sometimes still felt the crackle of that glass between her molars when she slept.

And then there were the dead girls for whom Mary had received no compensation. Only a deep well of wretched memory, a sorrowful roster of forever-gone names. Frances, Annie, May. Millie Henderson. Marjorie Ann Wise.

When Mary didn't sleep, when the tranquilizers delayed their effect, she lay awake, feeling the weight of lost lives on her bones. They stacked atop her like cinder blocks, pinning her to the mattress.

In the Starkings' entryway, the spasm of Sight had subsided; Mary needed to move. She reached for the painted white banister with an animal desperation to get away from Bernice's gutted expression.

"May I see Polly's room?" she said.

Get to the girl's bedroom, find anything she might hand the parents that could cajole them into offering her a meal, a place to stay. Mary could see Polly's portrait from where she stood. Surely you understand, she thought. Surely you have no reason to want me to starve.

Bernice pointed the way upstairs. "Suppose it couldn't hurt to try," she said.

It did, though. Hurt.

Polly's room was boyish—plaids and mellow woods, brittle achievement ribbons and a tipped pile of schoolbooks on the scuffed desktop. The bed was neatly made, and Mary's inner eye saw Bernice, scuttling hands pulling at the blankets, surveying the room with despair. Days had passed, though, and the blankets cupped at the spot where Polly's body was not.

Polly's pocketbook, on the bedside table, held just a change purse, a house key. Mary pulled a high school yearbook down from the closet shelf and paged through deliberately, coming at last to the photo she'd seen with her inner eye that morning, the same photograph of Polly in her full-skirted prom dress, legs akimbo as she leaned into a folding chair. Light bouncing off her necklace, obscuring its shape.

Next year, it might just be one of those maudlin "In Memoriam" pages, Polly flattened into paper again.

At a sound, Mary looked up, expecting Bernice's timid figure in the doorway. Instead, what swirled into focus was Polly, dressed in dungarees and her camp shirt, pulling open the top drawer of the lingerie chest in the corner.

The figure in motion so differed from the flat snapshots Mary had seen that she glanced between the photo and the apparition several times. The Polly before her had fluidity, an unscripted ease to her movements. The photograph felt like a trap—too small to hold the entirety of a human life. As Mary watched, the vision paused, closed the drawer, and walked across the room, past Mary, toward the closet—where she faded completely in mid-step. But as soon as that apparition had cleared, another began, Mary hearing the opening of the top drawer of the dresser, looking over to see Polly pause, close the drawer again, and walk back across the room. Three times Mary watched this, the yearbook still open across her palms. When Polly passed her the fourth time, Mary reached toward the vision with her hand, fingers curled as though to softly comb through the mist of her. Like a rubber band snapping, the apparition turned its head toward Mary, but the moment the two were face-to-face, Polly dissolved.

Polly's sadness draped Mary like a vapor.

Mary buttoned her sweater. She felt tears curve past her jawline to dribble onto her collar. An army of lost girls. Lost fucking girls. Eventually each of them became a pentimento that only Mary could see beneath the surface of this life as it carried on without them.

In the top drawer of the lingerie chest, Mary found tight rolls of bobby socks and stacks of neatly folded underpants. Pressed into a corner, a worn velvet jeweler's box. Mary cracked it open to find a religious trinket of tarnished tin on a cheap silver-plated chain. She squinted at it, holding it so close she could smell its old-penny odor. No markings aside from the figure of some robed saint she didn't recognize.

Mary palm-kneed onto the bed and insinuated herself into the Polly-shaped dent, her hand clutching the medal. Bernice, down-stairs, may have heard the guttural groan of the bedsprings, but no footsteps followed. Mary drew her customary cinnamon stick from the pocket of her sweater and pressed it to her nose. Of the scents she used to coax out the Sight, cinnamon was the least apt to cause nosebleeds. Nutmeg caused headaches; yarrow made her sneeze.

The Sight was a rabid creature with its own mind, more punish-ment than aid, but sometimes—if Mary squeezed her closed eyes until it was all green-edged blackness, if she grimaced tightly and concentrated on the thud of her own breath—the Sight would abide. Colors would throb into images, and silence would thrum into sound.

Fingers curled around the medal, Mary pressed the heels of her hands firmly against her eye sockets and focused on Polly.

In her stillness on the bed, the smell of cinnamon gave way to cool, bitter woods, and Mary felt her body rocking, a hammock, a canoe, the carriage sway of a horse's hips. The taste of soil and salt grew stronger; she could tongue at grains behind her teeth. The rusty odor of dried sweat deepened into an acrid musk. She still saw only the darkness of her own closed eyes but could map her surroundings with a different sense for which she didn't have a name.

Velvet-covered bark chafed her shoulder, buffeted a humid body whose only resistance was its own weight.

Mary became aware of the stretch in her inner-thigh muscles, the slick leather of the saddle, the bristle of the horse's short hairs against her damp and heartbeating skin. Everything was heavy, was granite, unmoving, unmovable, except the heartbeat and the whisper of air misting in and out of her cracked open mouth. There was an aftertaste of panic. With a competing familiarity and calm, she thought: The horse, at least, could be trusted.

Then, through slitted eyes, Mary saw slashes of color and ambling movement of the passing landscape. A soundscape of rhythmic footfalls rushed in, along with the hiss of wind through the fragile dead branches above. For what could have been a lifetime she traveled, moving and unmoving, over a slow road of mushroom and loam.

And then: a misstep, a stumble of horse hooves, and Mary felt the slump of her body, sensed her weight shift from centered to falling.

The impact was shoulder first; reverberations rang through her head. Time contracted around her.

The grate of soles against mud and pebble came suddenly. Mary's barely open eyes watched steel toes and mud-caked heels stop just a hair from her nose.

Paul.

Did she hear that? Was he talking to her?

"I don't have much use for these dramatic tricks, ma'am."

This voice, close and baritone, punctured Mary's stupor. She became aware again of Polly's bedroom, of someone standing in the doorway. She now lay supine on Polly's bed, her arms out wide in a rough approximation of crucifixion. Few possibilities for what had happened after those steel toes approached: A stomp from such boots could rupture a windpipe, shatter a jaw.

Mary opened her eyes with relief at being spared the witness of either.

A man. White and with a chest like the grill of a grocery truck, he stood between Mary and the bedroom door. In his sixties or seventies, he had a holster on his belt and a badge pinned to his suspenders. He didn't extend his hand, nor did he give an indication of how long he'd been watching her. With an acute sense of violation, Mary pressed her elbows to the bed to push upright. Her shoulder protested—echoes of the metallic pain from the fall in the vision—but she fought the grimace, put on an expression of indifference. She'd met this man, his kind, before.

"You make a game of weaseling your way into the houses of distraught mothers?" the man said, washing his hand down his face. Ugly, chapped lips like those would twist up before they spit at you.

Mary flicked her eyes toward Bernice, a specter behind him at the threshold to the room. "Rusty—" Bernice said, agitation in her voice. She looked at Mary. "Sheriff wanted to have a word."

Mary placed the soles of both shoes on the floor. "Mrs. Starking, I am happy to leave if I'm making you uncomfortable." She stood, closing the sheriff's advantage by several feet. Withholding her eye contact from the man, Mary looked only at Bernice. Built like that, such a man could press a girl into the ground with barely any effort.

"I told Rusty that you haven't asked for anything," Bernice said. She was a teacup jittering on its saucer. "I told him"—here her head swiveled to face Rusty—"I told you that she didn't want anything."

"I want only to be of service," Mary said. Her language came out stilted as she withstood the man's hard glare. The learned haughtiness of her Mid-Atlantic elocution irritated her.

Bernice dropped her forehead to her fingertips. Mary's night's lodging and next meal became more uncertain. She waited.

If this was exploitation, what Mary was doing, by God, it was reciprocal. These parents would want nothing further from her after she did or didn't find their daughter; she would be no more family to them than she was now. Some of them would pay out the reward, others wouldn't let her back in their home, but in that liminal space of anguish and hope, they would wrest from her anything she might offer.

Rusty said, "Bernice, may I trouble you for a cup of coffee? The boys at the station beat me to the pot this morning." Opening an ushering arm and starting toward the door, he looked back at Mary. "Come on, now." Mary allowed herself to be steered from the room.

In the kitchen, around a cheerful yellow Formica table, the trio sat with palms wrapped around mugs of gritty Chase & Sanborn instant. Rusty's assumption of authority over Bernice felt like Gurnie's had; Mary wondered why it was that no one wanted Bernice to speak to her without a chaperone.

Rusty filled up the kitchen with chatter about an impending rainstorm. Mary didn't say a word. She leaned back in her chair and imagined that chess pie she'd read about. Thought about her suitcase, still stowed at the Safe Lodge under the eye of the sleaze from last night. Thought about the unconscious rider and the horse from her vision, about a world full of pain just waiting to be visited upon any girl who wandered into it.

The sheriff raised his eyebrows into two sharp points, and his lip curled as he took a slug from his mug. "How many families you worked with?" His shift in tone was abrupt.

"Around twenty," Mary said, rubbing a finger on her top lip. Polly made thirty-three.

The sheriff slid his forearms forward on the table, leaning toward Mary and taking her mug between his hands. "I've been working every case of any kind in this county for twenty-five years," Rusty said. He spun her mug. "Time to time you folks show up, but only ever when there's a reward."

His voice was maddeningly calm. Like she was a small child in need of instruction. "Most often y'all just bring too much attention to yourselves and buzz around," he said, "getting in the way, tipping the families into upset."

Rusty sat up straight again, released her mug. "The reward money you saw in the paper, that's mine. I'm the one offering it, and I'll be the one paying it if need be. You'll bring to me whatever insights you think you have"—he waved his hand in the air—"and you'll leave these fine people in peace."

Mary's prospects for a warm meal and warm bed snuffed out, she flipped through her memory book, looking for park benches or churches she'd passed on the walk. She'd slept on church pews before, startling awake at the nudging of altar boys and flower-faced nuns. "I've no interest in upsetting anyone," she said. "Though I will need to talk to Mr. and Mrs. Starking for help with interpreting the images that come to me—"

Rusty spoke over her. "Everything will come to me."

And damn her, she stopped talking when Rusty began to. He threw back much of what remained in his mug. "And I wanted Bernice to know that this is our arrangement and that she is free to turn you away should you come nosing back at this door. All right, Bernice?"

"Whatever you think's best, Rusty," Bernice said.

The sheriff propelled himself away from the table and stood. "May I offer you a ride somewhere, Mrs.—"

"Garrett," she said. And damn her again, she'd told the innkeeper it was Graves. She stood, dignity and benevolence—a respectable woman—and smoothed at the pilled yoke of her cardigan. Her shoulder twinged. "That's exceedingly charitable of you. I'd gladly accept."

Mary was always apart from the families of these girls. Always the outsider to their private agonies. And yet it was Mary who lived inside these girls—it was Mary inside whom they dwelled. She became a well for their pain when they were no longer alive to contain it. And she wondered again and again whether this thing that she did, these searches she leapt into to ward off the worst overwhelm of the Sight, might not just be killing her.

If there were any other way to live her life, she would stop this. Everything was simply a choice between flavors of pain.

Peering into the sheriff's coffee cup, Mary watched the reconstituted grounds form into a spider and creep toward the handle on eight hairy legs.

The sheriff's vehicle, not the ancient pickup truck she'd have guessed Rusty would have, was a late-model Mercury hardtop. Mary remembered the ads for these. *Straight out of tomorrow,* they said. As though time were nothing more than a destination.

Newspapers and maps were feathered across the passenger's seat, and Rusty leaned in to clear them.

"If you don't mind," Mary said, "I get carsick in the front. I'll take the back if it's just the same to you."

The air inside tasted to her of cigarette smoke and bitter winter.

Mary had accepted the ride without a clear idea of where she might be deposited, with only the sense of wanting to ease the path between the reward and her pocketbook. Now that she was here, she couldn't imagine asking him to take her to Safe Lodge, letting Rusty make eye contact with that leering motel manager over the top of her head.

The driver's-side door bassooned open and Rusty settled himself in the seat, rocking his hips side to side. He placed his felt hat on the dash and keyed the ignition before twisting to look at her.

"Well, Mrs. Garrett, you figure I might pull ahead of the competition for your time if I asked you for a lunch date?"

Rusty took them back to the diner where Mary had begun her day. They jangled through the front door, and Rusty stepped past Mary to an open booth with a small enamel RESERVED table tent and slid in.

The same waitress from the morning, hard and deep-eyed, took their order. Mary averted her gaze, but the waitress said not a thing.

Rusty ordered egg salad, coffee, a plate of French fries, then asked the waitress to make that two of everything.

"The Starkings've had a world of trials these past few days," he said, tidying the sugar shaker and the Heinz bottle.

Thirty-three of these cases and Mary knew it like it was her own house, her own religion: the anguish, the drudgery of fogged-over days and weeks. Those left behind, hearing nothing but the beating of a hundred crows' wings filling the space between their heads and ceilings, the endless impressions of a wing, a shadow, a girl, edging into their peripheral vision.

Beryl Meager's grandfather, who had watched Beryl dragged by her hair into an idling roadster, had stumbled after her and broken his collarbone after dropping his cane. Teresa Alvarado, whose husband had cracked her daughter's neck, had to write her son in prison with the news. The Sight compelled Mary to witness it all, that girl's neck under the boot, the drawn-out snap of her spine as though through a loudspeaker, and when the moment of death came, it came wet and furious, and the Sight wouldn't let her look away.

Of course the Sight was a punishment. How could it be anything else?

The girls, though, the girls who went missing, were also there all along, for the whole agonizing experience of it. If there were true grace in the world, they would have been spared enduring their own disappearance.

Rusty didn't know trials—days that would only ever look like a girl-shaped hole in the world. Mary knew trials. She had died too many times already.

"Your prying isn't going to be of help, neither," Rusty said. He rolled up his shirtsleeves and tucked his tie inside his shirt. Mary resented the finality of his tone, his easy dominion over the whole world around him. Did he think she'd be so obedient as to meekly concede her own irrelevance?

"Certainly we can agree Polly deserves every effort we could make," she said, just as she had said to Bernice, just as she said to anyone who ever expressed reticence about her intrusion. The lunchtime din swelled at that moment, a man's laughter filling space like a tuba. Mary leaned in and raised her voice. "Because our aim here is the same, Sheriff."

"Well, I couldn't rightly say," Rusty said without emotion. He looked around the diner, lifted a few fingers in a wave of recognition at a pair of old ladies slurping cups of soup in the corner. The women moved so slowly, so out of pace with the frenetic movement of the rest of the room, they seemed unmoored in time. Mary might have been one of them, if life had moved in a different direction. She might have been a million things. Half-twisted in her seat, Mary waved in their direction. The women did not respond to Mary's gesture.

The sheriff laughed. "I wish I could tell you that our God-loving town welcomed visitors with Christ-like hospitality, but I'm afraid of trying to lie to a clairvoyant.

"In fact, I reckon you'll find most your time is wasted here. Some folk just prefer to take care of their own, and after all that's gone on the past year, we've had about enough of Northerners who take a mind to stride in and tinker with our relations," he said. The words were plain, but he delivered them with sugar.

"I'd like to change your mind on that," Mary said.

"No one here has been missing what you're peddling." Rusty worked at his canine with the edge of his tongue. "And if you're wanting to change my mind, best thing you could do would be to tell me something I don't already know. Isn't that about how this works?"

The diner placemat was crowded with advertisements for local businesses. Mary flipped it to the blank underside. "I have no interest in being enemies," she said. And she didn't, though she had no interest in being allies, either.

Rusty coughed and spit something into a handkerchief.

"Exactly where is this husband of yours?" he asked. "He lets you run after trouble like this?"

Mary met the sheriff's eye for a good long while. "What I know for what you know," she said, keeping any lilt of a question out of her voice. Rusty was hardly the first man to try to bully her, and she wanted him to know it.

She wondered whether her face betrayed her utter exhaustion, what it took to hold her ragged body upright, to pretend at authority and confidence when she knew full well what a defective savior she was.

But Rusty knew even less than she did; he seemed just to expect the world to bend to his expectation. Mary had no intention of bending for him. With snappish movement, she pulled a pencil from her pocketbook.

In careful block letters, Mary printed the information she had: the moments on horseback, the unconscious fall, the boots. She mulled over the voice she'd heard—*Paul*—but decided to hold on to that bit until she better understood the rules of this town, the underground lines of loyalty. She folded the placemat in half, then in half again, templed her hands over the tight square, and looked at Rusty with a forced serenity.

Rusty snorted and placed the handkerchief to his nostrils. His chapped hand was clumsy as he began copying information from his small notebook onto his placemat.

"I do wonder what draws a person to this type of witchcraft," he said. He spoke without raising his head. "There are six hundred different cons in the world. Why choose devilment and sorcery? Why not just rob the rich?"

"I suppose almost every little boy plays cops and robbers," Mary said, plain and soft. "How many keep it up into dotage?"

Rusty raised his eyebrows but kept his eyes on his hand. "Selling voodoo protection spells to the paranoid and wealthy," he said after a pause. "Advising on the stock market."

"Fireman, milkman, butcher, cook," Mary said. She sucked on her front tooth with a nasty snick.

"Perhaps," said Rusty, "we both are atoning for some grievous past." He drew out the word *grievous,* italicized it. He folded his placemat with sloppy attention and slid it across the table to Mary.

Mary covered the page with her palm; she wasn't about to let him read her face while she squinted at his bird scratch. And if the Sight was still hovering at her shoulder, she didn't want to be caught in another vision around him. Her skin itched at the idea. The intimacy of her visions was raw, was bruising, and she would not be put on display—not for this hot-air balloon of a man, not for anyone.

The waitress arrived with their sandwiches, and the sheriff tucked Mary's placemat into his breast pocket without reading it. Already she regretted giving him any information at all. She couldn't imagine he had been as forthcoming.

They ate silently, lunch with a finish line, moving French fry to lips before the previous mouthful was swallowed. As their plates were emptied of all but a dusting of salt, Mary made no movements toward her pocketbook. She pushed her plate away and centered her coffee mug before her, taking slow sips and eyeing the broad landscape out the window.

Each time she left New England, Mary was surprised all over again at how everything was three times the size she expected. Yawning-wide traffic lanes, grass medians so deep you could lie across them without danger. People's speech was that big, too, open and loud and unhurried. She was accustomed to clipped words, the pinched faces of people crowded at every turn, shoulders pulled tight to the ribs. Here, all these people's gestures seemed languorous, unbounded. It was tempting to see everything as looser than the tight straits that had bound her growing up, but Mary didn't trust rules she couldn't see. Not that she trusted much.

As a child, Mary had envisioned the South as nothing but cotton fields and bayous; the expansive green woodlands here had taken her by surprise. Once, two years ago, she had gotten off a bus in Phoenix, blessedly free of forest and with a nighttime sky that unfurled into a starlit big-top tent. Under the daylight, everything was laid bare. No shadows. Nothing hidden. It was an idea that she held close: getting back there, wearing linen, making pastel drawings and sun tea in the yard. Once she had the money, once the girls stopped disappearing, once she could manage to escape all that still bound her.

Mary drank her coffee to the grounds again, tipped her cup, and spun it on the saucer. She knew the sheriff was watching, but she kept her eye on the cup, flipped it up for reading. A horse, the rider's feet planted on the animal's back. A blink and the same rider, thrown. Betrayal, loss of innocence.

But Mary's mind was on the *Paul* she'd heard in her vision on Polly's bed. The man with the boots knew Polly well enough to speak to her in a tone that sounded something like regret.

Paul.

Mary had met five people in this town. She'd heard only one use that name for Polly Starking: her father, Gurnie.

A crack of laughter outside, and Mary turned to look. A line of people at the diner's walk-up window. The assembled people were all Black, a few women standing quietly with pocketbooks tucked under their folded hands, younger people dancing and joking. A darkened sky portended rain and all those people were about to be caught in it, without so much as an awning to blunt the downpour. As the first gigantic drops fell, the people waiting pressed their backs against the outside of the building, trying for shelter under the slim eave of the roof.

Rusty made a show of following Mary's line of sight to look out the window. "I suppose y'all up in Philadelphia or New York don't have your own ways of doing things, now?" he said.

She was disgusted by him and for a second forgot that he hadn't yet paid the lunch bill, that he still held the purse strings on that reward. She remembered both of those material conditions of her life before she landed on an appropriate retort. Just then, the waitress returned to refill Rusty's mug, pointedly ignored Mary's, and slapped down the check. As Rusty pulled out his wallet, he spoke pleasantly to the waitress about the traveling circus that had just rolled in to Lumberton.

Mary turned back toward the window. The gloom outside lit up the reflection of Rusty and the waitress, and Mary made note only of the cadence of their conversation, the rise and fall of expressions of surprise and certainty. She watched with the mild disorientation that comes with seeing things backward—the interior of the diner, her own upturned face planted in her palm, Rusty's hand clapped over the waitress's as she fingered at the bills on the table. Then, a turn: the waitress's fingers growing jerkier as her nails pressed into the table, as Rusty's grasp on her hewed tighter, his knuckles whitening, the waitress doubling over, Rusty's hand on the back of her neck pressing, pressing, pushing her cheek to the table, her knees giving way as she dropped to the ground, her cheek still on the table, her body shaking her body shaking, and still the steady cadence of syllables rising and falling.

Mary's eyes crossed, and it was no longer the waitress in forced genuflection but herself, her own young face smashed to a table, the handle of a butter knife jammed against her temple, the fur trim of her red parka sliding down her shoulder, the angle of her face obscuring the reflection of the man. She closed her eyes as the memory dizzied her, as the ammonia constriction crept up her throat and she tasted egg salad again. So many things she would never be free of, so many things not done exacting their toll.

Rusty dropped a heavy palm to the table and the memory's trap snapped open. Mary gathered her pocketbook and slid out from the booth, stepping behind the calm and weary waitress.

Mary leaned toward Rusty. "I'll be—I'm sure I'll be speaking with you soon." Maybe that's what she said. Maybe she said nothing, or maybe she screamed. And if Rusty was taken aback by the suddenness of her departure, if his ruddy face displayed any surprise or irritation, Mary was too far out the door to see, already at the end of the block, already dripping rainwater from her eyebrows and kicking up spray as she went, trying to outrun the thunderstorm inside her.

Hot heartbeat of her numbing hands pulling at the lock on the door and she had bolted from the room—carrying always the raw wounds that the Sight had opened up, the reminder of what happens when no one comes looking—*fevered running, back to the woods*—and she found the inn again, but she had no key, the lobby was empty—*she was escaping but also she was chasing*—she found Martha, dear—*soles of her shoes sliding on the leaves, the snow starting the snow slicking a branch*—Martha who let her into the room, who patted—*impression of a girl in her peripheral vision*—her shaking shoulder and told her to rest up, ma'am, who dropped—*loss like a boulder in her stomach*—the DO NOT DISTURB sign on the knob before leaving Mary to strip cleanly—*loss like no one would help her search*—to her slip, to crawl into the bed, scatter her hand across the nightstand for her tinking bottle of tranquilizers—*and then*—release.

Sneaker Footprints in Snow Speeding Mountain Search For Paula Welden

House to House Search in Fall River Area Starts as Police Follow Different Angle in Disappearance

A sensational new clue as to the whereabouts of 18-year-old Paula Welden was provided by Fall River Mass. police at one o'clock this morning when they told the Banner over the telephone they were conducting a house-to-house search for the girl after a lead provided by a waitress. On a tip a Banner reporter phoned Chief of Police John Mc-Mahon, Fall River, from his bed to contain a middle-of-the-night interview...

Fager Recognizes Photo

Danny Fager, operator of the College Entrance filling station, after seeing a picture of Paula Welden, reported immediately to newsmen and the girl's father as well as college officials that he saw Miss Welden walking down the college driveway Sunday afternoon and watched her as she headed toward Bennington.

'I'm Going on Long Trail' Girl Told Louis Knapp

Bennington Contractor Says He Gave Short Automobile Ride Sunday to Girl Resembling Paula Welden

Acting on a tip Wednesday night from a Bennington College official, a Banner reporter interviewed Louis Knapp, a building contractor living on Route 9 just outside Bennington near the Furnace Bridge. Mr. Knapp stated that at about 2:45 on Sunday afternoon he picked up a girl corresponding to the description of Paula Welden, 18-year-old College student missing since Sunday...

Foul Play Suspected

College Official Fears Girl Dead and Body Concealed; Three Questioned by Authorities

In a telephone statement last night College President Lewis Webster Jones said that the search authorities suspected that Paula Welden was a victim of foul play and that her body had been concealed.

Search authorities today will question closely everyone in the Long Trail district. All records will be employed to provide any...

Bennington College Student, Missing Four Days Known to Have Been Wearing Flimsy Footwear When Last Seen

By PETE STEVENSON

An intensive search for Paula Welden started at dawn this morning in a seven square mile area between Glastenbury and Bald Mountains. An even more careful search will be conducted in the area of the "Blue Trail" which branches off from the Long Trail and leads over Bald Mountain. A Bennington College faculty member Wednesday afternoon came upon footprints in the snow along the Blue Trail which appeared to be made by sneakers. Paula Welden was wearing sneakers when she vanished from the campus.

Sheriff W. Clyde Peck led the posse this morning which made up of over 125 Williams College students, Bennington College faculty members and students and a large number of local people who have volunteered to aid in the hunt.

MISSING PERSON

REWARD $5,000.00 IF FOUND ALIVE · REWARD $2,000.00 IF FOUND DEAD

Specimen of Handwriting and Printing

Paula Jean Welden, 18 yrs., 5'5", 122 lbs., blond hair, long bob, blue eyes, fair complexion with much color, features regular, nose slightly turned up, cleft in chin. Grayish scar on left knee, vaccination mark right thigh, small scar above left eye under eyebrow. Walks with a long springy step, has erect carriage. Athletic type.

DENTAL CHART ON BACK OF CIRCULAR

PAULA JEAN WELDEN

Paula Jean Welden, Brookdale Road, Stamford, Conn. a student at Bennington College, Bennington, Vermont, disappeared from college on the afternoon of December 1, 1946. When last seen she was wearing a red parka jacket with fur trimmed hood, blue jeans, white sneakers with heavy soles named Top-Sider, and a small gold Elgin ladies' wrist watch with narrow black band. This watch has repairer's marking 13050 ED, scratched on the inside of back cases. This girl likes skating, bicycling, hiking, camping, swimming, square dancing and playing the guitar. She is an art student interested in a mural painter and has done pencil and charcoal sketching, and has assisted in a mural design and done illustrations (black and white). She has also done waitress work.

REWARD, LIVING OR DEAD, $5,000.00 IF FOUND ALIVE, $2,000.00 IF FOUND DEAD. $5,000.00 reward for information leading to the whereabouts of Paula Jean Welden, resulting in her being found alive. $2,000.00 reward for information leading to the whereabouts of Paula Jean Welden and resulting in the identification of her body. Reward expires July 1, 1947.

Please forward any information to girl's father, Mr. W. Archibald Welden, Brookdale Road, Stamford, Connecticut.

SIX AND A HALF MINUTES

I come to on a mattress of straw-colored pine needles, wreathed by dying moss and splintered tree trunks. I try to wiggle my toes, notice my sneakers anchoring the blanket's edge. I wonder where my lover has gone, why I am waking alone, how long I've lain so crookedly and asleep.

A sash of light drapes across the wool blanket beneath me. I would expect my nostrils to numb to the chill and the smell of coming snow. I would expect to feel a shiver begin in my teeth and lower back, ringing the rest of me like a bell.

Instead, the chill of the woods drapes around my blanket but doesn't touch me.

For such a long time, the woods felt like a home. A place to hide, a place to burrow from the rest of the world. With enough concentration, you might pull on a taproot and remake the face of the earth. Scrape at the bristly skin of a fiddlehead and blanket a meadow in snow. There was a book once, a fairy tale of sorts, about a girl who could tug at a tulip bulb and make it storm.

My attention drifts. My forehead is tender and stiff. But I'm feeling too still to be concerned—not confused or fatigued, but *still*. I notice my spine on the blanket, the coarse warmth bisecting my body into safe earthbound back and vulnerable skyward belly. This is yours, I think. Your stillness, your contradiction.

My teacher says that I am too much a *girl painter* to scrape a copse of trees on canvas without knowing what someone will see there—Alice, bounding after the rabbit. Little Red, slipping the path. Ophelia, scratching purple welts onto her own soft neck as the vines wrap round and the creek water thunders down her throat. *Your woods must be unmanned,* my teacher says. My little jars of paint suddenly heavy in my lap.

I knew a girl painter, once, short brown hair and green paint smeared on the edge of her left hand. I followed her into the high school art room one day, as though I were some lost little lamb. I sat beside her, the instructor not noticing I didn't belong, a spare dry paintbrush loose in my palm. I remember a line of bluish sunlight slicing across her chest, the crystal of her wristwatch bouncing the refracted light around the room, into my eyes, down my shoulder. Like she was painting me with the sunlight.

Wind sighs through the trees: *Wise.*

The trees I slash with my palette knife don't hide someone else's tragic fairy tales but the tiny bead of perspiration behind that girl painter's ear, the bend in her back as she walked away from me.

Wise.

I'm drifting again.

In this moment, on this blanket in these unmanned woods, I find that I have a magical power to stop time: to command the sun to be still with me. The power to elongate a shortened winter's day into a week's worth of daylight, to press out any cat-footed thoughts of the missing lover, the impression on the woolen blanket, the shattered crystal of my watch face.

What power, to forbid wonder. Where is the creeping twilight? What are these brown spatters on my cuff? Why does this man trudging up the hill toward me avert his eyes? These are among the things I could forbid myself to wonder.

I liked to sketch my teacher while he dozed on the blanket, nude in the waning light. Never before him had I seen a naked man, and here was this one, red-haired and pale white and snoring humid circles onto my skin. I arrived at this college, frothing over with every kind of girl, every kind of giggle and accent and groan, and I ran straight at the first man whose eyes lingered on me.

I didn't even want him. I pretended, thought it was the thing to do. Be swept away, as they all say. And my false desire led me here, again and again, to this blanket in the woods, where my teacher had memorized every spur and shadow, where he pinched the weed wisps from my bare shoulders and held them up to the light, pointed at their edges or alternating branches to identify them. He made a fuss over which flower to call me, and I puckered my face in an approximation of a columbine, splayed my fingers into lilies.

My lover's wife was named Lily, though. Funny that I forgot that, even for a moment.

In this moment on this blanket, I am stretched into a lady's slipper, pearlized white petals blushing to pink veins. I'm a flower strewn on this coarse wool plaid, and the approaching man, sweaty and winded, looks right at me.

I've been playing at something the whole time, playing at sweetness and love and tarnished virtue. He doesn't know me, this man. I don't want him to, and I'm not sure that he could. I'm always looking past his shoulder for another figure in these unmanned woods, a smooth shape tucked between the mossy trees.

Wise, walking back to me.

When my teacher awoke on this blanket to catch me drawing him, I splayed my fingers and said, "Lily!" And his body turned to stone and his own face puckered. I placed my palms on his shoulders, pressed them down, away from his ears.

"It's nothing," I said.

"It'll be all right," I said.

In this moment on this blanket, among the things I might forbid from wonder: the pain like a second set of teeth grinding deep within my throat. The feeling in my body not of losing my breath but of being sealed, of unmoving air.

I wasn't sorry, though, that I had said it. *Lily.* It rang in the air between us, close and humid as we were. I soothed his skin with my palm, pressed my skull to the crease between his chest and arm. I plied him with my head until I won him back, until he folded over me, curtaining my shoulders with his long upper arm.

After the quiet stretched into the brittle winter woods, after the pattern of our breathing became a softened drumbeat, I said the name again.

"Lily. I sent her a letter."

For what would be the point of wonder in a moment like this, on this blanket in these woods on this day? What would be the point of wonder when the girl you love is gone and your lover, streaked in dirt and exertion, folds the edges of the wool blanket over you, ties the laces of your sneakers together and places them on your belly?

In my paintings, I might mask out the shape of a girl, leaving her unpainted form on the canvas. Saving her spot on this blanket.

At the sound of my voice, my lover's breath stopped and so I whispered to him, whispered into his neck, that Lily would see how much he loved me, *me,* and that surely she could understand. I didn't want him still, but there was something else of Lily's that I craved. The safety of being inside the thing.

"Lily will see," I whispered.

"When?" he said.

"This morning," I whispered again. "One of my drawings, too. She'll see. We can be free." Everything around me is ruin. I am the ruiner.

In that moment on this blanket, I was whispering still as his chest became granite against me, whispering faster as his thumbs grew hard against the soft spot at the base of my throat. I whispered until I was choked with whispering, until I could whisper no more.

Now my teacher knots the corners of the blanket and tosses into the center, onto me, a large rock, smeared rusty flecks along its ancient striations. It took seventy thousand years to form that rock. It took eighteen years to form me and only six and a half minutes to undo it.

My lover lifts the blanket, and my lady's slipper head is on his collar. His skin is wet and warm. Mine is already cold.

The short day's sun is finally setting.

In my paintings of the unmanned woods, the girl-shaped spot is fading.

Quick—hold me up to the light before it goes; identify me by my veins and by my branches.

SPELLS FOR SINNERS, PART TWO

Bᴌᴀᴅᴇɴ Cᴏᴜɴᴛʏ, Nᴏʀᴛʜ Cᴀʀᴏʟɪɴᴀ, 1961

Pink light was filtering through the pinholes in the motel drapes before the tranquilizers fully took hold and Mary slid into a damp sleep. She awoke in the drab green light a few times—the whispering slide of fabric on fabric gave her a shudder, the thought of someone else here in her room, and she felt her way over to slither the chain across the door. Once, she awoke at the sound of a clanging bell above her head, a trick of the senses. She took tablets of aspirin or more tranquilizers each time she crept toward awareness, not keeping track, not checking the time, until the brown glass bottle shook empty of all but the cotton.

The tranquilizers killed dreams, and memories, too, at least for the first few hours.

Mary is eighteen years old and she's still got her old name, and the snow hasn't yet begun. She looks through the Studebaker window at the man who says it's too cold out there and won't she have a ride and as she climbs in she says, *Call me Paul.* In that rocky southern Vermont accent they all have around here, he says that's no kind of name for such a pretty girl.

If she weren't on her own, she would laugh at that. She and her sweetheart, they used to mock men like him.

He says she shouldn't be out on her own. Says it's not safe. She thinks: It is true that it is unsafe to be around me.

Six miles down the road, she sees a sign pointing to the Long Trail, but the car just keeps on going, and when she tells him, *Mister, you missed the turn,* he says he's gotta take a piss something awful and there's a diner just up yonder. She's never heard a man talk like that and she feels a tick of concern. At the diner, his hand is on the curve of her neck, guiding her to a booth near the back. When he returns from the bathroom, he slides in next to her rather than across, and he crowds her against the frosted window. *What's your poison?* he asks, and elbows her in the ribs, maybe harder than he meant.

After coffee comes and then their food, Mary relaxes a little into the humid saltiness of baked potatoes and roast beef, and she giggles at the man when he shakes sugar onto his potato. *That's funny?* he says with a smile, but the smile dies before it reaches his eyes.

It's not a slam or a crack or any sudden movement. Instead, the man pushes her plate away and then his hand is on the curve of her neck again as he props his elbow on the back of the booth. Leadenly, he bears down, down, down, until Mary's head is pressed to the table, the chunky handle of the butter knife is wedged into her temple, and in the reflection of the window, where her own hot breath has evaporated the frost, she watches as he continues eating his sugared potato, not looking at her, not loosening his grasp on her neck.

How many times since has she wondered whether a glimpse at her coffee grounds might have told her what horrors were coming?

But they come.

And later—after her face is pushed to the hotel bedspread smelling of skin and bile—after she escapes not the room but her body
and returns to it again, now trembling in the dry bathtub until her
teeth are grinding metal—after she hears the sigh of his dozing slide
to the steady grumble of sleep—Mary slips out of the bath, rustles
for the car keys but can't find them in the dark of the space. Snow
has fallen throughout the night, and the sedan's tire tracks are already puffed over with a heavy layer. In her memory, she's far too
loud as she tries to sneak out—her ticking watch sounds like smashing glass, her breath an organ bellows.

The dream, dredged from bright hot memory, is the thing that
shoots her awake again and again—for years, for a decade—but it's
the other thing, the way the shards of her life fall back down to her
once she opens her eyes, that kept her lying there for hours, sleepless
and headachy and ashamed.

Mary had tried to train her memories away, had been working at it for
nearly half her life. For a few years, she simply refused to remember
her childhood, her birthday, her sisters' names, her own lengthy mis-
deeds. She kept all of it just out of focus, every burr and bruise from
the time before sliding into a blurred reflection of itself, made ano-
dyne and ghostly. If anything rushed at her, any clench of regret or
upset, she'd thump it away. Head to wall, hands yanking her hair, all
to flood her senses and scare memory away.

She'd gotten good at it, for a while.

For ten years, more, she'd worked as a shopgirl in Philadelphia,
paid six dollars a week for a shared room, and kept herself to herself.
She spent most of her spare time and money at the picture theater,
where the images and sounds ballooned enough to crowd out anything else in her head.

Then five years ago her co-worker's daughter disappeared. Angela
Whitaker, twenty years old, a college girl who answered an ad for a
house cleaner and never came home. On a coffee break, the girl's

mother pushed Angela's photo into Mary's face, and in that instant: Mary saw the basement apartment, heard the click of the man's empty gun, and felt the raw rub of the stocking tightening Angela's wrists to the bed frame. A fallen piece of mail, the man's address visible.

She'd saved that girl.

Mary felt no pride in it. A triumph measured only by a fleeting absence of her personal agony.

And then they kept coming, these visions of other girls, of other people's pain. And braided into them were all her own memories, everything she'd dammed away from her conscious mind for a decade. A wave of wretched feeling had rushed in back then, and Mary had stayed in bed for a week.

She was fired from her position at the department store. Movie theaters lost their allure, the films unintelligible over Mary's never-ending interior reel. It took her years to learn that if she focused on one idea, one feeling, the other noise receded for a while. She could concentrate. And sometimes the Sight gave her enough information to save someone.

Mary's own memories were never so obliging. Unbidden, they thrust themselves upon her like birds beating against a windowpane. She could only try to ward them off with her old tricks—head to the wall, hand tugging at her scalp—or, when those failed, sleep.

Mary slept for more than a day, and a knock on the motel-room door awoke her in what felt like late afternoon. Mary crept from bed to the door; it was easier than finding words to call out. She cracked it open and was relieved to see Martha rather than the innkeeper demanding payment that she didn't have or couldn't bear to give.

"I've got something of yours," Martha said, her voice sounding firmer than it had been before, or maybe just existing outside a dream.

Martha held up two of Mary's fortune cards. Mary's vision swam;

she was slow to understand. She reached out. Martha held fast to the cards—knight of cups and six of swords.

"Police and them are looking for a woman," Martha said. "Something's happened at the big market, and they're looking for a Mrs. Garrett who was by the Starkings' place yesterday." Martha tipped the cards toward Mary's fingers. "Pretty white lady, they say. Yankee, blond. Skittish."

Yesterday morning, the cards sliding beside the nightstand. Mary remembered now. She took the cards and crossed her arms in front of her chest, the cool breeze stiffening the downy hairs on her skin.

"You need to dress yourself and go on over to the market, ma'am," Martha said. She expressed the same polite softness Mary had seen the other morning but now somehow had the air of being trespassed upon. Up close, Mary could see deep lines drawing parentheses around the woman's mouth.

"Everything all right in there?" Martha said, and Mary followed Martha's gaze to the old bloodstains that dribbled down the front of her nylon slip, brown now from years of sink rinses. Mary's index finger pressed to the edge of her nostril before she realized she was doing it. Dry. She tried to turn the gesture into a scratch at the round part of her nose.

"I'll head over shortly," Mary said. "I mean, thank you, yes." It had just occurred to her that Martha might be doing her a favor.

Martha reached to pull the door shut. "It's out east on Broad Street. You'll be wanting a taxicab. Montgomery at the desk'll call Sigsbee for you."

Mary climbed into the cab wrong-ways, skull and palms first. The sky outside was gasoline-colored. She smelled the unbathed sourness of her own body, was aware of the yellowed inside of her blouse collar. Still deep in her sleeping self, she was a hibernating wolf moving by instinct and scent.

Mary held Rusty's scribbled placemat in tight hands; instead of information about Polly's case, he'd written, *Nobody invited you here. Get on home to your crystal ball why don't you.* She'd pulled the place-mat out during the never-ending sleepless night, had a fit, crumpled the page, and thrown it across the room, where it bounced lightly off the television screen. If this was how Rusty was playing it, why in the world had he summoned her today?

Mary parted with a precious dollar when the taxi driver, white and unshaven and reeking of gin, feigned not having change. The big market, Sure Foods, telegraphed the previous decade's commercial-ized optimism—all chrome edging and red flapping awnings. Cool, produce-moist air slapped Mary when she stepped inside, doing a great deal to awaken her at last. A uniformed cop stepped toward her with one arm open, saying something about a crime scene and the public. Mary narrowed her eyes and scanned the market's entry for a clue as to why she was here. She caught the broad slope of Rusty's shoulders from behind a stack of cans; he looked over and beckoned.

Rusty and a half dozen other white men similarly attired were gathered in front of a row of tall glass doors, behind which eggs and milk bottles and pink paper–wrapped cuts of meat lined the shelves.

Gurnie Starking was one of the assembled, hat pressed to his sternum. He nodded at Mary.

My Paul, he'd said.

"High time we got track of you," Rusty said, his jovial tone out of place among the dry faces. "Funniest damn thing, too, that not a one of our three motels, hotels, or boardinghouses had a record of a Mrs. Garrett checked in the past week. So I suppose you must've just di-vined yourself here."

Mary's stomach was empty, and with her wolf brain, even the raw pink pork loins at the neighboring butcher case tempted. Beneath the hunger, she felt a question about Martha, the one who'd pro-pelled her here, begin to form.

"As soon as we got this call, though, I knew we needed to get Mrs. Garrett here, since her insights will surely be highly valuable, indeed." Rusty spoke expansively, as though introducing her from a podium.

The men, conferring with one another, showed few signs that they were paying any attention to her. Gurnie was listening, though, and said in a low voice, "Yes, sir, I hope they will."

Rusty's hand was an upturned claw that he caught on Mary's elbow. "Your items for inspection can be found over here," he said, and led her to the steel butcher counter, on top of which a woman was stretched out, her arms draped over the edges, her ankles crossed in sacrificial repose.

Not a woman, though. The shape of her, arranged in empty clothing. A boy's-style shirt, a ribbed sweater, dungarees. Riding boots, caked and flaking. White, plain underpants, a grayed brassiere folded over what would have been a torso. Clothing that Polly's apparition was wearing in her bedroom yesterday. But who thought to lay out these things like a ghost?

"Gurnie's already told us as much he knows," Rusty said. "And Bernice's verified by telephone what Gurnie couldn't. Laundresses know all our secrets." His voice shimmered to somber.

Mary hovered over the clothes, her lip curling as she smelled at them, freezer-burned and dank. Rusty poked with the handle end of a meat tenderizer at the carefully laid impression of a body. What a game to play, with Polly's father standing right there.

"All can be traced to the Starking girl, of course. Her mother saw her leave the house that day, and her father bought her those riding boots not six months ago," the sheriff said.

"You found it this"—Mary waved her hand—"this way?"

"Wrapped up in a tidy little package, found right inside that egg cooler over there, folded neat as you please like someone's mother had packed her for camp." Rusty snorted as he gestured toward one of the coolers just to his left, tidy white eggs lined up like pearls. "We aren't sure how long it sat there. Polly had no particular connection to the market nor to any young man working here, so far as we can see. The package of clothing could have been placed in the cooler either from here or"—he tapped the glass with the tenderizer—"since these coolers have no back, direct from the stockroom."

The reward for finding Polly Starking dead was five hundred dollars. All the conceivable possibilities for that girl—she might have run away to Hollywood, eloped with a boyfriend, skipped town for adventure or sex—collapsed into one flat truth, a steel trap falling shut. Mary wished to move backward just ten minutes in time, when Polly could have been alive anywhere, even as surely as Mary had somehow known they'd all end up here. They so often did.

Mary willed insight. Focused her thoughts on Polly, pressed away distractions from the other folks around. Yet someone nearby was panicking—she could feel it, couldn't shut it out. Rioting-against-cage-bars kind of panic that rattled her as though it were her own.

"You have anything on offer, Mrs. Garrett?" the sheriff asked, leering a bit. "You asked to be included, and I am bound to oblige such a talented and generous volunteer."

She could easily imagine the perversion of the mind that would strip a girl's body and deliver her clothes to the cruel overhead lighting of a vast supermarket. The ritual of folding each item, of waiting for them to be pulled from the cooler shelf, shaken out and inspected.

Mary was neither witch nor wolf. She felt like nothing more than a vampire now, feeding on the drained life of this girl.

Rusty looked hard at Mary's face, then said, "Of course, no one was kind enough to tuck in a confessional letter. We're also missing a Saint Anthony medal her uncle gave her for Easter some years back, which Bernice says she's usually wearing." Mary's pocketbook grew heavier with the weight of that medal, pinched from Polly's room a day ago.

"Then there's the lady's wristwatch we found and that neither parent can identify." Rusty pulled his small notebook from his back pocket. "Elgin, black strap, repairer's marks scratched in the inside back cover, dated 1944," he said, looking up, eyebrows in exaggerated points.

Mary wrapped her right hand around her left wrist and found it bare. For sixteen years, that watch had tethered her to her *before* life, to her loss. She was never without it. She rarely took it off. Had she set it on her bedside when she fell asleep this morning? How had he gotten it?

She inventoried yesterday's path through the town—the motel room, Polly's bed, the diner. Bernice's kitchen table. Rusty's back seat. Had it fallen in Polly's room, gotten tangled somehow with her things? Maybe Rusty didn't even know the watch was hers.

But another look at his leering face made it clear that he knew and that Mary was meant to take meaning from the way he dangled it before her. That she was meant to feel frightened and exposed.

There was a metallic pinch at the bridge of Mary's nose, and she felt queasy from hunger.

"Is that all, then?" she asked. Her voice sounded far away, like her ears needed to pop.

The sheriff tucked away his notepad. "Would it help you now to take any of these items with you? Maybe some particular piece"—he drew out the vowels and the sibilant *c* with menace—"might could help you wrap your head around what you've gotten yourself into."

Mary felt a wash of disbelief that Rusty would offer to turn over evidence to a stranger, even her own stolen watch, even to be cruel. And he was doing it all for an audience. The gathered men, speaking to one another in low tones, scribbling notes and shooting photographs, barely flinched at Rusty's offer. This man had probably never felt unsure, unsafe, in his whole damn life.

"I have all that I need, thank you," she said, meeting his tone with a brazenness she didn't feel.

Rusty leaned in closer. His volume lowered. "You go on back and consult your tea leaves or those witch cards I hear you've got, and I think you'll find they agree with me: It's for your own good to let things lay. Know when to mark a loss."

"And the girl . . ." she said. A query too hopeless for the lift of a question mark. If she wasn't so preoccupied with her own safety, her own loss, Mary might have felt the heft of this concession. But she was as she ever had been. Looking out for herself.

Rusty rubbed at the grizzle on his neck. "We both know that window's closed now." He managed to sound regretful about it at least. Out came a plaid handkerchief. "You're treading on damn dangerous ground here, young lady. Next time it may just be this"—he gestured toward her shabby jacket, her yellowed blouse—"nice outfit of yours folded up in that cooler. 'Course," he paused, making a show of pocketing his handkerchief, "I'm no clairvoyant."

Mary's body went cold. It may have been cloaked in deniability, but she sure as hell recognized an invitation to get out of town when she heard one.

Rusty snapped his felt hat onto his head. "I'll be talking to you," he boomed. "Do come to me with whatever you are able to divine." He pulled her hand from her side and shook it with both of his rough ones. "We sure do appreciate your charitable assistance here."

The question, then, was for whose benefit this whole performance—getting her here, threatening her—was orchestrated. Who would be watching Rusty, who was being protected by his ham-fisted warnings?

"Mrs. Garrett." Someone touched her shoulder and she jerked away.

Gurnie Starking was behind her now, his outreached arm floating in space. "I appreciate you coming out this way. I know Bernice and Rusty have made arrangements on how your assistance will make its way to us, but I do hope you'll let me know if I can help you," he said. "Rusty let on you had a vision of my Paul, and I was hoping if you might tell me if she were scared, or hurting, or—" and he stopped, seeming as though he couldn't go on.

Mary eyed Gurnie. The wretched man was broken into pieces and glued back together; fine fissure lines scattered across his skin. He must have been the one to insist Rusty send for her.

If she could, Mary would have summoned one of her visions just then, either as an offering to Gurnie or an act of spite toward Rusty. But the Sight was unmoved by sympathy or smallness and did only as it wished.

Mary shook her head in apology.

Gurnie said, "This here's my brother, Clarence," reaching for the shoulder of the man beside him. *The amiable Starking boys.* The man lifted his chin toward Mary.

Gurnie went on. "Bernice isn't ready to put stock in what you do, but we understand it." Gurnie nodded and looked at Clarence, face shaded by the hat he hadn't removed. Gurnie turned back to Mary.

"When we were boys, Clarence snuck out of his bed. Couldn't have been more than four. The whole family searched for this boy all day into the evening, but it were our grandmama who lay down for a nap and dreamt of Clarence, tucked under the roost of the chicken coop three farms over. And of course he was right there when Daddy went looking."

The story had the cadence of calcified mythology. Gurnie glanced back at Clarence again and squeezed at his shoulder.

The Sight reached out and slapped at Mary just then—not with any of the insight she'd tried to conjure about Polly but with a useless movie-reel image of the Starking brothers' grandmother, sweating and crying out in her sleep, then taking a switch to a young boy's back legs. Mary pinched her arm to pull herself from the vision.

"I appreciate your confidence in me," Mary said. "I hope to have more to offer very soon." And she scanned the room for Rusty as she said it; he was twenty feet away, watching her over his shoulder.

"Well, I'm hoping you might join us for dinner tomorrow night," Gurnie said. "I'll smooth it over with Bernice, and you did say being with me and Paul's mama might could help your sense of things."

Mary wasn't ready to obey Rusty's nasty threat to leave town. Still, that sense of wild panic she'd picked up earlier pulsed around her, and she could hear that man's voice from the vision she'd had on Polly's bed—*Paul*, a voice so low, so defeated. She couldn't match the voices, not yet, and there was too much she didn't know. Could Gurnie really be such a monster as to pull the clothing from his own daughter's body and plant it for all the town to paw through?

Of course he could. Mary had encountered more-ghastly men than that.

"I'd be delighted," Mary said with a manufactured ease. "Anything to get us closer to finding Polly." She didn't know yet whether she was lying, whether she would still be in Elizabethtown tomorrow evening.

"Yes, ma'am." Gurnie pursed his lips and placed his hat on his head. With the movement of his waxed-cotton coat, Mary smelled an acrid sweetness like manure and earth. Clarence smelled of it, too, and something spicy and bitter. His light-gray trousers were stained a darker color below the knees.

"What time, Gurnie," Clarence said. His voice sounded like Gurnie's, like a train slowly rolling past.

"Six o'clock, let's say," Gurnie said, and reached forward to grab both Mary's hands in some sort of prayer. Mary hated being touched, and she swallowed against the sneer that curled her lips.

"You see something before then, though, you come find me at the farm. East of Jones Lake, off Sweet Home Church Road."

"I'll remember," Mary said.

"Clarence'll hear you, too, if you have anything. You just come up to find us. The old Turner place. You just come."

Mary looked around the market as the men started gathering themselves to leave, a ginger-haired cop folding Polly's garments into butcher paper. To the right of the butcher counter, almost past Mary's notice, stood Martha and a white-haired Black man in a shirt and tie, leaning hard on a wooden cane. They spoke to each other quietly, and maybe they were passing items back and forth, but Mary couldn't entirely see. She couldn't see because Rusty had walked over to where they stood and planted himself maybe six inches away, his back turned toward them and his arms folded as he swayed a bit, into their breathing space and back again, looking as though he were merely surveying the proceedings. When the Black man took a step to his right, so too did Rusty, shifting in his shoes. The ginger-haired cop finished up with the clothing and walked past with the wrapped items in a brown sack. Rusty took a sudden and deep backward step to turn and follow the young man, sending Martha and her companion tripping out of the way, Martha taking the man's cane in the shin as they stumbled.

Mary lurked near the front door waiting for the rest of them to leave first, Clarence closing Gurnie into the passenger side of the green Starking Bros. truck, the sheriff rocking his body into his sedan.

Only after all the men had left did Mary realize she'd forgotten to look at their shoes, to look for those steel-toed boots from her vision.

She walked the three miles back to the inn, her upset streaming behind her like a yard-long ribbon. There was too much to parse and Mary felt pummeled. How careless she'd been to let her watch, the only object that meant anything to her, slip from her hands. How careless to let it become a weapon to be used against her. She had often pried the back covering off the watch to trace the repairer's markings with a fingertip. The idea that watches, of all things, carried with them the material traces of their own history. Every stutter and error recorded by the hands that had fixed them.

The one thing she'd sworn to herself she'd never let go of.

How had Rusty gotten his hands on it? An object that usually sat so close to her skin—Mary wrapped her fingers around her own wrist again. And what he'd said about her clothes, that Mary's possessions would end up stacked in a cooler like Polly's had: Was he threatening to put his hands on her himself? No, she didn't believe it.

A prediction, a sideline bet among the boys at the station? *How long till the meddling Yankee lady ends up dead, washed ashore some lake? Two to ten days, on the outside.*

No one could possibly loathe Mary as much as she loathed herself. She strode faster along the gravel roadside, as though to escape her own contempt, heading west into the setting sun.

On the concrete porches of wide-spaced houses, people sat fanning away insects and watching the sky. Mary had said yes to dinner because she might well be on a bus to Chicago by tomorrow. She'd said yes to dinner because it defied the sheriff and might even earn her that five hundred dollars.

But it was villainy itself to sit down with that family, any one of them still hoping against proof that Polly was alive.

Mary walked now past the darkened diner, past the long row of windows on Leinwand's department store that offered up her own striding reflection. A thundering log truck passed, then a trio of vehicles, honking at her, voices of teenaged boys shouting through open windows. The third in the line was the same shiny pickup truck that had ferried Mary into town, the same lanky teenager behind the wheel, now a fist pumping up and out of the window as his passenger waved a transistor radio hollering Chubby Checker.

Mary was less than a mile from the motor inn, but she skittered across Broad Street to dip into the ungridded residential streets beyond, zigzagging to avoid headlights, to avoid the constant sense of being observed by people whose expressions were ever shifting from neutral to menacing.

Mary doubled back as the road unexpectedly veered and dead-ended into thin woodlands. Mary did not walk into woods, just as she didn't share the front seat of a car with anyone so long as she could avoid it.

She got herself awfully turned around on these un-sidewalked roads, which had been tarred over so often they rose above the patchy green grass in ankle-breaking darkness. Mary's inner elbows were sticky. The seesawing song of crickets rose up. Hunger roiled her stomach; in her pocket was a hard roll and a small wedge of cheese she'd purchased at the market with the last of her jingling change. Down to six dollars now, an inn bill looming, and not sure she had enough for bus fare even to Richmond. Eventually, though, Mary was squinting at the neon Safe Lodge sign from a half block away, and the idea of her snack, a bath, and a few minutes off her feet propelled her limping figure the last several yards.

Martha leaned against the low black fence near Mary's room door. Mary recognized the woman's posture from where she stood. The maid's back was turned and her head dropped down, looking as though she was in prayer. The older man, her companion from the market, was no longer with her. Martha jolted as Mary rattled the door key from within her jacket pocket.

"Good evening, Martha," Mary said. She felt cagey about Martha's presence here, out of her uniform. Martha might have been the one to sneak into Mary's room, pass Mary's watch to Rusty at some point; nothing was impossible. And, after all, Martha had pushed her to go to that market to be paraded before those men.

Up close, Martha's street clothes were as worn and threadbare as Mary's, though of a cheaper cut and textile. Martha's plaid knee-length skirt was held closed at the hip with a series of safety pins, and pilled wear speckled her sweater at the bottom curve of her bust. Martha's head had been bowed over a stack of finger-crimped photos. She wore an injured expression.

"I'd like to talk to you," Martha said, less deferential than before, when they had been dressed for their roles.

Hands like Martha's could hold a face beneath the surface of a cold bath until the body stopped flailing. Hands like Martha's could shove a person out the door of a moving car. There was nothing Mary hadn't seen. But with Martha between her and the door, Mary couldn't figure how to maneuver them elsewhere.

Mary nodded and unlocked the door using the key Martha had given her, feeling absurd about the pretense of security.

"If we were going to end up in the same place, you might have given me a ride home from the market," Mary said, turning on the ceiling fan. The bed was made, impression of a leaned-on fist on the blanket near the pillows; it occurred to Mary that Martha had made the bed, made the impression.

"I was with my uncle Rudy. He gave me a ride," Martha said.

"Well, I'd've been happy to make his acquaintance, too." The older Black man at the market had looked friendly enough, when Rusty wasn't blocking him.

Mary shook off her jacket and flapped the neckline of her blouse where it had moistened to her skin. "Especially if it might've saved me the hike." Pulling her shoes off stung even more than the aches in them, as the rubbed-off skin beneath her stockings hit the air.

"All due respect, but you'd be hard-pressed to find any Black man in this state fool enough to put a white woman in his car."

And now that it was said, Mary remembered that of course she knew this. Still, she felt insulted by it.

Martha sat on the rough wooden chair next to the low dresser and waited wordlessly as Mary excused herself to change. In the room's awkward silence, Mary powdered her underarms and neck.

"Mr. Ardell's been asking for you," Martha said once Mary had settled upright at the edge of the bed.

"Who's that?" Mary's mind was on the phalanx of men gathered at the supermarket.

"He runs the inn," Martha said. "Your gentleman caller from the other night. I've told him you picked up your suitcase and checked out and this room's been empty since that first morning. Far as he knows, there's nobody here."

Mary shook her head. "That's—"

Martha raised a hand and continued. "Now, that's not an easy thing for me, you must see. I'll be risking my job, the longer I let you stay." Martha pressed the fingers of one hand into the palm of the other. Her bare nails were the color of the inside of a seashell. "I'm a Christian woman and I believe in offering a hand to my fellow man, but I have to consider my own, too."

Mary waited for a pause.

"Yes, I do understand. I'm grateful for what you've done," Mary said. To her own ear her voice sounded patronizing, obsequious. She couldn't get comfortable.

Martha nodded in a clipped fashion. "Then I'd like for you to hear me out."

Mary had become so used to pushing away the sensations that swirled around her that she barely noticed she was doing it. But Martha's pain, what Mary had been holding at arm's length, probably since the moment they met, dropped on her with these words.

"You know the Quarter?" Martha asked. Mary shook her head. "The Colored neighborhood down Bladenboro, next town by."

Mary opened her mouth and Martha answered the non-question. "Where I live," she said. "Girl called Jack Washington, a real tomboy in the ninth grade, played on the boys' basketball team and all that— she went out to Jones Lake with her sweetheart and some other kids back before Thanksgiving." Martha worried at her cuticle.

Mary noted the cues—*tomboy, sweetheart*. A squeeze of sadness hit her sternum.

"There's a big diving rock, and you've got to climb up the bank and walk into the woods and around to get to the top. Kids did that jump all night, one after the other, until one time Jack climbed up the bank and into the woods and took longer than she ought to appear at the top of that rock."

Longer and longer, Martha said, until it became never.

Folks from the Quarter did a search of the park every day for a week, until one day they found Jack's swimsuit folded and pressed beneath her wicker sandals in the park's boathouse.

"Did you go—" Mary began, but Martha kept speaking, her voice lowering until Mary stopped talking.

"Other girls from the Quarter have gone missing over years," Martha said. "We've got sense better than to go to that sheriff for anything"—and here Martha's voice turned more fibrous, as though ready for Mary's challenge, but Mary was too wrung out to interrupt again—"but Jack's daddy wanted to drag the lake for her, and the county said he'd need a permit from the sheriff's office to do it. Instead, that sheriff just said Jack was a troubled runaway and closed the case. Sheriff's men have been patrolling the lake with an extra heavy hand since."

Troubled runaway. Some girls were destined for that label; Mary knew that better than anyone.

"And this Jack," Mary said, "you want me to read the cards for her?"

She could just about envision Jack, curled up on the forest floor with her sweetheart, slipping off through the trees, the sweetheart watching Jack's back curve as she walked away for the last time.

But no. They'd been swimming. Martha had just said that. The sweetheart would have been treading water, then, watching for Jack to crash back through the air, to break the lake's surface and rise up smiling, shaking needles of water from her hair.

"Repeat that," Mary said. She'd let her mind wander too far and missed something.

"Another girl. Evie," Martha said. "I've got an older cousin, and her daughter Evie goes to a college up North. Evie was home for January break and was supposed to leave for college again on the twenty-eighth."

"The same day Polly Starking went missing," Mary said. And Jack's disappearance at Jones Lake—Polly's horse had been found near Jones Lake.

Martha gave another of her clipped nods. She wore her hair in a bouffant with close-shorn sides, no jewelry. Mary wondered whether Martha reserved her frivolity for those who earned it. Mary could already sense that she was a disappointment.

"Last week the college telephoned my cousin to ask why Evie hadn't come back to school." Mary saw this—Evie's mother, a middle-aged Black woman answering the telephone with a hand on her hip. The anger on her face, the flick of her middle finger on the rotary as she dialed another number, her hard expression breaking into a grimace of fear.

"And you know nothing of where she could have gone?" Mary asked. "She's never done anything like this before?"

Martha hesitated and Mary took note. She was accustomed to getting half-truths and white lies from family members.

"She left the house for the bus stop when she ought to have," Martha said, her tone deliberate. "She only had a half-mile walk up to the corner of Main Street. Somehow the sheriff got wind about Evie disappearing, and he showed up like a thunderstorm, thumping on doors, asking questions."

Something in Martha's expression implied that there was more to it, more to the thumping and questioning, but Mary was at her limit. She hadn't asked for any of this.

"And now the sheriff's walking around saying there's no use searching, that Evie might have gotten off the bus in any town between here and Boston," Martha said. "That she could be someone else's problem now."

"But you think something happened here?"

Martha looked Mary directly in the face. "No one like you has showed up here before," Martha said. She clasped and unclasped the pocketbook on her lap. "Seeing as I've come to your assistance regarding the matter of lodging, I come to you in the hopes you might press your talents into service of a good family." Martha bumped her chin higher. "Never did harm to anybody."

Everyone has done harm to somebody. Just consider Martha. The only person here who had extended kindness to Mary was now before her, extorting her.

"There was nothing in the papers about these two disappearances," Mary said. Newsmen loved to lump missing girls together, reviving old mysteries when new ones appeared—Mary imagined all of those girls inhabiting their own secluded island, united by mystery and loss.

"It wouldn't be in the paper you've been reading," Martha said, and pulled a news clipping from her pocketbook, smudged and soft with folding. From *The Carolina Times,* what looked like a Black paper out of Durham, not among the newspapers delivered to the motel office. No images of the girls, but a report largely identical to what Martha had just said.

Backed up against a wall, Mary usually raged forth, but she was aware now of the trap she was in. She would remain cordial; she would try not to weep at the unfairness of what was happening to her.

"I prefer to choose my own cases," Mary said. She studied the news clipping again, then held it out to Martha. "Rusty must have had cause for closing these two cases."

Martha made no move to take back the clipping, and she was silent long enough for Mary's own words to echo back at her: She was defending the man who'd just threatened to run her out of town. It was a knee jerk, what she'd said. A reflexive statement, a reflexive thought. She had no idea what Rusty must have or might have done. Might do.

"You find a lot of girls who've gone missing?" Martha asked, though it hardly sounded like a question. She placed her pocketbook on the low dresser and folded her hands on her lap.

"I have," Mary said. "Only five of them alive, though."

"Mind if I ask, how many of these girls you looked for have been Colored?"

There it was, the question Mary didn't realize she'd been dreading since Martha started talking. The answer was none: She found the girls in the papers and on MISSING posters. All *white papers,* she supposed Martha was thinking, but where else would she have looked? When avalanches of information came at her through visions and sound, Mary focused on the stories she understood. It was the Sight that guided *her.* It certainly wasn't by design.

"I don't suppose your people have found a way to offer a reward?" Mary asked.

Martha stared at her so hard and long that Mary had to glance away. "We all have to eat," Mary said, and thought again of the roll and cheese in her pocketbook.

"There's no reward," Martha said.

"Why don't I just read the cards for you, first? See if there's anything to see." Mary sat back on the bed and drew her pack from her handbag. She motioned Martha to sit opposite and tucked her leg to tighten the coverlet between them. "You must understand that I have little ability to guide the cards. They may have nothing to say here."

She thought again of Jack and her sweetheart, treading cold lake water together, warm only where their skin touched. The long yawn of waiting the sweetheart must have felt when Jack climbed up those rocks for her dive and then didn't return.

Mary handed the deck to Martha with instructions to shuffle while concentrating on her cousin Evie. It might matter that Martha knew Evie, or it might not. They were a trick, the cards. They always were. A gambit to curry a little favor, to buy time for the Sight to waft down.

Mary laid out a simple past-present-future formation. Three figures. Three knights: Swords, ambitions. Wands, a rush forward. The knight of cups, the Polly card: the calm figure on the white horse, wine goblet easy in his hand.

Mary wouldn't pull out her divination notebook in front of Martha, so she puzzled over what was before her. She could see reason to think that the cousin, this Evie, had simply run away with a boy, though it wasn't coming from the cards.

Martha pointed at the cards. "Are these the three girls gone missing?"

Mary said, "I don't know."

What would Mary's life have been if she'd seen stories of joy rather than pain, of completed plans instead of those choked by circumstance? If the vision she was waiting for were of Evie arriving safely at school, of Jack completing her dive, rather than the devastation that likely lurked?

"Is one of these the Starking girl and her horse?" Martha picked up the knight of cups. "This card I found by your bed, does this mean Evie and Jack and that Starking girl— that the disappearances could be related?"

Martha's voice was suddenly pitched high; Mary's body tensed, and the movement shifted the bedsprings beneath them.

"Just let me think!" Mary stood and walked to the window. She was so thirsty, her voice cracked. She couldn't see what Rusty might have to do with a Black girl from the next town over. Or if indeed he knew whatever had happened to Polly. She wanted to pound at something, to smash glass. She moved to draw the curtain back, and she heard Martha's sharp intake of breath.

"Ma'am!"

Right. She was in hiding. She was a secret.

And she'd run out of choices.

"I'll need you to bring me some food." Mary spoke with a shadowed authority; she had little left by way of upper hand.

Martha nodded. "I can do that."

"But you can't be seen hovering at this door twice a day, now, can you?" Mary said. She paced the room. "So what is our solution?"

"I'll bring you a few sandwiches tomorrow morning," Martha said. "I'll leave them tucked into the doorframe right at seven o'clock. You'll need to grab them quick so as no one gets an eyeful."

"All right, yes," Mary said.

"And if you go needing something else, you'll be best off back at the big market. It's far enough out of town. Montgomery can get you a taxicab again. I wouldn't risk that long walk in daylight—too many chances to get spotted. And Montgomery's a good man. Discreet."

So Martha had heard Rusty tell her to get out of town. What else had she heard?

"You have a photograph of Evie?" Mary asked. Martha retrieved the snapshots she'd been clutching. Fingerprints smudged the glossy coating. In one, a Black girl was seated below the photographer, glancing off to her left. The glow of her face emerged from the pitch dark that surrounded her, and she beamed like a beauty queen, a self-aware smile and bright eyes. In the second photograph, the same girl, much farther away, her hair in short, loose Dorothy Dandridge curls, stiff beside her cousin Martha, arms linked at the elbows. The girl, Evie, was much taller than Martha and, obvious even with the distance, much younger. She wore a familiar-looking coat with a fur-trimmed hood. Even through the photograph, Mary could tell the coat was red.

And then the Sight: Mary saw Evie buttoning up the secondhand red parka that Martha had bought her even though it was sweltering that September day. Evie letting Martha's eyes shine with some small sense of ownership that already the girl resented. *Suits you:* Martha's voice full and proud. Evie letting Martha smooth her sandpaper hands down the front of that coat and tweak at the hood, letting Martha press two dollars into the pocket. Evie took from Martha the meat-loaf sandwich wrapped in twice-used wax paper. Evie knew already that she wouldn't write to Martha, Mary could feel it—that a letter would have to lie, and lying would make her guilt balloon. As much as Evie bristled at her family's overattention, it hurt tremendously to break from them.

Finally, when Mary spoke, her breath was short. "I had that same red coat," she said. She hadn't meant to say it.

Martha reached to take back her photographs.

"I haven't agreed to help," Mary said. "I haven't agreed to anything at all."

"Why don't you just think on it," Martha said. No *ma'am* this time. Martha picked up her pocketbook and stepped out of the room. "Once you decide, I'll bring you those sandwiches. And keep those curtains drawn."

The night had fallen to crickets and frogsong. Her stomach too tight to eat, Mary continued to sit awkwardly on the edge of the mattress after Martha's departure. Eyes closed, bra straps digging into her shoulders. Still so thirsty. The tight ache from earlier crept back to the spot between her eyes, the bridge of her nose, and quite suddenly large drops were landing, a rainfall of blood into her lap.

The chronic nosebleeds had followed Mary from childhood into adulthood. Her body unwilling to shake the habit, one of the few vestiges of her *before* life. They were the most persistent during her adolescence; how easily she could pull forth the sense memory of lying in the darkened living room in the middle of the afternoon, ankles crossed and elevated on the arm of the stiff brocade sofa, socks painted with blood splatter, a rough bath towel pressed to her face as the bleeding just kept on, her eyes watering, her breath tasting like the mildew in the threadbare old towel. The gagging feeling of hot blood running down the back of her throat. Sometimes, many times, she shared the drape-drawn room with her mother, Jean, who frequently sought its cool sanctuary to sit with a washcloth over her eyes. On those afternoons, Jean would transfer the cloth from her forehead to Mary's—*Paula's*—and, through the cave of her own breathing, Paula would hear the tumble of ice cubes, the liquid sigh of some clear spirit hitting the glass. Jean would sit on the sofa beside Paula's head, as often as not pinning Paula's hair to the cushion with her thigh, and press the cocktail glass to the bridge of Paula's nose. The pain of the cold was sharp metal, was the weight of five bricks, and receded only in the flashing moments when Jean raised her glass to her lips. Eventually, and with never a word exchanged between the two of them, Paula would roll to her side to check whether the bleeding had slowed. She would lie on her hip then, depleted, and Jean, refreshed, would fix another cocktail and leave for wherever she left for.

Paula would try to drift off to sleep, but her face was pressurized and she couldn't breathe. When she blew her nose, she would feel the clot in her sinuses, the slow pull of everything behind it, around her eyes, past her tear ducts, everything in her head coming out in the towel in her hands, and the bleeding would begin anew.

Sometimes, on the worst days, she would end up vomiting all the blood she had swallowed, a handful of what looked like bright-red blood jelly, the reason that she still wouldn't touch either ketchup or tomato aspic.

The grotesqueness of living inside this body knew no bounds.

In the motel room, where there was no one to tend to her, Mary pinched hard at the fatty part of her nose, dropped her chin to her chest, and wrapped her other hand around the back of her neck. She sidestepped to the bathroom to grab the bath towel and leaned against the sink as she waited. Ten minutes to stand, head bowed like a penitent. Ten minutes of shallow breaths through her drying mouth. But without her watch, she had no idea how much time was passing, and she stayed there for what might have been six minutes, what might have been forty.

Once the worst of the bleeding had abated, Mary climbed into the bath on kitten feet. Violent sobs choked her before she realized she was crying, and the weight of the whole god-awful day landed on her shoulders like iron, pushing her further down into the bathwater. She could barely breathe with the sobbing, and she hit her sternum with her fist over and over. She would have rent her garments but, naked and tender, she scratched at the skin of her throat, thudded her head against the tile wall.

Martha's accusation was so piercing that Mary couldn't bear to replay it. How dare, how dare she, how. How many had Mary not seen. How many had she saved. Five. Five girls saved. Mary had done that, and Martha had no idea of the life she lived, the constant terror of her nightmares and her visions and her goddamn memories. Mary had lived the horror of thirty-three girls' disappearances.

Thirty-four.

Jack. The image returned to her, the vision more imagination than divination, surely. Jack and her girl, the smell of each other's breath, the cocoon of infatuation, the cold spot on the sweetheart's skin when Jack climbed out of the water for her last dive.

Mary wrapped her hand around her bare wrist.

When the Sight had first begun, the small, incognito existence she'd made had splintered into this half-life she could barely cobble together. And in that five years, not once had the Sight delivered as clear a vision of a Black girl as it had half an hour ago. Mary hadn't noticed, somehow, that every girl she sought was white— it was everything else the Sight hadn't given her that she was watching for. The foresight that might have changed her life, that might have helped her avoid the wretchedness of the past sixteen years.

Mary had kept herself sane, alive, by pushing away—again and again—the overwhelming agony of others. And she had felt, at every moment, as though she might simply shatter, that each piece of her would soar in a different direction like a scattered flock of birds. As if the connective tissue that held her humanity together would simply wear away. Until the thing that had ruptured Mary's life into *before* and *after,* until the intrusive throes of vision and cacophony, Mary had never understood that pain could be an inescapable condition of life.

Mary keened, pounding a fist on the tiled walls, keened for Jack and her sweetheart and for Evie and Polly. *My Paul.* Mostly she keened for herself, the cold spot left on her skin when her own sweetheart had released her hand and walked away into the woods. She knew she had to be quiet, but the sound from her chest just grew. Mary jerked her knees and towed her head beneath the bathwater to escape the overwhelming sound—and descended into a vision of fresh hell.

Silence like a swallow. The girl she was now inside, bouncing in the back seat of a car, squinting as the car's headlights rippled on a ragged sign for JONES LAKE—NEGROES ONLY. Fear holding the girl's spine upright like a signpost. Arms inside the red parka, hands in its pockets. The car door, slick with humidity, a ragged metal hole where the inside handle should have been.

And then panic, propelling her up a tree-crowded hill and into the woods, heavy howl of breath, throwing arms against the whip of low branches, until Mary pushed her face back out of the bathwater, gasping, choking on it all.

U.S. Detectives Come to Montreal In Search of Missing Welden Girl

New York and Vermont detectives arrived in Montreal last night to direct a search in this district for Paula Jean Welden, daughter of a wealthy Connecticut industrialist, who has been missing for more than two months from Bennington College, Vermont.

A reward of $5,000 has been offered to the person who will find her alive, while $2,000 is the amount to be paid for her body in case she is dead.

Not long after she disappeared from her exclusive school, The Gazette reported that a girl resembling the missing sophomore student had been spotted by alert Canadian customs officials at Cantic, Que., on the Montreal-New York highway. The girl was on a Montreal-bound bus.

These reports were doubted at the time but numerous persons reported to police late in December and early this month that the girl, or someone resembling her, had been seen in Farnham and Montreal.

These reports were checked and proved reliable enough for several American detectives to come to Montreal yesterday, led by Det. Almo Franzoni.

The girl spotted at the border on December 12 was travelling under the name of May Gray and claimed to be a Washington stenographer. She told officials that she was going to Montreal for a week, although she did not know anybody in the metropolis.

She was very nervous, customs inspectors said. As her papers seemed in order, she was not detained and continued on her trip aboard the bus. It was only after the bus left that the officials noticed a resemblance to the missing girl whose picture they have.

The customs men notified the Vermont State Police as well as other police forces looking for the girl. It was a few days later that she was reportedly seen in Farnham previous to being seen in Montreal.

Miss Welden, daughter of Archibald W. Welden, a Stamford, Conn. industrial engineer, disappeared on December 2 wearing a red parka and hiking costume.

Anyone who could supply police with information relating to Miss Welden is requested to contact Det.-Capt. Ernest Francoeur, or the Detective Bureau at HA. 7171.

WHERE THOU GOEST

The nuns are built of shoes and skirts and dangling keys. Obeying an invisible upward gust, their habits balloon from their bodies. If someone, the hand of God, reached down, grasped them by their wimpled skulls, and shook, they would probably ring like bells.

The Girl has been awake for several weeks, unmoving on her cot. She doesn't speak, but she watches the nuns traffic around the infirmary floor. Every one of them walks with purpose—there is no dallying when faced with a divine to-do list, fifteen ailing nuns, and *her,* a mysterious girl with no name.

They speak of her and to her in unvarying volume. Sister Joseph, chin the shape of a lady's slipper orchid, complains that the Girl has increased her burden. The sister speaks with no apparent regard for the Girl's feelings.

The Girl has discovered a way to observe these encounters without interior consequence. She's taken to thinking of herself this way, as *the Girl,* and thus all happenings are filtered through the gauze of someone else's experience. The Girl's fever has spiked; the Girl's breath has turned to rotten eggs; the Girl's symptoms are resistant to Sister Joseph's penicillin. The Girl has no past; the Girl has no voice.

Sister Edwin is kinder, equally brisk, with a melodic Scottish brogue that reminds the Girl of her grandfather. Sister Edwin meets the Girl's eye as they change the dressing on her ankle and foot and tempers Sister Joseph's admonishments. "Lass, you must listen to Sister Joseph and stop fidgeting so."

"Aye," says Sister Joseph. "She can choose not to heed me, but she'll lose that leg most certain. I've already requested a bone cutter in the next supply order."

The Girl is not frightened. None of this is happening to her, after all.

When the Girl first awoke in the infirmary, there was another young woman occupying one of the cots: Sister Felix, the novice who had sprained both ankles in a tumble down the rectory steps. Sister Felix was a companionable presence and not the least bit dissuaded from her chatter by the Girl's persistent silence. No one else was answering her, besides; the other cots' inhabitants slept through the day, an untrained orchestra of aged soprano snorers.

"The Angel Brigade," Sister Felix said one day, catching a slight movement in the Girl's brow as a coughing fit erupted on the other side of the room. "They lie here, half alive, secretly pleased to be suffering so long for the Lord," she whispered. She gestured with her Bible at the splints on her ankles. "I might have a more sanguine attitude about my own confinement if I could believe my suffering was for the glorification of God rather than the polish on Father Helmsley's kitchen floors."

What was the Girl's suffering for?

Sister Felix's confinement wasn't indefinite, though. After two weeks, she was hobbling with crutches and a few days later was sent back to her own cell. Since her departure, she's returned just once to visit the Girl; she stayed only ten minutes, the Girl's silent companionship likely less appealing now that the wide world was open to her.

Before Sister Felix left, though, she placed a tarnished medal on the Girl's bedside table. The Girl's skin prickled with Sister Felix's closeness.

"Saint Anthony," Sister Felix said. "He's the patron saint of lost things and lost people. You must place the trinket to your lips and say—" Here she interrupted herself. "You may recite it internally, I'm sure. You must say, 'Saint Anthony, Saint Anthony, please come down. Something is lost and cannot be found.'"

The ditty was immediately caged in the Girl's mind, and now she has no choice but to hear it echoing—a trapped bird whistling, someone is lost and cannot be found.

The day that Sister Felix left, the other nuns started dying. It seems to the Girl, with her long tenure in the infirmary, that Sister Felix was a puff of air, and now that she is gone, the nuns' lungs have deflated. Three have gone in less than one week. Sisters Joseph and Edwin, unaffected by the passing of their charges, strip the cots down to the mattress ticking and remake the beds with coarse white sheets just in time for the incoming shuffle of new patients.

The Girl imagines that somewhere outside this room is a line of broken nuns, each waiting her turn to release her muscles on the stiff surface of a cot and relinquish the toil of existence to a wasting death. And it occurs to her that her presence might be keeping some overdue nun on her swollen feet, polishing the rectory steps that Sister Felix had scuffed as she fell.

The Girl can muster no guilt for this.

It is May now, Sister Joseph says. The infirmary's window is a relentless blur of raindrops, and newly returned birds sing unseen. The Girl has always loved May.

It is May and Sister Edwin is visiting family and Sister Joseph alone ushers the broken nuns into their beds and tidies the dead ones into the afterlife, where they doubtless stand in another limping line, waiting for space in heaven. The Girl suffers the loss of Sister Edwin's buffering kindness, and Sister Joseph is delighted to castigate the Girl over the care of her injured leg.

"The infection is not abating," says Sister Joseph. "I'm going to call in Dr. Hodges. He'll be in the infirmary next week to see to Father Helmsley's cough." Sister Joseph changes the dressing; the Girl does not speak. She has nothing to say that will satisfy Sister Joseph.

"The bandage is covered in dust," declares Sister Joseph. "Why is filth so drawn to you?" The Girl knows the answer, knows that she pulls tragedy to herself like a magnet.

The Girl is a ghost hunter.

It is languor, not locks, that keeps the nuns in the infirmary, and no one guards the doors at night when the Girl rises and drags her lame leg behind her across the infirmary floor. The corridor outside has never been electrified, and a single gas lamp burns near the window at the opposite end. The Girl spreads her wings and braces herself on the corridor walls as she moves toward the chapel nave.

Sister Felix has said there are ghosts in the convent. She whispered it to the Girl in the night: the dislocated items, the wailing outside the building's great wooden double doors, the cold spots in the chapel. Here, alone in the echoing nave, the Girl hears the ghosts wailing outside the doors.

Some nights, she opens her voice and keens along, hoping that one of them will hear her. Hoping that one will appear before her. But her voice is a hairy, foreign presence in the nave; it rises like a vulgar hymn, until it shatters at the ceiling and showers back down on her like a punishment.

And yet every night the Girl waits for one ghost, in particular, to finally appear to her, to confront her for all she has done.

Tonight, the Girl does not wail. She presses the Saint Anthony medal to her tongue like a Communion wafer. Someone is lost.

All during the war, Burtie, the boy next door, had sent her letters from Belgian APOs—heavy with black marker drawn through the details, a peppering of words (*dust . . . road . . . boys*) all she could see. Her parents always thought that she'd marry Burtie, and so did he, or at least his letters said. She would read the letters aloud to her lover as they lay bare-breasted on the cabin's dirt floor, the two of them holding the pages up to the light to try to decode the redacted words. But then there was no more lover; then there was no more war. The letters, though, kept coming: From a convalescent home probably not fifty miles from here they came, uncensored at last, blooming with gore and ash. Burtie wrote of the scent of burning flesh, the dread of waking up each day. The smell of friends on fire would never leave him.

"Battle fatigue" was his diagnosis, but the Girl hadn't known what that meant. Exhaustion of war. Weren't they all exhausted?— the ration coupons and curfews and forced optimism.

After fourteen months, Burtie was discharged from the Army at last, and certainly that was a long enough rest for fatigue to subside? He'd been so patient, he wrote, so faithful, and hadn't he earned her hand at last? Maybe he had; maybe all she was worth was this unsolicited fidelity. Maybe it was the deep well of guilt over his comrades' deaths. Maybe she recognized it.

It was easy enough to sneak out of her college campus with only what she could fit into her handbag. On the long bus ride from Bennington to Montreal, the Girl had knitted her fingers together on her lap and told herself he was still good old Burtie.

The soldier who had showed up in Montreal was not good old Burtie. The two of them stood under the blue light of the motor-inn sign in their moment of reunion, and rather than embracing her, Burtie ranted, knocked his skull, paced. He'd been followed, he said. A man on the bus, the driver's suspicious glare, the nurses who whispered about him. Through her own tears, the Girl had tried to calm him, palms on his jumping skin, a new blue tattoo on his forearm of a pit viper, coiled body, head rising to strike. The next morning, she stood beside Burtie in front of that judge as he trembled, damp on the collar, unable to return her gaze for more than a flicker of a moment. *Whither thou goest, I shall go,* she recited. *Where thou lodgest,*

I shall lodge. They had to repeat the verse for Burtie, who couldn't keep his focus on what was happening.

Someone is lost and cannot be found.

She and Burtie had lain in the side-by-side motel beds that night, even though they had been pronounced Mr. and Mrs.

But here. This is the pew where the Girl was found, weeks and weeks ago. A red parka, bare and brown-streaked feet. She was not sleeping when she was found, or at least her eyes were open, but she was so unmoving that the altar boy screamed loud and high, thinking her dead.

The Girl does not remember this. She does not remember the scream, or the pew, or the altar boy clanging the church bells and crying for help. She remembers only the nuns and the infirmary and Sister Felix's ghost stories. She remembers only getting on the bus headed back to New York, hoping to shed all that had happened.

But what happened is written on the Girl's body; she can still feel Burtie's hot breath on her face. Suddenly waking to find her wrists bound above her head with her own nylons. His hand on her throat, his urgent whisper—*Paulie, Paulie, Paula*—

He kept her there, in the motel bed, for two more days, barely touching her. Ranting. Weeping. Pacing, the battle hitch in his leg. He disappeared for hours at a time. Her cheeks tight with tears, dark flakes of dried blood on her upper lip. Smeared black makeup beneath her eyes, lipstick bleeding into the corners of her mouth. Red-faced and swollen. In her reflection in the large mirror canted across from the bed, she was monstrous.

And then on the third day, Burtie walked into the room whistling, bright-faced and jangling with nerves. He untied her wrists, then held her parka out for her like a proper gentleman. He wanted to take her on a date, he said. To celebrate.

There was a raw patch on her left wrist, where the nylon had pressed her watchband into the skin, and Burtie kissed it before looping her elbow into his.

They stepped outside and the Girl saw that it had snowed, the

whole parking lot and road beyond puffed and sparkling. She scanned
the horizon, looking for the direction of her escape, but then suddenly they had arrived: a diner, just one door over from the motor
inn, and already Burtie was ushering her inside, his elbow still
clamped around hers.

They sat at the counter and the Girl made eyes at the waitress,
who shuffled back and forth, thunking coffee mugs and heavy plates
of hamburgers and wilted French fries on the Formica.

Burtie sat sideways on his stool, his knees open wide to lock
around the Girl. He cartwheeled the menu in his hands.

"Shall we share a burger?"

"All right, yes," she said. She glanced back and forth from him to
the waitress, who avoided eye contact with studied perfection. Everyone in the diner, in fact, stared at their hands or their companion
or their meal, never looking up at the Girl with the smeared makeup
and the ponytail ratted up from three days on her back.

The Girl didn't scream. Why hadn't she screamed, pounded the
counter, stood on the stool, and grabbed the waitress's apron? The
Girl cannot understand it now, how anyone could sit there so meekly
for as long as she had.

When she indicated a need for the ladies' room, Burtie stood and
walked her down the back hallway and leaned against the doorframe.
He opened the door for her. "I'll keep watch, Paulie. You always have
been able to count on me to keep you safe."

What did *safe* mean, then?

Inside the green washroom: no windows, two wooden toilet
stalls, a janitor's cupboard with a bottle of bleach, white vinegar,
Borax, and, on the bottom shelf, a rusted green and red tin of Energine, skull and crossbones on the back, sweet smell of fruit juice.
The Girl held the tin and paced the cramped room.

She told herself it would just make him sick. Recited it aloud to
make it true: just sick enough that she could leave, go to the hospital,
find someone to take proper care of him. Keep him from danger.
From hurting himself.

Where thou goest.

The glass soap dispenser was empty, and the Girl unscrewed it and filled it halfway with the solvent. She wedged it into the pocket of her dungarees, loose and chafing after days of wear.

Then she screamed into the crook of her elbow and threw the empty canister across the room.

Burtie's lemonade or his manic mind must have disguised the taste of the cleaner, and the Girl salted and salted their French fries.

The door to the sacristy opens and Father Helmsley enters the nave. His presence is intrusive and blunt—the Girl has seen only nuns since she awoke. The sisters conduct their movements with an efficiency lacking in self-consciousness, while the father's demeanor is squarer and fills more space. He presses a light switch and obliterates the Girl's dark and calm. The Girl feels a tickle in her shoulders as he approaches.

Father Helmsley strides as if to take the empty spot of pew beside the Girl, then hesitates before seating himself on the bench in front of her, twisting around and hooking his arm along the back of the pew to face her.

The Saint Anthony medal in her mouth tastes like pennies.

"Sister Joseph reports to me of your progress," he says. "I hear there is renewed concern over the persistence of your injury."

The Girl has been seated so as to cradle her injured left leg on her right knee. She presses her hand to the heat of the bandage.

"Sister Joseph is a competent caretaker," he says. "Attentive. During the war, several dozen GIs were sent here each month from Fort Meade for care. I believe that many of them chose to live simply for fear of incurring Sister Joseph's disapproval." Father Helmsley chuckles in obvious self-pleasure, but the chuckle hicks into a full-throated cough that lasts for nearly a minute.

"I'm the one that brought you from this spot to the infirmary," he says, once he's recovered his voice. "Other than the soldiers, it's unheard of for us to take in members of the public. You are a lucky girl."

The Girl thinks of Father Helmsley's thick arm wrapped under her lower back, his hands on her hip and the skin above her knees.

He shifts in the pew. "Of course, I was—and we are—humbled to provide succor to any of God's children, yourself included."

The Girl has not earned succor.

Burtie retied the Girl when they returned from the diner. Already sick to his stomach, sweat dripping from his face to the Girl's as he leaned over her.

He fumbled the knots. Left them big. Sloppy.

He lay on his back with his head in the Girl's lap, talking about other versions of him, other selves whose draft number hadn't come up, who'd registered as a conscientious objector and spent eighteen months stationed at a mental hospital in Florida. As the poison cramped his abdomen, as his stomach distended, he whispered. "We might have ended up anywhere," he said. "And if we had been anywhere but on that road, maybe our boys wouldn't have died."

Burtie spent much of that night moaning from the motel bathroom, and the Girl worked those knots for hours, until she was free.

Climbing back to the bed on all fours, Burtie whispered, *Paulie,* breeze through a corn husk. The whites of his eyes a deep crayon yellow. She wasn't sure he could even see her.

She gathered Burtie's things from the dresser. Traded her sneakers for Burtie's Army-issue boots, pressing socks into the toes to make them fit.

There was no light that faded from Burtie's eyes, no sudden wind in the room at the departure of his spirit. There was just the sound of his whispering, and then there was not.

She took Burtie's wallet. She took the motel key. She wiped the makeup from her face and retied her ponytail. At the front desk, she paid their bill through the following night.

She took a walk. She did not look for a police station or grasp the arm of the cop she passed. She did not call the hospital from a pay phone. She did not send an ambulance to the motel. She bought a bus ticket and left all of it behind.

She has not earned succor.

"You spoke that night," Father Helmsley says, his voice cracking the silence and commanding the Girl's attention. "You cried out the entire length of the corridor, and you moaned from your cot all night long. When Sister Joseph and I asked your name, you said you had none. When we asked about your home, you said you had none. But when the boy first brought me here to this spot where you sat, I asked you then if you were ill. You looked not at me but at the door and said, 'I am seeking wisdom.'"

The Girl does not remember this, but she knows that he is wrong.

"Such a curious response," he says. "Wisdom is found only in the Lord's grace. But here, you may at least find healing."

The Girl is not here for wisdom. She has not come for healing. She came to find Wise.

Getting on that bus in Montreal, wanting to leave everything behind, the Girl tried to come back to the beginning, to the place where Wise was lost. To the moment the Girl became the type of monster who cared for no one but herself, who could end Burtie with barely a regret.

Where thou goest.

The Girl's heart is beating through her injured leg.

She wonders whether even Father Helmsley recalls that the wedding vows come not from Jacob or Abraham or Adam but from the Book of Ruth. A woman grabbing the hand of her beloved companion, Naomi. *Where thou goest, I will go. Where thou diest, will I die.*

What the Girl wouldn't give to clutch Wise's hand to her breast again.

"In Luke thirteen, Jesus transforms a woman who had been crippled for eighteen years." Father Helmsley ticks a finger toward the Girl's bandaged leg.

The Girl's leg is not the part of her that needs to be transformed.

"And in Matthew nine, he heals a crippled man begging outside the synagogue," he says.

The Girl is willing to sit here, to be a beggar, to wait as long as she must for Wise's ghost to hear her keening.

"In Mark seven," says Father Helmsley, "Jesus heals a mute by spitting on his own finger, touching it to the man's tongue, and saying to him, 'Be opened.'"

The Girl notes Father Helmsley's use of the present tense, giving the impression that the events happen on a constant loop or that Father Helmsley doesn't understand that there is a point at which past rushes into present and ends.

Father Helmsley places his fingertip on his tongue. "Shall I?"

The Girl withdraws.

"Ahh," says Father Helmsley, wagging his damp fingertip in the air. "Then prayer is the best course for you."

There is no amount of prayer that can restore all the Girl has lost.

He pushes himself up from the pew. "Consider these miracles as you say your prayers, my girl, and have faith," he says. He raises a flat hand in the air, canted as though to slice between them. "In nomine Patris et Filii et Spiritus Sancti," he says.

The Girl does not move as Father Helmsley crosses back to the sacristy door, shutting the light at the threshold.

The Girl spits the Saint Anthony medal into her hand and wings it hard across the chapel, where it pings off an altar candlestick. Someone has been lost.

The Girl has no name and no home. *Where thou goest,* she whispers, quiet enough for the ghost to hear. *Where thou lodgest, I shall lodge. Where thou diest, I shall die.*

And there I shall be buried.

She stretches out on the pew, her back to the cool hard wood.

SPELLS FOR SINNERS, PART THREE

Mary rose from her motel bed and was startled by someone across the room moving toward her.

Damn it. It was just the reflection of her own stooped figure. With all the mirrors in motel rooms these days, it was impossible to have any privacy.

Last night's vision, the girl in the red parka bouncing along in the back seat of a car, still sat on Mary's joints. She reached for her clothing and the roiling fear returned—the panic of feet stumbling up a root-rugged hill. The vision was so close to Mary's own unburied past that it might as well have been Mary herself, lurching through the woods in waning light, running after or away from someone, wrapped in that red jacket.

Mary looked through the motel door's peephole: No one strolled along the motel walkway. Crouching, she cracked open the door. A gritty doorframe, empty mat. No sandwiches. Martha had been serious, then, about her conditions for helping Mary.

You hungry?

All night long Mary had watched on a loop her eighteen-year-old face reflected in a car window, a mid-forties maroon Studebaker sedan filled with cigarette smoke and wet heat and a tinny Benny Goodman coming from the push-button receiver. *You hungry?* asked the middle-aged white man when he stopped, leaning across the bench seat to press open the passenger door for her. *I've got some sandwiches and soda pops my daughter packed for me. More than I could eat on my own.*

Call me Paul. Her own voice, younger and more obsequious, lilting up at the end in a way it no longer did. She'd wanted to hear someone call her that again.

And so she let her foolish desire draw her into that passenger seat, Benny Goodman swirling, condensation building on the car's side window, the first timid snowflakes falling outside. *Paul's no kind of name for such a pretty girl. It's not so safe to be walking around looking as pretty as you do.* She'd answered him that she was familiar with the trail, that she'd just hiked it last month. She hadn't understood safety the way he meant it. Not then.

Mary was a haunted house, filled with all manner of horrors, half of them her own.

Now she wrapped her head in a snagged silk scarf. Above the sagging bed, reflected in the wide wall mirror, the knockoff van Gogh that Mary had noticed the first morning, the woodland landscape with the fairy-tale girl.

Except now: The figure, the girl, was missing. A blank spot on the canvas. As though the girl had simply faded away, leaving behind all that surrounded her in the image.

Mary snapped her fingers to shake herself from the vision, but the girl's absence remained. Mary faced the painting, climbed standing onto the bed to run her fingers over the canvas. The girl was gone.

The Sight would never fail to remind her that there was one lost girl, at least, whom Mary could never find. She reached to twist her watch but found the wrist bare. All around her was loss. She cut off the choking sob that threatened.

"Enough," she said aloud. "Enough." She grabbed her pocket-book and strode to the motel door, yanking it open without checking for passing guests.

On the other side stood Martha, key in hand, Hoover leaning against her thigh. Her face opened in surprise but closed back to neutral just as quickly.

"You're still here," she said to Mary, a flat tone to her voice.

"I am," Mary said. She stepped back, expecting, she supposed, that Martha would reach out with a white sack of sandwiches. But Martha merely wheeled the Hoover into the room and plugged it into an outlet near the dresser with the snappy and sure movements of someone who performed the task a dozen times a day. Martha grabbed her supply bucket from the walkway and stepped past Mary toward the bathroom.

"On your way out, though, I suspect," Martha said, not turning to her. "So many places to be."

Mary moved her pocketbook from one hand to the other. "Just coming to look for you," she said, projecting so that her voice would carry into the bathroom, but Martha returned in the middle of Mary's sentence. Martha's eyes were trained on her toes, following, Mary came to see, a dotted pinstripe of blood that trailed from the bathroom sink to the foot of the bed. The very spot where Mary had sat when her nosebleed came on so suddenly last night.

Standing halfway across the room, Martha glanced up to meet Mary's eyes. "Looking for me?" she said, and her tone was musing, far less urgent than Mary felt.

"There—" Mary cleared her throat. "There was mention of some sandwiches," Mary said, and loathed each syllable as it left her mouth. Her indignity laid bare in this shabby room, on this carpet painted with her weakness.

Martha's lips twisted, as though she was biting the inside of her mouth, and she brushed past Mary and down the motel walkway. Mary hesitated, worried about that sleazeball owner, but hunger and desire won out. She followed Martha into the lobby, empty of guests.

Montgomery, the day clerk who had called for Mary's taxi yesterday, sat behind the high reception counter, reclining and smoking a hand-rolled cigarette. He was a lanky Black man with a mustache and deep parallel lines between his eyebrows. He paged through *The Carolina Times,* the Black newspaper Mary recognized from Martha's clipping last night. Mary squinted at the headlines from across the room but couldn't make anything out except a blurred back page of red-and-black advertisements.

Montgomery came straight to his feet once he noticed her. "Mrs. Garrett," he said. "Good morning, ma'am." Mary turned away from the forced humility of his posture and watched instead as Martha unlocked a small storage cupboard behind the desk. The clock on the wall read 11:55. Morning, but barely.

"My understanding as I left last night was that we were under no enduring arrangement." Martha's voice, coming from inside the cupboard, was muffled when she spoke. She turned back, holding a tin of Energine stain remover and a pair of peach-colored rubber gloves. She shook the tin hard as she locked the cupboard behind her. "I was under the distinct impression that you were uninterested in accepting the case of two missing Colored girls." Martha hit the last three words slant, as though twisting them.

Mary's eyes flicked in Montgomery's direction. He still stood at attention, and he made some noise by picking up the telephone receiver. "Something I can do for you this morning, ma'am?" he asked. Mary didn't know him from Adam. Did she imagine his snide undertone?

Or was she simply angry at herself, standing useless and penniless, waiting for Martha to bestow a modicum of attention? A motel room and a cloak of secrecy yanked away unless Mary could conjure some vision about Martha's missing cousin, Evie. It was absurd and inevitable, and it infuriated her.

With her unruly Sight, Mary couldn't even be certain that last night's vision had been about Evie. She was inside that girl as she ran and couldn't see her.

Martha pressed open the glass lobby door with her hip and took a step into the walkway. "And now I just find myself wondering what in the world is keeping you from gathering your belongings and vacating your room." Bells rang, small tinkly bells, as Martha exited.

Mary followed, looking again at Montgomery, who twitched his mustache and made a snicking sound with his lips as he replaced the telephone receiver.

Martha carried the green tin of Energine into Mary's room and rummaged through her supply bucket for a large saddle brush. Dropping fluidly to her knees, Martha began working at the streak of Mary's blood on the pale-beige carpet.

"I had a vision last night," Mary said. Her tone was petulant, she knew; she couldn't help it.

"That so," Martha remarked mildly, and returned to her task. She scrubbed her right arm away and back, leaning her body into the movement, pausing only to squirt more of the clear liquid from the tin.

"There was no need to try humiliating me in front of that man," Mary said. "I'm low enough already." The apple-juice odor of the cleaner filled the room.

Martha didn't answer, her arm still stroking back and forth, her hips rocking with the effort.

"You think this town sprang into being the moment you walked in?" Martha finally said. "Folks here have had whole lives, whole generations, you know nothing of. You think you're privy to anything folks here don't already know?" She shook her head and squirted liquid from the tin. "What a piece of work is man," she said, and scrubbed some more.

Lord, Mary couldn't parse this town, these people. They wanted, they didn't want. They opened, they closed. They watched her constantly but averted their eyes. The beast in her empty stomach yowled; Mary stepped toward Martha.

"I saw that red coat of hers," Mary said. "Evie's coat."

But Martha just kept on scrubbing. The smell of the cleaner was sickly sweet.

"The coat you gave her." The words left Mary's mouth like a punch, but still Martha didn't reply. Mary was mad and wanted to make some sort of angry gesture, but she couldn't bring herself to walk past Martha's crouched figure to slam the bathroom door, and there was nowhere else to go. She stepped out of the motel room and, fool that she was, she pounded hard, twice, at the doorframe, pounded and growled shortly through gritted teeth. Her body could betray her in a hundred different ways, and here was one of them: It had to lash, to smash, to pound or throw when it couldn't hold everything in.

Over her shoulder, Mary watched a man in a lightweight rain jacket amble up the walkway toward her, his mouth wrinkling in judgment. She turned and marched ahead of him. He could be one of Rusty's men. He could be no one. He could be the man chasing that girl up the wooded hill. Mary didn't know a damn thing, not really, worth a five-hundred-dollar reward for a dead girl or a packet of sandwiches. She was fooling herself to think she was anything more than a vulture.

Mary turned the corner when she reached the end of the building and paced across the strip of mulch at the far side of the parking lot. The other hotel guest stepped inside and, through the lobby window, she watched him speak to Montgomery. She kept her head turned from the road, watching too in the window's reflection for any sign of Rusty or his car.

"All right, now."

Mary jumped at Martha's voice, close and impatient.

"You got me out here. What more do you want to say?" Martha peeled the rubber gloves off her hands and punched them into the pockets of her uniform dress. That curled red script on her name badge, the *Housekeeping* Mary had noticed, faded into white in the sunlight.

Mary worried at the knot on her scarf and opened her mouth.

"Hold up," Martha said, and held a hand out while looking over her shoulder. Without touching Mary, she led the two of them around the corner into the motel's carport, away from the road and the bank of room windows. Mary's relief at the hiding spot was tempered by her suspicion that it was Martha who didn't want to be seen with her.

"Go on. Say your piece," Martha said. Mary had squandered any generosity Martha might have felt toward her last night, and this unvarnished version of Martha disquieted her. Every day is a new opportunity to learn something about oneself, and on this day Mary was learning she preferred that even her extortionist be cordial.

In a measured tone, Mary related last night's vision: the girl in the back of the car, the red parka. The missing interior door handle. The headlights sweeping past the Jones Lake sign. And then the panicked run up the hill—but there she stopped, because what could lie beyond that run that Martha could stand to hear?

Martha mashed her fists into her full pockets. She looked out toward the slim patch of light bending around the corner of the building. Mary's stomach grumbled and she clutched at it with both hands. Martha showed no sign of having heard.

A dizziness overtook Mary—a combustible cocktail of exhaustion, hunger, despair. Shame. Eyes she couldn't trust. And more—Martha's pain, which last night had been raw, pure sensation and loss, pulsed off her now, waves of anger and disgust.

"Just what am I supposed to do with that?" Martha said to the sunlight. "Just wh—" And she tilted her head back on her neck. Her face collapsed into itself, and long and low and unbending, she bellowed.

The heartbreak of it crashed down on Mary's shoulders, and she backed against the wall and slid to a crouch. She had felt the anguish of dozens of families; she had endured cracking thunderstorms of it echoing inside her head for days. But somehow she'd failed to expect it here. She'd failed—

Spilling around Mary was every sweet memory Martha'd had of Jones Lake now warping in its opposite—like water on fire. A gathering of Black men in white shirtsleeves standing waist-deep in the lake, plunging person after person into the water in a gesture that held violence and grace in equal measure—cold wash of brown water, expanding lungs at the wheezing rise back toward the white heat of the sun, the tea-colored stains on the clothing, the promise of being brand new.

Smooth bare feet hopping, one to the other, off the hot rocks waterside, the rising clatter of a dozen children's voices, begging, hooting, scamming nickels off the aunties to pay the swimming fee, then the shock of the cold splash, toes stubbed over rocks half buried in the sand.

The hot sun evaporating water from a shoulder, leaving a coat of caked sand behind on the skin.

The willing weight of a married man's body on Martha's as the ferns fingered through her hair like other lovers, as the sun set over his broad back, as her desire found its rhythm and gasped.

Martha's memories all skimmed past on Mary's interior projector as they became corrupted by this new knowledge, this new pain. Someone had drilled to the safest, most tender place and there had begun their campaign of brutality.

Martha's keening quieted; the memory reel had spun to empty. Mary wiped away the wetness from her cheeks and rubbed the empty spot on her wrist where her watch should have been.

"I'm sorry, I'm so sorry," Mary said. Would all of this flatten her, flatten them all, before it ended?

"So you've got no sight on a driver? No eye on the car?" Martha pressed her lips together.

"No." Mary knew she had delivered just enough information to devastate. She felt the squeeze of her empty stomach again, a hammering behind her eyes. "I've . . . I've been where you are, I know—"

Martha stared at Mary just then with an expression of such hatred that Mary's words, whatever they would have been, dried up.

"You think any of these families care about that?" Martha said. "About whatever happened to you that pushed you to live like"—she gestured, an angry finger from Mary's head to her toes—"like this? You think I care if you can see enough of yourself in me?"

Martha shook her head, looking at her hands as she pulled the rubber gloves back on. "No, sir, I can't say as I give one damn." She glanced back up at Mary. "But if you're itching for someone to confide in, then maybe you can get that sheriff to buy you lunch again."

Rusty is my enemy, Mary thought to say. It took her a few heartbeats to understand everything that was intended with that sentiment; somehow, she'd still figured Martha had food squirreled away for her in a locker somewhere, that Martha had bet on Mary and Mary would be taken care of.

"He was here, your man, this morning," Martha went on. She waved a gloved hand in the air. "Came by to make sure you'd checked out."

Martha wasn't giving her a single minute to figure things out, to catch up. "And you told him what?" Mary said. She didn't know whether she was hurt or angry or afraid, but her voice came out hard.

Martha met her eyes. "Montgomery'll take that room key whenever you're through with it," she said, and turned to walk out of the carport.

Martha had left Mary's room door open, and Mary returned to the spot at the end of the bed, gazing down at her feet and the dark-brown mark left by the cleaning liquid and her own spilled blood. Every space was haunted by something. She felt the residual clenching of muscle, the high pitch of the silence. Mary looked at the mirror, the reflection of the empty spot in that painting above the bed.

She hadn't been looking for herself in others. She hadn't. She'd only ever been looking for Wise, the girl missing from the painting. The girl missing from her life.

Mary fished yesterday's stale roll out of her pocket. Hot water from the tap and the sole tea bag in the courtesy mug. She steeped weak pink tea and soaked the roll bit by bit until it was soft enough to chew. The idea of giving up her room was laughable, the privilege of a woman with options. Mary had none. No future, either: Her empty mug offered no tea leaves to read, no smudges of half-truth.

She wouldn't spend the night on a depot bench somewhere, not if she could help it.

She must have dozed off. She turned to the bedside alarm clock, parked at 3:25. On closer inspection: The clock's second hand hesitated, ticked forward, then back, then back again. Even time was untrustworthy here. And with her watch ripped off her wrist, all for Rusty to finger it with malice, Mary herself was unmoored in time.

She crept out to the covered walk and checked the lobby clock through the window, keeping herself out of sight. Now 5:52. It was a dreary evening, the gray sky mixing with the dusk, rain falling steady and cold.

"Mrs. Garrett."

The voice behind her was low, and the whisper of it crept up her neck like an itch.

"Mrs. Garrett, I don't mean to startle you." Clarence Starking stood behind her in his trench coat. "Gurnie sent me over to see if you might still be here, on account of the rain. Him and Bernice didn't want you getting soaked on your way over for dinner." Rainwater pooled in the brim of his hat.

She'd forgotten all about dinner, but her stomach grumbled at the idea.

"Ma'am?" he said, and gestured toward the green pickup, where a blue tarp had been tied over the forest of spiky farm equipment.

Mary didn't let her face show the revulsion she felt at the idea of squeezing into the cab of that Starking Bros. truck with a man who smelled of livestock. A rush of water hit the awning above them, and the fabric stretched into a bowl that dipped low enough to brush the top of Clarence's hat.

Mary looked down at Clarence Starking's feet, shod in dark-green galoshes.

She nodded and allowed Clarence to run ahead of her in the downpour to open the passenger door. Inside the truck, everything was slick and humid. Mary kept both fists visible in her lap, her pocketbook tented against her chest.

And just then the Sight took her, offered up again that distressed grandmother in a replay of the vision Mary had gotten at the supermarket, the clairvoyant grandmama who reached out to switch the back of a young boy's legs, who now slapped at the adolescent version of that same boy in a fit of fear or frustration. Then that gesture of rage faded into another moment: One of the Starking brothers, face younger and rounder than that of the man who carefully closed Mary's car door, brushed past the old woman shoulder first, in a rough gesture that tumbled her to the floor. From the rug, legs awkwardly beneath her, the old woman wrapped her arms around herself and twisted her lips to shout in the direction of the door, through which the young man had already left. The vision played like a silent film, and then the image faded to gray, and there was only this man sitting beside her, keying the ignition, and pulling into the driving black rain.

File of Missing Persons

It looks as if the case of Paula Welden might go into the unsolved file of missing persons—a file that is thicker than many persons realize. Unsolved disappearances are relatively rare but there are enough to show that, small a world as this may be, it is big enough so that many things can happen without attracting notice.

Most of the search for Paula Welden has been based on the assumption that she started on a hike on the Long Trail. But Bennington College is some miles from the Trail entrance and it was 3 o'clock when she left the campus. Would she be likely to start a journey of such length at such an hour, knowing darkness would be falling in an hour and a half?

There have been other and equally baffling disappearances around her. A few years ago Jerome Collins of Westminster, a middle-aged apple grower, vanished from sight. His car was found beside a road in the Ludlow section and no other clue was ever uncovered. Nobody ever came forward with any explanation for his disappearing.

An equally baffling and interesting case was that of Paul Bishop. The family lived here for some years in or about the 1920's but had moved away when this young man disappeared on the way to his wedding. He was to meet his fiancee at the Church of the Trans-figuration, better known as the Little Church Around the Corner, in New York but he didn't show up. Clues cropped up spasmodically for some years afterward but none ever proved tangible.

There are others right within this little area. Some are complete disappearances. Others are cases of persons who just left town and never took the trouble to notify anyone and some never came to public attention. And, of course, there are celebrated national and international disappearances. Justice Crater of New York left a night club, got into a taxi and never has been seen since. Rudolph Diesel, a German and inventor of the engine that bears his name, disappeared from a ship in the North Sea.

Undoubtedly numerous persons disappear deliberately and perhaps greatly enjoy intensive efforts to find them. But there must be others, and these may be the majority of cases, where a person meets with an accident under circumstances where a body is never recovered. Possibilities on this score are manifold.—Brattleboro Reformer.

Cause of Color

The iridescent color of a duck's wing patches is not due to pigment, but to submicroscopic prisms breaking the light on the surface of the feathers.

PAPER DOLLS

Lynn had hoped George might have a companion for her before he left for his most recent trip. He'd been too busy, he'd said, and now Lynn sat alone in this house with nothing but a boring old puzzle for company.

"Too busy sharpening your ice pick," she'd said, knowing that he hated when she used that name for his medical tools. With his back to her he had said, "You know, if we'd had children you wouldn't need me to pay someone to be your friend." Nasty man, sometimes.

Lynn had never wanted children, told George that his two sons were enough. His sons and her birds. Just enough space and love to share.

Anyway, George treated her like a child much of the time. She hated it, and she relied on it.

She'd done little more today than sip salty cinnamon tea and page through her book of leaf pressings. She'd never loved George's boys all that much. They were quiet and studious and forever dissecting frogs. She hid in her rooms once they returned home from school, until it was time for dinner.

They didn't live here any longer, though. They were men now, quiet and studious men, and the older, Samuel, had three more boys of his own—one set of twins, which Lynn's mother always found terribly vulgar. *Humans should not have litters,* she had said. The younger and cleverer son, Cyril, worked at a laboratory, where he dissected bigger things, calf brains and piglets, she supposed.

Lynn's upper lip twitched. In her solarium, dim in the waning evening light, Lynn spit onto the floor. She rubbed her bloated stomach, always empty, always looking full and heavy. When she pushed the wrought-iron chair back, it honked like a goose. From their cage, her Gouldian finches meeped and flicked their wings in reply. Through the glass on the other side of their cage, a large house cat stalked through the low grass.

The air was thick and perfumed today, and the fronds from the potted palm stuck to her bare shoulder as she passed. She liked the click of her hard-soled shoes on the tile. Click. Click click.

In the kitchen, someone new. A companion after all? But no, the someone new wore a blue uniform dress and stood sorting dry beans with red, chapped hands. Click. A cook, then. Click click. White-blond hair frizzed out from her downturned face.

"I'm Lynn," Lynn said. "If you're new, there are things you should know. I am allergic to bananas and bee stings and cheese. Turning thirty-five made my stomach a traitor to corn and also to nuts and seeds. Aspic makes me queasy, and dying animals make me cry. If you come across a dying animal, you must hide any evidence of it and deny that it ever was."

Lynn squinted. There was something funny about those beans.

"I don't like exotic meals," she said. "My father used to eat haggis and goose eggs for lunch, and just looking made all us girls squeal. I prefer dry toast and soft-boiled eggs for lunch and light suppers except for on Sundays. Is it Sunday? Never mind. Whatever you're making will do for tonight. Are you from Tallahassee?"

The new cook just nodded a bit without looking up from her task. Lynn was not one to manage her domestic help with as heavy a hand as her mother had, but this struck her as somewhat insolent.

Lynn sat her empty tea mug on the counter and spun it a bit, looking for patterns in the dregs.

"I suppose Dr. Frank hasn't returned yet from his outing?" Lynn couldn't remember where he'd gone; ever since the Remarkably Successful Procedure that corrected her broken mind, afternoons could vanish from memory without warning. She felt disoriented—without the past, how could she know where she was? It was certainly nearing dinnertime, though; the light was a golden pink, and she could hear the mosquitoes knocking against the screen door to the back patio. She thought to sniff the air—was dinner ready? Had she already eaten? But no, she smelled only lemons—it was winter, then, and the sun was setting early.

A motor sputtered outside the kitchen door. Who would mow the lawn at dusk? The mosquitoes alone!

"I was in love with a soldier once, and he was in love with me," she said, still spinning her mug. "The day they told me he died, I fell down on our dining room floor and didn't get up for two days." He had lived next door to her family, and before he left for the Army, she would watch him out her bedroom window.

Would George's boys join them for dinner? She looked over her shoulder toward the dining room, scouting for signs of their dissection tools. The room was dark, heavy drapes drawn against the sunset.

There used to be a large rectangular mirror on the wall behind the dining table. She remembered standing on the patio, smoking a cigarette, and watching the reflection of the sunset behind her, tiny blinking orangewhite sun changing the color of the entire sky. She remembered standing behind George's boys and watching the mirror image of them pinning open a frog smaller than her palm. Where had that mirror gone? She pressed her dry lips together: When was the last time she'd had a cigarette?

Her first cigarette, she could remember that: breathy laughter behind the school building, hands and dungarees covered in paint, stinking of turpentine, and the other girl, the other painter, fumbling with a matchbook, her watch crystal winking in the sun, cigarette moving like a conductor's baton as she screwed her lips in concentration.

Both of them so young, so, so beautiful. It was an image that floated past Lynn's eyelids with some frequency. Before her Remarkably Successful Procedure, she might have known why she clutched at it so, but now it passed by like a bird winging past her window.

Lynn touched her palms to her cheeks, fingertips to the pouches beneath her eyes. She made believe she was a blind person, creating the image of her face with her hands. She closed her eyes. She conjured a mystic, a carnival crone with drooping jowls and deep-set eyes, heavy and sparse eyebrows, skin that felt like wrinkled wax paper.

If she dug in with the tips of her fingers, she could feel the gristle of scar tissue deep behind her eyelids; she once again remembered awakening from the Remarkably Successful Procedure with eyes that looked like eggplants and swollen lids that drooped into her vision. For two days she had been able to see clearly only when she looked down.

This was in fact the part she remembered best, the weeks in which she looked like an unlucky prizefighter. Even though George had promised her that she wouldn't, she remembered too the slide of the metal ice picks into her eye sockets, both at once, chafing that tissuey skin right beside the bridge of her nose.

George didn't like her to mention that part, the bruises or the temporary loss of sight, or the weeks when she couldn't remember how to tie her shoes or how to toilet herself or the words for any of the things she knew or loved.

Lock it away—snick-snick sound with his tongue and teeth—*lock it away with the other unpleasantness. Your life is a miracle. Tell yourself that story instead.*

George had his own favorite story. From the New Testament: Jesus heals a mute by spitting on his own finger, touching it to the man's tongue, and saying to him, *I open you.* When finally Lynn's words had come back to her, when she spoke to the nurses and her sisters calmly about her preferred bloom for corsages, George said it was like she was a mute rendered vocal again. *I open you,* he whispered to her.

Lynn ghosted around the kitchen now, opening the low cupboards and drawers of hodgepodge, looking for—what was it? Her packet of cigarettes.

"Cook," she said, "have you seen my cigarettes?"

"I didn't realize you smoked," the woman said. "It's hard on the nerves, and the heart, too. Perhaps I could make you some cinnamon tea or you could work on your puzzle."

Her jigsaw puzzle was scattered across the dining room table. She'd forgotten. Cook must have noticed, or she'd been watching Lynn.

"I won't be the subject of surveillance in my own home, you know. I have a right to stand on my ground. I'm an American citizen." Lynn clicked her heels on the kitchen's red tile floor. And because she so liked the sound, she did it again. Click.

The new cook was counting out funny-looking beans.

Outside, a motor whirred to a stop. Someone would have to pick that puzzle up if the whole family was to eat here tonight.

"A soldier was in love with me once," Lynn said to Cook. "And he died, and I was so Troubled and Excited my father shook me by the shoulders until my chin hit my chest." She sat on a counter-side stool. "The war had already ended, so he couldn't have died, then his letter arrived two days later. Handwriting as clear as though it were my own, and he said he was coming home. How could he have died if he said he was coming home? I have his letters still; I keep them in my book of leaf pressings." She didn't like the look on Cook's face. "I'll show you."

Lynn clicked back to the solarium for her book. The sun had

moved to the other side of the house, and the solarium was as gray as if coated in ash. In the solarium's wide white birdcage, the pair of finches flitted when she drew close. In the dim light, she couldn't see their colors or the movement of their eyes, but they meeped and hopped. Lynn tugged a loose thread from her red cardigan and shimmied it through the bars. The female finch dropped off her perch to pick it up; Lynn had been secreting nesting materials into there, hoping they might get broody.

Someone had spread fresh newspaper bits along the bottom of the cage. Lynn spotted the date. December 1. Why, that was her Disappearance Day. Her own private little anniversary, and she'd nearly missed it.

Lynn tried at length to fingertip the shredded bit of dated newspaper out of the cage. The bird must have disliked the intrusion; she swooped down to nick Lynn's fingertip with her little beak.

On her Disappearance Day anniversary, Lynn liked to think about how much people had missed her. An idea like a warm blanket. When she was still in the hospital in Hartford, she collected all the clippings about her disappearance. She made a quilt of them and burrowed underneath it, smelling the unwashed scent of herself, delicious with the feeling of hiding inside the world. She could distract herself from her past that way, though even then the reasons behind her being there had grown walled off in her memory, amidst the ice baths and sedatives. She still felt acutely the rip of loss, though, and there was a wicked satisfaction to seeing the rest of the world search for her, to see her own devastation broadcast upon their faces. *More people miss me than I remember knowing,* she had said to the sweet-smelling nun who visited daily. The nun patted her hand and whispered at the nurses' station about poor Miss Coleman, who was fixated on that missing college girl. *What harm to let her have the articles?* the nurses whispered. And Lynn was pleased at her unexpected skill in hiding.

On December 1, 1946, Paula Jean Welden put on a bright-red parka and left her dorm room.

Indeed she had, but the newspapers all left out the brawny men in white shirtsleeves who'd clamped her elbows and rushed her into the back of a long black car while everyone else was in class.

Lynn clicked to the table for her book and clicked back toward the kitchen. In the glass of the French doors, her reflection.

She had been pretty once.

At thirty-nine, Lynn's mother had still been smooth-faced and trim, two babies born and two more to come.

After Lynn's Remarkably Successful Procedure, the muscles in her face worked differently, some of them not at all. Her left side drooped when she smiled broadly, so she avoided smiling altogether. If she went missing now, no one would look for her. In the dining room, where there used to be a mirror, there now hung a portrait of George and Lynn. In the painting, Lynn was settled near George's knee, and his large hand wrapped the back of her neck. She hadn't sat for the portrait; George said it would be too much of a burden and didn't she have her puzzles and her leaf pressings, and they used instead her old high school photo, the one that appeared in the papers all those years ago. She recognized the likeness but didn't see herself in it.

Someone else had painted her portrait once, the same someone who had lit her first cigarette. That portrait had also been a terrible likeness, Lynn's face muddled, a Caravaggio stream of impossible light hitting her bare breasts, her hands and feet disappearing into shadow to cheat the painter's own shortcomings. The hiss of the match, the ticking of the painter's watch as she cupped her hands around the tip of Lynn's cigarette to shield the flame. Tick, tick. The flaring smell of sulfur mellowing into the catch of the tobacco threads, tick, tick, the painter hovering her hands longer than she needed to.

Click, click click, back to the kitchen.

A man entered through the side door. He was dressed in khaki short pants and a green shirt, wetted to his chest with perspiration. His ears stood out pink against the pale brown of the rest of his skin, and water drops slid down his neck. Was this George? She examined him further, his carriage and heavy breathing. No, no. This man was from the gardening company. There was a yellow tree insignia on his shirt, over his right breast. He put his hand on Cook's shoulder, a gesture of familiarity, then leaned into the kitchen sink, where he drank water right from the tap. Without so much as a by-your-leave. Was she no longer here? Was she no longer the mistress of this house?

Never mind, though, because she had her book of leaf pressings. Cook had in fact made her a new cup of cinnamon tea, and Lynn sneered a bit at it before opening her book.

"Dr. Frank back yet?" the young man asked. Lynn lifted her head to answer him, perhaps to scold him for failing to address her properly, then saw that it was Cook to whom he'd been speaking.

"Tomorrow evening," Cook said quietly, so quietly that Lynn had to lean forward to hear. "He gets into Sarasota at six, and his son will fetch him from the airport."

"I lived in Sarasota, you know," Lynn said, looking down at her book, thick and puffed with treasure, a grimoire. She turned the stiff pages so that it would appear as though she didn't care whether she had their attention. "I lived there in an institution that my husband ran. For special girls, girls too tender for this horrible world." The kitchen heated under the setting sun. "It was quite elite. I've always been very tender."

Lynn reached for her mug, then remembered what was inside and withdrew her hand. "Dr. Frank gave me this album while I was there, in fact. I'd never seen such plants as they had in that state."

"You are in Sarasota right now, Mrs. Frank," Gardener said. Cook shot him a foul look.

"Is that so?" Lynn said. She sucked on her fingertip. She'd punctured it somewhere, and it was aching.

"Are you cold? You're shivering," Cook said, and pointed to Lynn's hand, which was, come to see, tremoring slightly.

"I've always been quite tender," Lynn said, and she tucked her hand into her skirts, deep in the warmth between her thighs. Throughout most of her childhood, her nose would bleed torrentially and without warning. *Whenever you don't get your way,* her mother would say. Since moving to Florida, she no longer got nosebleeds— the humidity, George said—but even when she couldn't remember how to tie her shoelaces, she could remember how the painter taught her to tend to the nosebleeds, to pinch the soft part of her nose and drop her chin to her chest, how the painter would wrap her hand around Lynn's neck and hum.

Outside the screen door, a mist of insects rose up from the grass just as the sun hit the rooftop of the brick building that ran the length of the lawn. A woman in a blue uniform led a stumbling line of drab-dressed women toward the dining hall. One of the women stopped to pluck a blade of grass.

Gardener looked at Cook and whispered, "Where was he this time?"

Tick, tick.

"Cleveland, I think," Cook said, her voice only slightly softer than regular volume. "Was a piece on the radio this morning on the drive in about some fool demonstration he gave, standing onstage and poking at some lady's brain with an ice pick." Cook raised her eyebrows and flicked her gaze toward Lynn, all of which Lynn watched. "He's a right piece of work."

"It's called an orbitoclast," Lynn said, but really there was no difference. The instrument George had used for her Remarkably Successful Procedure had originally been pulled from George's own icebox, his father's initials carved into the wooden handle, the veneer worn gray in spots.

"What time is dinner tonight?" Lynn asked Cook, using a schoolteacher tone of voice to draw the woman's attention back to her assigned task.

"How long ago was it that you and Dr. Frank married?" Cook asked. The question was impertinent, wasn't it, totally aside from Cook's work.

"We married in 1951. Seventeen years ago this spring," Lynn

said. "I wore a smart plaid suit and carried a small button bouquet. My husband wore a top hat, and the judge performed the ceremony in my husband's office at the institution. My parents were there, and my sisters. We had petit fours with lunch. Later that night I threw up my chicken salad sandwich." Her mother once had told her that men expected certain things from wives, but Lynn had simply not been prepared. She had always been quite tender. After that first night, she had slept with George's ice pick under her pillow for years.

Following the ceremony, she and George had posed alone for a photograph in front of the judge's American flag. She moved her head at the last moment and her expression was blurred, barely a face at all. She wore a smart plaid suit, linen, and the painter's Elgin watch was on Lynn's wrist, hidden in the photograph by her bachelor's button bouquet (*Centaurea cyanus*). George wore a top hat. Their wedding bands were thin and gold. Lynn had that news article somewhere: PSYCHIATRIST WEDS MODEL PATIENT.

When her parents had sent her from the hospital in Connecticut down to the special institution in Florida, Lynn had been forlorn. Before her Remarkably Successful Procedure, she experienced constant Troubled Excitement—over her dead beau, they told her. Over the accumulation of losses from the previous years. She missed her sisters and her dorm room at Bennington with the window that looked out onto the gravel walkway winding toward the Barn, where all the classes were held. She missed her henpecking roommate, and she missed the short-lived pretense that all those girls—*we girls*—existed not for the pleasure of the men who would be their husbands but for their own pursuits. She missed stolen afternoons in the woods. Men expected certain things from wives, but Lynn had only ever let the girl painter drive deep into her most tender spot.

The painter, Wise, who had once plucked a stray thread of cigarette tobacco from the tip of Lynn's tongue. *I open you.*

Lynn pushed the teacup away. "I want some brandy," she said.

"No, a hot toddy." Her housekeeper used to rub clove oil on her gums whenever her teeth hurt.

Cook and Gardener exchanged a glance—don't think I didn't see that, Lynn thought—and Gardener pushed himself out of his counter lean. "I'll take care of that for you, Mrs. Frank," he said.

Lynn's book of leaf pressings was on the counter in front of her. Not just leaf pressings, though. She kept all sorts of precious things tucked in the back pocket, and no one ever bothered to look. She pulled out a weathered news article, one of several dozen, and burnished it flat with the round part of her fingernails.

PSYCHIATRIST WEDS PAPER DOLL PATIENT, one of the captions had said. George had taken that one away.

Lynn and her little sisters once made paper dolls from Mother's beauty magazines and suffered a switch that had them sore and sleeping on their stomachs for a week.

Gardener pushed a glass of warm milk across the counter toward her.

Lynn had once burrowed under the articles about her Disappearance Day, but the news clippings in her leaf book were of a later time: after her Remarkably Successful Procedure, when she and George (oh, he was still Dr. Frank to her then, though) traveled by rail all around the United States, as far north as Minnesota (state flower: *Cypripedium reginae*). She was a lunatic célèbre—that's what the papers called her. Dr. Frank's model patient, cured of her depression and bouts of hysteria and still so poised and calm. She would perform arithmetic on big green chalkboards at the bottom of cavernous lecture halls and sometimes draw portraits of the attendants in oil pastels, all to show the Unaltered Character of Her Intelligent Mind. And Dr. Frank would have her bring out and read for the group one of the dead soldier's love letters, to prove the Eradication of Her Troubled Excitement.

"Whether Dr. Frank's transorbital lobotomy would garner equal success in a member of the lower or racial classes is still untested. Dr. Frank attributes Miss Coleman's quick recovery of her wits in no small

part to her cultivated upbringing and fine Scottish heritage." Lynn read
that part aloud, from *The Arizona Republic* article in her hands.

How funny that she could appear in the papers twice in her life
and no one noticed that she was the same person.

"You aren't the same person, that's how," George had said. "When
you left college, you became Lynn Coleman. And when you took my
hand in marriage, you became Mrs. George Frank. Why, you're not
the same person at all."

If she wasn't the same, then how was it she remembered all of
it? She could recall that once, knowledge of her lover's death had
pulled despair with it like a comet tail, could recall the wretched
emptiness of her own loneliness, her own bad deeds, the Troubled
Excitement that had been with her long before it had a name. She
could recall smashing a mirror out of grief, recall becoming a thousand reflected versions of a self she could barely stand to see. She
could recall learning that her college dean had been speaking with
her father about her Upset and how she became so angry she shattered the lamp in her dorm room and went to sleep that night grinding bits of glass between her back teeth. She could recall howling
at the sky when they moved her first to Hartford, then to Sarasota,
strapped to a gurney like a maniac. She could recall George showing her his tool case filled with blood-splattered ice picks before
her Procedure and how she clamped her palms over her eyes and
shrieked like a child. It was curious to her how distressed she had
been once, when now she could simply decline that feeling.

(Her Troubled Excitement had been the full size of her body,
anguish pulsing from crown to toes. Where had it disappeared to
after her Remarkably Successful Procedure? Somewhere, did a
Lynn-shaped cloud of Upset live a separate life, troubled and excited
but unscarred?)

George, though, he got plenty distressed still, when Lynn made
mistakes and forgot her words again or had an accident in her night-
clothes. Lynn read every paper that appeared on the counter and

clipped every article with George's name. Every so often, George crushed the article into a ball and threw it across the dining room. He slapped her on one of those evenings, when she asked what *un-credentialed* meant, and sent her to her room. She slept with the ice pick in her hand that night, though it had disappeared when she awoke.

Where was George? Was it near dinnertime?

Lynn refolded the news clippings and slid them into the back folder of her leaf book. She kept all manner of things in here, like her wedding photo and postcards from her sisters and the last letter her soldier sent, the one that arrived after he had died. She kept it there, the girl painter's watch, flattened between the weight of all the pages.

It was

It was meant to be right here.

It was

Where was it. "Where is it?" she said to Cook. "Wise's watch. Did you take it?" Gardener took a step toward the kitchen door, still facing Lynn. "Did you?" she asked him.

"Now, Mrs. Frank, you've been right here with us the whole time. You know we didn't take anything of yours." Gardener crossed his arms in front of his green shirt. "Don't get excited."

"Who's Wise?" said Cook.

What were they doing, these two? Why were they here? Lynn felt a storm brewing up from her stomach.

"I'm not Excited," she said, dropping her hands to the counter. "I'm not angry. I promise that no one will be in trouble. Just tell me where my watch is. Just tell me where George is."

Both these people in her kitchen started talking at her at the same time in infuriatingly dulcet tones, like she was some wild animal to be calmed.

Someone was always taking away what mattered most to her. She had found her ice pick again, a year or two ago, and she kept it hidden in the pocket of an old red parka that hung in the back of her closet. She still might need it someday. She had lost more people than she remembered knowing.

She looked into the dark dining room, where Samuel and Cyril had left their dissection tools again, left one of her Gouldian finches pinned open on the dissection tray.

"Someone's going to have to clean off the dining room table if we are to eat tonight," Lynn said. Her voice sounded round and close. "And someone's going to have to tell me why I'm here." She leaned onto her leaf book.

"Tell me about those," Cook said. Those? Her clippings. Lynn tilted the book up.

"I collected these when we traveled across the country," she said. "One from every state."

"But none of them are labeled," said Cook, leaning toward the waxed sheet.

"Leaves are labels enough," Lynn said. She ran her fingers across a spread of pages. "Basal leaf formation, parallel venation, linear shape—this one's a daylily, *Hemerocallis.* Here, basal formation and filiform shape—that's *allium,* wild chives." She flipped through the cardboard pages. "Rosemary, pansies, fennel, columbine."

"Venation, what's that?" Cook asked. Lynn didn't care for her tone.

"Veins, veins, like these," she answered sharply, and slapped at her bare inner wrist. Used to be she wore a watch on that wrist, but now she had no reason to track the time. "Really." She closed her book. "Is dinner ready soon? I may like to go take a nap first. My stomach is still upset. In fact, I may not eat tonight." Sleepiness dropped like a stage curtain. Her head swayed a bit.

It wasn't a finch but a *Cypripedium reginae,* a lady's slipper orchid, pinned open on the dissection tray, the pouched labellum split and flattened, sticky pollen scattered across the tabletop.

"I may just rest until George is home. Someone will watch the boys, won't you?" Lynn could still feel the finch's beak prick on her finger. She could still feel the fingertip on her tongue. There were paper dolls scattered all over the dining room table. Someone would need to clean those up. Someone would need to raise those boys. Above the dining table, the mirror was missing and in its place a portrait of George and some woman. She had felt the ice pick in her brain. A portrait of George and no one at all.

SPELLS FOR SINNERS, PART FOUR

BLADEN COUNTY, NORTH CAROLINA, 1961

The ride to the Starkings' house was blessedly brief. The rain stirred odors Mary hadn't noticed when Gurnie had given her a lift: spice, like a peat fire. Some green bitterness she could nearly taste. And the damp and muddy smell of Clarence's ancient trench coat. Clarence glanced her way only when making right turns, and he didn't try to start a conversation. Mary studied his profile and the stiffness of his carriage. The expression of the younger man in her vision had been neutral, impersonal, as he'd shouldered the small old woman aside.

What to make of all these impressions that kept raining down on her? The Sight was as truculent as ever, offering sucker punches instead of answers.

Gurnie Starking was out on the porch, smoking a cigarette, as the truck's headlights swept the yard and the front of the house. He stubbed it out and grabbed an umbrella to usher Mary in.

"Sorry about this inclement weather, Mrs. Garrett," he said. He said the word, *in-clement,* in such a way that Mary understood its structure for the very first time. Unmerciful. She'd always thought it meant threatening, looming. She thought everything was threatening, even the weather. But unmerciful was far worse. As though the power to grant mercy were in one's grasp, and one could simply withhold it.

The house was humid and yellow under a half dozen table lamps. The steamy smell of cooked carrots lingered in the front entryway, where Mary scrubbed the soles of her shoes on the welcome mat. She heard the clatter of meal preparation under the yawning sound of a radio hovering between frequencies.

Gurnie showed her to the same sofa she'd shared with Bernice earlier in the week. He shut off the radio and sat across from her, a tin man on a brocade chair. His shoes were a softened and grayed old buckskin.

"I brought some of Polly's things out for you," he said, and pointed at the low coffee table. Mary nodded and reached toward a scattered stack; she'd forgotten for a moment that she was here to work. To perform.

Clarence entered in stocking feet and shirtsleeves and sat in a stiff chair near Gurnie. While Gurnie leaned toward her, elbows on his knees, Clarence relaxed, his deep brow shadowing his eyes.

Gurnie pushed a photo album toward Mary. "Try here, ma'am. Bernice has always kept a good album. She keeps a good house, is a good mama."

Mary paged through the album without much expectation. Photographs were lies, fabrications of wellness and calm. There was nothing about *her* true self that would have appeared in her parents' photo albums. They'd just as easily tell the opposite story: that Paula Jean Welden was a doting eldest daughter, that the house clattered endlessly with the bright sounds of four girls, that her father's mountainous stature signified reassuring strength, her mother's smile was sweetness and release. Her family's album couldn't convey the astringent smell of clear liquor that wafted off Mother's skin or the tight hold her father had on them, the way his roar echoed through the house when he was home at all, and it would have kept hidden

Paula's greatest loss, her months of desperate searching, the same grinding task that had prepared her for this—Mary's—current life. Paula had carried her hatred of her parents on her back like a boulder, but not one of the family portraits would have shown it.

Mary had always been resentful of the grace offered to missing girls' parents, as though the girls' disappearance suddenly made their families blameless. Plenty of these families had been like her own: places that no one would ever dream of returning to.

The real insights that Mary needed were most likely found locked inside the minds of these family members, or Rusty, if they were to be found at all—whether Polly was somehow connected to Martha's girls, Evie and Jack. Which man had whispered *Paul* the day she fell from her horse. Why Polly's clothing had been tucked so coolly beside the flank steaks at the market.

Until one of the Starkings unzipped their skull for Mary to poke around, she would just have to wait for Polly, who knew all the secrets and was doling them out at an excruciating pace.

The album held snapshots of Gurnie and Bernice before Polly had come along, just the stiff posed photographs that so many people had: the cheap wedding photo where the seams on the photographer's backdrop showed, the smeared happy faces on the church steps, awkward arms holding up a first pair of house keys. As Mary turned the page to Polly's birth certificate and her tiny, inked footprints, she shouldn't have been the least bit surprised to find that each of the photographs of Polly held only a blank spot where the girl should have been, as though someone had cut out her image with a knife and replaced it with white paper.

The blank Polly spot started small, a swaddled bundle on a sweet-faced Bernice's lap, then elongated and filled out as the pages progressed, until the blank spot was lanky and stretched over the back of a horse, until it was standing between Gurnie and Clarence as they grinned beside a hitching-post shingle that read TURNER FARMS in block letters. Gurnie held up a smaller, hand-printed sign: *Starking Bros. Farm*.

A missing girl rewrites an entire story the moment she disappears. Really, no one could know that better than Mary. Who was she but a second draft?

"Bernice took that one," Gurnie said, pointing at the snapshot of the brothers with Polly. "The day we bought our farm in the sheriff's sale. Polly ran and picked out the stall for her horse right after and spent two days painting the walls with sheep and cows and roosters, so as her horse would never feel lonely." He broke on the last few words.

Mary flattened a snapshot with her palm and braced herself for a cold splash of vision. But the Sight kept her here, face-to-face with the Amiable Starking Boys.

"Maybe you would like to touch some of Paul's favorite things," Gurnie said, rearranging his pile to nudge forward a worn-out cloth rabbit.

"Did you happen upon any more information, Mrs. Garrett?" asked Clarence, speaking as though weighing each word.

"She'd tell us if she had," Gurnie said, still looking at Mary.

Mary rubbed at her left wrist, missing her watch. Between these two men existed decades of hurts and secrets and minor grudges, plus all the history that felt withheld to Mary simply because she hadn't learned it yet. Martha had accused her of swanning into town as though the place had sprung into being with her arrival, but Mary knew better than this—she knew well the endless undoing and redoing of old betrayals and promises that marked every family's history. And the tangle of resentment and sadness and regret between Clarence and Gurnie enveloped her now, as though she'd wandered into the smoke from someone else's fire.

She wouldn't trust either of them with her life, or with Polly's.

Fully grown for more than a decade now, Mary still always sided with the girls, full of soft adolescent ideas, vulnerable for a million reasons that men like these could never see. A girl like Polly had the capacity to dream an entire world, a whole future, into existence with a dedication that adults would scarcely believe. Mary had never fully released the world she had dreamed at that age, no matter how far her life had strayed from that ideal, no matter how much loss had blossomed inside her like a cancer. That vision of a future had been one of her few escapes from the heaviness of her home life, from wartime, from womanhood and all it would mean.

Mary reached forward and picked up the cloth rabbit. Immediately she felt a stab of pain. She looked down to see a sewing needle protruding from her fingertip, a bead of blood seeping into a stain across the cloth rabbit's ear. *I'm sorry,* she looked up to say, but it was no longer the Starking brothers sitting across from her. She was up in Polly's room, a crib in place of the bed, a changing table in place of Polly's desk. Inside the crib, the soft shape of a sleeping baby, bottom in the air and cheek to the sheet.

Mary's own body was rocking, not side to side as on Polly's horse but forward and back, gentle movement of an old rocking chair, and her hands weren't her hands but another woman's, shorter fingers and spool of thread in her lap.

"Adaline, you're bleeding." Mary looked up to see Bernice at the door of Polly's room, a younger Bernice with the swollen chest and loose housedress of a new mother. She shuffled as though still pained from birth.

"I'm right as rain," Mary heard herself say, and her voice was no-nonsense and sure.

"The baby's all right? No, don't get up." Bernice peered over the edge of the crib. She reached in to rub at the baby's back. "I think Gurnie wanted a boy. You think so? I wish she were a boy. I'll never stop worrying about her. Girls bring so much trouble." But Bernice didn't look disappointed, didn't look like she wished Polly were anything other than who she was right then.

Mary drew her finger up to her lips, where she sucked at the blood still dribbling.

"Boys bring many of their own troubles, Bernice." The old lady's voice was unwavering. "And they don't end, neither."

And Bernice nodded like she knew just what the woman was saying.

A clatter and a thump from the kitchen, and Bernice's voice—

older, and angry—called Gurnie's name. Mary was back in the Stark-ings' muggy and sad living room, alone now with Clarence as Gurnie went to answer Bernice's call.

She continued to finger at the cloth rabbit. No fresh bloodstain, but she imagined that she might see a faded, nearly scrubbed-out spot on the rabbit's ear.

"This was sewn for Polly by her grandmother? Adaline?" Mary looked up.

"Adaline was my grandmama. Mine and Gurnie's. Polly's great-grandmama. She died about ten years back." Clarence stretched his fingers and laced his hands together.

"The same grandmama who had the—" What had Gurnie called it again? "Who had dreams? The angel on her shoulder?"

"At her back. Yes, ma'am." He looked nearly liquid. Face neutral, eyes still shaded. And again Mary saw her vision from the truck, the old woman being shoved aside with a rough knock of the shoulder.

Gurnie came in with a forced nonchalance and a platter of celery smeared with cream cheese. "Bernice is fixing to join us. Begs us to go on have a seat at the table."

How many of life's secrets were found in the arrangements of human beings around a dinner table? Mary followed Gurnie to the oval table at the dining side of the room, keenly aware of not taking Polly's seat. She allowed Clarence to select and pull out a chair for her, and she scooted close to the table. It was set with deliberation, but everything was in the wrong place. The lace tablecloth was up-side down, the spoon where the fork ought to have been, and a stick of butter sat lopsided on a saucer. It was Mary's intuition rather than her gifts that let her see that Bernice wasn't too pleased to have her over and that Gurnie had tried to lift some of the burden by assisting in an arena he knew nothing about.

The first time Mary had set the table incorrectly, she'd taken a smack to the eye. The scar, carved by a corner of her mother's diamond ring, was still visible just under Mary's eyebrow. Her mother hadn't even spoken to her or corrected her. Had just lifted her hand and struck, before pushing all the silverware to the middle of the table and saying, mouth corners cemented in place, "Again." Paula Jean had been only eight or so then, and the littlest sister not even born, but Pamela and Stephanie, so small they shouldn't even have been touching the knives, helped her start over. Mary can't remember now if they'd gotten it right or what they even had eaten that night.

Conversation around the Starkings' table was stilted as they waited for Bernice, and Mary steadily pushed celery into her mouth, holding one stick while chewing the piece in her mouth. Whatever happened next, she would face it with a full stomach and with strands of celery string between her back teeth.

Bernice carried a platter piled with pink meat and carrots to the table. She was red-faced and damp. "Gurnie, the potatoes," she said. She was less of a husk than she'd been the last time Mary saw her; then again, she'd had no choice. Mary's company had been foisted upon her.

But as Bernice began grabbing at plates and serving Mary and Clarence, Mary could see that Bernice was raging. Her arm movements might have zinged; she was sharp and impatient, thudding plates down the last few inches to the tabletop and dropping into her own chair before Gurnie returned with the bowl of mashed potatoes. He circled the table to spoon them out, apologizing for his sloppy serving.

It must have been the tension of the moment that kept thrusting Mary back into her own childhood, the frisson of family arguments around the dining room table under flickering bulbs. After a childhood lost to raising her mother's children, Mary would have been happy never to spend another moment at a family table, happy to eat French fries and watery soup from bus-depot diners for the rest of her life. When Paula was twelve, Mother had come to the table with red eyes and a bottle of sparkling wine, and she had sloshed the foam into all three girls' water glasses. Paula lifted the whispering glass to watch the bubbles break the surface, and Mother announced, winging the bottle around by the neck, "Make room for one more, my darlings. Mother is expecting!"

The news had hit Paula like a bottle on the nose, and she looked up at Mother just as a small red drop rolled to the edge of her own upper lip and splashed to the tablecloth. She had thought that her job of raising her sisters was getting closer to ending, that finally they were all learning to become friends, that they would help her with the meaningless tasks Mother constantly threw her way, and now suddenly she was facing years of diaper pails and spit-up and Mother under the covers for days at a time. Paula tucked her index finger beneath her nostrils, and Mother sneered and tossed the wine bottle aside, where it bounced onto the carpet.

"You always get a goddamn bloody nose when you don't get your way," Mother had said. "You are always set on ruining everything."

Mary was still the great ruiner, it seemed. Here, at the Starkings', the discomfort in this dining room emanated from Bernice, a woman who looked to be past her breaking point. If Mary could have made her exit smoothly, she would have. With fistfuls of celery in her stomach, a meal seemed far less urgent than it had an hour earlier.

Gurnie sat down, and Bernice reached out to grasp Mary's hand. Were they to pray? But Bernice just squeezed Mary's fist and rocked their wrists back and forth like they were schoolchildren.

"I suppose Gurnie has already told you that Rusty and them have called off the search," Bernice said. "I expect the mother is always the last to know anything. Suppose I should have gotten out there myself, but now they say with this rain everything will be washed away." Her anger seemed to grow as she spoke, and she thudded Mary's knuckles against the table.

A hiccuping vision overlaid Mary's sight, a downpour pounding at the surface of a lake, a river, swelling and breaching its banks.

And then it faded and she was just staring at Bernice's anguished face, telegraphing helplessness and fury and despair.

Gurnie and Clarence wouldn't look at Bernice; they both scraped at their plates and pressed slivers of ham into their mouths.

Mary said, "Giving up the search seems to be a habit with Rusty."

Damn dangerous ground, he'd said. Well, here she was, stomping across it.

"What's that?" Bernice said. She released Mary's hand and stood to root around in a nearby china cabinet. She emerged with a half-empty brandy bottle.

Mary shoveled a forkful of mashed potatoes into her mouth. "I've heard that the sheriff's office has cut short a few other searches for missing girls in Bladen County."

Still only the scraping of forks on china, the pop of Bernice's brandy-bottle cork.

"Two Black girls," Mary said, and took another bite. The food was bland, but it was food, and warm.

"I don't know anything about that," Gurnie said, and leaned back in his chair. "But Rusty's been a good friend to this family. I regret that he's made this decision here, and Clarence and I and some others will be out searching regardless, but I don't see any reason for the disrespect."

Echoes of the speech Mary had given to Martha last night. Less convincing even than when she'd said it, especially now that she could picture Evie's red coat, the way Jack's slick fingers caressed her sweetheart's cheeks as they treaded water in the lake.

The rest of the meal passed without conversation. Bernice made no move to clear the dishes; Gurnie and Clarence ambled back and forth from the table into the kitchen with lost expressions on their faces, as though never before had they been expected to clean up after themselves. Bernice sipped at the same small pour of brandy and propped her head on a palm. The rage was still there, but she was slipping inside herself again; Mary could feel it.

"Bernice." Mary smoothed at her napkin. "Did Polly know these two missing girls? Jack and Evie?"

Mary felt exposed here, having said their names, having taken a swipe at Rusty without knowing the consequences. And likely for little good—her own mother wouldn't have known where Paula spent her afternoons, impressionistic and hungover as her mother's days usually were. Even after all that had happened, all the wreckage Paula's mother had caused, she hadn't been able to remember Marjorie Ann Wise's name. *I wonder whatever happened to that girl,* Mother had said over the morning paper one day, after Paula had already spent weeks searching.

In this dining room, Bernice lifted her hands to shade her eyes from the chandelier. She stared at the brandy bottle, then said, "I just can't, Mrs. Garrett. Until my girl is home safe, I just don't have it in me to feel for some other girl's mama."

Until my girl is home safe—Bernice still clung to the idea that Polly could walk back into this dining room, naked and reborn. Mary flashed again on the churning river, and she yanked at the hair close to her scalp, yanked herself from the vision before the Sight could compel her to see some destroyed version of Polly rising from that water.

From the entryway, the sound of the front door opening wide and bouncing against the wall. Mary tensed and thought: The wind has picked up. Then the scratch of feet on the welcome mat and Rusty's big voice taking dominion over the entire house. "Nasty night for it," he called out, and must have made his way into the kitchen. Cold dread lodged somewhere near her shoulders, Mary listened for his movements, squinting her eyes with the effort. Near silence from the other side of the house, whispers or meaningful expressions among the men that didn't carry to the dining table. Mary glanced at Bernice, who still sat with one hand shielding her eyes; with a fingertip on her other hand, Bernice traced a lily on the lace tablecloth.

In strode the man Mary'd been avoiding all day for fear of she wasn't sure what.

Rusty entered the room with both arms open, as though welcoming Mary into his own home. "Mrs. Garrett, I could have sworn you said you were on your way out of town. Here I've been mourning your absence all day." He took Clarence's chair at the table. "How relieved I am to see we've not yet been deprived of your company."

Gurnie followed him in. "Sheriff just stopped by to check in," he said, and leaned a hand onto Rusty's wide shoulder. "Mrs. Garrett was kind enough to join us for dinner and spend some time with Polly's things. In case if she might could see anything that leads us to Paul."

"And did you meet with success?" Rusty asked.

"Excuse me," Bernice said, and she dropped her napkin onto the table as she rose. She shouldered away from Gurnie as he reached to touch her back and marched up the entryway stairs toward the second floor of the house.

"Mrs. Garrett will correct me if I'm wrong," Gurnie said, looking right at her, "but I believe our session was not fruitful in the way we'd hoped."

Truth was that Mary longed for the opportunity to tempt the Sight by pawing through the Starkings' home, digging deeper into the family's closets. To find out whether Martha was right and Evie and Jack's disappearances were related to Polly's. Mary still needed the reward money. But at this moment she was driven just as much by spite. Besides, now that Rusty had seen her, she had no incentive to scurry away like a cockroach under daylight.

"I'd like to try again," Mary said. And she did feel better now that she'd eaten, now that her head was temporarily quiet.

"I'm afraid that's a bad idea," Rusty said, and pressed himself to standing with his palms on the table, tilting it off its far legs as he did. "Storm doesn't show a sign of breaking tonight, and there's already flooding along Broad Street. I should probably see you home now if you plan to get out of here at all."

"Ah, well, ain't that a shame," Gurnie said. He sounded sincere, but Mary hated how malleable he was, how deferential. He was letting go too easily, giving up on Polly in the face of the mildest resistance. Unless he was the culprit, unless he'd orchestrated this entire evening just to see what she knew.

A chill rang up Mary's back to her shoulders.

"You'd best skedaddle now, too, Clarence, unless you're fixing to sleep on your brother's sofa tonight," Rusty said. "No family needs two tragedies, and anything that gets lost out there tonight ain't bound to be found for weeks."

Mary stood from the table. She could take a bum's rush with dignity. "Maybe I'd best take a taxi. I can imagine you might be needed this evening, given the storm."

Rusty adjusted his belt. "Too late to catch Sigsbee tonight, I'm afraid. And foolish to try to walk in this sort of downpour. Lucky thing I'm here to escort you." He snorted.

Clarence's voice rolled into motion. "I'm happy to run her on back to the Safe Lodge," he said.

"I want her to stay." Bernice's voice, cracked and exhausted, came from the threshold. She stood with one palm to the doorframe, for once not worrying at anything. "She'll stay the night. You go on home, Clarence."

"Seems you've gained quite a following, Mrs. Garrett." Rusty shifted his hips in a manner that Mary read as discomfort. He didn't want her to stay. "Do you have a preference?"

To answer that question would require Mary to pin down some understanding of the circumstances and oblique motivations that hurricaned around her. What Clarence or Rusty might do to her alone in a car, what Gurnie might do to her while Bernice slept, what slow madness might creep over Mary with another night in that motel room, what prompted Bernice's sudden about-face, whether there was safety or peril to be found deep in the overnight of the Starking house. Just a few days ago she'd been so desperate for such an invitation.

Mary could hear the storm blustering, the rain drumming the windows.

Bernice's eyes were red-rimmed, and she met Mary's gaze full-on for the first time. She moved her head in one of her slight, nearly perceptible nods.

"I'll stay," Mary said.

Bernice escorted Mary upstairs to Polly's room. It was not even gone nine o'clock, but the thundering storm gave the evening a midnight feel. Gurnie walked out onto the porch with Clarence and Rusty, and from the stairs Mary could feel the gust of clammy wind that shouldered in when they passed through the door.

In the days since Mary was last here, Bernice had returned to Polly's room to smooth the rumples Mary had left in the bedspread. The louvered closet doors were closed, and the tall lingerie chest stood tidy and shut tight.

"Sheets are clean. I just changed them this morning." Bernice wrapped her arms around herself and leaned against one of the bedposts. "I want it to be nice for her, when she gets back."

Mary kept her pocketbook tucked under her arm; it felt indecorous to put it down here on any of Polly's furniture with Bernice watching her like this.

"Mrs. Starking, why did you change your mind, about me, about my trying again?"

Bernice stared at an invisible spot on the carpet, then straightened her back and walked toward the door. "What makes you think I did?" she said, and shut the door behind her.

That woman was so determined to keep Mary out. This whole family with its mental privacy fences and its come-here-go-away posture. If Mary had twenty goddamn dollars to her name, she would sneak out of town at midnight and forget she'd ever heard the name Polly Starking. Mary dropped her pocketbook to the carpet and wedged open the window sash.

Polly's room occupied the front right corner of the house, and the window overlooked the street. Mary couldn't see the front porch, but the indistinct rumble of Rusty's gusty voice carried even through the rush of wind and cars sheeting water. She pressed her ear to the screen.

A low and somber voice that Mary couldn't pick up, couldn't identify.

"Eh—" Rusty interrupted with a syllable of disgust, and Mary could imagine him waving an arm in dismissal. She heard the tink of raindrops, an alto plop of water hitting the brim of Rusty's hat. The crunch of gravel beneath shoes, the bassoon creak of his car door. She listened next for the sounds that would indicate which of the Starking brothers stood on the porch, but Bernice breezed back in then with a glass of water and a folded garment. She stopped short.

"I'm sorry. I suppose I never have knocked on Polly's door. She slept in here as a baby, you know." Bernice placed the glass of water on the side table and held out the fabric object. "A nightgown. One of mine. Not sure anything of Polly's would fit you, and to be honest I don't want anyone else wearing any of her things."

Mary's position at the window seemed to have escaped Bernice's notice. Mary stepped forward to accept the nightgown. She slept in her slip most of the time. "Thank you, Mrs. Starking." She tried hard to catch and hold the woman's gaze.

"Good enough," Bernice said, and turned to go. "'Night."

Whatever had been going on outside was over when Mary returned to the window. She left it open a few inches and enjoyed how the wet wind danced the lightweight curtains toward the bed. Mary slid open Polly's drawers, leafed past the pleated skirts and camp shirts hanging in the closet, riffled through the two or three carbons tucked under the typewriter. Nothing more revealing than that medal Mary had found when she was here last. It was still in her pocketbook, and she pulled it out and fastened it around her neck. In Polly's bed, in Bernice's nightgown, Mary felt like anyone but herself.

She pressed her face deep into Polly's pillow, and beneath the harsh detergent she could smell something else, something human and distinct. For months after Marjorie Ann Wise had disappeared, Mary—Paula—*Paul*—had slept with Wise's paint-stained cardigan under her head, wanting to inhale whatever of Wise might be left there, whatever skin cells or turpentine or perfume. Paul had wanted all of it. And then she'd worn Wise's watch every day, had slid into sleep at the sound of its ticking, right up until it had disappeared—had been taken from her, just as Wise had been.

Lying in the bed of a missing girl always jolted Mary back to that place, the ripped-open grief of loss, so much rougher, so much more shameful, than anything that had happened to her since. If Wise hadn't disappeared, what might life have been?

And why hadn't the Sight come to her early enough to save Wise?

It came now, Mary's vision, finding her on her hands and knees, naked shins against the soft green carpet. Above her head, bare wood of the underside of a table. The scalloped hem of the lace tablecloth dripped over the table's edge and obscured her vision of the room. The same table at which Mary had just eaten dinner. Everything bathed in a white-blue sunbeam hitting slant through the living room window.

Where was the Sight taking her?

Her mouth tasted like a cherry lollipop, and two of her fingers were pink and sticky.

Across the floor, she could see a woman's stockinged ankles crossed in front of the sofa. She smelled cigarette smoke. One of the chairs facing the sofa appeared occupied, but it was canted away from her.

"Boys back yet?" The voice, an old woman's, wavered.

"I told you, Adaline, Gurnie's up in Fayetteville looking at a new tractor, and Clarence is on his way back from the farm." Bernice's voice was raised, as though placating someone hard of hearing.

"Oh no, he's not," said Adaline. "Oh no, oh no. He's not." A strong intake of breath.

Mary's hand, a small child's hand, reached up to pinch at a necklace around her neck, to run it along its chain; she felt the small vibration like a buzzing bee. Mary pinched at it again, trying to feel for its shape. The same medal she'd put on before bed. A thread between her and Polly.

And then suddenly Mary was somewhere else, was high above the ground. On a horse, the same horse from her earlier vision from Polly's bed. High above the ground and looking down a steep embankment toward a body of water. A flash of bright red down below, and then Mary awoke, wailing.

Mary tried to memorize the image, the flash of red that must have been Evie's red parka. The flash of red that connected Polly Starking to Evie—Mary gasped, sobbed against her will, seized with another girl's terror.

Mary felt a depression on the mattress behind her and tensed;

she turned to look back over her shoulder. Bernice, in a nightgown nearly identical to the one Mary wore, placed a hand on Mary's shoulder. She soothed at Mary's crown. "Shh shh shh," Bernice whispered.

Did Bernice know it was Mary here, or had she come by pure loving instinct, groping in the dark to answer her daughter's cries?

"Shh shh shh," Bernice whispered again, cool palm on Mary's hot head.

Mary loathed being touched—it broke her too easily. How hard it made her work to hold herself together. To not unbind her muscles, release her rigid neck. To not fall into fragments at the relief and the simple warmth of another person's skin.

Mary fixed her jaw tight and set her face against the waves of repulsion and desire. She could feel a small humid circle on her cheek where Bernice's hot breath landed over and over. Mary exhaled to a count of six. Inside her eyelids: Jack and her sweetheart, pressing together pruney fingertips. The sounds of the water moving around them, the contracting woods at night.

Mary looked up at Bernice's face, her red-rimmed eyes, and another vision: Bernice, wearing the same pleated skirt and Peter Pan blouse as she'd worn the first day Mary entered Polly's room. Day was breaking in the vision, and Bernice stood at the stove in the yellow kitchen, avoiding her reflection in the window. Gurnie walked into the room and poured himself a cup of coffee from the percolator. He put a hand on the back of Bernice's head.

"Clarence swung by for the truck right early, but he'll be back to pick me up. Any chance for some eggs?"

"What did he need the truck for?" Bernice said. Her voice sounded deadened, distant. Mary could feel her hollowness, edged by sparks of something else—suspicion, rancor. Bernice pulled eggs from the fridge and lit the burner beneath the skillet.

"Making another search pass through Smith Swamp," Gurnie said.

Bernice hiccuped a sob, and Gurnie wrapped her up in his arms.

Time passed like a blink, and Bernice and Gurnie sat at the kitchen table with empty dishes before them. Mary could taste the salty egg yolk on the back of her teeth. The wide swinging sound of the front door opening. Gurnie stood up as Clarence entered the kitchen.

"Anything?" Gurnie asked.

Clarence removed his hat and shook his head.

"Did you really look?" Bernice said, suddenly, aggressively, rising from the table.

"Bernice?" Gurnie said.

"Did you really look, or did you just disappear like you do?" She stood facing Clarence, her soft hand curling into a fist. "Disappear and come back stinking of mud and sweat like some animal?"

Gurnie moved between Bernice and Clarence, but Bernice stretched to speak past his shoulder. "Did you go do whatever it was that made Adaline scream in the middle of the night? The thing that made her so sick at the end, the thing that made her refuse to go to sleep? Did you—" She lost herself on the last word, lost the muscle control in her legs and slumped toward the ground, where Gurnie swooped to catch her.

"What foolishness is this?" Gurnie whispered at her. "You know this man loved Paul like a daughter. You're hurting, sugar, you're just not yourself."

And the Bernice in Mary's vision, sobbing deeply into Gurnie's flannel chest, gave way to the Bernice bent over Mary in Polly's bed. "Okay now," Bernice said, stiffer than she'd been a moment ago. She turned to go.

Watching the woman's back, the sweep of her shoulder to her low spine, the small freckles on her upper arms, Mary wondered with some measure of anger what it was that Bernice and Adaline suspected, and what they might have been able to stop.

Charlie—Homeroom Representative (10). Future—United States Armed Forces.

PAULA JEAN WELDEN

The friends who are most stimulating to us
are those who disagree with us.

"Paul"—Classical Seminar (11), Debating Club (12), Le Cercle Francais (11, 12), Yearbook Art Committee (12), Hospital Project (12-Co-Chairman). Future—College, Art School.

Agent (11),

BOSTON POLICE CLUE PETERS OUT

Michael Houlahan, lieutenant of the Boston police department, called The Banner this morning at 2:30 with a report that the following want ad was running in the Boston Traveler newspaper:

"Bennington College student available part time job. January, February and March." Lt. Houlahan said that the return address attached to the ad was Virginia Butler, Box 9758. When informed of this development, President Jones of the College informed The Banner that no such student was being carried on the roll of the College at this time.

Two 18-year-old girls were being held Tuesday night at the office of the Traveler's Aid at the LaSalle Station in Boston. However, it was determined that the two girls were from North Adams and had no known connection with the case of Paula Welden.

IN MEMORIAM

We offer sincere tribute to the memory of a fellow classmate who, because of her loyalty and integrity, exemplified to the highest degree the characteristics denoted by the word—friend.

Throughout the years to come, we shall always cherish in our hearts the remembrance of our esteemed comrade, Marjorie Ann Wise.

31

GHOSTWRITER

> Your true reflection is found at the outer bounds of what you will do.
>
> —Virginia Butler

> Rescued from obscurity by a devoted advocate, Virginia Butler now holds the record for number of volume requests at the New York Public Library . . .
>
> Eerily prescient . . . distinct voice . . . Life shortened by ovarian cancer over twenty years ago . . . Her overlooked and later celebrated first novel in which a young girl escapes the bounds of a wartime feminine existence to join the ranks of the natural world, nymphette of the forest . . .
>
> —*The New York Times,* October 3, 1996

In Virginia Butler's first book, a girl goes missing from her boarding school. It's 1916, and the girl climbs to the top of a hill in her drab school uniform and burrows deep into the earth using only her fingers. Inside the hill, the girl builds herself an underground palace with tree roots for a hammock and a bouquet of lightning bugs for a lantern. She can make it rain with the right tug on the tulip bulbs, and if she presses on the embedded stones, boulders rise from the ground like standing figures to shadow the valley. In the story, the girl is free and she is god.

Paula Jean read that book in high school, lying on her stomach on the dirt floor of an old boys' camp. Wise, who had pressed the book into Paula Jean's hands in the first place, lay on her back beside Paul, smoking a cigarette with her blouse unbuttoned, shoulder pressed against Paul's arm. Over time, that old camp cabin in the woods, shuttered because of the war, became their burrow away from the rest of the world, where they were free and they were gods.

And then Wise was lost and Paula Jean ran away and somehow decades later Paula Jean is here, in Virginia Butler's empty house, standing at the dead woman's stove, scraping the teakettle to the front burner and turning on the heat. It almost seemed that Virgie had called Paul to her all those years ago, as though she had known what would come: Paula Jean studying Virgie like a specimen until Paula Jean could impersonate Virgie as easily as she could be herself.

And so easily had Paula Jean become Virgie that it seemed preordained: Three volumes of forged correspondence, much of it between Paula Jean and Virgie. Two *posthumously discovered* novels. A half dozen reissues of Virginia Butler's early work, with prefaces by Paula Jean. She'd slid into Virginia Butler's place like a hand into a glove.

But the publishing house, once Virgie's and now Paula Jean's, has decided to send someone to pay her a visit.

The letter arrived today.

On our insurer's insistence, we have instituted a new standard of due diligence . . . required to validate and photograph all of Virginia Butler's original correspondence and manuscript drafts . . . apologize for the intrusion . . . unable to reach you by telephone . . . arrive on the 23rd . . . sorry for the inevitable inconvenience.

Paula Jean thinks better of the tea and pours three fingers of whiskey into her mug. She stabs at a lemon wedge with pointy clove studs.

The back door slams open on its own; the flames beneath the tea-kettle bluster and go out. Strong smell of gas. Paula Jean dead bolts the door and relights the burner. Her old bones creak. It's easy to imagine it, an open door to a different lifetime: a muggy lover who's just dropped beneath the faucet of the farmhouse sink for a gulp of cold water, smelling of sweet grass and diesel. A neighbor delivering a chess pie beneath a blue-gingham napkin with a wordless wave. In this life, though, it's just Paula Jean standing alone, watching steam rise, willfully shackled to this kitchen where she begged for crumbs for too many years. She had come as a girl to escape her small miseries, and then up from the floorboards grew lashes that wrapped her ankles and held her in place for forty-four years.

She fingers the envelope. The Boston publisher—or more likely the secretary that types his mail—has addressed the letter to Paula *Walton.*

They misspelled it on the first book, too, missed her penciled correction, and just like that she became *P. Walton, editor,* unsexed and anonymous. In retrospect, she's not sure why she let them take her name away so easily.

When she was in high school, it was Wise who had given her a new name. *Paul.* The sound of it still felt like Wise tucking a strand of hair behind her ear.

"God no, not Paul. That's no name for a writer," Virgie had said. The exasperated tone, the authority of it. As though Virgie were still standing right over Paula Jean's shoulder.

Paula Jean had been filling Virginia Butler's mug, her other palm resting on the egg-slicked diner counter between them. *Paula* embroidered on her waitress uniform in red script above her right breast. Fall of 1951. She had seen the leaflets in the library announcing Virginia Butler's visit to Stamford that week, had long ago memorized the contemplative pose from her author photo on the jacket. The news of the visit, then Virgie's appearance here, in Paula Jean's diner, felt like a message from Wise. It had been five years since Paula Jean's splashy run away from college, inspired—she'd never admitted to Virgie, as though Virgie hadn't puzzled her out immediately—by that book Wise had given her. Seven years since Wise had gone.

"I'm not a writer," Paul had said.

Virgie—though she wasn't yet Virgie, she was Miss Butler, *Dr. Butler,* she endlessly reminded people—tipped a snowstorm of sugar into her mug and stirred the coffee with the lead end of her pencil. "I think we'll see about that," she had said.

Paula Jean hid her smile. A spark! The first notice anyone had paid her since she'd run away and watched her disappearance spill across the papers, since her mortified return home to Stamford six days later. Paul's parents had quietly shut the bedroom door behind her and called up *The Stamford Advocate* to persuade them to drop the story. Her father wrote a check to cover the cost of the detective the paper had hired, threw in a bit to grease the wheels of the printing press. And then nothing was ever said about it again.

In that diner, after years of her parents' averted eyes, Paula Jean had felt greedy for the attention, but Virgie had lost interest in her already, was marking up a manuscript with her dampened pencil tip.

This was one of the reasons it was so easy to take over after Virgie died: No one had ever gotten to know Virginia Butler. No one but Paula Jean.

Be me, Virgie would say when the telephone rang, echoing through the rotting old house, and with pleasure Paula Jean would oblige: to the gas man, the oncologist, the editor's assistant at Virgie's publishing house.

Photograph all of Virginia Butler's original correspondence and manuscript drafts. This, out of the deep blue. After twenty-five years at this, Paula Jean has long since stopped lying awake at night over fears of being found out—and now here is the fear, frog-walking in on some Boston man's legs.

After the first manuscript Paula Jean had sent to the publisher, the "collected" letters between herself and Virginia Butler, she'd sped home from the post office in Virgie's ancient Cadillac to puke and sweat. But over time, seeing her words under Virgie's name made sense. Her life as a champion for Virginia Butler's legacy—*edited by P. Walton*—became its own kind of truth. Its own kind of home. Paula Jean had created some of the most anthologized, beloved, and discussed books of modern times. People named their children after Virgie's—after *her*—characters. What further proof must that Boston man demand?

Even still, it's that first novel of Virgie's over which Paula Jean feels the most ownership. It had cast a spell over her first love affair, had been the first thing she'd ever said to Marjorie Ann Wise, the swaggering painter she'd been following to art class for weeks. *What is that about?* Wise sitting on the low wall outside the high school grounds, hair cut short the day after senior photos, three cigarettes tucked into her bobby sock. The soft tick of Wise's wristwatch filling the silence after Paul's question. Wise closed the book without marking her place. Her fingers were short and streaked with oil paint. *You're in Lawson's third-period art,* Wise said. She held the book out for Paul to take. *Get it back to me on Friday.*

Paula Jean had never read a book so quickly in her life. Within months she'd memorized it as well as she had memorized every mole and mark on Wise's body, the dark hair that grew at the nape of her neck, the aluminum squeeze of happy pain she felt when Wise drove her fingers between Paul's legs. Everything, the good and bad of them, came from that book, and didn't that make it just as much Paul's as Virgie's?

It did. It must.

And yet Paula Jean's stack of notebooks, in which she has kept painstaking notes of her decades of fabrication, will condemn her to anyone who looks. Her own rough drafts of Virgie's letters, outlines of the posthumous novels, diagrams of Virgie's sentences. The man behind the curtain, so to speak. Paula Jean thumbs through them now, seeking in them some evidence of her own righteousness. Shouldn't all the work count for something? Shouldn't it prove her authority? What could be more intimate than poring over the details of another's life, than resurrecting her? Virgie didn't have to spend years studying herself, memorizing her own tics and tells. Paula Jean knows Virgie better than Virgie could have ever known herself. Paula Jean has constructed a legacy, and she's given every bit of the credit to a dead woman. She's taken barely anything for herself, and of course no one has ever thanked her.

Paula Jean shuffles into the kitchen and shoves the notebooks into the cold oven. She can spin stories out of air, but material truth is less malleable.

Paula Jean's already finished her toddy, and a woody sliver of clove is swimming around in her mouth, prickling her tongue and soft palate numb. Her mother taught her to make a hot toddy when she was only six. From a housekeeper, Paula Jean had learned to put clove oil on a cotton swab and press it against the gum whenever her sisters complained of toothaches. Her baby sister, Heather, slept with a cotton ball doused in the stuff pressed between her eyes for the six days Paula Jean was missing from college. "Eye ache," she'd said over and over. "I ache, I ache."

Paul and Wise had always hated the end of that first novel. A sign of an early and unsure novelist. A twist: not a god at all but a girl who slipped on ice and cracked open her skull before she made it a hundred yards from her dormitory, the sylvan euphoria nothing more than the fevered death throes of adolescence. They had rewritten it dozens of times, granting the girl the love affairs and conquests stolen from her by Virginia Butler's limited imagination.

A few years ago, Paula Jean wrote an introduction to the reissued edition of the book, and she declared the ending *a dozen pages best edited out of Butler's legacy.*

The author's promise to her protagonist—you may be shaped and known by the adventures you have, you and the world may change each other in equal measure—has yet to be fulfilled, in our literature or our world. When is a girl no longer a girl? It's an old joke, and Butler is too cowardly to change the punch line. [P. Walton, introduction, *Her Home in the Burrow,* Virginia Butler (Penguin Classics, 1988), vi.]

Paula Jean had clacked it out on Virgie's own Smith Corona, digging in the insult with each pounded key.

Nothing she did could touch Virgie, though; Paula Jean has been shadowboxing for twenty-five years. Everyone here but Paula Jean is a ghost; even Lewis, the mean old tomcat who showed up on her porch five years ago, matted and smelling of salty earth, died last spring. Paula Jean used to look out the back window, watching the cat stalk around in the dust after voles and mice, his thick tail rigid and parallel to the ground. She still calls for him from time to time, attributes the wooden creaks overhead to his heavy footfall.

She'd rather a house filled with ghosts than one haunted only by solitude.

Paula Jean came here looking for a home, for the imagination that had spun out the most beautiful world she'd ever touched, and found instead a wolf in a nightgown. All those years ago, avoiding the rotten wood on Virginia Butler's front porch as she pressed the bell again and again. That moment itself a funhouse reflection of the night nearly six years earlier she had stood on her parents' front stoop after hitchhiking back to her hometown, fur-trimmed parka hood pulled up to hide her face from the streetlights. The blank look on Virgie's face when finally she peeked past the curtain in the front window, filigreed with black lace made of mildew. The sagging cot reluctantly offered, the same cot Paula Jean would sleep on for more than twenty years. The way Paula Jean found all the letters she had written to Virgie, only one of them ever opened, tucked into a tottering pile of manuscript pages. Everything here always threatening to become kindling.

Much better is the version Paula Jean has told for so long that she nearly slips and believes it sometimes: a conversation about art and the lingering coolness of Virgie's hand on Paula Jean's elbow, the extravagant tip, the invitation to look her up if ever Paula Jean was in North Adams.

By the time Virginia Butler had come to Stamford, Paula Jean was an old maid at twenty-three. Bored and broken by all that had come before.

"They never did find me," Paula Jean had said as she refilled Virgie's mug across the diner counter. "They climbed three mountains and hiked the Long Trail and never looked in the room next door." Red-faced, snuggled against the damp body of that French girl in the dorm room next to hers.

"Villagers and their pitchforks. No reputation for intellect there," Virgie had said.

What was the name of that girl in the next room over? Paula Jean can't remember. The girl had been so jumpy, so nervous about the detectives and the attention, and after a few days, she'd had enough of being an outlaw and pushed Paul out.

The first time Paula Jean had slept in Virginia's bed was the day she'd left Virgie's cold body in a Pittsfield hospital. Paula Jean palm-kneed into the indentation in the center of the mattress, that distinct chemical hospital smell lingering on her skin. Still, Paula Jean was thrilled to see the implications in the reviews of Virgie's posthumous volumes, edited by P. Walton. *In the great tradition of spinsters making home together.* It felt like the truth. A shared life, whether or not Virgie would have admitted it. Paula Jean had built this for them both.

But this Boston Man will march in now with his camera and some bureaucratic insistence that Paula Jean prove some part of herself. He'll demand entrance into her home and her history, Virgie's history.

He's coming to break them apart.

Paula Jean looks at the house as he might demand to see it. Here are the letters I sent to Virgie in 1952, she'll say. I reckon they are older than you. Here is my own copy of her first book, which in the end I never even asked her to sign. Here is where I scraped molasses off the pantry floor with a nail file. Here is where I found a rat suckling her puppies, and here is the incinerator where I put them all.

Here is where I pulled the waxy ends of Virgie's bob into a fist in the middle of the night as she heaved into the sink after chemotherapy. Here is the oven with the broken pilot light, and inside are the notebooks I won't let you see because they prove my deception. Here is the dial on the cooktop that I often forget to twist completely to the right, and here is what gas smells like, if you close the doors and windows tight.

Here is Virgie's will, which I altered with the perfect mimic of her signature so that probate wouldn't take the house, because that old witch died without leaving me one red cent for my decades of trouble. Here is the telephone that used to ring once or twice a week, a sound that would lift Virgie's head from her typewriter and make her say to me, "Be me."

Be me.

Be me.

Be me.

Paula Jean became Virgie in Virgie's own home—the letters Virgie ought to have written back to Paula Jean, the books Virgie might have written had she lived—and what may have begun as a shot at revenge became a shared life, of sorts. *Intimacy takes many forms,* she might tell the Boston Man.

Might the Boston Man wonder what had kept her here? Leashed to a woman like this one, battered by an unrelenting ego, an affect unsoftened by age, by art, by the length and loyalty of Paula Jean's companionship?

Paul imagines—an imagining now pliant from frequent use—it had been her and Wise burrowed away in this rambling old house in the country. Stair treads propped up with dictionaries, bed frame still made of pine and rope. How luxurious these forty years might have been, how textured their life. Wise's half-finished canvases leaning against every wall. Notes left for each other on every surface. Cackling together at *That Girl* reruns and reading aloud—*don't forget your pill, you're always up to something, spaghetti again?*—and Lewis too somehow alive with them, jumping from one gentle lap to the other. At the beginning, perhaps, Paul had imagined adventure and sex and art and food until they were breathless, but after decades here she finds herself craving a more tender sort of solace.

She'll make herself another toddy. She lights the burner and has the fleeting idea of poisoning the Boston Man, of slipping kerosene into his tea. They grow refined, conservative men up in Boston, just like they did in Stamford; he probably wouldn't say a word about the bitter taste.

But he'd be too big for the incinerator, and Paula Jean isn't strong enough to dig a grave.

In one of Virgie's books, a parlormaid stole laudanum from a stable hand who'd been kicked in the back by a horse; she dosed her abusive master's nighttime sherry with four teaspoons of the stuff. She stood behind the curtain, listening to his breathing become labored then stop.

At the hospital, Paula Jean had stood behind the curtain between Virgie's bed and the door, listening as her Cheyne-Stokes breathing lengthened and rattled. In memory, Paula Jean feels the bottle of laudanum sweating in her palm, in a tangling of real and unreal. In this moment, she cannot remember which of them wrote that scene, which memory or fiction mirrored the other.

But she knows she'd never have had the courage to kill Virgie. She's just the brand of coward who only steals from the dead, who only betrays when a back is turned.

Paula Jean fiddles with the watch on her wrist, Wise's old Elgin that she's worn every day since forever.

Virgie freely stole elements from Paula Jean's life and wove them into her novels. And once those details were driven into Virgie's stories, Paula Jean felt stripped of them, a little less flesh and memory than she'd been. Her little sister's clove-oil cotton ball, the way her mother pressed a cold cocktail glass to the bridge of Paula Jean's nose whenever it bled. The flare of her own disappearance from college and her pink-cheeked hiding spot in the French girl's bed. Paul kept Wise to herself. Virgie had never earned that story.

The fire under the burner is out again. Striking a match to relight the stove for the kettle, Paul remembers the first time Wise lit a cigarette for her. A spark, the briefest shift in the color of Wise's face, a burst of warm tones. The sound of the match strike would wake Paul when she'd doze off in their burrow in the woods, when the waning sunlight would start to filter in gray and she'd smell that sweet-salty scent of the extinguished match head. They had pounded an old nail by the cabin's door, and there they hung Wise's watch—stolen, it turned out, from her father's car, where his mistress had left it behind. The watch became the wall between them and the outside world, the ticking the persistent reminder of all that was on the other side.

Paul still wears the watch, though it hasn't kept time for years.

In the dining room, Paula Jean takes her old seat at the table, her *before* seat, just to the left of Virgie's elbow, and presses her forearms into the streaked wood. Sitting here, Paula Jean would watch herself and Virgie in the warped mirror over the chest of drawers, a false fly-on-the-wall view of her life, Virgie chugging out pages from that old Smith Corona. In the mirror now, Paula Jean looks like she did then, a lady-in-waiting, a perched finch. If life had been reversed, would Virgie have hooked her hands under Paula Jean's arms to hold her during the heaving? Would Virgie have cradled the memory of Paula Jean, no matter the risk?

Paula Jean imagines the Boston Man sitting across from her, at what would have been Virgie's right elbow. Dark-gray suit, a slick briefcase. Poised to expose her.

It had happened more quickly than she could have expected. These computers, these mechanical memories, these new ways of capturing crooks and forgers.

But what the computer can't capture is the space between Virgie's tissue lips whispering, *Be me,* and Paula Jean's dutiful embrace of the role.

The way to be someone else, she could say to the Boston Man, and she'd lean in close, *is to make the other person's skin your landscape. You could draw the pattern of their chicken bumps and chin hairs better than your own. And they become your own.*

You obliterate yourself in service to them, she would say.

But you didn't obliterate yourself, the Boston Man would say, sly in his suit, cheek twitching. *Your name is on all those books. "P. Walton, editor." You're both Frankenstein and the monster.*

But it's not her name, is it? P. Walton is no one at all.

God no, not Paul. That's no name for a writer.

She is a writer, in the end. A builder of story.

She's a goddamn Pygmalion.

You always get vulgar when you're up against a wall, Virgie had told her more than once. *Avoid poker and contract negotiations.*

Paula Jean hears that voice now and looks to Virgie's habitual seat. Virgie's there, as she so often has been over the past twenty-five years, Virgie before the cancer shrank her, when she still had the energy to be as mean as she ever was. Now, here, she's sizing up the Boston Man, raising an eyebrow and pursing her lips.

Even Lewis the mean old tomcat has taken a seat at the table, a piano stool with a needlework top, threadbare and warped. It squeaks as Lewis digs into his paw with his snaggly teeth.

From her vantage point, Paula Jean can see the whole table reflected back in the dining room mirror. All four of them are there. Paula Jean's hair could use cutting. She usually does it herself in the bathroom with a pair of kitchen shears. Time must have gotten away from her. She fiddles again with the wristwatch. "Did you know that watches carry their histories with them?" she says aloud, because if the ghosts are here, they may as well listen.

Virgie, older than Paula Jean, older than dirt, rolls her eyes. The Boston Man, though, is a child. He gestures for her to continue.

"Every watchmaker makes a mark inside the back cover to memorialize the repair." Paula Jean uses a ridged thumbnail to pry off the back of the watch case. "Like rings of a tree trunk." She's only taken the wristwatch in for repair a handful of times, but that first marking, that was from the repair shop that had it when Wise disappeared. It had simply stopped one afternoon, and then four days later, Wise was gone.

Back in 1951, in the diner, pouring sepia-clear coffee into Virgie's mug, Paula Jean had said, "They climbed three mountains to find me, and now that I am back, they cannot look me in the eye." Her parents had lived and died mortified by the tempest she'd caused by disappearing; more than once after she'd returned, they introduced her as one of her younger sisters. Her sisters treated her as a spinstery old aunt from the time she was twenty-one. When Paula Jean returned home from her run-away, she became a secret someone had spoken out loud, and everyone did their level best to pretend they hadn't noticed.

After she left for Virgie's, she never spoke to her parents again. Her letters to her sisters started coming back *Addressee Unknown.* One disappearance a tragedy, two disappearances a relief.

Virgie pulls a slim packet of cigarettes from her sweater pocket and gestures to the young man from Boston for a light. Virgie was an occasional smoker, reserving the habit for completion of manuscripts or moments of temper. Paula Jean does not expect the spark of the Boston Man's lighter or the red beacon of Virgie's cigarette to have a corresponding smell, but she tastes the butane and the ash at the back of her tongue. She could always taste the cigarettes on Wise's mouth. Paula Jean slugs her toddy.

Virgie says to the Boston Man, "Forty years ago, this paper-doll girl shows up on my front porch, smelling of fried potatoes and coffee. She demands a position, says that she has come upon my own invitation, and simply won't leave. I never hired her, I don't recall paying her, and still here she was each morning, wiping at something or scrubbing at something else."

The Boston Man raises his eyebrows at Paula Jean.

Paula Jean says, "Every love story has an origin."

Virgie tilts her head back. "Yes, every love story."

Paula Jean looks from Virgie to the Boston Man and back again. "I did this for both of us, you know," she says. "Your legacy would have disintegrated. The world would have moved on."

"If only I'd died young," Virgie says. "Dying in one's early old age is ordinary. No tragedy in it. I should have been like your sweetheart and gone at seventeen."

"She was eighteen," Paula Jean says. Eighteen and a senior in high school. Wise was going to join up with the WAVES after graduation. Wise's entire family—father, brothers, uncles—had been in the Navy. Paul hadn't understood it, wanting to be like your family, wanting to be near them.

"See?" Virgie says, speaking around the cigarette suckered to her bottom lip. "Very romantic."

Paula Jean is suspicious about which version of Virgie is seated with her—Virgie as she was, or Virgie as Paula Jean has built her? She wishes she could check a tag or a manufacturer's stamp on the bottom of the apparition's bare foot.

In the mirror across the room, Paula Jean is the oldest of the assembled, ropy tendons under silk-scarf skin, wooden bones poking at the seams of her clothing, teeth too big for her face, belly that sits like a cat on her lap. Lewis's ghost snores beside her, tiny eruptions of grumble and air that she's missed these past six months.

A spark, then a fire. Being seen—not as a mother's helper but as a girl. Desired. The aching distance between Wise's lips and Paul's. And then, years later, the second spark across a diner counter, just a dim reflection of the first. But it was all that Paula Jean could grasp at, her only chance to remake herself after limping home in shame.

They climbed a mountain for me, Paul had said, pouring thin sepia coffee into Dr. Butler's cup, splashing it onto the bodice of her diner uniform. *And they never looked next door.*

Sounds like an impulsive, spoiled child lashing out, too pitiful to know how to go about making a life, Dr. Butler had said, not looking up from her papers.

"You were such a disappointment to me," Paula Jean says now, and her voice is mournful and defeated even to her own ears. "You were the author of my childhood."

"Those stories were all mine, you know," Virgie says. "Nothing was ever yours."

But something *was* hers. Paula Jean remembers: The rusty smell of skin and the scratch of the hair on Wise's shins, her hair sticking to Wise's damp skin, Wise wrapping a hand around Paul's neck to tilt her head forward, pressing on the soft tip of Paul's nose. The stink of clove on a cotton ball, *I ache I ache.* Tugging on the tulip bulbs to make it rain. A sharp metallic pain at the back of her head, everything so cold but the liquid heat sticking her hair to the back of her neck. The spicy, boozy smell of laudanum. The ache, the ice.

"Do you smell gas?" asks the Boston Man, pushing up the sleeves of his suit coat.

Dark is dripping down outside the kitchen window, and the kettle has whistled itself to empty. She twists the knob to the left.

Through the wooden slats of the blinds, her fractured reflection.

Still, the smell of gas.

This was the life Paula Jean had made, the funhouse mirror of the life she could have had with Wise. And now this Boston Man would take even this one away from her. Leave her with only a half dozen books with someone else's name on them.

In the grease-streaked window of the oven door, Paul catches not her reflection but her shadow. She opens the oven and a wall of gas sighs out.

The notebooks are not even warm to the touch. Paula Jean creaks slowly down to sit cross-legged before the open oven, door nearly in her lap, and drags the notebooks toward her over the ridges of caked grease. Deep in the stack, that copy of Virgie's first book. The one Wise pressed into her hands so many years ago.

Inside, on the flyleaf, Wise's tight, spidery handwriting, the black ink faded to an orangey sort of purple. The only love letter anyone had written to Paul, captured between these covers. The book began them and it had ended them. Hadn't it already taught them that they wouldn't get to keep what they had found? That the burrow would give way to the cruelty of all that was outside it?

The heavy kitchen door is bolted shut, and the faded turquoise paint glows gray under the ceiling fixture. The windowpanes in the door reflect back the other pinpoints of light in the room. How many times has Paula Jean knelt before this oven, hand and knees, sawing her right arm to remove the drips of roast grease, the grit on the floor pinching her nylons, her knees? How many hours—

Has her whole existence been a death throe?

"Oh, whose hasn't."

Virgie's unsympathetic voice in her left ear, hair standing on Paula Jean's arm now.

Paul hears still the spark of the lighter, the lapping rhythm of Lewis's phantom tongue. In a house that usually whines with the silence of its waning years, these snicks and dins rise up like a flimsy symphony. Everywhere spirits, except the one she longs to see. These spirits will fade, though, leaving just Paul and her empty house and her expansive aloneness. Not even a cloak made of spiderwebs, not even the company of dust mites or fleas.

Paul feels the boozy rush of the toddy, the gas of the oven, the cloying sweetness of the clove. The earthy mix of blood and late-autumn mud. It had been a Tuesday in November the last time Wise walked away from her. It was March before Paul had stopped looking.

She aches.

When is a girl no longer a girl?

When she becomes a memory.

But couldn't Paul really learn to control what happens on the hilltop and the valley below from inside her burrow? With the right kind of tug, she could make mountains rise, make ideas catch fire. She could be free and

Be me.

"That's no name for a writer," Virginia had said.

Wise nodding in that appraising way she'd had. "Paul, then. Call me Wise." The spark.

The kitchen reeks of gas.

Everyone here a ghost.

Paul closes her eyes, and she can almost hear the ticking of Wise's watch as Wise pushed at the round tip of Paul's nose against a sudden nosebleed.

Everything shut tight.

No one here but her.

And who is she? She wrote herself into existence. Her history is kindling.

That last moment, Wise crunching away from her, out of their cabin, disappearing into the shadows between the trees.

Paul has spent years rebuilding that burrow with Virgie's ghost. And now even that will disappear into shadow.

"Why couldn't it have been you I brought back?" Paula Jean says.

Wise doesn't answer. She couldn't. Even these ghosts are just figments.

Paula Jean breathes in and envisions the gas dancing around in her lungs.

The kitchen matches have been in her hand so long they've become damp. It takes several strikes, her right arm sawing forward and then

a spark.

SPELLS FOR SINNERS, PART FIVE

BLADEN COUNTY, NORTH CAROLINA, 1961

The spinet piano at Evie's deaf old neighbor's house held its tune for only six months at a time. For five years Evie had whined to Cousin Martha that all her babysitting money went to Sam Paltry, the church organist who tuned the pianos of the fifty Colored families who had them. Sam was the one who taught Evie to read music, though. He was near ten years older than she, but Evie thought for a while about making him her beau, just because he was so reliable and because it might lower her tuning costs. But then he married prissy Molly Ann Bell, who lived over in Lumberton and who took a hot comb even to the lace on her socks, and he moved out of the Quarter. Evie was left wishing she'd stolen his tuning key before he went off.

Nonetheless, the piano and Mrs. Smith's profound deafness granted Evie space she couldn't get at home—a space silent enough to compose music of her own.

When she sat in the whining quiet of Mrs. Smith's house—no

endless babies' crying there—even from the time she was twelve, Evie could be lifted up by the very idea of a song. Something like a magic carpet ride must feel, aloft but unafraid. She would begin with a motif from a church hymn, some *ding-dang-dang* she found in Mr. Smith's (may he rest) abandoned Baptist songbook, letting her mind repeat it, reverse it, play with it until it became a phrase, a beginning. And then she would thunk around on the piano keys until she could find a few chords, and Mrs. Smith would wander over to the spinet and place her palms on the top of the instrument and smile as though the vibrations were telling her secrets.

Evie and her brother Ronny found a dented old dinner bell in a trash heap outside the cotton mill, and they dragged it on home in Ronny's red wagon, coughing on the dust that swelled up around the wheels. Her daddy rigged it up for her, and from then on when her family needed her right quick, they banged on that bell rather than disturbing Mrs. Smith or trying to shout over whatever tune Evie was plunking out. For five years that bell was the sound she was always listening for, the true metronome to her days.

By and by Evie's legs got long enough to reach the piano pedals, and Mama and Daddy's new favorite joke was that they'd never worry about her making time in the back of some boy's truck since she spent all her free hours with the widow next door. Mama began talking about how some boy's family would be mighty pleased to have such a musical daughter-in-law and that maybe playing the piano would make it easier for her to find a job after she finished her teaching degree—a degree her parents had always told her she'd get. She'd be the first Lawrence to go past high school.

"It's a tight world out there, and you best take any small advantage you can get," Mama said all the time.

And yet Evie was a fairly miserable piano player—she never was able to make the music come out of her fingers the way it ribboned and dove in her head. She couldn't even whistle. Instead, Evie drew her music, illustrated it in spikes and wiggles, an improvised language of sound. She used a blue pencil to count out her beats, to circle moments that should swell, to loop those that should slur. She sat next to Sam Paltry on the church organ bench and they translated her drawings into sheet music, and then he'd tease out her song on the organ almost as it had played in her mind. She took out the only two books on musical notation in the Spaulding Monroe school library, both published before 1910 and with someone else's marginalia all through.

Evie never stopped drawing her music, though. Her language was closer to the truth of the song, anyhow.

Mrs. Smith's tidy house offered an unwatched mailbox, and it was there that Evie received the music school brochures she sent away for, and it was Mrs. Smith's address she wrote on her Boston Music College scholarship application, accompanied by her composition portfolio, which owed as much to Sam Paltry's patience as it did to Evie's imagination. When in late April the scholarship offer came—with a self-important handwritten note from the director of admissions that she and one other in her cohort would be "the first Southern Negro girls" to matriculate in the school's thirty-year history and wasn't that "quite an accomplishment for everyone involved"—Evie had just a moment with it before the big bell next door clanged for her to come home. She pinned the letter to the inside of her pocketbook and carried it everywhere for a week.

Sitting after Sunday school with her ankles up on the long living room sofa, Evie announced to the family that she'd been awarded a scholarship to a two-year teaching college in Boston. The music college was too tender a secret to be marched before her parents' ire and expectations.

"There are five Colored teachers' colleges in North Carolina, you selfish girl. There's no need for you to go farther than Elizabeth City, unless you are hiding something from your family." Mama's fist on her hip, her upper-arm flesh drooped over her elbow crease. Vertical furrows already deeply carved above the bridge of her nose. Mama was their house, both shelter and confinement.

"Scholarship or no, who will buy the bus tickets to Boston, who will buy the books? Who will teach these blessed ignorant children right here in this town to read? Not Evie Lawrence, that's for sure, isn't it." Daddy took a slow pull from his ginger beer, as though to prove he wasn't the puppeteer giving Mama voice.

There weren't enough teachers at Spaulding Monroe, the sole Colored school in Bladen County, and often enough students from the teachers' colleges filled in for semesters at a time. And it was a shame, and Evie would have done something about it if she could, but her one body couldn't solve that big problem, and she wasn't suited to teaching, besides. She was going to make music.

The next week at Sunday dinner, Cousin Martha's hand on her elbow, sandpaper with those blunt-cut nails, Martha pressing her face to Evie's ear, "Go on, get out of here, sugar pie." Martha, with her rainy-day savings and *I can take a few more motel shifts a week, and just write me each weekend to tell me what you're learning.* "Two educations for the price of one," Martha said.

Somewhere inside Evie ought to have been the humble part that would find herself unworthy of Martha's sacrifices, poor unmarried Martha, whom the family described as "very devout" when trying to persuade young men to take her out (and then divorced men, and then widowed men). Martha was always on the edges, taking care of people so that they'd pay notice to her, and Evie saw that and still she accepted the help, still she lied to them all.

If Evie had let it, the guilt would've grown up around her ankles like lashes to tie her in place, hold her to this town, this family ground, and sure as Sam Hill she wasn't going to allow it.

Evie's suitcase, full that first time with her diaries, her music, and a nickel recorder her brother Ronny had abandoned, was placed in the bed of Uncle Rudy's black truck, and Martha riding in back to keep it from tumbling out. They took her all the way to the bus depot in Fayetteville that first time, for more ceremony to the journey, and insisted upon sitting with her in the dripping Colored waiting room for over an hour. The bus was late and Martha was in danger of getting fired from her job over at the Safe Lodge, which would have ruined things for both of them, wouldn't it.

Evie wrote to Martha once that first term, a lonelier letter than she had intended, after a grueling dressing-down by the instructor for confusing *lentando* with *legato*. It was an entirely new language, not just the Italian but the terminology, the dominant seventh, the tonic note, and she was one of the few students without years of private musical instruction. She skipped the two-day bus ride home for the Thanksgiving holiday and had an egg salad sandwich at the diner near campus with priggish classical pianist Priscilla, the other "accomplished Southern Negro girl," who absolutely knew the difference between *lentando* and *legato,* who chewed quiet as a cow as Evie spent an hour talking herself out of quitting school, out of swallowing poison in mortification, out of running away to the circus to run the calliope. Evie went back to the empty dorm that night and pulled out the pink floral stationery her mother had given her when she graduated from high school.

But she couldn't write to Martha of what was really happening, so she wrote instead of an imagined math class, how the white teacher did trig so differently than they had learned at Spaulding Monroe, how the cafeteria food was dry as a bone and bland. She didn't write of how all the other students knew Debussy and Bartók and she knew mainly church hymns. She didn't write of the men, white men, Colored men, who followed her out of the T stations, catcalling, grabbing at her arm, or the way she was free to walk into any downtown bar, through any door, but only if she was willing to withstand the white folks' impassive stares pushing her back out like a gust of wind. She didn't write of how shabby she felt that first month, wearing the only two dresses she had, both light and flouncy, while the Northern Colored girls had snug wool skirts and smart twinsets that never wrinkled under their instruments. She wrote of how the Northern girls cut their hair close at the sides with the tidiest edges she'd ever seen and no one wore perfume to cover the stink of the subway. When Evie returned home to Bladenboro for winter break that first year, Martha's standard bun had been replaced with a thin puffed bouffant and close-cut sides, and she insisted on having her photo taken with Evie, just the two of them.

"Will you have to give back those textbooks?" Martha asked over Christmas Eve dinner. "Did you bring any home with you? Oh, you must have, though—you must have studying to do while you're here." Evie knew that Martha had taken a notion to a secondhand Northern education. Evie demurred, made it sound as though she had given her books to another girl at school; she promised to bring home the next batch, though, and she nearly believed herself when she said it.

"We'll be lucky Evie comes home again this summer," Mama said, spooning mashed potatoes onto Ronny's plate. Mama always had her number, even when she only knew half the story.

"Now, Evie'll be home for Easter for sure," Daddy said, shredding the darkest-red pieces of ham with his fork. She'd missed that deeply bitter, salty smell.

"Daddy, it's a two-day bus ride. We don't get that much time off classes."

"We'll just see about that," her daddy said.

"Cover your lap, miss," Mama said, gesturing with the potato spoon and splotching the table linen with butter. "Don't go and ruin that fine college-girl dress."

Packing her new wool dress had been a big mistake. She'd already endured the needling about her hairstyle, her shift in enunciation. And, anyway, life in Mama and Daddy's house had a way of staining on you, mustard or a little kid's snot, a homemade smattering that irritated Evie to no end until she got back to school, where the idea was sweet and forlorn. She tucked the dress back in her suitcase, beside the other belongings she planned to ferry to school. Piece by piece she would move herself from Bladenboro to Boston, and then when she graduated she'd move on to New York. She was sure her mother would notice the lighter drawers, the books tipped into now-empty space, but if she did she didn't make a peep.

And in the end, Evie kept her promise to Martha about the

books, which turned out to be a clever way to disguise how many of her possessions she carted up North with her at each visit. She scrounged abused texts from the Friends of the Library sale, filled a grocery sack to the top for twenty-five cents. On her visits to Bladenboro, she meted out the books: *American Standard Reader, Advanced Geometry, The Complete Shakespeare.*

At school, Evie gave in to Debussy and Bartók's String Quartet No. 2 as well as all the early Ellington her parents loved, probably the only music other than church hymns that had taught her to listen. She made Italian flash cards—*capriccio! pesante!*—illustrated in her own special language. She visited the hallway outside the string practice rooms and sat half-distance between two doors, drawing pictures of what she heard, until she could draw the music to command the double bass and violin in her head. Evie learned to play the piano better: She was bound to, with her tutor holding sharpened pencils beneath the keyboard to train her from dropping her wrists. When another student dropped out of the spring showcase in October of her second year, Evie was invited to fill in. Rumor, always rumor, was that a handful of Madison Avenue types came up, scouting for jingle writers. *This* would be her magic carpet ride, a more reliable gamble for getting to New York than hopping into bed with an A&R scout, particularly with Evie being her mama's daughter: tall and thick-waisted and plain.

She had a plan that started with working summers at an advertising agency and then doing the other hustle in her senior year, getting music into the hands of a piano man in a downtown club, working her way toward the labels. Each term, students left after being "discovered," but Evie wasn't giving up a minute of her free college education. Her future would come either way, and it could just wait another two years.

As Halloween approached, though, Evie got antsy. Her scholarship would cover her for four years, but she couldn't count on any more money orders from Martha once she admitted the imaginary nature of her two-year teaching degree. She took a part-time position shelving books at the school library and spent months listening for a motif in the squeak of the book cart, the thump of the stamp, the thud of falling books. Student composers for the showcase had their pick of musicians for the performance, and suddenly all the Northern boys, Colored and white, who'd rolled their eyes at Evie's accent or ignored her outright were running to catch up with her, stopping her mid-stride by curling their hands around her waist and turning her whole body toward them, playing her an accompaniment *alla marcia* as she walked across the lawn to the residence hall.

All the while, Evie noodled with her blue pencil, trying to find the song that could snag the ad men's attention. To find the song that could drown out the withholding little goblin inside her that stomped her mad feet and called every misfortune a punishment, that told her she'd end up right back in Bladen County.

Evie worked her way through evening library shifts and T rides listening to the music her mind made, taking notes on the soft inside of her arm with an eyebrow pencil. By the time Christmas break arrived, she'd made just enough progress to feel like a genius and a fool, depending on the time of day. She sat on the bench seat at the back of the bus for the two-day ride, drawing her chord progression in the frost on the window with a fingertip, running the *legato* melody in her mind.

In Philadelphia, a stooped old auntie with a proper-brimmed hat frog-walked up the back steps of the bus and paused to look around her, huffing onto her dark walnut cane. Like some Sunday funny, she lifted that cane in Evie's direction and swung it through the air.

"What are you doing at the back of that bus, child? Don't you know we can ride in the front now?" Granny shook her cane, not entirely in control of its trajectory.

Evie sat up straight like a shot. "Yes, ma'am. I only wanted to spread out a bit." She gestured toward her suitcase. Truth was there wasn't a point in settling in up front when she'd just have to move back at the Virginia line.

Granny's cane swung in the direction of the lavatory door, just three feet from Evie's knees. She huffed again. "You'll be regretting that in about two hours."

Granny wasn't all wrong.

Daddy picked her up from the bus stop, and Ronny was ringing that dinner bell as they pulled into the gravel drive. The littlest of the babies were in grammar school braids now, and Ronny was talking about joining the Marines. They ate dinner at the picnic table in the side yard, and Mama told her she could skip the cleanup just that first night. Evie sat alone in the dark and listened to her family, a domestic riot of mismatched sounds, clanking and scraping and wood-chair feet and Daddy whistling "Joyful, Joyful, We Adore Thee." For the first time, Evie recognizing that tune as Beethoven's Ninth.

The frigid Boston winter closed the world, but in the humid Bladenboro winter Evie could walk along the Cape Fear River and blow her pitch pipe and listen for her song in the squawk of waterbirds. She took lunch to her daddy at the worksite and leaned on elbows, memorizing the scrape of the trowel and the clank of the red bricks. At church, she borrowed Mama's lipstick to draw the flick-flick-sigh of the handheld church fans on the inside of her arm. But her family was leaning on her heavily over the holidays; Mama said near every day how relieved she'd be once Evie was back home. Daddy made a point of circling two employment advertisements in *The Carolina Times,* both for schoolteachers within twenty-five miles.

Her parents insisted that she take Ronny with her anytime she'd be out after dusk, on account of another Quarter girl gone missing in the fall. If only they knew how often she walked home from the practice rooms well past midnight, how often she and Priscilla had gone out to hear a new horn man and drink whiskeys at Connolly's until three.

After New Year's, Cousin Martha came over for coffee and cake, and when Mama got up to break up a fight between the little ones, Martha leaned forward. "I read that Shakespeare book," she said. "Which was your favorite play?"

"You read that whole thing?" Evie asked. The volume had taken up nearly half of her suitcase last spring.

Martha nodded. "Winnie at the Spaulding library lent me a study guide to help with the difficult parts." She shook her head. "I promise you I had no idea why he was so esteemed when I started, but then I started to understand him. If not his words, then his rhythms." Martha helped herself to another cup of coffee. "It's easy enough to pick up on what's going on if you pay attention to the rhythms," she said. "Even when you can tell you aren't getting the whole story."

Evie felt the flesh in her cheeks and arms run hot.

"Is it actually Boston, where you're living?" Martha asked.

Evie had only ever imagined it being Mama who figured it out, Mama shaking some damning piece of evidence, demanding an explanation as Evie cried in desperation. But Martha spoke in a calm and unhurried tone.

"It is," Evie said, trying to match Martha's tone, and failing. She sounded as caught out as she felt. "But I'm in school, a good school. I had to lie, I had to, or Mama and Daddy would have made me stay here." How did Martha know? Evie ticked through it all in her memory—her letters, the library books, something she had said?

Martha arched her penciled-in eyebrows. "The fault, dear Brutus," she said, but Mama walked in just then and collapsed into her chair. Martha leaned back and sipped at her cup.

Later, as Martha pulled on her gloves, Evie followed her to the front door. "What fault?" Evie whispered. "I had to."

Martha chucked Evie's chin, the gesture feeling sillier and more demeaning with Martha being so much shorter than Evie.

"How did you know?" Evie whispered, brushing Martha's hand away.

"Lots of little ways, I suppose, but mostly, you're far too happy to be going to teachers' college."

Evie squeezed her shoulders. "Are you gonna rat on me?" she asked. Martha was nearly old enough to be her mother, but Evie had only ever talked to her like a sister. Had taken for granted her loyalty like a sister, too.

Martha pinned her hat on. "How you take care of your parents' hopes is your business. But this 'had to' nonsense is too much. You're making your own decisions, Evie Lawrence, and any one of those decisions is going to change the lives of your family. You think, once they find out, your mama and daddy going to let any of the little ones leave this state for school? You think that whatever it is you're studying up there is going to pay you enough to take the burden off your daddy?"

Martha pulled Evie into a hug and rubbed a kiss onto her cheek. "You're a clever girl. Until you show you see how family works, though, don't expect me to keep up with extra shifts to send you money. There's folks here more in need of that than you." She patted Evie's arm. "But I'll keep your secret, for the time being."

Just a few days later, Daddy asked how many tickets Evie would get to her graduation ceremony. "Your mama's planning to bring the whole lot of them," Daddy said. "We were thinking of coming up in a little motorcade, us and Uncle Rudy's truck. Your mama wrote to the Y up there; we may even stay a whole week." And then the day after that, Mrs. Smith brought over a note requesting that Evie come play for her, and Evie was not there more than a half hour when the dinner bell clanged for her return.

In Boston, Evie was an *I*. Down here in Bladenboro, she would always be a *we*, one of the four Lawrence kids, one of the sprawling Lawrence and Mason families.

The bus to Fayetteville, where she'd catch her transfer to Boston, came through Bladenboro at 5:15 in the morning. Evie walked alone up Seaboard Street to the corner drugstore with her suitcase and hatbox, past her old school and the ancient pile of tires on the corner of Grief Street. Farm trucks rumbled past on the dirt road, shiny from the oil slicked over it. Her suitcase was heavy with a framed photograph of her parents, one of the few in which they were captured laughing, at her uncle's wedding, the two of them loose in dance and beer and the spring sunshine of Jones Lake. Photographs were spells, conjuring taste and the sounds of voices rising.

For a year and a half, every man she had met assumed she was a dummy, or a pushover, or provincial, or a Jezebel. Even her piano tutor talked about the soft cocoon of her accent, the warm honey of it, the seductive lilt that he said wrapped around him like a long blade of grass even when she first telephoned him to ask for an appointment.

No: If Evie's speech, if her *music,* had a flavor, it wouldn't be honey. It would be the pungent green-algae taste of the air near the lake in early spring or the first gulp of the water each summer, fresh from the high jump and tasting of bitter adrenaline, fish skin, and silt. This was the secret part of her that would never be known so long as she stayed up North. A part neither sacred nor profane but secret all the same.

Down here, no part of her was secret. But no one had ever assumed she was a dummy.

The leatherette handle on her suitcase—heavy also with her summer sandals, her Sunday school Bible—was tearing from the weight, the pale-ivory netting that undergirded the leatherette stretching from the stress. Evie leaned against the lamppost and rested her bag in the pool of light, stacking her hatbox on top. She thought about the third chord in her progression, thought about how often that clanging dinner bell layered over her playing at Mrs. Smith's piano. Thought about how that sense of waiting crept over her music, listening as she always was for the summons elsewhere.

Always waiting to be called home. Evie's mind on Martha again, who'd treated her to small looks of disapproval ever since Evie had admitted her lie. Still, Martha had held her secret—no doubt to it that if Martha had breathed a word of Evie's deception to her parents, Evie'd be locked up in her old shared bedroom instead of on her way back to school.

She breathed into the buttoned-up collar of her red parka to warm the skin on her nose and chin. It would be colder in Boston. She sneezed ice crystals up there.

A flock of migrating birds scratched and dug at a patch of brown grass a few feet away. Every so often one would hop, a straight-up-in-the-air pop with no apparent muscle movement.

Evie checked her wristwatch. How many more times would she make this walk? How much of her life would be spent in anticipation of that dented-dinner-bell clang? Would she end up living Martha's life, tied by duty but yearning for more?

A truck slicked past on Main Street. Evie didn't look up fast enough to make out the lettering, but she saw the brake lights flare in the dimness of the hour and heard rattling get louder as the truck backed up, *lentando,* to stop just in front of her on the street.

Paula Double Identified

Girl Mistaken for Missing College Student is Elizabeth Graves, Now at Montpelier.

PAULA DOUBLE—20

Due to the resemblance to missing Paula Welden, a close double who was recently interviewed by Connecticut state detectives, has asked that her identity be made known as she continues to be mistaken for the Bennington College girl last seen on December 1.

The girl is Miss Elizabeth Graves, 19, of Brooklyn, N. Y., who has a summer home at New Haven, Conn., and recently enrolled at Vermont Junior College in Montpelier.

The Montpelier Argus writes of her identity as follows:

Miss Graves told the officers at the time of her examination and repeated also to an Argus reporter, that she was the daughter of Dr. and Mrs. Arthur H. Graves of 39 Praza street, Brooklyn, N. Y., where he is director of the Brooklyn Botanical gardens. The family also has a summer home in New Haven, Conn., where he was formerly a professor at Yale University.

Another coincidence in addition to her striking resemblance to Miss Welden was that she was in Montreal on skiing trips on two occasions, one about two months ago and one about a month ago Miss Welden had been reported in Montreal and Detective Franzoni made a trip to the Canadian city to check on the report. It is possible that Miss Graves was mistaken for Miss Welden there.

She has confirmed that she had been considerably annoyed by being constantly mistaken for the missing Bennington College student and emphasized that she desired to get the record straight. Her assertions in this respect were fully confirmed by the state investigator, who declared he and other authorities were convinced that she was not the Welden girl in spite of the fact that, as he put it, her description was almost identical.

Many Montpelier residents who have seen Miss Graves on the street have noticed her similarity in appearance to Miss Welden, which has, as Miss Graves said, become embarrassing. She wears a red parka coat similar to one which the Bennington College student was wearing when she disappeared.

Elm Tree Inn

MAIDEN MOTHER CRONE

Everyone's mother dies, this much is true, and Bitsy is no different, it seems. Twenty-six hundred miles away her mother tosses in a fever, and Bitsy slumps in a molded plastic seat in the Phoenix bus station, waiting for her Greyhound connection. Vegas and the circus now a full day behind her and her mother's muggy Florida deathbed three days down the road.

A mother she's not seen for thirty years.

Bitsy's not left Vegas since she got there decades ago, so she's never had this vantage—looking back at the circus and thinking of it as home.

The chairs in the station are bolted to the floor in a circle, inducement to watch one another rather than glare at the bus clerk who keeps changing the numbers on the departures board, extending this yawn of time into infinity in ten-minute increments.

Across the room, a faded mural advertises Greyhound's City of Lights line. A performer once snapped a photo of the mural for her, but this is the first time Bitsy's seen it herself. A corny Vegas collage, the mural features a twenty-year-old poster for the Great Vegas Circus (*Five rings of awe and strength!*). And on the poster, zooming up from the lower left-hand corner, is Bitsy Graves, great feather puff exploding from her head, silk reins easy in her hands, heels dug into the backs of two circus horses. A painting of a photograph, holding an impossible pose for two decades. Even without the passage of time, no one would've recognized Bitsy on horseback. She barely recognizes herself.

A decade since she's gotten onto a horse. After the fourth ankle fracture, she couldn't mount without an assist, and they reassigned her to the viper tent, where she learned to dose a snake behind its head, to move it convincingly as though it were awake; to remove its fangs and venom sacs while it slept, replace the fangs with white chalk, filed down to a point. She wore a low-slung belly dancer's costume, flat medallions sewn along the hips, and sweeping blue eye makeup, a vision pulled from Elizabeth Taylor in *Cleopatra*. Alfredo lit her with red gels on the lamps, and she put rouge on her nipples for the "Gentlemen Only" late-night revues. She fooled herself into thinking she was fooling them and that it wasn't just the drink and the desert and the Wild Western feel that made them hoot and holler so.

But the white spiderweb age lines crept over the swell of her breasts, her neck slipped from supple to slack, striated lines that she recognized from her mother's morning face. The men hooted still, but the sounds spiraled into jeers, and this time it was Bitsy's idea to move on. To climb into the fortune-teller's red scalloped caravan and crocheted shawl. To grow out her fingernails and use putty to sculpt her round nose into something aged and hooked and persuasive. Bitsy knows she shouldn't enjoy the caricature, but there's relief in disappearing into someone entirely new. The costume is heavy— thick rings and humid layers of scarves and skirts. The world can't reach Bitsy's skin when she's wrapped up in it. Now and again, she even forgets to drop her muddled Soviet accent between shifts. "Stop it," says her roommate, Pilar, shuddering over her Sanka. "I feel like I'm being interrogated by the KGB."

Two hours until the sticky bus to Austin for the next leg of the journey, and Bitsy's already done the *People* crossword and filed her nails from their sharp points into daughterly ovals.

Bitsy's not sure she knows how to be a daughter anymore.

Her mother only treated her as a daughter when it served her to. All other times she was just a nursemaid, a nuisance. Bitsy drank those roles away years ago.

From her suede fringed bag, Bitsy pulls her sister Pamela's last letter, florid script on dark-rose stationery, although the rereading doesn't soothe her one whit.

I haven't told Mother you're coming, but I'm trying to get her to hold on a bit longer. Trying to drum up some excitement over the grandchildren's spring pageant, talking as though she might be able to attend, even though there's little hope of her ever leaving the house.

Her memories are confused and out of order now, and so I don't think you even need to worry about shocking her. I've told Steph, too, and she's promised me absolute secrecy upon punishment of ostracization. We aren't telling Heather you're coming, not yet. She's too close to Mother to see much outside herself anyway right now. Half the time we can't get her to climb out of Mother's bed and give her some rest.

I do wish that other detective had found you before Da passed. I look dearly forward to embracing my big sister after so long.

How to be a daughter, a sister, to a family that blames her for the weakness in her father's heart, which plagued his final decades?

Not one of them knows what she knows: that he told her to go, to take that tiny bastard growing inside her and find someone else to take care of her. "No daughter of mine would dare bring this trouble home at the holiday," he told her over a crackling and lagging long-distance connection.

He would not wire her money for a train ticket, didn't care to see her at his Thanksgiving table. So she wept in her dorm room for two days, then hitchhiked to New York, where no one, including the man involved, was any more sympathetic than her father.

She'd been sitting on a bus-station bench in New York, red and streaked face, when a crowd sidled up, asked her if she was that missing Bennington girl in all the papers, then police and station managers and her father driving down from Stamford to look her in the face, station manager's hand turning Bitsy's head this way then that, pointing out the upturned nose and dimpled chin, the small scar on her eyebrow. Her father nodding, mighty grateful to them, such a trying time, but no—here, looking her square in the eyes—this girl was no daughter of his.

She cannot be blamed for the weakness of his heart.

Was it her foolishness that broke them apart for good? Had her father always been that hard man, or had he suddenly become him?

If any one of her sisters asked, she might tell them that his death wasn't punishment enough. He should have lost each of his teeth. He should have lost all of his daughters. He should have been stripped of his name.

A boy, maybe nine, walks the outer circle of the bus-station chairs, heel to toe, ramrod back, peacocking for the uninterested travelers. He wobbles over a bolt in the floor. Bitsy wonders if Mother still drinks, if even on her deathbed she wears the heavy rose perfume to hide the smell of gin. Or if everything since has just been encore to the eighteen years that came before, everyone grimacing as Mother grows loud at the dinner table with a story she's already halfway for-gotten, averting their eyes as she walks from the room on the balls of her feet and disguises a slight stagger with mincing side steps.

Bitsy, too, became accomplished at disguising her imbalance, even atop those massive white horses. But her hit-bottom moment, as they called it in AA, came with her final ankle fracture during a performance that she didn't remember at all. She merely awoke in the free clinic in loads of pain, the doctors withholding even Tylenol because her labs came back at dangerous blood-alcohol levels. Then: the wretchedness of detox, the shame of being demoted to snake lady, the deeply humiliating memory of her own stench as she woke in the hospital bed, and Bitsy left the booze behind for good. Inside her hip pocket, Bitsy's ten-year AA chip presses against her pelvic bone as she shifts in her chair.

The bus clerk shuffles to the departures board and replaces a two with a three. Ten minutes closer to never.

Bitsy had known her mother was dying before the telephone rang, before Pilar rattled the green phone receiver against the cardboard accordion door that separates Bitsy's bedroom from the rest of the trailer. Prickle to the scalp and a flash of image—Heather curled around their mother's sweating bed-bound form—hit like lightning.

Somehow, Bitsy had given birth to the flashes at the same time she gave birth to the child. Then the child was taken and she drank the flashes away.

Bitsy had forgotten about them by the time they reappeared, in the months after she got sober. The first flash hit while she held the delicate head of a doped-up pit viper, and she had the sudden fear that somehow through the power of wistful thinking she had turned her weak tea into whiskey. The flash—a squeeze behind her earlobes, as though Bitsy's head were wedged between two rocks—of seeing herself standing beside her own likeness on this Vegas poster, had only made sense just an hour ago.

Bitsy stands to stretch. She is wearing Pilar's cast-off pantsuit, a wild paisley number that makes her feel much younger than her layers of crocheted shawls and cheap metallic scarves. Bitsy lifts her suitcase (also borrowed from Pilar; *no one has regretted rushing to a deathbed, Puff*, she'd said, holding it out) and takes a slow walk across the glass-walled depot, pausing before the City of Lights mural. The suitcase is nearly empty, more for show. Bitsy has little she can wear home to a dying mother, so she's borrowed two plain dresses from the circus seamstress. The last time Bitsy was at this depot, she was waiting for a Utah-bound bus; she'd been starting to show and had layered a cable-knit sweater over her blouse, zipped her heavy red parka over her torso. Her bus ticket, purchased by a Catholic ladies' relief society, damp from her hand. She remembers too clearly walking the perimeter of the depot, sweating beneath her breasts and down the sides of her face. She was dodging curious eyes then and felt some peculiar relief when people would notice the tin wedding ring she'd bought from a man outside Penn Station.

Bitsy stands side by side to her portrait, the frozen funhouse version of her other, younger self, cheeks flushed and round with youth and the mistaken idea that one's past could be drowned, could be trodden down with iron horseshoes.

"You been to Las Vegas before, miss?" The boy from earlier. "My first time, and my uncle Rod is going to take me to see the fire-eaters. You ever seen fire-eaters?"

Bitsy had kissed a fire-eater once. Her breath had smelled like kerosene.

"I have. And I've seen fire-breathers, too. And men who can lift entire caravans over their heads." Bitsy mimics the motion with her suitcase. The boy bounces on flexing ankles. He is beautiful, light-brown skin with dark eyelashes that turn his eyes into showstoppers.

"I can lift my sister," he says. "And I can almost lift up my dad. My mom is heavier, so I have to get stronger before I can lift her." And he turns and whooshes away, arms out like he's a twin-engine airplane.

On Monday afternoons, when the circus tents are dark, Bitsy likes to lie in her bed nook at the back of Pilar's trailer and listen to the big jets from California swoop past on their way to landing, listen to Pilar and Alfredo make love to each other. When Bitsy has sex, she never manages to scratch her deepest itch, to get to the obliteration that booze used to offer. She closes her eyes and all of it is still there—lost daughter, dead first lover, estranged family, shame and destruction. And time, glugging away like water down a tub drain.

In her candlelit roulette over the scarf-draped table, Bitsy holds tourists' open palms in hers, tracing valleys with a long red talon, guessing at their lives from the smell on their jackets, their postures and skin stains. The flashes are useless here, cannot be called down for anything; when they do come, she can't always describe what she's seen. A ripple of fabric, a cut-off peal of laughter, an eyelash on a cheek.

Pamela, the oldest of Bitsy's sisters, renewed her efforts to find Bitsy after their father died six years ago. The goon who hung around the shadowed back of the tent on "Gentlemen Only" nights, tinted lenses and empty pipe, showing up every night for weeks without tipping a single girl, watching Bitsy like she glowed—he turned out to be Pamela's detective, Burton. Would Bitsy have fucked him that first time if she'd known? Maybe yes, maybe no.

Seated in the waiting-room circle, there's a man who looks like Rock Hudson. He watches her. His terrifically full mustache moves in a sneer of appraisal.

Before the fortune-telling, before the AA chip, she had run into men like this one, who caught up with her in tight corridors, who stepped out from pools of darkness as she left her show tent. She was a snake handler, a horse wrangler, confident she could manage those she didn't want and give in to those she did. Still, she felt unease at every footstep from behind, at lighted matches and cleared throats in the dark. Large hands on her stomach through her spangled leotard, on her naked flesh above her belly dancer's medallions.

The thing about fire-eaters is that they don't actually eat the fire. They take it into their mouths and they extinguish it. It never reaches their core.

To chase away vanity, the mistresses of the maternity home shaved every one of the girls' heads. "Girls in need," the mistresses called them. No one was ever called Mother. Curfew at 6 P.M., though the home was in the desert and there was nowhere for them to go. There were knees on hardwood floors and dawn readings from the Book of Mormon. There were ballet stretches and bars of shea butter rubbed on growing bellies. Clipped-short fingernails and hard carrots in corn syrup.

Girls who got close to their times slept with bags packed, shoes on, ready for the birthing room in the basement, then the bumpy ride to the mother-and-baby home in Rockville. The girls palmed one another's stubby skulls, joked about the good sleeping to be had here in St. George, even on the thin repurposed Army cots, and the screaming symphony of tiny lungs awaiting them in Rockville. Few wanted to stay in St. George, though. Whether they were keeping their babies or not, the girls were ready to leave the sharp edges of the maternity-house mistresses, always reminding them of their wicked nature and the lifetime of atoning that lay before them.

And somewhere outside this home stood a line of girls in similar troubles; the moment a baby was born, a girl's cot was filled by another peeking pinkly over her rounded belly.

Bitsy had never seen anything like St. George, white temple blossoming above green grass in a desert, transubstantiation of sheer Mormon grit.

It was those red-banded mountains, though, rounded like doubling bread dough, bowls of aged earth, that made Bitsy feel harbored and held. Propped up on elbows to see over her swollen stomach, all of them looking to her like the curved backs of women in repose: women sleeping, women thinking, women kneeling, ready to rise.

The squeak and release of another bus pulling up. A flash, and Bitsy sees a teenaged girl laughing and twirling under the arm of a taller girl before landing lips to lips. Then a glass depot door swings open, sunlight bounces, and in comes the girl from Bitsy's flash, younger in this moment, adolescent, pimpled. She passes Bitsy's mural without a glance. The girl drops to one of the hard seats and props her ankles on her bag. She crosses her arms over a Sweathogs T-shirt and picks at a scab on her elbow. Not a moment later the girl is up again and at the pay phone, her back turned, a stripe of sweat between her shoulder blades. She moves as though utterly unaware of the eyes on her—Bitsy's, Rock Hudson's, the zooming little boy's. The girl runs a hand through her long stringy hair.

In bed last night, naked from the waist down and limp on top of his damp and yeasty sheets, Bitsy asked Burton not to give her Pamela's number, even if Bitsy called him begging. *You never beg,* he said, reaching to turn the last of his bedside bourbon into a coffee mug.

If I have her number, I'll flake out, Bitsy whispered. Only the image of her sister waiting at the bus station in Sarasota, long purse strap held against her side, would keep Bitsy from changing her mind, from ditching the buses and heading back to Vegas, to her trailer, to Burton's bed, where she knew how to become whatever thing was expected of her.

After so many lonely decades, Bitsy likes that there's someone besides Pilar who knows nearly the whole truth of her. *I don't want to be found,* she'd told Burton when he revealed himself five years ago. She'd thrown his pants, heavy with the leatherette belt still looped through the waist, to thud against her door. *I didn't want them to know.* But it was too late; he'd already written to Pamela with Bitsy's name and address, and it was just a week later that the first letter arrived. *"Bitsy Graves."* Pamela had dropped sneering quotation marks around her name on the envelope.

Bitsy hadn't had a flash of that. She hadn't seen Burton revealing himself; she hadn't seen herself borrowing money from him to buy this bus ticket.

Six years ago, though, she had flashed on her father dying, clutching his left arm. She'd learned to trust the truth of those flashes by then, to understand them as glimpses of some likely future. And when she flashed on her father's death, Bitsy went to an AA meeting rather than picking up the phone.

Rock Hudson has moved his mustache and himself two seats closer to the Sweathog girl's heavy duffel. He pokes at it with the tip of a suede shoe. He wears a striped polo shirt and light-blue trousers. His breast pocket boxes into a packet of brown cigarillos. Bitsy is forgotten.

It is the end of April. Bitsy is forty-seven, but really she is not: She has spent too many years playing nubile waif in bare legs, too many years playing old lady in fringe. She's flattened her lifeline, and she stands timeless in the center of a circus ring, seeing all versions of herself at once.

Burton, who plays at being hard-boiled, is a marshmallow. He reads Erich Segal at night; his pillowcases are dotted with salty tearstains.

He cried, too, when Bitsy told him her story, after a year of steady one-night stands, after he silently put his door key on her key chain and started packing egg salad sandwiches for her to take to work. She hates egg salad, but she is fond of Burton.

She'd never liked being the oldest sister. Mother handed the babies over to her nearly the moment they were weaned, and she lost most of her own childhood to wiping noses and reminding her little sisters to brush their teeth and write thank-you cards. It was a broken wartime world they were all growing into, and a busted, unmothered family.

Then she turned around and became her own drunk, unmothering mother.

The mustachioed Rock Hudson worries at a shirt button and props his ankle on the opposite knee. The Sweathog girl hangs up the phone and drops back into her seat. She is not meeting Rock Hudson's gaze, is digging through the side pocket of her bag.

When she relaxes against the back of her chair with a box of jelly beans, Rock clears his throat and leans forward, his long hand open.

"Care to share?" he asks. His voice is both serious and not, dangerous and not. The girl shrugs and shakes the box over his palm.

Bitsy wants to cast a spell over the moment, where the girl is still a girl, where the future that Bitsy has just seen is still possible. To carve away anything that could interfere: the man, the bus, any unforgiving parents lurking in the wings.

For years she couldn't imagine why the flashes had come to her *after* the baby, *after* her father left her weeping on that bus-station bench, *after* Mother sat with that precious novel open to Wise's note on the flyleaf. To have had the power to avoid the argument with Wise that led to the apology note inside the book. To have seen how the youngest, Heather, would go through Paul's things and pull out the book, how Mother's mouth would twist as she called Paul grotesque. To have seen how easily she would cave to Mother's disgust. And how every other rotten thing that happened would cascade from that moment. Bitsy had spent twenty years drunk as a skunk to try to drown the memories.

She had skipped step nine, in AA. Making amends. As far as she was concerned, it was still the world that owed her. The only one she owed an apology was long gone.

Bitsy closes in on the pair of them, the girl and Rock Hudson. In the smudged metallic reflection of the pay phone, Bitsy is a flower.

She sits down on the girl's other side. "Hi, sweetheart," she says. No put-on circus Soviet accent. Instead, channeling her mother, full-throated Connecticut grande dame.

The girl turns, shaking the jelly-bean box. "You want some, too?"

Bitsy makes a bowl with her open palms. "Thank you." Seven jelly beans drop in her hands, land in the shape of a mountain. She cracks through the shell with her front teeth and sucks on the filling. Clove.

After going sober, Bitsy had sugar cravings that came like lightning strikes in the middle of the night. She would tiptoe past Pilar and Alfredo's sleeping bodies and lean against the kitchen table, licking a finger and dipping it into the sugar bowl.

The girl says to Bitsy, "You waiting for the Las Vegas bus, too?"

Rock Hudson leans forward, elbows on knees. "That where you headed, sweet thing?"

The girl looks over her shoulder at him and nods. "My dad moved there after my folks split. It's my first time visiting."

Rock Hudson moves one seat closer. "It's a long ride. Not safe for a pretty girl on her own."

The girl laughs shortly, and Bitsy detects unease. "Well, mister, it's just a bus. I've already taken two just to get here." The girl runs her hands along the back of her neck, lifting and dropping her long rope of brown hair. Her T-shirt is damp beneath the arms, and her small breasts shake. The lowering sun is blasting heat and white light through the wall of windows. All three of them squint.

The girl's bus to Vegas leaves an hour after Bitsy's eastbound bus. On this Tuesday afternoon, the station is sparsely populated, no more than a dozen people milling.

"Lucky for you, I'm headed the same way," says the man. "I'll even give you the names of some great spots to check out with your old man, or whoever." He shimmies a leather-wrapped flask from the inner pocket of his blazer, draped over the arm of his chair.

"You enjoy a cocktail?" He takes a pull from the flask and shakes it toward the girl. She giggles.

"I'm only fourteen." Sweeps her hair to the front, toys with the ends.

The man makes a show of looking around. "Your old man's not here, sweet thing. You look old enough to me." He wiggles it again. The girl accepts it with a shy smile, but she hesitates once the mouth of the flask brushes her lips. She looks at Bitsy.

"Would you?"

Bitsy's ten-year chip vibrates in her pocket. "No thank you, doll. I'll stick to jelly beans."

The girl takes a short swig and her face collapses into a pucker. She swallows a cough as she passes the flask back.

Fire-eaters extinguish fire in their mouths rather than swallowing it, but Bitsy remembers how a fireball of grain alcohol would pitch down her esophagus to her stomach, landing like lava, warming her muscles just enough to mount that white horse.

The boy is still zooming around the bus station as his parents lean against each other, poring over a guidebook, and Bitsy lures him over with a few of the jelly beans. She's thinking, some part of her, that she ought to get the two children side by side. To make obvious how young this girl is. To say, *Steer clear.* But the boy just snatches the candies from Bitsy's hand and takes off again. His hand snags the girl's hair and flips it into the air. The girl grabs up, leans forward to smooth her hair, and the man reaches out to help her. Catches Bitsy's hard warning look and purses his lips into a baiting smile. When the girl sits back, he pats her on the shoulder.

"What's your name, now, pet?" he says. He swigs at the flask, but Bitsy sees that his Adam's apple doesn't move. He holds the flask back out to the girl.

Across the room, a skewed, intoxicated version of Bitsy's earlier self gazes on.

It's for your own good, girl. Someday you'll want to do it the right way, husband, family. You are free for that future now, and the baby is free of your shame. It'll be a new beginning.

Bitsy spent four months learning to make lace. She was making a christening gown. She finished two days before she went into labor.

She still has it, the gown, tucked beneath her mattress. She still has the book with Wise's note in it, though she hasn't opened it in years. She'd rescued it from the trash bin in the kitchen the night after her mother called Wise's parents and destroyed everything that mattered to her. Wise was gone the very next day.

Longing takes so many shapes. It can be curling into bed beside a sweaty, dying, never-quite-mother whose life was wasted on anger and gin. It can be daily repeating the maternity ballet routine, willfully sleeping on the hard lump in the mattress. Declining to cry at a father's death. Trading in an eastbound bus ticket for another headed back West. Not extinguishing fire but swallowing it.

Longing, like this jelly bean on her tongue, can taste like kerosene.

How ever could Bitsy return to being a daughter now?

The day after her daughter was born, the day after they tricked Bitsy into signing papers and took her baby away, the day after she found out that the mother-and-baby home in Rockville was a fairy tale: from the car window, breath feathering mist, Bitsy watched the mountain women. Bitsy's daughter was taken even before Bitsy got to place her daughter's tiny palm in her own, before she got to whisper a name in her daughter's perfectly formed ear, and for twenty-nine years—every single day for those twenty-nine years—Bitsy has called her daughter May, after the month she was born.

But on that raw day of being torn open once and then again, when the car chuddered west and the punishing light burned white against Bitsy's swollen eyelids, as they wound past the red-banded rock formations, those mountain women stood. Just as she'd been waiting for them to do for months, they rose up one by one onto granite legs and crossed the terrain on great square feet. Standing between the burning horizon and the snaking two-lane road, they shadowed Bitsy, offering her a momentary shelter from the blazing, unkind sun.

The sun is slipping down below the streets outside and Bitsy stands at the pay phone, facing the wide glass wall. The girl naps lightly, unbothered for the moment. Bitsy's Austin bus leaves in a few minutes. The Vegas-bound bus leaves in an hour. The Rock Hudson fellow stands at the wall of windows, smoking a cigarillo and watching Bitsy. She can smell the sweet smoke from here. She turns her back to the man and does some deep pliés, as low as the coiled metal phone cord and snug pantsuit waist will allow her to go.

Burton picks up, sounding gruff and PI-ish, but his voice goes smooth like a tumbled gemstone when he hears Bitsy's voice. "Where you now, baby?" he asks.

Bitsy and Rock Hudson stand stark before the sunset. Bitsy shields her eyes. She does another plié.

As low as she can go, she holds her pose. She asks Burton for Pamela's number.

A curtain is dropping on the eastern sky now, a circus tent the hue of a deep bruise. Her shadow elongates as she stands from her stretch.

Her shadow reaches nearly to the napping girl's knees. In a week and a half, it will be May.

Bitsy cannot be a daughter now.

She sits back beside the sleeping girl and coaxes the girl's head onto her paisley shoulder. The Bitsy in the mural, still on fire inside from a Molotov cocktail of loss and shame, disappears into a reflection of the stark white light bouncing off the eastern wall.

Bitsy could just try to talk to the girl, warn her of men and flasks and unnecessary touches to the knee.

Or Bitsy could turn away. Or she could defang the man like a pit viper.

The clerk calls for the eastbound bus.

Bitsy moves her shoulder to block the girl's inclined face from the last blast of setting sunlight. Eight hours to go from Phoenix back to Vegas. To hold a pose for that long.

SPELLS FOR SINNERS,
PART SIX

BLADEN COUNTY, NORTH CAROLINA, 1961

The next morning, Mary folded Bernice's borrowed nightgown and left it at the foot of Polly's bed. She smoothed the bedspread. She had too much to think about. Already her visions from overnight were blending into one another and her dream life.

A flash of red. She needed to write it all down. Evie's parka. Polly had seen Evie's parka, and maybe—probably—it had happened the day they both had disappeared.

Mary opened her pocketbook to retrieve her notebook, but it wasn't there. Of course. She'd left it in her motel room. She hadn't expected to be here now, to need it.

The sheriff's diner placemat with his nasty note was still in there, though, and she pulled it out, casting about for a pencil. Nothing in Polly's desk drawer but old sticks of gum.

Mary padded down the carpeted stairs with her shoes in her hand. The light was gray and early morning-ish, but Mary had no idea what time it was. She rubbed at her bare wrist.

The first floor of the house was silent but for the ticking of the refrigerator.

Out the kitchen window: The driveway was empty. Gurnie surely kept farmers' hours, had probably left before daybreak.

The Starkings' kitchen table was a mess of old newspapers and clipped coupons. Under a discarded pair of scissors, a red-inked ad for Sure Foods glowed. FAMILIES RELY ON SURE FOODS. STARKING BROS. HAM 39¢/LB. Mary skittered her fingers about. At last she found a pencil tucked into an old church directory. Drawing a big X through Rusty's scrawl, Mary scribbled, her fingers tripping to keep up. Red parka. Evie. Polly, flash of red. Bernice, Adaline's anguished cries. What else? Mary picked through her memory for details. The flavor of the lollipop on young Polly's tongue as she knelt beneath the dining table.

A car engine turned over a few houses down and Mary jumped, dropping the pencil. Nothing felt safe here. She still didn't know if Bernice had intervened with Rusty and Clarence last night to save her. To shelter Mary from whatever might have happened to her if she had left with one of them. And not a thing was stopping any of these men from swinging back here this morning. Polly had disappeared in broad daylight. Hadn't Evie been walking to the bus stop in the early morning?

None of Mary's previous searches had involved this much uncertainty, this much danger. She'd been sticking her neck out for ghosts since she got here. Was she overreacting? The one thing Mary had always been extremely good at was protecting herself.

A school bus rattled past the Starkings' kitchen window. Life moving along just as it always did. As it always had. The day after Wise disappeared those many years ago, Mary had been awakened by the clatter of trash collectors and lay in her bed, stunned and fuming that anyone could do anything so commonplace when she could barely breathe for the weight of the loss and shame that sat on her sternum.

Upstairs, Bernice might be feeling just the same.

Mary folded the placemat to return it to her pocketbook, her fingertips landing on another Sure Foods ad like the one in the newspaper. Red ink blazing. FAMILIES RELY ON SURE FOODS. Saltines. Harris Farm beef. Canned carrots. Starking Bros. ham.

Mary read it a few more times before she finally saw it.

The Amiable Starking Boys. Gurnie and Clarence had business at that market. They had reason—excuse—to be behind that bank of coolers where Polly's things were found.

Mary felt as though cold water were running down her neck. She must have been the last person to put this together. She must— Mary glanced in the direction of the staircase. Bernice really must know a lot.

Beside the Sure Foods ad on the placemat was an advertisement for Safe Lodge, and Mary dialed the number. As she listened to the rotary dial click through, she stood with her back to the corner of the room, watching the driveway and listening for cricks overhead. The small kitchen clock showed the time as 7:05.

"Safe Lodge." It sounded to Mary like it was Montgomery, and she could imagine him leaning back in his seat, paper open on his knee.

"Can I speak with Martha—" Mary had no idea of Martha's last name, of Evie's last name. "Martha, who is on your staff, please. This is Mary Garrett." She whispered the whole thing while trying not to sound like she was doing it.

"Mrs. Garrett, of course," Montgomery said, and his tone turned interested. "Martha's just gotten in, and I'm not at all sure she's available right now. May I place you on hold?"

Mary nodded, then blinked and shook her head. "Yes, thank you," she whispered.

Agitation made Mary's skin feel as though it were fluttering.

"Yes." Martha's voice on the line, no question mark at the end of her greeting.

Mary opened her mouth, but she hadn't thought further than this. She'd just cast a line in the direction of the only other person she knew in this town.

"Go on, then," Martha said. She sounded matter-of-fact. Not yet impatient.

"It's Mary Garrett. I'm at the Starkings' and I need a ride." Her whisper hid the shaking in her voice, but the receiver vibrated against her ear. She couldn't stop shuddering. "I didn't know how to find a cab, and my things are still over there."

Martha sighed, and Mary could hear the rumple of fabric and muffled voices as Martha must have pressed the receiver to her body and spoken with Montgomery. Mary kept her glance darting, watching for movement near the stairs, in the driveway, feeling like a bird smashing against the wrong side of a windowpane. Mary was startled when Martha's voice returned.

"Do you have any money?"

"Hardly," Mary said. She had six dollars, and she wanted to hold on to as much as she could for her bus ticket. "I've got some things to tell you, though."

Martha harrumphed, expelling loud air into the receiver. "As useful as what you laid on me yesterday? You can keep it."

"More useful. Maybe. I don't really know, I'm sorry." Mary felt overwhelmed, on the verge of tears. "But I'll give you everything, every morsel of it, and then I'll get the hell out of town, I promise. I can't—" And she faltered, because what was it she couldn't do? Stand up to these men, whichever of them she should fear? Choose these three missing girls over herself? Find the courage or the right questions to crack Bernice open? Relive her own loss again and again and again?

"I can't just slink through backyards and shadows to get to the motel without being spotted, can I?" Mary said. "Can you send Sigsbee over here, please?"

Silence.

Mary ticked her gaze back to the empty stairway. She dropped her voice again. "Someone here had something to do with all of it. Please."

The sound of Martha clicking her tongue. "I'll send him over. Meet him at the corner of Pine in five minutes," she said. "You better have at least fifty cents."

Mary replaced the receiver as stealthily as she could, then fingered two quarters and a nickel from a small dish on the windowsill. She tiptoed toward the front door. A creak behind her and she turned to find Bernice on the landing at the bend of the stairway, bare feet on blue carpet. Robe wrapped tight, face twisted tighter. Had she heard Mary's phone call?

Mary's hand was on the doorknob. She remembered Bernice's palm on her head, the closeness of her skin and breath from the night before. It had unlocked something for the briefest of windows.

"Must have gotten what you came for, then," Bernice said. Her hand drifted to the banister. Mary took all of her in, the exhaustion that was aging her, the slight petulance to her voice that made her sound so young. Mary might have been Bernice, she supposed, if her life had been what her mother had prescribed for her.

Mary cleared her throat. "It has occurred to me, Mrs. Starking, that no one seems to want us to spend time alone together. Which one of us is it who could tell secrets?" Mary wanted to sound conspiratorial, as though they could still be allies.

"I don't know a thing about that," Bernice said. "And no secrets as I can see that have anything to do with your business with us." Her veil of distrust back in place.

"Nothing you can tell me about your husband's family? Nothing that you can't tell Rusty or maybe that he already knows but won't act on?" Mary wanted to ask, *Why did you holler at your brother-in-law in your kitchen three days ago? What tortured Gurnie's grandmother so, left her terrified of these amiable Starking boys? Why am I getting these flashes of family history when all I want is to be free of all of this?*

Bernice took one step down, then stopped. "Do you understand that I would do absolutely anything in my power to bring my Polly home? Do you believe that to be true?" Her hand cuffed the banister as she spoke, then she waved her palm in the air with dismissal. "Actually, it doesn't matter to me at all whether you believe that to be true. You just go on, now."

Bernice stepped back up to the landing and climbed the rest of the stairs. Mary waited to see if her silence could coax Bernice into saying something more, something helpful or damning or clarifying, but she heard only the sound of a door shutting.

Anything in my power. Mary recognized that cage. She'd lived inside it, too. *Anything in my power* meant that Bernice had already run the risks, had already decided how little power she had, what was and wasn't worth saying. What would make a difference, and what would just make life more unsafe, or unlivable, for her.

It would be cold comfort ten years, fifteen years, down the road when Bernice was lying in bed, realizing she'd traded away the possibility of finding her daughter just to protect this pitiable existence.

Sigsbee pulled up to Safe Lodge, and Mary watched the car's reflection glide along in the lobby windows in the drizzly beige light of the early day. She handed over seventy cents and scooted across the back seat to get out on the driver's side, closest to the building. "I'll give you an extra quarter if you can come back in an hour," she said, trying for sweetness.

Sigsbee touched his hat. "Yes, ma'am," he said. He swerved the car into a parking spot, and she watched him reach into his jacket pocket and pull out a flask. She could only hope Rusty didn't drive past and wonder at what Sigsbee was up to.

In the lobby, Montgomery held his usual post. The entire back page of the newspaper in his hands flashed with another red and black Sure Foods advertisement: STARKING BROS. HAM 39¢/LB. Montgomery accordioned the paper to wish Mary good morning. Martha leaned against the desk, drinking from a Styrofoam coffee cup.

"Morning," Martha said.

Mary nodded. "Thank you for the taxi." She shuffled her pocketbook from hand to hand. "Is there more coffee?"

Martha took a sip of hers. "You're welcome to make some." She exchanged a glance with Montgomery.

"It's— Never mind," Mary said. She'd said something wrong already.

"You look a mess," Martha said. Mary scanned her tone for snideness, but Martha sounded merely observational.

"I'm . . ." Mary stuttered. "I'm in over my head on all this." Saying it aloud was excruciating. She felt stripped.

"Hmm," Martha said, and she sipped more coffee. "Seems that way."

Mary tried to see herself as Martha might—arrogant, unwilling to listen. Unfairly advantaged with the Sight, which Mary just may have been misusing all along. And Mary realized how much she wanted Martha's approval—a desire she didn't fully understand.

"Can we sit?" Mary asked, and walked to the table in the corner of the lobby. Martha followed.

Mary dropped into a chair, catching that sunburn-on-the-face feeling of interrupted sleep. All the butter and pork fat from last night's dinner turned over in her stomach. The stale smell of coffee on Martha's lips made it worse.

"Sit, please," Mary said.

"Very kind of you," Martha said, and Mary's face warmed further.

"I'm doing it wrong, I know," Mary said. "I've done all of it wrong. So I'd like to give you whatever I can about Jack and Evie, and then I'll go."

Martha didn't reply, but she put her coffee aside and folded her hands on the tabletop.

Mary pulled the placemat from her pocketbook. Flattened it across the table between them, like poring over a map of all she'd seen since entering this town. She talked through her visions and added notes with Montgomery's ballpoint pen—Rusty's rush to the Starkings' to keep Mary from plucking some secret from the air, the canceled search party, the Sure Foods ad. Her missing Elgin watch turning up with Polly's things in the market's egg cooler.

"I don't think Evie is still alive," Mary said, with some hesitation. Martha's jaw tensed. "And I think Polly saw whatever happened to her, and then died for it. Whoever is doing this, it's not for capture."

Martha cleared her throat, and Mary could hear the sob at the base of it. When Mary had learned that Wise was dead, she'd smashed the mirror in her bedroom, a hundred jagged versions of her face howling back at her. Now she busied herself with smoothing the placemat until Martha spoke.

"So who, then?" Martha said. Her voice was thick.

"I think it must be one of them, or all of them," Mary said, and she too was on the edge of tears. "It happens, so much more than you'd want to think." Doses of lye in morning oatmeal, shoves down stairs. Girls packed off to relatives, to convents; girls locked away.

Martha shook her head. "Some family is going to silence their own girl just to— No, I don't believe that."

Mary might have said, *People have sacrificed more to protect much less.* Such things didn't take a monster. Just a coward.

"That family, what would they have to do with Evie? With Jack?" Martha said.

"I don't know," Mary said, and tried to press the wetness from her eyes without Martha's notice. "I was in Polly's house, and she could only show me what it was that she knew." Mary's limitations—not those of the Sight but of Mary's own movements and manners—felt suddenly unavoidable.

"Could those fortune-telling cards of yours tell us?" Martha said.

Out of deep habit, Mary nearly offered to fetch them and do a full reading, but she knew it would be mere theater. The visions she'd been getting were too inhabited, too rich; the cards would just look like the party game they were. And none of it would change what she already knew was true.

"Do you still have those snapshots?" Mary thought to ask. "Of Evie?"

Martha shook her head. "They're at home." She looked over at Montgomery, who was following the conversation with naked interest. "Should I go get them?" Martha's question was directed as much at Montgomery as Mary.

Mary felt pressure on her sternum. "I can't wait around for all that, I'm sorry," she said. The lobby clock somehow already read

8:15. She could almost feel Rusty's approach. She'd likely managed to turn Bernice against her this morning. Who among the people she'd met didn't wish her gone?

Martha's demeanor shifted at Mary's words. Whatever sympathetic connection might have been forming between them, Mary had shattered it.

"I see. You're on your way out, then?" Martha said. She stood from the table with stiff movements. "This is just the end of it for you."

"It's not safe," Mary said, her voice breaking on the last syllable. She closed her eyes and it was Jack she saw there, treading water with her sweetheart, weak blue moonlight curving down their shoulders.

"Never is," Martha said. She drank down her coffee and tossed the cup into the wastebasket.

From Mary's chair, she could see the streak of coffee grounds climbing up Martha's cup: a silhouetted figure, finger pressed to her lips. A secret kept. Something Martha had known that might have led to Evie's disappearance or in some roundabout way could have prevented it.

"You'd better gather up your things," Martha said. "Mr. Ardell is due in at nine."

"What will you do now?" Mary asked, still seated.

"What would you do?" Martha said, and studied Mary's face. "What did you do when your girl went missing—she was your sister? Daughter? Niece?"

She was everything. Wise had been everything, and everything had been about Wise since the moment Paula Jean followed her into the art room in tenth grade.

"I did—I did this," Mary said, and gestured around her.

Martha nodded, and Mary wished she could see inside this woman, see her thoughts and follies and all that she seemed to understand that Mary didn't.

Mary could feel the regret, the sadness, the shame, though.

"If there's nothing else, I'd best be getting on," Martha said, and turned toward the storage cupboard. Montgomery reached for his paper.

Mary left the placemat on the table as she stood to go. "You should steer clear of Rusty," she said, to Martha, to the room.

Montgomery was the one to respond. "You take care of yourself, Mrs. Garrett," he said, and shook out his newspaper as he turned the page.

"No doubt," Mary thought she heard Martha say from the storage cupboard.

Well, she would. She was the one who got to leave.

She was always the one who got to walk away.

Inside her motel room, she dropped her key onto the bed, still mussed from yesterday's late-afternoon nap. A low buzz from the fluorescent lighting in the bathroom.

Mary checked behind the shower curtain, behind the bathroom door.

No one.

She clicked on the bedside lamp and the bulb burst, showering the tabletop with fine white glass shards—and drawing Mary's attention to her own lost watch, laid out on the table with care. She held it up to the light from the window: The crystal was smashed.

A sharp pain hit the bridge of her nose; her eyes flashed to blind. Then, with a sweep of her arm, Mary flung the watch across the room, where it bounced off the television screen. She pulled the pillows from the bed and whomped them onto the carpet. With her pocketbook, she took aim at the bedside lamp but dropped her wrist and let the pocketbook clatter to the ground, where it skated across the room. She dropped to the bed and sat heaving in the dreary gray morning light.

The watch had first stopped when she was in high school, when it had still belonged to Wise. A few days before Wise disappeared. And so Paul was late leaving their cabin in the wilderness. Late getting dinner on the table that night. And she had taken such a belt to the backside that she bled through her nightgown. Her mother always got good and drunk before she called for the belt, and when she was particularly angry, she'd swing it buckle side down. There was no reason why it mattered more on that day than any other that dinner was late. The girls' father rarely even came home from the city by then.

Paul could have let Wise take care of her the next day. She could have stripped out of her thick tights and let Wise tend to the injuries, could have taken what little comfort was available in her shitty life. Instead, she'd picked a fight. Wise, meeting her for a cigarette in their camp in the woods, making sweet-faced jokes about school and sex, reading Paul's face and dropping the laughter, just reaching for her, *but, Paul, what is it?* And Paul had thrown words at her instead. *You made me late on purpose; you don't understand me; you're possessive. Common.* And Wise had unbuckled the watch from her wrist— such an elegant movement, with her cigarette still held between two fingers—and tossed it toward Paul. *You be in charge of yourself, then.*

Wise was gone before the watch was even fixed. In Mary's mind, it had stayed Wise's watch, and wearing it had always been a reminder of why Mary's life was what it was. All that she had given away.

Who had slipped into the room overnight to leave this clumsy threat? It could have been any of them. It could have been anyone.

Mary surveyed the carpet, littered with thin bulb glass. A squeeze behind her eye sockets and she lay a finger below her nose out of instinct. Dry.

A month ago, Mary might have walked away, just done the thing she needed to do to keep herself moving, pretended not to notice the mess she was leaving behind. But now she thought of Martha— Martha on her knees scrubbing at Mary's blood on the carpet, Martha crouching to pick up delicate pieces of white glass. Dropping to the ground, Mary began fingertipping the tiny flakes of glass into the wastebasket. The carpet still smelled like stain remover. A sliver of lightbulb embedded itself in her finger, and she pinched it out with her teeth.

In the knockoff van Gogh above the bed, the girl was still missing.

A shimmer in the corner caught Mary's eye, and she expected to see Polly again, impatient and sore. Instead, the shimmer stayed a shimmer—fractured, dancing light and nothing more. Perhaps it wasn't even there.

All these years at this, and Wise had never appeared to her. Some part of Mary had always believed the Sight had come from Wise. A curse that she couldn't break, no matter how many girls she found.

"What else is there to do?" Mary said aloud to the room. "I have no killer to catch, no idea how to do such a thing." No one to turn to. Who, besides Rusty, had power in this town? A mayor, maybe. A mob. The world was filled with these injustices, filled with hands and shoulders that would crush some girl like Polly Starking for seeing, speaking. There was always somewhere else to be—there was always a reason, a way, to leave.

Mary cleaned up her mess, packed her suitcase, and left the key on the bed. She asked Sigsbee, breathing out gin and boredom, to take her to the bus depot. As he pulled onto the wide road out of downtown, Mary scooched down in the back seat and watched the world fly past in the taxi's rearview mirror.

She wanted to focus on whatever would come next for her—a meal, a propulsion forward, out of the morass of this town—but she couldn't stop chewing on everything here. Jack's sweetheart, waiting alone in that water for Jack to dive down. Polly on her knees under her parents' dining table, listening to her great-grandmother's anguish. The fortune cards, the image of churning water. Rusty's endless posturing, his heavy hands, his pretense at caring. Polly's saint medal, which Mary was surprised to find still fastened around her own neck. If Jack and Evie had been ended by the same man, then how many of them had come before? Jack, treading water; Wise, walking into the woods. The intrusive shame when Martha had held that mirror up to Mary, probing her about never seeking Black girls. A cancellation to the balance sheet Mary had been keeping in the back of her mind, of all her good deeds, all her selfless deeds, waiting for them to outweigh her mistakes.

From her pocket, Mary drew her smashed watch. She ran her thumb over the fractured crystal, the well-worn leather strap. Had she ever needed this talisman to remind her of why she'd chosen this miserable life?

What would happen to her if she just let it go?

Mary sat up straight. She cracked open the back window, held her breath, and pressed the watch through the opening. Still not breathing, she followed the watch's movements in Sigsbee's sideview as it whisked into the tall grass at the roadside.

The car made a hard turn and rolled to a stop, and Mary looked forward to see that they were idling in the Sure Foods parking lot. Bright-yellow signs painted with red letters filled every window, and she unconsciously scanned them for the Starking name. "I thought we were going to the bus depot," she said.

"No depot in town, hon, but the Trailways ticket counter is inside the market. Buses pick up out front here." Sigsbee gestured to a bench to the left of the entrance.

Of course they did.

To market, to market, to buy a fat hog.

Mary bought her ticket: $5.05 would get her as far as Atlanta if she waited for the four o'clock bus. Left with nothing but a jingling fifteen cents, Mary placed her suitcase into a shopping carriage and wheeled around the market's aisles to pass the time.

A nation unto itself, Sure Foods shut Mary off from the crucible of the past several days. Here everything was comfortingly the same, bright and sanitized. Still, she was aware this was the place where Polly's clothing had been laid out like a corpse. Where Mary had unwittingly participated in Rusty's parade, in his play of valor and innocence.

A man in a light-blue smock sprayed water on a mountain of iceberg lettuce. When he turned away, Mary grabbed a strawberry from a carton and wedged the entire thing into her mouth. She pushed her carriage toward the butcher counter, eyeing the expanse of stainless steel where Polly's things had so recently been. A hand-painted sign, *Starking Bros. Ham—39¢ a Pound,* was just at eye level, and Mary couldn't believe how easily she'd missed it the other day.

She stared too long and the boy in the pink paper apron winked at her, working at the toothpick in his mouth. When wasn't she being watched by someone? When wasn't her every move in this goddamn town scrutinized by a never-ending line of people searching, people hiding, of ghostly girls shrieking in her ear in tones she couldn't hear?

But then she forgot about the butcher boy, because what was that—what was that thing that didn't belong on the bottom shelf of the tall milk cooler beside her?

She stared. A pile of bright-red fabric wadded between two bloody butcher boxes. There was movement behind the glass, behind the shelves—the turn of mud-caked boots, a ghost, a memory.

Mary knew what it was, what it had to be. Her hands tightened on the shopping-cart handle. She must have been looking for this, or something like it. Why else hover here? Why else swan around the market like she had been?

A relentless mystery with only dead ends. She could pull that red parka out of the cooler, but what would it get her? She'd given all she had to Martha. She'd been turned away by Bernice.

Mary backed away from the milk cooler and turned down an aisle. She dropped a box of saltines into her shopping cart. Just to the left of the crackers, an odd impression: The girl on the Dolly Madison cupcake boxes was missing. Like the painting in her motel room, like Polly's photo album: just the background, an outline of where the girl had once been. The shelves on the other side offered up the Morton Salt container, with a bare spot where that little girl in boots had stood. Mary reached for the canister before noticing that, just beside it, the Aunt Jemima pancake-mix box had only the empty silhouette of a woman's figure on it. Next to it, the Vermont Maid's face had faded from the syrup label. Everywhere she looked: blank spots where the girls had been. Mary tried to remember them all—pink dewy cheeks on the Sunbeam girl. Pert, blue-tinted nose of that Gerber baby.

She tried to picture the missing girls of Bladen County: Polly in her glasses, Evie with her Hollywood haircut, Jack with her tomboy swagger. She could hold in mind only the haziest ideas of them. They were fading so fast.

She wished she could have taken them with her, somehow. Gotten them out of this place that had killed them—that had, at least, allowed them to be sacrificed for secrets someone didn't want to face.

Mary rubbed tears from her right eye, but she wouldn't allow the sob to break from her chest to her throat.

The Sight was being as clear as it ever had been: More would come. More missing girls would be lost here, more ripped-apart lives, a lake that would keep swelling, that would breach its banks from the volume of horrors it held.

And she could outrun it, save herself, arms wrapped around like a pill bug, always a reason and a way to leave. Or she could cast her hands outward and, charging forward, meet the mean world as it came.

Paula Welden
Disappeared Dec. 1, 1946.

Grill Youth in Disappearance Of College Girl

Cambridge, Mass., Dec. 24 (U.P.)—Carl William Rockel, 23-year-old art student of Roxbury, was ordered held in $20,000 bail today for questioning about the disappearance of pretty Paula Welden from the Bennington (Vt.) College campus two years ago.

Rockel pleaded innocent to a charge of armed robbery and assault with a dangerous weapon when arraigned in connection with a 59-cent robbery here Sunday. His case was continued 10 days and he was returned to Cambridge police headquarters for questioning by Vermont investigators.

Police said Rockel acknowledged having been in the Glastonbury Mountain area of Vermont where the 18-year-old girl vanished during a Sunday afternoon hike. But he denied he knew anything about her disappearance.

Rockel was linked to the girl's disappearance after police discovered two drawings in his room, one of which bore a striking resemblance to Paula. Police said he also carried a newspaper clipping about her disappearance.

Miss Welden, an art student, was the daughter of a prominent Stamford industrial engineer. She disappeared from the college campus Dec. 1, 1946.

Carl William Rockel

Western Union Messenger Claims Paula Welden Signed for Package in New York City

Is the Paula Welden of Bennington college still alive? A Western Union messenger in New York city claims a Paula Welden signature for a package he delivered at the Empire State building.

In a letter to Bennington county's sheriff he gives his information and says "Will you please check up and try to find out if she is the missing Paula Welden?"

Sheriff John H. Maloney has sent the letter on to Paula's father, Archibald Welden, Brookdale road, Stamford, Conn.

The missive is as follows:

"On Nov. 26, Sunday, I read in the newspaper about the disappearance of Paula Welden from Bennington college in 1946. I believe I know her whereabouts. I work for the Western Union Telegraph Co in New York city.

"One day I delivered a package to Mooresville Mills, 67th floor, 350 Fifth Ave. at West 34th st., New York city, N. Y., also known as the Empire State building.

"The girl that signed her name—Paula Welden in small writing. I only looked at her for a few minutes and judging by the way she looked I'd say she is Paula Welden, the missing daughter of Archibald Welden of Brookdale rd. in Stamford, Conn.

"On the day she disappeared she might have hitch-hiked a ride to New York city. Let me know by return mail what the results are.

Yours truly,
Harold F. Wilderman,
221 East 18th st.,
New York City, 3, N. Y.
Room 1

P. S.—I read in the news that there is a reward of about $8,000 for information leading to the whereabouts of Paula Welden alive or dead.

The girl I delivered the package to had blonde hair and looked in the early 20's, about 5 feet 5 to 5 feet 8 inches tall. She is right-handed. That's all I could remember."

2 Waitresses Not Missing College Girl

Two waitresses who were believed to be Miss Paula Welden, missing Bennington college student, have been checked by the sheriff's office and city detectives and found not to be the missing girl.

One of the waitresses, who gave her name as Miss Lois Kling, alias Dwyer, is being held on a vagrancy charge pending further investigation, police said. She told detectives she arrived in Schenectady from Cleveland and had been hired as a waitress in an Erie boulevard restaurant last week.

The first girl investigated by the police was not identified. Sheriff William H. Dunn said he received a call from a man who had been served dinner by a girl who resembled the missing school girl.

A reward of $5,000 has been offered for return of the girl if alive and $2,000 if found dead, according to police. She has been missing from the Bennington campus since Dec. 1.

George F. Bambach, re

Lead Still Sought In Disappearance

Vermont officials are continuing their routine investigation of the disappearance of Paula Welden, missing Bennington College student, hoping to find some worthwhile "lead" which might substantiate the belief of the girl's father, W. Archibald Welden, of Stamford, Conn., that she may have been the victim of foul play.

Information from Williamstown, Mass., reveals that representatives of the Schindler Detective agency of New York who have been active in private probe of the case have left their headquarters at Williams Inn where they have been working secretly for several months. Even the hotel authorities did not know their identity and believed them to have been FBI men, according to the North Adams Transcript. The Schindlers were active in the Harry Oakes murder case probe in the Bahamas a few years ago.

time they had one relating to divorce.

ret. B. Altman & Co.; etc.

56. **Pressure Cooker; $15.95**
des. W. Archibald Welden
mfr. Revere Copper & Brass, Inc.
ret. Bloomingdale Bros., Inc.; etc.

57. **Dutch Oven Roaster, "Dreamline," 4 qt.; $3.71**

58. **Chicken Fryer, "Dreamline," 2 qt.; $3.94**

OBJECTS OF FINE DESIGN

New York, New York, 1950

Monday after Thanksgiving, 1950. Lois was standing at the file cabinet in the center of the office floor, filing endless invoices for lumber orders and construction requisitions, when it happened. Under her thumb as she flicked through the folders: her father's name. An innocuous file folder. Crooked type on a pink requisition sheet for an exhibit at the Met: *One Hundred Useful Objects of Fine Design, 1948. Catalog number 56, pressure cooker. Designer W. Archibald Welden.* Lois's scalp prickled. Her father's name had to be a harbinger of trouble; she could feel it all the way down to the tip of her mostly numbed toes, wedged into secondhand office-girl pumps.

"Miss, you authorized to sign for this thing?" Before the heat had even left her cheeks, some short-stack courier with a Long Island accent was thrusting a clipboard in front of her face. She grimaced and jerked back a step. "Miss, come on, I'm already backed up here," he said. The courier waggled a brown package with his other hand.

Lois let the sheet feather back to the open file drawer but didn't take her eyes off her father's name, that *WELDEN* glowing a mean and angry red.

"Packages for Mr. Krenshaw on the mail table," she said. She held out her hand for the courier's pen and scribbled a signature, looking at him for the first time as she did. He was bright pink and damp above the ears. Baby-faced.

As the courier turned away, Lois plucked the pink requisition sheet from the folder and palmed it as though it were evidence of all her secrets. At the sound of her boss's hand on the knob of his office door, Lois dropped to her desk chair and drifted her fingertips over her typewriter keys.

Krenshaw stepped out of his office. He had large black eyebrows—Lois had it on good authority that he darkened them with shoe polish once a week. That Krenshaw was unreasonably sour when it rained supported the theory, too.

"Meeting and then out for the day," Krenshaw said, shrugging into his overcoat.

"A package came for you." Lois pointed with her pencil.

Krenshaw pulled a box of scotch from the brown paper. "That's a fine bottle," he said. He weighed it in his hand. "Put together a note thanking Marshall for me."

Lois ate a sandwich at her desk while pretending to page through the new Sears catalog. Once the floor emptied for lunch, she pulled an unlabeled green envelope from her locked bottom drawer and tucked it into a stack of incoming mail. With the stack in hand, she kitten-stepped into Krenshaw's office and pressed the door until the latch snicked into place. Newspapers fanned over the leather armchairs, and Krenshaw's amber glass ashtray spilled out onto the walnut desktop. She dropped the mail and the scotch on the desk.

Lois squeezed her eyes shut and tried to remember every detail of her father's Midtown office—back then it was all chrome and deco and curved lines. Archie Welden designed shiny cocktail shakers and fondue forks with Bakelite handles. He would have guffawed at the blended sludge Krenshaw considered fine scotch—when she was a kid, every time Archie opened a bottle of peaty Ardbeg, she would sniff the air, certain some part of the room had caught on fire. She tried now to remember the pressure cooker her father had designed, catalog number 56, useful object of fine design—but she couldn't conjure the shape.

The last time she'd stood in her father's office, she was seventeen, a freshman in college, surrounded by hard-faced adults leaning toward her like carrion birds. *Can't go on this way. Diseased. Abnormal.* Some fink in her dorm had given away her love affair with her college roommate Beth; their parents had been called. *Compulsion,* Paul's mother had said, lips twisting, pouring herself a vodka from the bar cart. *Leave childish things behind.* Archie had said nothing, just read through the stack of papers given to him by one of the stern doctors, whipping his signature across the page without looking up. Never did meet her eye. Handed the stack back to the man and said to Paul's mother, "This *will* be the end of this." Didn't even rise from his seat when the doctors escorted her out, her reflection warped and oblong on the chrome lampshade on his desk.

Krenshaw kept an envelope of cash stashed in his desk drawer. A rich man's habit; her father used to do the same. After the first time Krenshaw squeezed her breast as she leaned over the desk, Lois started skimming from the envelope. Never more than 10 percent, an arbitrary figure that helped keep her rage in check; getting canned wasn't an option.

The envelope usually held a few hundred bucks, so she lifted a solid thirty a week, doubling her weekly wage into the left cup of her brassiere. Once, when Krenshaw groped her, she had heard the bills crinkling. Krenshaw hadn't noticed.

A dismal five bucks in the envelope today. Christmas shopping? A fur, maybe one of those round television consoles. She had hoped he'd send her to the department stores, like some of the other men did with their secretaries; those girls always managed to misplace enough change to pick up a pair of gloves or a brooch, which they modeled in the ladies' room like brazenly kept women.

Beneath the envelope of cash was a letter, typed on distinctive green stationery. Lois had slipped it into his daily mail pile before the holiday. All about Krenshaw's illegitimate daughter. Certain parties had taken notice. Certain parties would be in touch.

She knew what it said. She had typed it, after all.

Lois had been the one to intercept a letter from the daughter over the summer. Marked *Personal,* in sloppy script. The daughter wasn't wise enough to ask for cash or to lay it on thick; she just wanted her long-lost father to know she was marrying. Perhaps he'd care to attend.

It was unlike Lois to exert herself for anyone else's benefit, but she had a particular ire for fathers who failed their daughters. She'd forged Krenshaw's handwriting on a wedding card and put a whole week of her own skimmings into the envelope. Nearly fifty bucks. Included a note that the girl was far better off with money in the bank than a shiftless, disclaiming father.

And then Lois had done what she'd been required to do with what she had learned. Everyone was getting shaken down by someone.

Now Lois tucked the five-dollar bill into her brassiere and dialed Ruth at the Dutch Treat Café.

Breathless, a familiar voice on the line said, "Dutch Treat."

"It's me," Lois said. "You going out tonight?"

"I'm meeting Hannah and Freddie at four," Ruth said, shouting over the lunchtime din. "Why? Everything all right?"

Ruth was always meeting friends. Lois didn't keep any friends, other than Ruth.

"A funny little thing happened. Got me off-center, is all," Lois said.

"Come by, then."

"Maybe." She was selfish about Ruth's attention, even after so long. "Maybe you should just come over after."

Ruth sighed. "Lo, I can't face that god-awful woman tonight. Come to the bar. Be sociable." The god-awful woman, Lois's landlady, was forever lurking at the front door, waiting to catch one of her boarders sneaking a man past the threshold. Mrs. O'Connor never ate; she was fueled instead by the potential for evicting a girl for immoral behavior.

Lois returned to her desk just as an elevator full of secretaries spilled out, a dozen girls purring in brightly colored wool. Two glanced her way—Sherman's girl and Sandra, the clerical head—and Lois looked away with affected nonchalance. It hadn't even been two years since she was in the papers last. She kept her hair dark like Elizabeth Taylor's to avoid recognition, which had worked for the most part. People still looked at her a bit too long at times, lingered as though she were some starlet whose name was just out of reach. When Lois took this position last summer, Sandra had given her the washroom key and stood for a moment with her hand on Lois's shoulder. "I am so certain we know each other," Sandra had said. "Are you a Bryn Mawr girl?"

January 1947

The first time Lois met Raymond Schindler, he was sitting at the lunch counter of the Everett Spa, where Lois was a waitress. She handed him a paper menu and sloshed thin sepia liquid into a mug in front of him. It was winter, just a month after she'd left school. Raymond was white-haired with a broad carriage and looked every inch the private dick he was. Only Lois hadn't known that yet.

He came back three days in a row and asked her benign questions about her neighborhood. She lied most of the time, but he found her.

One evening, in the back barroom of the Annex, where half the girls were playing penny poker and the other half were pressed chest to chest on the dance floor, Raymond Schindler stepped in. Somehow he hadn't been made for a cop, which, fair enough, he wasn't. But he might have been made for a husband, of which Lois had already seen a few steaming into the Annex, curling their lips at the boys out front. This night, when Raymond Schindler walked through that backroom door and stood with assumed authority over the proceedings, the Black girls looked at Lois and at the other white girls on the dance floor with impatience.

"Miss Paula Welden, your family's mighty worried, young lady," he said. "Is this what you've thrown them over for?" He reached into his breast pocket and lit a cigarette from one of those little silver cases, reveling in the attention he'd garnered.

"No last names," someone hissed into her beer bottle.

Lois, in a bare-shouldered gown she'd rented from a woman on Perry Street, stepped away from her dance partner. She'd been on pins and needles over being found, the very idea of it tasting like electricity and rubbing alcohol. Watching over her shoulder for her father's shadow for the past month and a half. But look here at this pain in the ass—was she supposed to be cowed by a self-important thug surrounded by dykes?

"I think you must be mistaken, old man," she said, and lit a cigarette of her own from one of the poker players' packs. She hadn't smoked since high school. "This right here is my family."

One of the poker players, an older Jewish woman in a full skirt and tight white blouse, cackled and drummed her short red nails on the table.

"We sure are, mister," the woman said. "I'm Granny." She gestured and said, "That's my boy Junior"—pointing at a round, busty blonde in lace gloves—"and that's Uncle Sam," nodding at the next poker player, a handsome Black person who leaned back in her chair, wearing pleated trousers, a heavy silver watch, and a crisp pink shirt unbuttoned to flash a white undershirt. The poker player chuckled and nodded at the man.

"Surprised you didn't recognize me," she said.

Of all the ways Lois had seen power wielded—restraints, belts, cruel expressions—she'd never before seen it as lashes of laughter.

The savage look in the man's eye told her there'd be consequences.

The bartender leaned into the back room just then. "This your problem?" he asked, his gaze landing on Lois.

She exhaled smoke through her nostrils and nodded. "Taking care of it."

"Take care of it down the block, then," he said.

Lois grabbed her pocketbook and walked past Raymond Schindler, through the bar's maze of high-top tables, up the half flight of stairs to the street, and down to the wide corner at Seventh Avenue. Under the streetlight, she turned to face him. She'd already started with the dark hair dye by then and used scarlet lipsticks and dark brows like a divorcée on the make. She looked at herself each morning in the mirror and Paul Welden seemed miles and years away.

"All right, then," Lois said, stubbing the cigarette beneath her shoe. "Is my father here?"

Raymond Schindler, though she still didn't know that was his name, shook his silver head, and the light from the streetlamp streaked. "No, missy. I'm the only one here, though your intuition is correct. Your father did send me. Your father and *The Stamford Advocate*, to put a finer point on it."

She nearly choked. "The newspaper? Are they out of their goddamn minds?"

"I suppose you've not been keeping up with the locals, then," Raymond Schindler said. "Your disappearance is still the primary matter on the imagination of most everyone in your hometown. And there's a reward, in fact."

"Naturally," Lois said. "My father wouldn't have it appear any other way."

"It's a mighty high reward, too. Seven thousand dollars, at last count. Well, high for some." Raymond Schindler ran a hand along his lapel.

"Buddy, I think—"

"'Course, the money would really be secondary to the victory, having found the famous little coed who made people climb three mountains in search of her." He snorted lightly. "Would have to change the tale about where you were found. Considerably so."

"I'll not go to bed with you," Lois said. "If that's where this is headed." She sounded far more confident than she felt on the matter, for she knew what awaited her back in Connecticut. Confinement, needles, more electroshock therapy. In the face of that threat, her morals and dignity were moving targets.

Always had been.

"Now, keep that voice down," Raymond Schindler said. "I've known your father for years and I met you as a little girl. No." He shook his head with some disgust. "I'm thinking through an alternative arrangement. If we were to put together a simple payment plan, you slip me say fifty dollars a month—"

She barely made that much.

"—it would be a decade before you'd be able to compensate me for losing that reward, and that's not accounting for interest accrued on that seven thousand dollars."

It was after one in the morning, and the only people around were couples ducking into alleys, drunks in doorways. Lois stood with Raymond Schindler, stark under the streetlight as though performing a play. Lois couldn't believe this conversation was happening out in the open.

Her fear tasted like pennies. Had done, ever since the electroshock.

"You're well raised. Pretty in an unobtrusive way." Raymond Schindler's manner reassumed the sovereignty he'd lost when those women in the bar laughed at him, now that he was no longer outnumbered. "You can gather information for me. Easy job, no training required. And to remind you of the bargain, one of my men will stop by each month to pick up that fifty dollars you owe me for keeping your location and indiscretions to myself."

Oh, she'd love to slug him.

He lit another cigarette, taking his time, opening the case, tapping the cigarette, snapping the case closed. Lois leaned against the streetlamp and wondered with a start whether her father had offered a reward for finding her dead, too.

All she'd wanted was to get away, from the constant surveillance and the taste of smoke and metal, the threat of lobotomy that had wavered across the telephone line the last time she spoke to her parents—*They take an ice pick to your eye sockets, girl,* her father had said, *and these compulsions of yours will disappear. Is that what you want?* What she'd wanted was peace from the constant brutality, not the new intrigue of dark street corners and extortion.

It was a wet cold, and Lois had left her secondhand overcoat in the bar. She wrapped her arms around herself, palms spread wide to cover her bare upper arms. Raymond Schindler made no move to offer her his coat.

Good. She had no interest in pretending they were friendly.

"Can we agree on such a bargain, or shall I place a long-distance call to Stamford?"

"I'll run," Lois said.

"I'll catch you," Raymond Schindler said. "I caught you here once already. And you'll hardly run in this getup—" He gestured with his cigarette. "One of my boys is watching your boardinghouse already."

Lois tried to find something cruel enough to match him. Her scalp prickled.

"On the other hand," Raymond Schindler said, "I suppose I could wander back into that bar and start collecting names and addresses of the patrons. Make sure my trip wasn't a lost effort."

Lois shuddered and shook her head.

Raymond Schindler flicked a business card at her, then snagged a taxi just dropping off a tumble of barflies.

"Hey, sister," Lois heard. Her whole body lamppost-stiff, she turned to face the stairwell down to the Annex. The blonde with the bosoms—what had that woman called her, *Junior*—crouched, stage-whispering, "Sister, I've got your coat here." The woman's voice had a crisp, bilingual articulation, something European. She straightened, patted at her tight hairdo, and walked over, shifting her hips in a leonine manner.

"I know who you are," she said, as she handed the tatty coat over. The woman, Ruth, had been stopped just last month on suspicion of being one Paula Welden, she said, along with six other blond girls sitting on benches at Grand Central. Ruth had a dark complexion, was thick and bow-lipped, and short of the bleach job had no passing resemblance to Paula Welden at all.

"Don't I just look like a Vermont girl to you?" Ruth said wryly, wiggling her torso like a dashboard figurine.

The gal was too much, for sure, and Lois was defenses down when she ought to be battening her hatches. Lois hadn't told a soul her real name, her old name, not since getting to New York, and here she was, suddenly vulnerable to a slick private dick and a hot-to-trot blonde. She may as well be handing out calling cards.

"Say, you know who that Raymond Schindler fella is, don't you?" Ruth asked, her voice sounding concerned now.

"Knows my father, he says." Lois thumbed at his business card.

The gal clucked her tongue against the back of her bright front teeth. "He's big league. Loaded. His own table at the 21 Club, just worked on that big royal-murder case in the Bahamas. You don't read the papers?"

Lois didn't. And she couldn't quickly piece together why he pretended to care about fifty bucks a month if he really was rolling in it.

"You must be in deep, then," Ruth said, and reached out a hand to pat Lois's arm.

She hadn't been, a day ago. But now, "I guess I am," she said, and turned toward the Christopher Street subway entrance. "Thanks for my coat," she called over her shoulder.

Under the streetlamp, Ruth looked dazzling, doe eyes and sorrowful concern. Lois poked through her pocketbook for a subway token. Now was hardly the time for that nonsense.

But Ruth called out, "I'm famished, you know."

Lois turned back.

"I know a guy," Ruth said, and pointed at a diner so dimly lit that Lois would have guessed it closed for the night. "My treat."

And Lois, God bless her, walked with Ruth through the beginning of a winter drizzle to the spot across the street, where Ruth needled at the owner to fry up a few free eggs, there's a good sport.

It wasn't until she got back to her room at the boardinghouse that night that Lois raged—threw a chair across the room, pulled her old red parka from the closet and tore through the gabardine, pulling off the hood, ripping the seams.

The next morning, the house mistress stopped her on her way out the door. Out at the end of the week, the mistress said. Whatever that ruckus was last night, it had no place here.

When Lois arrived at the Everett Spa for her shift, one of Raymond Schindler's goons was already seated at the counter, with a green envelope that he slid to her under his mug. Inside, a typed note directing her to apply for a clerical position at a travel agency in Midtown and a falsified letter of reference to match. She only had to stay at the Y for three nights before she found another room; turned out it was much easier, as an office girl, to find respectable accommodations.

Monday After Thanksgiving, 1950

In the mild evening, Lois walked with her coat over her arm. She twisted her wristwatch band.

Electric shock had meant stars in her head and light-headedness for days. A side effect of the treatments, besides the short-term retrograde amnesia: a sort of corruption of memory. The memories revealed themselves unpredictably, Technicolor pieces of her life that startled her with their unfamiliarity, something like seeing a photograph of herself in a place she knew she'd never been.

The memories had mostly proven false—enchanting and convincing episodes from some life she hadn't led. Her roommate Beth had been transferred to a different dormitory by the time Paul returned to school, had suffered no consequences of their affair but no longer had an appetite for Paul's company after all the dramatics. Still, Beth would pick up the hall phone when Paul called, trying to puzzle out what was real (*Did I have a love affair with my art teacher? Did I have a baby? Who drives a Studebaker?*). Lois's first year alone in New York had been painfully uncertain. No one to remind her of who she wasn't. She just walked along foreign streets, trying to carry herself as someone whose sins were myriad and undiscovered.

But eventually she had Ruth, and Ruth was willing to laugh out loud when Lois asked odd questions. *Have I ever killed a man?* Lois had asked after a cold memory dropped on her last week, a hot motel

room and a man with yellow eyes crying out her old name. *Not today,*
Ruth said, and wrapped an arm around Lois's waist. *But the next time*
Krenshaw paws at you, you could dose his coffee with poison.

A prickle on Lois's scalp would be her only warning that something amiss was coming to mind, that some odd idea was trying to
shoehorn into her memory. The images were impossible, some of
them—Lois, middle-aged, standing side by side with a younger version of herself. Or holding the hair of a lover who must have been
Ruth as she dry-heaved into a sink, Lois's own shockingly aged face
looking back at her in the mirror.

Was it possible that Lois was actually on the *other* side of things,
looking back even on this time in memory? If that were the truth,
then at least she had Ruth for a lifetime. She'd rather have that future with Ruth than any future without her.

There were other memories, of course, that Lois knew were hers,
that she wished she could disclaim. The ripped-open pain of finding
out Wise had died in some convent only three hours away and that it
was Lois's fault. She'd've gladly traded that away for a bottle of gin or
a subway token.

It was just past five and the Annex was packed shoulder to shoulder. Lois stood on the low bar rail and spotted Ruth waving her into
the back room. Lois shimmied between heated bodies, inconspicu-
ous in her office drag. She closed the backroom door behind her.

At the high poker table, drawn together as though threaded with
a cord, were Ruth and her people—Hannah, Melinda, Freddie, and
three other girls Lois didn't know. The newcomers must be from
what Lois called Ruth's "Red Lady Brigade," her Morningside Communist friends, not Annex regulars like the rest. Their faces were
close and the table scattered with bottles, newspaper, and stationery.
Ruth reached out for Lois, wrapped an arm around her shoulders.

Under Ruth's other hand was a distinct green envelope with
crosshatching—one of Raymond Schindler's.

Lois knew these envelopes well. She'd been slipping them into
employers' drawers for nearly four years; she'd just fingertipped one

into Krenshaw's mail stack this afternoon, for chrissakes. Raymond Schindler had one business model—extortion—and the appearance of his green stationery meant life was about to become dire for someone.

Now for Ruth.

Ruth's fingers curled around Lois's wrist. Lois had made no secret of how jumpy she was about Ruth's Communist Party membership, particularly since the Subversive Activities Control Act had passed over Truman's veto just this fall. Ruth was in danger of losing her citizenship. Being shipped back to Poland, where every single member of her family was dead, villages burned. Or being detained indefinitely in some dank underground cell.

Ruth rubbed her thumb against Lois's watchband. Ruth knew the watch had belonged to Lois's first lover, also knew not to ask too many questions about it, or her. Lois could be a real monster, of course she knew that, and Ruth bore it with more grace than Lois ever could have.

"We shouldn't have paid him after those first letters," Hannah said, and pounded a fist on the table. "We're just the suckers he thought we were." Hannah, a tall Jewish woman, had white hair that flew around like a wind sock. Lois had made that observation once, and Ruth held Lois's hand for a moment before saying, "That's fine, Lo, but Hannah was field-dressing soldiers in Spain while you were learning penmanship."

And, credit where it was due, Hannah was the one to laugh at Raymond Schindler when he'd followed Lois in here nearly four years ago.

"What were we supposed to do?" Melinda said, placing a hand on Hannah's forearm. "Take the risk that he'd tell our landlords? Your boss?" She sneezed loudly into her elbow. Freddie, dapper as ever in her suit and suspenders, held out a handkerchief.

No question that the girls could lose their apartments, their jobs, if their Party membership got out. Raymond Schindler's scheme was built on that guarantee.

"Who all got letters?" Lois asked. She'd never particularly won-

dered how a cannonball in the stomach might feel, but she was finding out just the same.

"Me, naturally," Hannah said. "Patrice, Freddie, Dorcas, Rose."
She pointed at the letter in Lois's hand.

Only two of the recipients were Annex regulars. Lois turned to
Ruth. "But not you?"

"Not me." Ruth released Lois's wrist and took a long pull from
her beer.

"But you knew? About these letters? The"—Lois lowered her
voice—"blackmail?"

Ruth nodded, lips still on the bottle.

"'Course she knew," one of the white girls said. "Think any one of
us had two hundred fifty clams squirreled under the mattress?" She
laughed and drew a frowning Hannah into an embrace.

Lois extended her hand. "I'm Lois, by the way."

"I remember you," said Rose, the Black girl. "From the meeting."

"Me, too," said the other white girl, offering a small hand with
blunt nails. "Dorcas."

Well, she'd rather be taken for a Communist than pegged as
Paula Welden, any day of the week.

The predominantly Black Morningside Women's Communist
League branch had taken Ruth in when she'd arrived in New York in
1943 as a Polish Jewish orphan. They found her exotic, she said, and
she knew Marx and found him appealing enough—and the free
coffee and pastries at the Morningside meetings the most appealing
of all.

Now these girls were Ruth's family.

"Paying up just let them know they'd scared us good," Hannah
said. She talked about Raymond Schindler as though he were a force,
a system. Lois supposed only *she* knew who the blackmailer was: a
man, a greedy and malicious man, who had no hesitation about de-
stroying a person's sense of peace.

"It's been done," Ruth said. "Gotta move on."

"What does he want?" Lois asked.

Ruth gave her quite a look. "The letters all made the same demand," she said. "They want the Party's donor roster."

"Eh," Dorcas said, and took the letter from Ruth's hand. "Editorial license. They want to know who *has* the donor roster. She who just happens to be—" Dorcas tapped Ruth's arm with the envelope. "Ding ding ding."

After a year of fighting the state house on registering Communist Party members and fighting Congress on Subversive Activities, the Morningside branch had dispersed its files among key party members, scattering the target. Turning Ruth into a target for Raymond Schindler, in the end.

Lois spun her watchband. She couldn't be held responsible for every extortion line Raymond Schindler had running in this city; there had to be a hundred chumps like her, just doing what they were told on threat of exposure, jail time, social humiliation. And most of those folks who got one of Lois's hand-delivered envelopes were dirty anyway, had a nasty deed they wanted kept under the rug.

But Lois had done other things for Raymond Schindler before. Jobs she regretted. Jobs with consequences. And now her chickens had come home to roost.

What a nightmare. And how familiar a sensation.

In whispered pleas, Lois prevailed upon Ruth to leave the Annex with her at around nine.

The landlady was at the door before they'd finished climbing up the stoop.

"Quite a bright dress for evening," Mrs. O'Connor said to Ruth.

Lois ducked under Mrs. O'Connor's arm and ushered Ruth in. "You remember my sister, of course," Lois said. "We'll be certain to keep it down, Mrs. O'Connor. Have a good evening."

Mrs. O'Connor didn't move. She tilted her head. "Half sisters, was it?" She gestured at Ruth in that way self-appointed guardians of the white race had. It was something Lois hadn't noticed before Ruth named it for her.

"Good evening, I'm sure," Ruth said, not bothering to hide that she was sore over it. She kept her short hair a brazen white-blond and drew her brows in high arches to make her look like Judy Holliday. She didn't.

"Now, wait a moment, girls," the landlady said. She hovered a moment before locking the door and turning to face them squarely. "Lois, you've entertained your sister several nights already this month. Margaret's mother is staying with her for the week, and you know you two share a wall. I think perhaps it's—"

"Mrs. O'Connor," Lois said. She wrapped her arms around Ruth while turning her body toward the other woman. "My sister"—she lowered her voice—"has been ruined by a no-account scoundrel. We're working out how to break the news to our parents without causing any sudden illness, which is a danger, as you might imagine." Lois began guiding Ruth up the stairs. "We're deeply appreciative of your discretion."

Inside Lois's room, Ruth stage-whispered, "Well, ain't that a swell cap to the evening! The old crow's a Catholic, and here she thinks I'm unmarried and expecting."

"Oh, damn it all," Lois said. She turned and flopped onto her bed. Ruth dropped alongside her, casting about for Lois's hand.

Lois let the quiet settle for several minutes before whispering, "Just give them the names."

Ruth, who must have been waiting for that sentence all along, spoke over her. "And he'll ruin each and every one of their lives, too. Losing jobs, losing kids. And if we give him nothing, or put up a fake name, it's more of the same."

Lois let herself feel angry, knowing it was small, was false and unfair. She couldn't feign surprise that Ruth would be someone's sacrificial lamb, but did it have to be for one of these other women? Lois and Ruth had plans of their own. "We have to protect you," Lois said. "It's Raymond Schindler."

Ruth rolled on her side to face Lois. "I knew it was from the beginning. But knowing it was him didn't alter the fact that these women's lives could be ruined."

Lois's scalp prickled.

Just this morning, it had been the fear of her father's shadow looming over her life, then Connecticut and the psychotherapist, and shock therapy again and forever. Lois remembered in flashes the sweaty heat as she rioted against the restraints, panic like a needle of adrenaline to the heart, eyes of the doctors and nurses who looked only at one another, never at her. Seeing her father's name had deposited his presence into her new life, had made all of it possible again.

Now Raymond Fucking Schindler had sidled back in, he whose puppeteering hands were constantly moving Lois to another job, pulling her strings to snoop through file drawers, copy down account numbers, keep phone records. And still she was paying his goons that hard-won fifty bucks every month, wherever they showed up, rain or shine. Until she'd started skimming from Krenshaw, paying that monthly amount had meant skipping lunch three times a week, letting handsy middle-aged men from accounting court her with gifts of diamond bracelets that always turned out to be made of paste.

Lois had seen what happened to the people who didn't pay. Even Raymond Schindler's goons were missing fingers at the knuckle. One wore an eye patch.

Her last boss was hit by a car just a week after refusing to pay the amount demanded by one of the green letters she'd slipped onto his desk. Lois—and, she imagined, the others in Raymond Schindler's ranks—had been particularly attentive to his demands over the months that followed.

Now it was Ruth, despite all Lois's effort to put space between Ruth and Raymond Schindler's racket; it was Ruth who was in his sights. Ruth who knew almost all of Lois's secrets, who kept time for her, kept memory. Ruth who loved Lois better than nearly anyone Lois had ever met. Sweet, fierce, hot-blooded Ruth, who had never been under a man's boot in her life.

They would have to run. Someone would give her up sooner or later, and they would have to run.

"I supposed you gave all your savings to those girls to pay him off," Lois said. "That's just what you would do."

"It just as easily could have been me getting one of Raymond Schindler's letters," Ruth said. "Should have been. I've been involved in the Party years longer than the others."

Over three years of bedtime whisperings, Lois and Ruth had made a sweet little plan for running away, for saving up and changing their names for good and driving out West. Shaking Raymond Schindler's men and making it all the way to Arizona, where they'd make sun tea and splash enormous watercolor paintings on canvases leaning against trees. Twist long gray hair into braids and wear lacy white nightgowns like aging Edwardian matriarchs. *Our grandmother house,* Lois called it. *White girls always want to run to the West,* Ruth had whispered the first time. *Why is that?*

They would need to be able to make quick decisions, couldn't afford to linger at bus stops or filling stations on anyone else's clock. Ruth could drive. Lois had managed to save three hundred thirty dollars, most of it lifted from Krenshaw.

"A car," Lois said. The words came out like a finger pointing. "Is three hundred enough for a car?"

Ruth combed Lois's hair with her hand, curling her fingers into long brush bristles. Lois breathed and Ruth kept combing, catching small snarls in her soft knuckles. "Don't say you won't leave," Lois whispered, desperation sounding like anger, fear tasting like pennies. "Don't say it."

If a car cost three hundred bucks, that left them thirty for gas, food, rooms, from here to Arizona. A week, maybe two. Sleeping in the car. Saltines and ketchup soup. Lois had learned about living hand to mouth in the past few years, but she couldn't imagine living on even less than she had now. Somehow Ruth never seemed distressed about money.

"I won't disappear on them altogether," Ruth whispered, her breath sour and smoky. She stood and undressed, dropping her stockings and skirt to the ground, pulling on Lois's peacock-blue dressing gown, a gift from Ruth on her last birthday.

Lois heard Ruth's garters dangle against her thighs. Lois wanted to press her lips to the creases on the backs of Ruth's legs where they swelled into her bottom, curved into the silk of skin where her thighs pressed together.

"I can get us a car, but I won't disappear on them." Ruth brushed her short hair with Lois's saddle brush. Static clicked in the silence of the room. "I'll give Freddie a means of contacting us, and we're going to send them cash as soon as we can."

Lois stood and undressed to her brassiere and slip. She folded her clothing with cruel little movements.

"Even after you go on the lam for love of them, we're to keep funding their revolution?" Lois felt mean and she felt implicated. Cold, too. She wished for her dressing gown back.

Ruth sat on Lois's desk chair and crossed her legs. Her expression stayed neutral.

Lois's face relaxed. "I'm not as heartless as I sound," she said.

Ruth stood and guided them to the bed, where she opened the dressing gown to drape them both inside. "I know, dum-dum," she whispered.

Lois pressed her back into Ruth's embrace. She closed her eyes to sketch out how Ruth's shorter, chimney-stack body pressed to hers, the firmness of her clavicles and sternum, the welcome humidity of her breasts, the purpled curves and divots worn into her skin from the stays and seams of her brassiere and girdle. She imagined Ruth's knuckly toes knotted together, the way her ribs filled from the back with each breath.

Lois—*Paul*—and Beth, back when they were only roommates, used to lie this way together, curled into each other and always on the verge of comfort shifting to caressing, the soft flick of a wrist turning an embrace into something more.

Then it had turned to more, and the more she loved Beth the more fearful she became of losing her the way she had lost Wise, and then Lois *did* lose her in the end. Lost her to interfering adults and hospital restraints and the cold reaction of their classmates.

And Wise, of course. Always Wise. All of Lois's stories began with Wise.

"You don't have to run with me," Ruth whispered into Lois's hair. "This problem doesn't have to be yours."

Ruth didn't understand how close Lois always was to losing everything. How easily they could lose each other.

"Where you go, I go, sister," Lois said, her voice cracking.

Ruth pressed her thumb to Lois's temple and whispered, "Then sleep."

At the first crank of a bakery-truck door, Ruth crept out of bed for her early shift. As neither of them had a telephone at home, she would call Lois at work once someone at the Red Lady Brigade managed to find them a car.

"You're sure they can find one?" Lois whispered as they stood at her bedroom door.

"Cricket, this is what we do," Ruth said. She touched her fingertips to her own lips and left.

Lois shimmied her old suitcase from beneath the bed and stuffed it with underwear and stockings and two wool day dresses and a pair of sturdy but scuffed shoes. She set out an outfit for the day—a smart red suit she'd purchased at a consignment shop—and spared a thought for Arizona, where she would wear dungarees spattered with paint and plaid camp shirts and never again roll a stocking up her thigh.

Lois twitched at a slight knock landing on her door. Her watch read 6:15. She hesitated, and the knock fell again, this time with the needling voice of Mrs. O'Connor. "Can I have just a moment, Miss Kling?"

Lois wedged the case under the bed with one foot. She cracked the door.

"I saw your light. I'm on my way to Mass, but I brought you the name and address of a maternity home in Utah that has accepted—"

A pause. Lois, no intention of lubricating the awkward and demeaning transaction, stayed quiet.

"—unfortunate girls from our parish in the past, and I thought you may want to write to them." Mrs. O'Connor's voice was soft; her lip twitched. "They take good care of their girls, and your sister would do her share of the chores, but they would find a devout family to take in the child."

Mrs. O'Connor pushed the notepaper through the door opening. She seemed to expect a response from Lois, and when none came, she expanded. "There are homes in the city, but"—hand flutter—"waiting lists and whatnot, and I do think it prudent for a girl to leave the place of temptation. It shows a certain respect to her betters if she takes care of her difficulties elsewhere, don't you agree?"

Lois tucked the nasty little paper into the pocket of her pajamas. "I'll pass this on." She pressed the door shut. If it was the last time she saw the old crone, she wouldn't weep for the loss of her.

Taped beneath a dresser drawer, Lois's savings. She rolled the three hundred thirty dollars into the left cup of her brassiere, where it became dull pressure against her goosepimpled flesh.

Lois arrived at the office early enough to stash her case on a top shelf in the coatroom.

It was barely eight when Lois looked up to find a small pink man marching toward her desk. She rose to greet him, a professional smile on her face as she puzzled out why he was familiar, why he moved with such purpose.

"Hey, angel," he said. "Remember me?" A grating accent tweaked his speech. He put his hand on her elbow with a sense of ownership and began moving her backward toward Krenshaw's office door. "He in?"

"What?" Lois couldn't think quickly enough whether some lie or the truth would save her from this man, this joe she'd just recognized as the courier from yesterday. He caught her wrist and reached behind her body to turn the doorknob. He shuffled them both inside the dim office and shut the door. The man released Lois and dragged a chair in front of the door. He sat squarely, knees apart, face in shadow.

"What is going on here?" Lois said. Her voice wavered between irritated and inquisitive, unsure of the power differential at play.

"I have something to show you, but I've got this story to tell you first."

Lois tried to clock whether she ought to try for the scotch bottle and bean him over the skull or if he was just angling for a date or a job. She might hit him with the scotch either way.

"I've got a cousin up in Boston. A guy I'd give my life for, if you don't mind me getting a little sentimental." Why were men always playing so loose with her time, as though it were their resource to expend?

"We watch out for each other. And not two years ago the son of this cousin of mine, a Roxbury kid with a head full of nickels, he gets pinched by the cops with photos in his pocket of some young piece, a coed from a fancy New England school who ran off."

The man pulled a newspaper clipping from his jacket pocket. "Got into the papers, in Boston, in New York, even down in Florida. And they all ran that coed's photo with the item." He waved the clipping in the air. "Care to see?"

Lois crossed her arms. She'd seen that photo plenty.

The man looked down at the clipping. "Seems to me they should have just gone to New York, you know? Girls like that, bored of being good, always running off to the city for a thrill." He glanced back up at her. "Don't you think?"

"What does any of this have to do with me?" Lois asked. She measured each word, stripped it bare of emotion. She wasn't giving this weasel a thing. No time for this, for him. Whoever he was.

"I'm mighty glad you asked that, lady. Because the damnedest thing—I mean, I couldn't have predicted such a turn. But then yesterday, when I was delivering a parcel to your boss here"—and he pulled another page from his inside breast pocket, a yellow carbon paper—"why, the coed in question happened to sign her name for it."

She'd practiced her new signature over and over before starting this job. *Lois Kling. Lois D. Kling. Miss L. D. Kling.*

But one glance at her father's name, at the accusatory *Welden* on that pink Met requisition sheet yesterday, and she'd become Paula

Welden once more. She could recognize her signature on the carbon from here.

"And you know, I've always been entrepreneurial," the shrimpy guy started up again. "And I had this thought: Say, maybe some investor out there would like to compensate me for this idea of mine, this idea of looking in New York City for that run-off coed."

She laughed. There was nothing left. All she still had was this: She could look at him and laugh. It wasn't supposed to be this weasel, this molehill, who came along and stole what she'd scraped together. It wasn't supposed to be anyone but Raymond Schindler getting the drop on Ruth and everyone she loved; or not anyone but her father, presence of a mountain range, striding across the main floor of the office, flanked by surly policemen with ready nightsticks.

Now this weasel strode across the room and slapped her face, hard. Her nose felt like it might explode. "Don't go dropping into hysterics, now," he said. He clasped her shoulder, but Lois was taller and she squirmed away from him, half-leaning and half-sitting on Krenshaw's desk.

"My thought is we can come to a friendly arrangement." The weasel stepped back and put his hands in his pockets.

"I can give you twenty dollars to leave and forget this scheme," Lois said. "A very friendly twenty dollars, in exchange for that carbon, free and clear." She could only imagine being free and clear for twenty dollars.

"Our friendship is just beginning, Miss Welden," the man said. She could imagine him in front of a small shaving mirror in his rented room, trying out sneers for her benefit. "I anticipate we'll be meeting frequently. I'll need to keep you updated on your investments, naturally."

Krenshaw's telephone was jangling and perhaps had been for some time. Lois rolled her watch band to check the hour, but the courier grabbed both her wrists, hard, and shook her slightly.

"This is enough messing around, little darling. Let's get that twenty dollars now. No putting me off until lunch or clocking out. It's now." His face reached only to her sternum, and she could see straight down the mean tunnel of his throat. The telephone, after a moment's silence, took up its insistent ring.

"Yes, all right," she said. "Let me go and I'll get it for you."

He released her after a pause, and—whizzing calculations, *could she get to her handbag could she slip money into her hand could she take such a risk*—she twisted away from him to wriggle her fingers into her brassiere, to try to peel twenty dollars while leaving the rest tucked away. It was an optimistic effort, as the man's fingers were inside her blouse immediately, plying her soft breast tissue with purpose, squeezing her own fingers together and pulling from her brassiere the entire roll of cash, nearly four years of skipped lunches and whispers across the pillow about the small desert town west of Phoenix where she and Ruth would find a room of their own with sheer white curtains and a bison skull on the windowsill.

His elbow jerked against Krenshaw's bottle of scotch; it fell to the floor and shattered.

The man counted the money in a glance and smiled up at her. "My idea is paying off quite well, yes, sir," he said. He backed his way to Krenshaw's door, stubbing the leg of the chair, kicking at it. "I'll see you right around Christmastime, Miss Welden."

He left.

Lois's sobs were silent at first, great bites of air that doubled her body, that sucked the breath from her lungs like inverse bellows. She fell into Krenshaw's desk chair, her hand to her diaphragm as the involuntary spasming continued. All these fucking men.

Stupid girl, she should have gone to Krenshaw's envelope for the twenty instead. She pulled the envelope from his drawer. It was empty. Of course. She had emptied it, and the five she'd pilfered was now in the hands of that nameless shrimp with the thumbscrews.

Lois leaned back in Krenshaw's chair. Her lungs hitched with the aftershock of her sobs. A hammer started behind her eyes. She pressed two fingers to the base of her throat. Breathe.

A hard fast knock, the doorknob twisted. The cauliflower nose of the VP's new girl poked into the opening, and Lois dropped her cheek on her hand to cover the blossoming redness. "Oh, but you're in for it," the girl said, and wrapped her hand around the edge of the door. "Krenshaw's called twice. Just imagine him walking in and seeing you at his desk. What happened, some Romeo throw you over?" The girl's glasses fogged up in eagerness over some bona fide dramatics in this boring-as-sawdust office.

"Something like," Lois said, and reached for Krenshaw's phone. "He's at home?"

"No way, honey," the girl said, her mean little teeth hitting her bottom lip as she grinned. "He's on his way here. I'd give it twenty minutes, tops. Best clean that mess up quick or he'll tan your hide." The girl nodded meaningfully at the broken scotch bottle and the amber booze bleeding all over Krenshaw's white rug. She left Lois to the mess.

Lois lifted her lip into a sneer. The upset had made way for rage. And rage was the mother of invention.

She pulled yesterday's green envelope from Krenshaw's mail stack. She carefully peeled back the flap and pulled out the letter. Back at her desk, working quickly and not meeting the eye of the VP's girl two desks down, Lois retyped the letter, changing the pickup details and the amount.

Each keystroke was a sock to some man's eye.

Hello, Proud Papa. You've seen our proof. She's a lovely girl, looks so much like her daddy. Would your wife agree? Wouldn't you know, we'd be happy to ask her for you. We've got your phone number right here. Or perhaps you'd prefer to keep certain indiscretions to yourself. In that case, we're willing to forget what we know, for

Raymond Schindler's original letter demanded two hundred dollars a month, with the first payment due tomorrow, Wednesday. How much could a man like Krenshaw get in an hour? Whatever Lois asked for, she was mugging right from Raymond Schindler's pocket.

> $600, due to us on Tuesday. Our courier will come by your girl's desk at 11 a.m. sharp. Cash. No IOUs. No second chances.

By the time Raymond Schindler's goon showed up on Wednesday afternoon, Lois and Ruth and Krenshaw's cash would all be long gone.

Lois had just gotten the new letter onto Krenshaw's desk and gone to the supply closet for a tin of stain remover when Krenshaw stalked in. She was a few steps behind him as he threw his overcoat and hat onto her desk.

"Not sure what happened in here last night," Lois said primly, and dropped to her knees beside the shattered bottle. Krenshaw, green envelope already in his hands, glanced over.

"Shame," he said. He angled so that he could get a good look down her blouse.

Lois felt enraged anew by how easily things of value slipped in and out of these men's hands with such little care.

She gathered the chunks of curved glass and winced as a shard bit her on the forefinger. She flipped the top on the tin of cleaner with the other hand and had just squirted the liquid when Krenshaw slammed a fist on the desk.

"Take care of that later, Miss Kling. I need to make a call." He slammed the office door behind her.

It took him less than forty-five minutes to get back from the bank with the money. As he knocked around inside his closed office, Lois answered the phone.

"It's me, dum-dum," Ruth whispered. "We're gonna have to scoot, and quick."

Lois eyed the clock—10:15. "I might need some time," Lois said. "There've been wrinkles."

"Some girl gave up my name, Lo. There's a hunk in here I'm pretty sure is straight from Raymond Schindler's goon patrol, been eyeing me for a few hours. Freddie just dropped off the car, so I'm gonna scram. I'll take a few loops around the park in case he follows me, but I need you waiting for me. I want us out of the city as soon as possible."

Lois was under no delusions that Raymond Schindler was unaware of her relationship with Ruth, that he'd piece together right quick what exactly she'd pulled on him those few years back.

What exactly she was pulling on him right now.

Krenshaw came out of his office just as Lois was hanging up the phone. "Are we paying you to conduct personal business, Miss Kling?" he said, leering again down her blouse.

Lois leaned back in her chair. "Of course not, Mr. Krenshaw."

He held out the green envelope, thick and stiff. "A courier is coming for this at eleven. It is imperative that he receive it. Heads will roll, Miss Kling," he said, leaning a fist on her desktop. "I expect you to sit here and wait until that courier has arrived and then bring me a signed receipt. After that's completed, you may finish attending to the stain on the rug and bring me a fresh cup of coffee."

Lois remembered Ruth's idea about poisoning Krenshaw's coffee and imagined with satisfaction dumping the whole tin of stain remover into his mug and standing by blithely as he choked and fell onto the stained white carpet.

Even in her imagination, she wasn't as dastardly as any of these men she had met. Death was apples compared to a lifetime of fear.

Then again, she'd done nothing to absolve herself of her compliance, her own bad deeds. Lois snuck to the coatroom for her suitcase and pressed the heavy green envelope full of Krenshaw's cash into her pocketbook. It was her own weak will, her fetish for self-preservation, that had set the whole thing in motion. Since seeing that green envelope in Ruth's hand, Lois had been attempting to convince herself that it was merely one of those false memories, but she knew what she had done.

August 1947

The basement of the Church of the Master, on the corner of Morningside Avenue and West 122nd, smelled like mouse droppings and truly terrible coffee. Lois had never been this far north; in the eight months she'd lived in New York, all the snooping and prowling she'd done for Raymond Schindler, she'd rarely made it past 90th Street, and only then because she'd gone home with some girl from the Annex.

The crowd inside the church basement was modest, and Lois noticed immediately that only two other white women stood among the gathered, each in conversation with a smaller group of Black women. The older white woman, her face framed by a nimbus of frizzy gray hair, glanced at her watch and called the meeting to order. Lois took a seat in an empty row at the back.

As the women at the front of the room worked their way through administrative matters, Lois repeated to herself every name she heard—Mrs. Watts, Mrs. Stewart, Miss Katz—to commit them to memory. She felt a sequence of breeze, movement, and body heat beside her.

"Hi, sister," the newcomer said in a breathy, accented voice. "Didn't expect to find you here."

It was Ruth, the bosomy peroxide blonde Lois had gone home with a few times, the same one who'd brought out Lois's coat the night Raymond Schindler showed up at the Annex. Lois leaned over and accepted Ruth's hug and kiss. "Hello to you," she said.

"Let's take roll," said the woman at the front of the room. "Starting with our new face. Ruth, who've you got back there?"

"This is Lois," Ruth said. "I can vouch for her. Swell girl."

"All right then," the woman said. "Stand up, swell girl. Lois what?"

"Dwyer," Lois said after a moment's hesitation. Raymond Schindler had changed her last name on her a few times already. "An interested party."

"We welcome the curious and the committed. We're pleased to have you, Miss Dwyer."

Lois spent the rest of the meeting working to memorize every name on the roll, reciting them to herself and adding details as they emerged—neighborhoods, husbands' names and jobs. The moment the meeting broke for refreshments, she excused herself to the ladies', where she sat and scribbled out every nugget she could remember. When her stubby pencil began to form the round arc of Ruth's name, Lois stopped. She tapped the page. She could always add the name later.

TUESDAY AFTER THANKSGIVING, 1950

Rain drummed at the roof of the leaky old pickup truck Freddie had procured for them. Lois didn't even ask how Freddie had gotten the truck so quickly. Being in this tight space with Ruth suddenly felt claustrophobic and raw. Lois cracked the window and breathed in the misty cool air, the smell of diesel and seagulls.

"You all right?" Ruth asked, looking over from the driver's seat.

The feeling of a sunburn on her cheek reminded Lois of the slap, the courier, the bruising pressure of his fingers against her breast as he took everything she had saved. In her lap, the green envelope from Krenshaw, cash splayed out. Lois wrapped the bills in that pink Met requisition sheet with her father's name on it and jammed it back into her pocketbook. She pushed the empty green envelope out the window and watched it wing away in the slow-moving traffic.

A prickled-scalp memory overlaid the gesture: Wise's watch whisking out a car window. Lois tensed and reached for her wrist. It was okay. It wasn't real.

Lois rolled her head toward Ruth. She wondered how much Ruth could withstand knowing.

"Lo?" Ruth said, taking her eyes off the road.

"Just hungry," Lois said. She wrapped her arms around her stomach. "You?"

"I'll be hungry once we hit New Jersey," Ruth said.

They didn't stop in Jersey, though. Ruth took them on back farm roads that meandered and hairpinned and rollicked around flattened brown fields. Somewhere in Pennsylvania, Lois insisted they pull into a Fuel & Eat just off the potholed county road.

Old men were scattered about the tables, two young Black families petted French fry–faced children, and two old white ladies shared a booth at the back.

"Get something to go," Ruth said as she held the door for Lois. "I don't want to stick around anywhere too long." She walked back to the pay telephone, and Lois slid into a booth near the door. She put her head down on crossed arms.

Ruth hadn't said it yet, had only held a thin-lipped expression when Lois spilled everything that had happened that morning—but Lois knew Ruth would want to send their surplus cash back to the Morningside ladies. The money made Lois deeply uneasy, and she sat now with her pocketbook under her thighs. Lois had taken it right out of the mouth of the lion. She could end up dead for it or dragged back to her family in Connecticut if Raymond Schindler found her. Her Ruth rescue mission had been transformed into an escape hatch for herself. She'd never dared defy any of Raymond Schindler's schemes before. Lois and Ruth ought to board a steamship for Greece and disappear forever.

Forcing herself to think about that Morningside basement three years ago was like grinding glass between her teeth—Raymond Schindler directing her to attend what he called a *meeting of subversives*. Detailed instructions to identify every attendee: names, addresses, places of employment, race, approximate age. At the time, she'd been indifferent to the task. She'd presented the names to Raymond Schindler's goon without a qualm. Her fingers pressed to the stubby pencil drawing a straight line from that church basement to this godforsaken moment.

In the window, Lois focused on her own reflection. "Be better," she whispered.

"If you're suffering, I've got antacids and coffee in three shades of battery acid. And one meat-loaf special left." The waitress, a hard fifty if a day, lit a cigarette from a nearly empty book of matches. Lois placed an order for two egg sandwiches. She wanted fries but questioned whether villains deserved them.

"And fries!" Lois called to the waitress's back.

Ruth returned just as the waitress delivered a greasy white bag and the check.

"I have an old friend in Baltimore who can give us a spot to stay tonight," Ruth said in a low voice. "It's safe, and we won't have to pretend that we're sisters."

"We could stay at a motor inn," Lois said. "We don't have to scrimp now at least."

She craved anonymity, always had. But then again, the longer she was alone with Ruth, the more she was bound to confess it all, and would Ruth stand to hear it?

"Who's renting a room to a single woman, much less two, with nothing smaller than a fifty-dollar bill?" Someone clattered a spoon behind them. "Besides which, I have some business to take care of with this friend." Ruth dropped three dollars on the table, grossly overtipping.

Lois wished she could blink herself forward in time, could prickle her scalp and awaken in forty years, wrinkled and absolved, in that big white bed in Arizona. Ruth had heard that the mountains were red and rounded there and the spaces between them felt like bowls, or the great laps of stone women. To awaken in such a lap.

"Look at them," Lois whispered, and nodded her head toward the two old women in the booth. They were both relaxed into the wooden backs of their bench, and one reached out to knock an errant bit of lettuce off the other's lapel. Lois watched for the hitch in the woman's movements that might indicate what she really wanted to do was reach for her companion's hand. "They could be us. We could be them."

Ruth appraised the women. "Maybe, Cricket. But let's not be them yet." She grabbed the greasy bag of food.

They took winding back roads again, and it was gone 9:30 when they arrived in the suburb outside Baltimore, a sea of squared-ranch sameness that, Ruth said, had been built for the returning soldiers. "Your friend is a soldier?" Lois asked with some alarm. She'd assumed they were visiting a woman.

"M.J. was a WAC," Ruth said, "and her husband was Army. Civilians now." She consulted her handwritten directions and eased the truck into a dead-end turnaround at the end of the street. She cut the engine and tucked the keys into the visor. "Let's walk," she said, and pulled the pillowcase with her belongings off the floor.

They crunched gravel for two blocks, Lois's pocketbook with Krenshaw's—Raymond Schindler's—cash growing heavier with each passing streetlight. Lois tried to speak a few times, but Ruth shushed her. Lois wasn't sure whether she would have asked questions or made a confession.

The porch light glowed above a low stoop and a windowless front door. As Ruth's foot hit the step, the door swung wide. At the opening stood a woman around Ruth's age with wavy brown hair, wearing a glinting Star of David necklace against the expanse of her bare freckled sternum. Blue-white cigarette smoke plumed from her other hand, and a second woman emerged from its veil—tall, blond, white, extremely Protestant-looking, and easily Lois's mother's age. Both wore wildly bright Japanese-style dressing gowns that seemed garish and out of place from the plain little front stoop.

"Come in, dum-dums," the dark-haired woman whispered, and she made ushering gestures, ribboning smoke around the entryway. Dead-bolting the door, the woman flicked on the hallway light and leaned back with crossed arms.

"You look dreadful," she said to Ruth, and reached out to tweak her blond hair. "Is it a wig?"

Ruth swatted the woman's hand. "I'm the most fashionable diner waitress you've ever seen."

The woman, whose voice was deeper than Lois had expected, turned next to Lois. "Don't mind us, pussycat. Welcome!" She was a handsome woman, with a square jaw and an air of party-gal conviviality.

"I'm M.J., and this is Pinky." M.J. tightened the belt of her robe, then threaded her elbow through the other woman's. "And if I'm not mistaken, everyone is terrifically parched."

Lois followed the women down the hallway. The carpet was plush, but the floor creaked beneath their feet. Sun-faded patches of wallpaper revealed where framed objects had been removed. The chrome living room smelled heavily of lilies and tobacco, and Lois's eyes watered.

The blonde, Pinky, stood beside M.J. at the drinks cart and toyed with the other woman's hair. Everyone seemed to look up at Lois at once.

She helped herself to a seat on the stiff yellow brocade sofa and tucked her pocketbook beneath her knees.

Pinky leaned to place a cool glass in Lois's hand. "Welcome," she said in a bed-pillow voice. Her yellow hair was bookended with a subtle white at the temples, and she draped one arm over the other as though posing for a Coca-Cola advertisement.

Spread out on the coffee table were a dozen or more photographs, and Lois reached for them.

"Ah," said Ruth. "Someone went on an archeological dig this evening." She scooped the photos into a stack and flicked her way through.

Over Ruth's shoulder, Lois saw that the snapshots all seemed to have captured the same giddy masquerade party. Women in WAC uniforms and feathered masks, others in just brassieres and panties, double exposures with knees and legs thrust up into the frame of the picture. She saw younger versions of Pinky and M.J., Black girls, white girls, Chinese girls, all of them in uniform, a girl in a showgirl outfit who might have been Ruth.

"Is that—"

"Yes," Ruth said. "I became quite the pet of the teletype operators of Fort Des Moines." She lit a cigarette from the pack on the low table. "We all served in our own ways."

Lois couldn't imagine a life that looked like that, women and freedom and unabashed sex and glee. The familiarity of the women's touches, the curl of a hand over another's abdomen in a gesture that was like neither a sister nor a lover but somehow both.

That life might have been Wise's, if she'd lived to see it. *All those WAVES are just like us, I'll bet,* Wise had said—in a memory Lois knew was real—cracking her knuckles and slapping her knee.

"Pinky, love, can you rustle together some crackers or olives. Or do you girls want eggs, maybe? I think we have two. Gerald will be by in the morning with a fresh dozen and a campaign donation."

Gerald. Lois had forgotten there was a husband in the mix. But didn't he live here?

"M.J., don't go overboard. We aren't lost puppies—and don't you dare think of giving us more money."

More money. Lois's head whipped toward Ruth, who watched her cigarette tip and shrugged in a small way. Had Ruth tapped M.J. already, for the first of Raymond Schindler's extortion letters to the Morningside women? And here Ruth hadn't even told Lois that any of it was happening.

"I'm wrung dry, dolls," Lois said, and handed her drink over to Ruth. "It's been the most exhausting day of my life. Can I—"

In a feminine flurry of apologies, M.J. and Pinky led Lois to a spartan guest room, just a simple double bed on locking wheels and a wooden chair in the corner. "Our decorator put us on a budget," M.J. said in apology, and kissed each of Lois's cheeks. "Have scandalous dreams and don't get up early. Being on the lam is exhausting business," she said.

Pinky pulled Lois into a tight, back-caressing hug and whispered, "It's gonna be all right, sister."

Lois had loved only three girls: Wise, Beth, and Ruth, and each of these affairs was an island, not an idea that she'd held beside another. She'd never had friends with appetites similar to hers, and it had simply never occurred to her to look at that sea of women to whom she wasn't attracted and see potential for companionship; she was busy guarding her secrets. She couldn't puzzle out how to act in front of M.J. and Pinky, or, here, even Ruth. They moved so easily in front of one another. Intertwined.

And she was resentful, too, of the nostalgic spell cast by those photographs. She'd done everything she could to become brand new when she boarded that bus from Bennington to New York City, and she wasn't fond of the reminders that Ruth had stories longer than the one they shared. Only seven years older than Lois, Ruth seemed to have lived several lives by the time they'd met.

Lois was the corrupt party, though. The villain. She had no right to be resentful or small.

Sometime later, Lois was dimly aware of the shift of the mattress under Ruth's weight, of the slide of the sheet over her hip. When she awoke, the bed was empty. She rolled to pull her pocketbook out from under the mattress just as Ruth came in, water from her hair dribbling down her neck to the shoulders of Lois's dressing gown. It didn't close as well as it did on Lois, and as Ruth sat on the edge of the chair, Lois could see all of Ruth's naked body, the crease beneath her breasts, the swell of her pear-shaped belly, the fold of skin beneath her navel, hint of darkness and hair below the robe's sash.

"I should just give that robe to you," Lois said, and shoved her pocketbook beneath the pillow.

"We'll share custody," Ruth said.

"Of our debts, as well?" Lois said. There was a hairline fissure that shimmied crookedly across the plaster of the ceiling.

Ruth toweled at her hair. The room smelled of Ruth's face cream, roses.

"I wanted you to meet them," Ruth said. "They are extraordinarily generous people. They sent hundreds of dollars without a question."

"They seem fond of you," Lois said.

Ruth creaked open her compact and laboriously applied her dark eyebrows. "Does it still feel as mysterious to you, how Raymond Schindler had all the Morningside ladies' names except for mine?"

Lois sat upright and clenched and unclenched her fist into a bed pillow—what exactly had Ruth figured out?—then she flopped the pillow onto the carpet, where it landed with an unsatisfying whomp. Singlehandedly bankrupting all the dykes and Reds on the Eastern Seaboard, and Ruth had known all along.

Be better.

Ruth turned her back to Lois as she finished making up her face. Lois watched the movement of Ruth's arm, her shoulder as it sloped into nape; how well she knew Ruth's flat and low rear end, the ridges in the skin above the back of her knee. She knew the fullness under Ruth's chin, and the kinkiness of the little hairs that grew at the base of her neck, exactly where the peroxide ended and Ruth's true hair color began.

Once, she'd memorized all of Wise's body, too. They had lost each other while it was still new enough for Paul's throat to catch at the sight of Wise tromping toward her through the woods, at the sight of Wise's back as she disappeared into the trees. What happened to those memories, to all the energy she'd found for wanting Wise? To all the love? It had filled Paul's entire body. Was it walking around without her somehow, still in the exact shape of her?

"We're all of us on the same side of this, Cricket," Ruth said into the compact mirror. "I'm saying that to remind us both."

"Come here to me." Lois's voice caught. She waved her hands.

Ruth dropped her compact and approached the bed. Lois wrapped her arms around Ruth's midsection, sliding hands under the dressing gown to the still-damp surface of Ruth's skin. Usually Ruth's body was dusted with a jasmine powder, but this morning she just smelled of herself, of salt and skin.

"Will I ever stop disappointing you?" Lois whispered. After everything, after all she'd let herself be used for.

Ruth placed her palms on Lois's skull, drifting fingers down to the soft spot between her collarbones. "I want to pay them back," she said.

"Let's go to Greece," Lois said. "Let's live on the beach."

Knuckles in Lois's wet tangles, Ruth said, "And just forget all of them?"

"We could be so far away from Raymond Schindler that no one would be able to pronounce his name. We can become new people. New hairstyles, new names. Never let another man interrupt our life lines."

Lois insinuated her knee between Ruth's legs, lightly kneaded the tender skin on the inside of Ruth's thigh where the hair grew wiry and intentional. Ruth caught Lois's hand in her own.

"And just forget all the people we're part of?" Ruth said.

"They're yours. I'm not a part of them," Lois said, and tipped her head in the direction of the rest of the house.

"You could be," Ruth said. "Don't you ever want to be?"

"I just want you," Lois said, her mouth pressed to the moist underside of Ruth's breast.

"I don't just want you," Ruth whispered, and petted at Lois's shoulder.

"Not even sometimes?" Lois whispered back, and slid her right hand toward the heat and shadow between Ruth's legs. Ruth opened her mouth but said nothing. She softened the bend of her knees, shifting her pelvis slightly onto the heel of Lois's palm. Lois drew shapes with her fingertips, and the dressing gown shuddered with the slow rocking of Ruth's hips.

Neither of them heard a knock, if there was one, but both Lois and Ruth heard the round-mouthed "Oops!" and the thunk of the door shutting again. "Sorry!" M.J. yodeled out from the other side. "Take your time!"

"Should we stop?" Lois whispered.

Ruth's neck released. "Guess so," she said. But neither of them lets go of the other, and then neither of them stopped.

After, Lois slid the tangled dressing gown down Ruth's shoulders and tossed it aside. "All I want is to confess to you," she whispered, still shiny and tight from lovemaking. "You're some kind of witch."

Ruth laughed and brushed hair out of her eyes. "Tell me all your secrets, then." Her voice softened to serious by the end of the sentence.

Lois rolled to her side and nestled against Ruth's body. "Wise," she began, and she felt Ruth start.

"I— Go on," Ruth said.

"Wise died."

"I know," Ruth whispered, and brushed a kiss to the back of Lois's neck.

"My mother got her hands on a note, a letter Wise had written to me inside our favorite book. We'd had a fight and Wise wrote me a love letter." Lois took a deep breath. She'd never told anyone, not even Beth, the whole of it before. "I denied it. I—" She was reliving it suddenly, the anvil in her gut, the heat flash of her cheeks, the metallic pain behind her eyes that told her she was about to have a nosebleed. "I told my mother that Wise had a crush. A fixation. That I'd barely spoken to her. It was a delusion."

Ruth's hand stilled its caresses, sat lightly on Lois's hip.

"My mother called Wise's parents. They sent her away." She had searched, gone to the police for help when Wise's parents had put the phone down in her ear. Had endured the chuckles of the cops who made jokes about girls from Wise's part of town, who talked to one another instead of to Paul. Her nose had started to bleed as she stood at that station desk, and not one of those men had even offered her a handkerchief.

Ruth rolled away from Lois, onto her back. Lois felt Ruth tuck an arm under her head. Maybe Ruth was staring at the same fissure in the ceiling.

"They sent her to a convent," Lois said after a moment. "And she refused to eat." Lois choked on those words. She could never decide why that had happened—whether Wise was despondent, betrayed, or was a fucking bruiser who wasn't about to give those nuns what they wanted.

"And then?" Ruth's voice had an edge, and it made Lois's face crumple to know that Ruth was thinking about her all the things she'd been thinking about herself for years.

"And then they force-fed her, and it was too much, and she—it was heart failure, they said. And she died. And she was alone, and—" Lois took a hiccuping breath and rolled to look at Ruth.

"And I can't lose you." She whispered it. "Not to Raymond Schindler. Not to—"

"This is real? Not one of your trick memories?" Ruth said.

"It's real." Lois could tell Ruth how many times she'd wished, hoped, it was false, how many mornings she'd started awake with what felt like the new realization that it might not be true.

"You were a kid, yeah?" Ruth looked at her, and Lois saw the lines near the corner of her eyes, the way the skin on her neck was slack from a certain angle. Most of the time, Ruth looked so baby-faced that people were surprised by her certainty, her easy bearing.

"A kid, but it's not the last selfish thing I've done." Lois reached to take Ruth's hand. Ruth allowed it, but she didn't return Lois's squeeze. "But never ever again would I do that to someone I loved."

"It's a hell of a thing," Ruth said to the ceiling. "It's a hell of a thing to ask someone to feel safe after that." She bit at the skin around her thumbnail.

"Everything I do is to keep you safe," Lois said. "Remember Arizona. Our grandmother house. Mountains like women."

"Uh-uh." Ruth shook her head. "Don't railroad me with fantasies. I'm not ready for that yet." Ruth was turning back into the tough cookie she'd been when they met, shiny armor that just dared you to try to push her around. Lois hadn't seen this version of Ruth in some time.

Ruth sat up and reached to the bottom of the bed for her slip. "You're willing to sacrifice others for your own safety. And what about them?" She began to dress herself. "What is safe for them?"

Lois didn't respond but stood and began rooting through her suitcase for a change of clothing.

"There is no such thing as safe," Ruth went on, snapping her stockings into place. "Never will be."

Lois sat back on the bed and balled her clothing in her lap. She thought she might weep, that her nose might start gushing, that she might compress into a hard little ball from the shame and dread that vised her.

"All you've succeeded in doing is making yourself alone. Separated from the people you're willing to discard." Ruth tossed her makeup bag into her pile of clothing.

Lois reached toward Ruth with both hands. "I'd never discard you."

Ruth walked to the door. She looked back at Lois. "It's not that I worry you don't love deeply enough." She sighed. "But broadly enough." She shook her head. "I'm going to help with breakfast," she said, and shrugged in a small way before closing the door behind her.

Lois felt her scalp prickle and a sensation like a brick slamming onto the bridge of her nose, and she lay back on the bed. She *knew* that she'd traded Wise away for nothing—that she'd defended herself to the same two people who would pulse electricity through her brain a year later. Who thought she needed to be belted, and repaired, and contained.

Wise's watch ticked at her from her wrist, as it had for the past five years. The watch had outlasted Wise, outlasted Beth, and might outlast her time with Ruth. She couldn't fight Ruth's accusation that protecting herself had just left her alone. Those false memories she'd had of her future—her own face, softened with age, standing beside no one but herself. What if she could keep herself going for twenty, forty, more years but she had no one? She'd had that nightmare before, but it was always of Ruth being taken from her, never of driving her away.

Lois wanted to be angry; she would have preferred it to this feeling of wrongness. She could shout, pound her fists. *What should I have done, then, with Raymond Schindler? Refused to go to the meeting, refused to turn over all your friends' names? Given him yours, as well?* Except that—except that her anger would be false, even to herself. If she'd decided differently, she would have figured out what to do, wouldn't she? Ruth might have helped her.

Lying there alone, Lois raised her eyebrows with the realization that all of those women might have helped her, if they'd known.

Lois could taste the blood running down the back of her throat, the hot, thin, metallic flavor of it. She sat up, leaned forward, pressed the fatty tip of her nose, just as Wise had taught her. *Ten minutes to think about how much you love me,* Wise had said every time.

As she hunched over, something rustled in her pajama pocket: Mrs. O'Conner's note about the maternity house. Well, wasn't that about two lifetimes ago.

Plops of bright red dripped onto the balled-up dress in Lois's lap. She breathed through her mouth, listened to the tick of Wise's watch. She never had any idea how long ten minutes took.

And while she hunched there, she tumbled into a new idea, one of her out-of-order memories, a memory of *after.* Of sitting in a fabric-covered bus seat, dressed in a brightly colored jacket that looked like a bouquet of flowers, and someone—the sun blinded her, but it must have been Ruth, she felt the soft sureness of her, she needed for it to be her—beside her, sun-washed face turned to the window as they watched the landscape, the sky layered purple and blue, the colossal pink stone women pretending to be mountains.

A funny taste on her lips, like sugar. Like cloves. Like kerosene.

Her nose now dry, Lois stood. There was something to be done.

She dressed, then held her heavy pocketbook in her hand as though weighing it. She reached to tuck it back beneath the mattress—no, in her suitcase—and started for the hallway. Then, no, she turned back and pulled out the stack of bills, wrapped like a cut of veal in the pink Met requisition sheet imprinted with her father's name—remember *that* nightmare; the past forty-eight hours really were the longest year she'd ever lived—and pushed it into the deep pocket of her dress. It made a noticeable bulge, which she tried to camouflage with fists in both pockets.

At the bedroom door, she realized there was no lock. She had never before dared take a girl to bed without a locked door between her and the rest of the leering world.

In the hallway, Lois stumbled right into a man opening the front door. Solid, with a ripened-fruit face, he shook snow from his hat and overcoat before stomping his feet on the mat.

"Happy blasted Christmas," he said. "It's not even December." He draped his coat over an empty chair and pulled off his shoes. He turned to Lois, a carton of eggs in his hand. "You are not my wife," he said, shaking a finger.

"Darling!" M.J. said, and walked through the living room to reach arms up in his direction. He leaned over to accept kisses on both cheeks, then turned back.

"You must be Lois," he said, and tipped his fingers to his hairline. "I am Gerald Hollander, man's man, newsman, aspiring flâneur, and second sergeant honorably discharged."

"A pleasure," Lois said. "I'm Lois Kling, formerly Dwyer, formerly Jones and Alt, exploited woman, ersatz secretary, and houseguest on the lam."

"A true scandal to have you in our home," Gerald said, and raised an imaginary glass. "Alas," he said, "something is wrong with this champagne."

Ruth marched over and swung herself onto Gerald's neck. "Hello, old so-and-so." She left a wide red lip mark on his cheek. He patted at her hands.

"Getting taller, I see," he said.

"Every day," Ruth said, and reached over for Lois. It must have been from habit, because Ruth hesitated once she had Lois's hand in hers, then loosely unlinked their fingers. "All right," she called into the kitchen. "Will we ever be fed, or shall I set out in search of snow-buried apples in the yard?"

"Coffee?" Gerald asked.

"Translucent," M.J. called back. "It's a Charles Dickens winter."

"Did it all go well?" Pinky asked. Her champagne-colored trousers swished as she crossed the room.

"Not as well as we hoped, but we weren't robbed, either," Gerald said. Noticing Lois's interested expression, he shrugged. "Lightening our load of a few old family pieces. How many mirrors does one really need?" He turned toward the kitchen. "Eggs!"

"Skillet's hot!" M.J. tilted into the living room and gestured for him.

As Lois and Ruth set the table, M.J. dropped into a dining chair and leaned elbows onto the tablecloth. "I'd been hoping we could have one of those breakfasts that bleed into lunch cocktails that swim into dinner and dancing, but I'm afraid there's been a snag."

Ruth froze, her hands in midair. "Did you get caught up in it?"

M.J. sighed and picked at the fabric. "Gerald received a letter at the office this morning. Green stationery." Lois's face flooded with heat.

"Sister, none of us is surprised. We all knew the risks. And Gerald thinks he can put the guy off for a few days."

"What's the demand?" Ruth asked. Her voice was as serious as Lois had ever heard it.

"A classified ad in Gerald's paper," M.J. said. "Something about domestic services available. Very cloak-and-dagger."

Gerald walked into the dining room, tie tucked into his shirt, sleeves rolled to elbows. He set a dish heaped with scrambled eggs on the table. "With the war on, we're all on alert for hidden codes. Obviously this gent isn't trying to bag part-time work as a lady's maid."

"How did he find you?" Lois asked. Wasn't this what everyone else wanted to know?

"Finding Ruth means finding us," M.J. said matter-of-factly. "Maybe this gonif has eyes at Western Union, or maybe he's had Ruth's name longer than he let on. Doesn't much matter. We've got it well in hand."

"But it does mean we need to get you out of town on the double," Gerald said. "If your man's operation has already reached Baltimore, he could have people on the street, watching this house. I've got you two bus tickets to Raleigh for now. You'll have to plan your route from there. I'll pull around the block and you two will skip through the backyards to meet me there. Heads down until we get to the bus station, and then you'll be on your way. We'll handle getting the truck back to Freddie."

"So eat quickly, pussycats," M.J. said, and spooned eggs onto Lois's plate.

Even with the tension and the looming getaway, the party ate merrily. Lois watched M.J. and Pinky tease Gerald, watched Ruth go pink at small jokes based on years of friendship, and, rather than jealousy, she felt something more like harbor. Like being offered shelter in another's lap.

M.J. raised a toast—"To my basherts, all of you!" she said, swinging her coffee mug to acknowledge each in turn—and Lois took Ruth's hand in her own, nearly shifting at the last second to pick up Ruth's spoon before remembering that it was all right.

Almost all right. Ruth allowed her hand to be caught, but her expression was still guarded.

Pinky reached across the table for a cigarette packet. "No more smokes?" she said, shaking out confetti of tobacco.

"Not until payday," Gerald said.

"Fuck," said M.J.

"Don't intimidate them with your piety, my darling," Gerald said.

M.J. threw her leg over Pinky's lap. "Oh, stop pretending to make love to me," she said, over-enunciating as though onstage. Gerald reached out and pinched her cheek.

"Speaking of." Gerald placed his billfold on the table and drew out four ten-dollar bills, straightening each as he built a slim pile.

"That's all?" M.J. asked.

"For now, I'm afraid. Start collecting nuts." He turned right away to Lois and Ruth. "Don't you begin to refuse it. Teasing M.J. just gives me a thrill."

The watered-down coffee, the missing mirrors. Even in all her isolation, Lois had been connected to this happy, frightening web of people who gave until it hurt.

"We'll wire more in a month, when things have cooled down," M.J. said.

Ruth clenched at Lois's hand. "You're champs . . ." Ruth said, and trailed off.

"Oh, don't get suspicious just because something gets easy for a moment," Pinky said. "There's plenty of impossible coming your way. Both of you."

Lois could see where the mirror must have been. An expanse of empty wall faced the dining table. Lois could imagine seeing her own reflection as she sat here, could imagine looking herself in the eye. *Be better.*

Lois met Ruth's gaze and squeezed her hand. "It's all right," she said.

She turned to the rest. "It's all right," Lois said again. From her deep dress pocket, she pulled the stack of Krenshaw's fifty-dollar bills and sat them in the center of the dining table.

They all gaped but for Pinky, who raised her juice glass. "Well, three cheers to the moneybags!"

"You shouldn't suffer for your kindness," Lois said. "It won't take much to get us to Phoenix. And we'll send help back to the Morningside ladies before we go." She would get a job, join a circus, hustle for their bread. She could sell off her possessions—she looked down at Wise's watch. Her only possession. She would fret about money and Raymond Schindler. That could just be her role in this. Everyone had a role.

She squeezed Ruth's hand once more and nodded, then closed her eyes and for just a moment let herself return to that earlier memory: the colossal pink stone women disguised as mountains, the sky layered purple and blue, and the orangewhite sun winking at them from the horizon, bathing them in heat, setting them aflame, until the entire bus was a trundling ball of fire, everyone's skin still smoldering as they arrived at their destination, each of them as someone altogether brand new.

SPELLS FOR SINNERS,
PART SEVEN

The grocery boy's toothpick must have been dipped in cinnamon oil. The smell peppered at Mary's nose when she returned to the Sure Foods butcher case. She squatted before the milk-cooler door. She could see the outline of her own reflection there, layered like a pentimento over the red coat inside.

If she could meet her own eye, what would she tell herself?

Mary's throat tightened at the saltless air inside the cooler as she opened the door. The gabardine was stiff from the chill. She shook the red parka out onto her lap, and the fur-trimmed hood fell limp to the ground.

Mary's shoulders and head were propelled back against the glass of the door by a sudden vision: elbows grabbed from behind, pressed toward each other in a way her body wouldn't allow. The shocking pop of shoulder joint and tearing pain. The rough yank of suitcase from fist so that the handle tore, too. She heard fabric unstitch itself at the shoulder seam. The trilling of a hundred small birds scattering

upward to the tree branches above. Then she heard hoarse screaming, felt the tautness of muscle over rib, the shortness of breath, a
body slammed into a green metal door. A soft face smashed into its
own reflection in the window, a face Mary had seen in Martha's well-
loved photographs.

Evie's eyes stared back at her, and then the vision ended like a
hand releasing Mary's throat. She tasted kerosene. She tasted pennies.

But no. Not pennies. On her tongue, Polly's medal, still on the
chain around Mary's neck. Given to Polly by her uncle Clarence.
The medal Polly's gauzy bedroom apparition had led her to take. The
same one that had gleamed white in the camera flash in the photograph of Polly that Mary found in her yearbook. The answer Mary
had been looking for was there all along. Something else Mary hadn't
seen.

The butcher boy leaned over the top of the counter, shoulders
loose and arms draped, the toothpick still working its way around his
tongue. "You all right, ma'am?" he said. "Can I get you a glass of
water?"

Mary let the medal drop from her lips back to its chain. She nodded, as much as anything to break the spell of his gaze on her.

What are you going to do now? she goaded herself. You going to
just turn your back on Martha and Bernice and everyone else who
loved these girls? You going to put on Evie's bright-red parka and
walk out of this town, disappear again?

But she just might. She knew herself well enough to predict that.
Of all the people Mary had looked at with suspicion and fear, all
those hands and faces she could imagine doing unspeakable things,
Mary feared herself the most. All the things she had failed to do.

The girl she had abandoned. The suffering she had caused.

If Mary vanished with Evie's coat, there'd be no evidence that
Evie had died in this town. People, those who even paid attention,
would still say Evie had just run away. As though that absolved everyone else.

Mary's ribs and shoulder still throbbed from the violence in the vision. My shoulder, she thought. Evie's shoulder. The porous partition between her body and the other girls' had been so frightening to her for years. In this moment, she was reassured to be feeling anything at all.

The boy appeared with water in a stained mug, and when it rushed down her throat to her stomach, Mary was reminded of how long it had been since she'd eaten, aside from that little out-of-season berry now somersaulting inside her belly. She tilted her head back against the cooler door.

"Ma'am, miss. Ma'am, you're bleeding." The boy recoiled from Mary and pointed to her face. She could feel it, the warmth of the blood pooling in the divot of her upper lip, the tightness of the muscles behind her eye sockets. She made no move to touch her nose, to cup a palm to catch the drops.

The boy pulled off his pink apron and held it in a ball to her face. She could smell the rotty sweetness of animal blood, the oiliness of lard. Like a butchered animal, Mary bled into the boy's apron, Evie's red parka tented over her knees.

From halfway across the market, Rusty's voice boomed. "Now, Mrs. Garrett," the sheriff said. "Will wonders never cease." He leaned against the butcher counter and pushed a fist into his trouser pocket. His white shirt was speckled a grayed peach along the collarbone, where spots of perspiration rendered it translucent.

"I'm obliged, Edward," Rusty said in a tone of dismissal. The boy lingered before plodding through the swinging door.

"What's this?" Rusty gestured at Mary, now pressing the boy's apron to her own face. She could feel the heat of the accumulating blood, the light-headedness starting to creep up the back of her neck. She tipped her head forward and pressed at the end of her nose. She didn't look at Rusty, didn't answer him. He didn't appear to give a damn, picking at the cuticle on the thumb of his free hand.

"Some new divination to share, then? Your time at the Starkings' yield any new insight?" He knuckled at the brim of his hat.

"What are you doing here?" Mary asked, her voice venomous at the last syllable, muffled by the boy's apron.

"What's that you've got there?" the sheriff said, blending the syllables into one long melodic word.

Mary dropped the apron to her lap. "It's a jacket." She slid the uneven weight of the parka up her arms and onto her shoulders, and so climbed into an old memory: lifting the coat from ivory tissue paper on a Christmas morning in 1944 in Connecticut, pulling it on over her pajamas, swinging her middle sister by the hands in her matching navy version, the magnesium snap of her father's flashbulb and ready flare of her mother's hangover.

In one movement, Rusty reached a hand down and took Mary by the crook of her arm, pulling her up and out of the market as quick as she could keep up. She tried to twist backward toward her shopping carriage, to her suitcase and handbag. Rusty's grip didn't give, and Mary's ribs felt like ice.

He hadn't ever put his hands on her before. Somehow, she hadn't expected that he would.

"I'm on my way out of town," she said. "I have a bus ticket in my handbag."

"How you gonna catch a bus if you can't tell what time it is?" he said, and tapped his thick finger on her bare wrist.

Well, there was that mystery solved. It didn't really matter how Rusty had gotten her watch; he'd gotten it, gotten her, all the same.

Outside, through the front entrance, the white clouds had rolled to velvet gray. Mary pulled away from Rusty, scraping the side of her shoe on the asphalt.

He grabbed her again with a grip like a vise. His vaguely pleasant expression didn't change; he only lowered his voice slightly as he kept smiling at the few patrons now stopping to watch.

"Sugar, you just walked right on out of that store without paying for merchandise, and I'm going to have to place you under arrest for petty larceny."

"What merchandise?" Her hands were empty.

"Produce. Consumed while on the premises."

The strawberry seeds still between her teeth.

There wasn't a moment she was unobserved.

Rusty walked her to a black-and-white finned squad car, and he opened the back door. "As I recall, you get carsick in the front seat." He pushed her roughly into the car. As she dropped against the stinking seat, he shut the door, closing out the ambient street noise.

He disappeared into the market and returned with Mary's suitcase and handbag. He loaded them into the car's trunk while holding court outside, loudly announcing to the rubbernecking shoppers that he had apprehended the shoplifter and the situation was well in hand. "I managed to persuade the market to withhold charges if I promised to escort the thief to Fayetteville and put her right on an out-of-state bus."

Rusty glanced over his shoulder, making eye contact with Mary. "A strict husband's hand might could set her straight," he said. "No business running around on her own, anyway. Not safe."

Mary pounded on the car window like she was pounding on his contemptible face. She didn't care what these people thought. She scanned the crowd for Bernice, for the Starking brothers. But then she stilled her fist, thinking, maybe, that she saw Martha. That Martha had followed her here. Had come on her own to investigate. A squinting group of white people kept shifting on their feet, blocking Mary's view of the few Black people scattered behind the crowd. She banged on the window again, pointed at the red parka sleeve.

"Evie," she shouted. "Evie."

Rusty walked around and climbed into the driver's seat. Mary didn't even know for sure whom she'd been yelling at.

Her scalp prickled and she got a replay of the vision she'd had the first morning in this godforsaken town. The innkeeper, rough, grabbing at Martha, looking about ready to take advantage of her.

Martha must have been desperate, entirely at her wits' end, to risk angering that innkeeper just to keep Mary around long enough to offer the feeble help that she had.

It took effort to not see these things.

"Don't stop hollering on my account," Rusty said as he backed out of the lot. "Better out than in."

Mary's hand dropped to her lap. She looked down at her arms sleeved in the red parka, and then at the car door—where there were no interior handles.

No way out.

Everything she had done to protect herself, to scare away this very possibility, and still this was going to happen. Her earlier bathtub vision of the moment flickered: It had always been her. The girl trapped in the back of the car, the girl in the red parka, the girl running for her life, had always been her.

The vision overlaid on this moment, marched forth, and the Sight and her real life merged.

Rusty pulled the car onto Route 87 back toward town. He cracked his window and the humid air streamed into the back seat. The sky looked about ready to let loose again.

Mary summoned her grandest New England inflection, the college-girl voice she'd dropped years back. "Certainly you have more important things to do, Sheriff. I don't know why you're bothering with some alleged petty larceny."

Rusty laughed at her. He laughed!

"Well, I'll tell you what, Mrs. Garrett, the sum total of what you do not know could overflow Jones Lake."

Brown water breaching its banks, churning with mud and pine needles.

"Am I wrong that your job is to keep your citizens safe?" she said, her mouth in a grimace of disgust.

Rusty snorted. Kept his eyes on the road. "You are beyond your ken here, Mrs. Garrett," he said.

Mary had been wrong so many times. The bloated confidence in Rusty's every gesture, what she'd taken for bluster. Empty threats. Now it was too late.

She looked at Rusty's thick fingers on the steering wheel and remembered again how she had defended him to Martha. Martha had come into her room to ask for help, and Mary's instinct was to rationalize this man's disregard of Evie and Jack's disappearances. She had thought it would matter to stay on his good side. He had the power, he *was* the power, the very definition of it. She'd thought— fool, fool, foolish, how she hated herself now—that was how she would stay safe. And then she'd thought, somehow, that hiding from him could keep her safe. Why had she assumed there was any way to be safe?

She never had been.

The image, the one haunting her for days—Jack treading water with her sweetheart, eyes glowing in the night, shoulder blades slippery as she left the lake to climb the rock for her dive—was there, behind Mary's eyelids when she blinked.

Where in the body did fear reside? In the base of the throat, the diaphragm, the pelvis. Whatever its source, it crept upward, constricting Mary's breath.

And then she was in another vision, or, rather, a sensation—a tight squeeze from behind as she fought against strong arms, a grapple, an attacker driving her face and shoulders into the cold lake, a wretched and burbling cry as her panicked gasps drew dark water into her throat and lungs.

"I thought we were on the same page for a while there," Rusty said. Mary choked on her breathing as he drummed his fingers on the steering wheel. "Thought we were going to avert all this bother and heartache, but you couldn't leave well enough alone." He met her eyes in the rearview mirror. "We might have moved on from this."

She gulped air, swallowed against a dry throat.

"What does that mean, Sheriff? You going to kill me off?" Mary could feel the dried blood from her nose caking her upper lip and cheek. "Folks saw you put me in this car."

Rusty snorted a laugh. "You know by now that people see what they want to see."

The Sight again, pounding her skull, Evie's skull, to the side of a truck. Everything in Mary's head bleeding into her waking life, everything getting muddier.

Lightning fractured the purpling sky.

The corners of Rusty's lips moved up and down like a shrug. "But I've no intention of laying a finger on you," he said. "Never have. Unlike you, it just turns out I'm able to predict the future."

And then it was an old memory intruding into the moment: Reflected in the car window was Mary's own soft, youthful face, her hair the light strawberry blond it hadn't been in years, the scar above her eyelid somehow younger, too. She had been watching herself, back then, in the Studebaker—watching her face in the window as that man's hand had pushed roughly between her legs. Not wanting it, but thinking it made sense that she would be punished this way for what she'd done to Wise. Always just staring at herself, always locating herself and her worst decision in everything that surrounded her.

"What I can't seem to figure out is why you'd go and risk yourself for something that's none of your concern." Rusty made a wide right turn onto the bridge crossing the Cape Fear River, following a large truck laden with timber. The air shattered into rattling noise, and Mary couldn't tell what was thunder and what was the rough jogging of hard pine against chains.

Mary'd been trying for sixteen years to find Wise. As gutted as she was that Wise had never appeared to her, that the Sight had never granted her one goddamn minute with the only person she'd loved in this world, she feared having to face her, having to withstand Wise's unforgiving glare.

But Mary's visions, her memory, her imagination, were all turning against her—and so there of course was Wise, sitting in the passenger's seat beside Rusty, twisting around to leer into the back. Wise, hollow-eyed, something smeared down the front of her chin, wholly conjured from Mary's mind.

"Almost as though you're using these girls for your own purposes," Rusty said. "Though it's hard to imagine what that purpose might be."

"She's a magpie," Wise whispered. "Collecting girls' horrors, as though that could heal her." Her once-bold voice was hoarse. "As though that would absolve her."

"I saved five girls," Mary said. "Don't I get credit for that?" She was so quick to defend herself; it happened without a thought. It was like breathing.

"Bless your heart," Rusty said.

"What about all the others?" Wise whispered. "What about these three?" And then: Mary saw *them*, though she had felt them there for some time, for days. Their weight on her shoulders, their agitation under her skin. Looking into Rusty's rearview mirror, she saw reflected the three of them hip to hip in this back seat, Evie, Jack, Polly. Their solid reflections where hers ought to have been.

"I couldn't help them," Mary whispered.

"Don't recall anyone asking for help from you," Rusty said.

"What might you have offered them instead?" Wise said.

Jack, shivering in her swimsuit, jaw tense, elbows on her knees as she leaned forward from the middle of the seat. Polly, without her glasses, muggy in her camp shirt and ribbed sweater, her riding boots flaking pale-gray mud onto the floor. Evie, pulling her red coat to her chest, twisting the button placket with a squeezed fist, leaning her head against the window, her breath brushing white fog onto the glass.

"They were dead before you got here. No saving them. All they've asked from you was to see them, and you tried to twist yourself into their battered hero." Wise was shimmering, looking less real even than the three Bladen County girls.

Every cruel thought Mary had been accruing, all the lashes she usually wielded toward herself for betraying Wise, for being not enough, coming now from this figment.

It had taken so much effort to not see. The overwhelm of stories that had pelted her—the loss pulsing at her from every direction, from every person who passed her on the street. Town after town. Year after year. Girl after girl.

"Stop looking for yourself in the mirror," Wise said.

"Your true reflection is found at the outer bounds of what you will do," Mary whispered back. Their favorite line from Virginia Butler's book—*their book*—about the girl in the burrow. A call to bravery, a chide for action. Everything had seemed possible at fifteen.

Mary knew her outer bounds. She remembered her own young red face, the feeling like she was covered in a sunburn, hiccupping with tears, denying to her parents her love for Wise, denying even knowing her. Bringing Mother the telephone book to look up the Wises' number, sitting with her head pressed to the study door as Mother's voice slurred across the line, calling Wise *diseased, an inappropriate influence*. All of it a sharp and cutting weapon against the tenderness of Wise's hand tucking Paul's hair behind her ear in the humid and earthen refuge in the woods they'd kept for a year and a half. Everything that she had ruined in that moment, the walls of their burrow crumbling around them—*that* frozen moment had been her true reflection for all these years.

How desperately, *physically,* she craved absolution—like she'd been on fire for half her life, flames licking at her organs, charring everything. No matter how many girls she had saved, she could do nothing to earn forgiveness.

In this back seat growing sultry from the hot breath of all these girls, Mary felt the knowledge build in her in the same place as the fear had been—in the throat, the pelvis, the diaphragm. Shame had made her small. Grasping for heroics was the meekest of gestures in the face of endless loss, endless injustices.

Her body, already stiff and clammy, became more rigid. She looked up in the rearview mirror at the three girls' reflections, each of them deep in the country of her own loss.

She could stop trying to not see. What if she just did that.

Mary closed her eyes. It was like trying to unclench a muscle, the release excruciating.

What crept in first was coolness, the mineral smell of fresh water on rock. The girl she was inside now must be Jack, shivering from the wet, from the nighttime chill in her swimsuit. Jack turned fast at

the sound of branches clattering behind her. The hooting of preda-
tory owls ran goose pimples up her arms. Shuffling footsteps dis-
placed dry leaves, but Jack couldn't locate the sound, kept turning
her head left and then right. And then it was the flap of an overcoat
as an arm raised high and struck her.

A riot of pain in the back of her head.

Even as Mary still sat in the back of this patrol car, she was also
staggering to her knees as Jack, pressing her palm to the dry forest
floor, no moment to understand the drop or the hurt because it came
again, another blow, hard and brassy. Mary simultaneously felt the
leather seat sweating beneath her thighs and the grit and slick of wet
rock beneath her falling knees as she dropped. This girl she was inside could not keep her eyes open under the drain of disorientation.
But Mary could see the steel-toed boots, smell the ripe and the sweet
that tickled out from the folds of the attacker's coat and feel the sudden shock of no breath, of Jack's throat closing, of green-edged blackness taking over her vision.

Mary awoke to herself, arms wrapped around her chest and with
a pinch in her throat from the attacker's grip.

Her sight came into focus. Wise was gone from the front seat.

Mary was sweating now, beads down her neck, drips from her
eyebrows onto her hands, darkening the red fabric of Evie's parka.
She pushed it down her arms, but its weight was wrong. There was a
hushed thud from one of the pockets.

Mary fingered the parka pocket, keeping her eyes on Rusty. She
hadn't noticed this in the market, the object wedged into the pocket.
She spider-walked along it—a wooden handle, varnish worn away in
places. A long metal shank, narrow girth. A screwdriver? She felt for
the tip with her forefinger and withdrew suddenly when something
sharp pierced her skin.

An ice pick.

Was it real?

She looked again at the girls in the back seat with her. It was at
least as real as they were.

The car made a hard left into a low-lit lot, and Mary's stomach swung. The headlights bouncing on the sign, just as they were supposed to, just as the vision had shown: JONES LAKE—NEGROES ONLY.

She pulled her hand from the pocket and watched bright red blossom from the tip of her index finger. She put her finger in her mouth, pressed the soft pad to the flat of her tongue.

Be opened.

She didn't know which of the girls had said it.

Mary pressed her forehead to the dull cold of the window in a gesture that mirrored Evie's. Air in, heat out. A sound, Evie's fingertip on the glass, drawing musical notes in the fog of her own ghostly breath.

The engine ticked to silent. The woods draped around them like stage curtains. Rusty pulled a folded newspaper from a pocket in his door and opened it across the steering wheel.

"We'll be attended to shortly here," he said, his lips twitching into a smirk.

Mary looked down at her hands, the tip of her index finger still an angry red. Hands that had once brushed small weeds from Wise's shoulders. Hands that had passed dozens of handkerchiefs to weeping mothers. Hands that had balled into fists when Martha challenged her. No one left to save. What else could these hands do?

She wrapped her palm around the ice pick, still in the parka pocket.

Another vision, Martha's arms wrapped around a woman, Evie's mother, both of them rocking, dried out of tears, expressions gone, as though their muscles had given out from the grimacing. In Mary's torso, the abrupt feeling of a speeding train slamming the brakes—all the pain she'd thought she carried now real and truly landing on her for the first time. Rage, disappointment, regret, fury, sadness, silence, all rattled against her ribs like jail-cell bars. Wailing, weeping, she bent forward and retched.

"Goddamn it." Rusty rocked out of his seat and came around to open her door. She leaned to the ground and vomited up the bile, the water, that single February strawberry. She vomited up Polly's breakfast eggs, the coffee cake Evie had pinched from the kitchen, the sudsy pink soda and cold lake water Jack had swallowed. Mary heaved onto the gravel lot, imagining the feeding tube down Wise's throat, the churning of hot liquid, her heart thrumming somewhere behind her right ear.

"For fuck's sake," Rusty said, and he stepped away to light a cigarette. Mary heard the engine of a second vehicle, the crank of a brake, the slam of a door. She didn't look up. She gripped the red parka to her abdomen, shimmied the ice pick from the pocket. The metal warmed in her hand.

"You're in the doghouse this time, Starking," Rusty said. "We've got a real right mess on our hands now. I'll not be the one to take care of this one. I've cleaned up enough after you." From her peripheral vision, Mary saw Rusty flick ash from his cigarette. She kept her head down, trying to fight the spinning.

"I know it," said Clarence Starking, and Mary heard the whoosh of his overcoat as he moved suddenly in her direction. The blow to the back of her head was swift and unexpected. She fell onto the heel of her palm, the bottom half of her body twisted into Rusty's car, the other hand still hiding the ice pick. She hadn't seen this. Or she had but she hadn't understood.

The mud-caked boots were inches from her nose. The smell of what she realized was hog shit and sweet hay. A rough hand grabbed the hair at the nape of her neck to drag her through the puddle of her own sick and out onto the gravel.

The wrenching grip suddenly released, and Mary tried to get purchase. The grit and pebbles dug into her shins.

Dread yawned open, and a fire washed over her skin.

Mary curled to a pill bug to shield herself. Clarence Starking reached down toward her throat, his face so deadened, so impassive. He wrapped his fingers around the medal's chain on her neck. Snapped it right off in a gesture that burned, and only when he stood and looked down at that medal he'd given to Polly did his face twist into something else—half of his upper lip curling, looking nauseated, disgusted, so purely hateful that Mary couldn't turn away. Rusty smoked his cigarette, gaze elsewhere, and Clarence raised his hard boot to stomp at Mary's side. She whipped her head away from the blow and a vision intruded, projected on the inside of her eyelids—

Polly Starking, ignoring the NEGROES ONLY sign, guiding her horse onto the high path above Jones Lake, ambling along and coming upon Uncle Clarence—seeing him knee-deep in the brown lake water, hovering over a Black girl whose bright-red coat glinted in the early morning sun. Polly called out to him before the deadweight of comprehension dropped in her stomach—before jerking her confused horse backward and away, before looking back over her shoulder and not seeing the coming low branch.

Mary was losing herself.

She could hear Jack's voice, Polly's voice. She was surrounded by them, all the girls she hadn't found. Those she had. Were they cheering? Were they keening? With so many of them, it sounded like a siren. How many? Thirty-three. Thirty-five with Jack and Evie. Thirty-six with Wise. Hundreds with all the others she had never looked for.

The Sight came at her like a flip-book now, Clarence looming over other girls, again and again, the season and time of day changing, Clarence's face aging, but always him bearing down on them. Nearly always in this place, the sinister drape of leaves behind him as he stepped toward a girl who was already dropped to the ground, already dizzy or confused or in pain.

Their agony was heat, and Mary was burning alive.

Adaline tossing and turning in sleep, seeing her grandson Clarence as the lost little boy in that chicken coop—but not sleeping beneath the roost, no, *stalking* the chickens, twisting his soft and pink hands around the necks of those birds as they battered against his body, feathers whipping in his eyes.

Adaline had watched Clarence for the rest of her life, watched in craven silence as he grew increasingly compulsive, increasingly bold.

How many Black families had Adaline abandoned to never-ending grief, choosing this boy, this man, over them all? How many people would bear the consequences of no one stopping this man?

How many girls had Mary not seen.

It was Wise behind Mary's eyelids now, Wise clutching her throat, her chest, tears sliding into the creases of her eyes, fighting strong arms, crying out. Mary felt it, she felt Wise's devastation, Wise's laughter and rooster preen shriveled to something hollow and choked.

And then Mary saw Bernice, humming in her kitchen, stirring powdered rat poison into a thermos, handing it off to Clarence with a tight smile, feeling the regret, the resolution. Had these things happened?

Clarence Starking yanked Mary up to her knees and she fell forward, bracing herself with a foot. The gravel was wet, the rain falling now, hitting her body like cold metal but failing to extinguish the fire on her skin. She staggered upward, forward, her body a projectile. Her body a weapon.

No such thing as safe.

Nothing now to lose.

She swung, making the choice as her body moved. Her arm hinged, a viper striking. The ice pick sank into Clarence Starking's eye socket, jogging to the left as it hit bone. Mary fell forward on her own power, knocking them both to the ground, slamming her forehead into his, driving the ice pick further.

Starking cawed and flapped like a downed bird, hands on his face, repetitive syllables that amounted to no words at all. Mary stumbled up to the flats of her feet, the hot spots where the soles of her shoes had worn thin. Rusty moved toward them, and his face told her he didn't know which of them to come for. And so she began to run, into the woods, of all godforsaken places.

Time accordioned, and five days—three years—sixteen years—folded onto this moment. Past slamming into present, opening up again as though on a loop. It is sixteen years earlier and she is watching Wise walk away from her for the last time. Only now Mary is chasing her, is chasing them all—stomach full of ball bearings, sharp turns of ankles as her feet slick over half-rotted branches that blossom with ashy green spores. Orchids unfurl from the forest floor like lady's slippers. That bitter spice smell on Clarence Starking's coat was these woods—Mary runs, and the trees' heady incense dizzies her. She can see just immediately in front of her, or maybe not even that. Heavy boughs skate past. She is outrunning the raindrops, but she can't catch up.

Billowing around her are new sounds and images: Men calling out from high tree branches, happy splashing and sun-warmed rocks, the smell of bonfires and sticky sweet booze and kids making duck calls through curled fists. Women wrapping arms around each other's waists and so much laughter it sounds like thunder.

In this place that is a braid of past and imagined, she can see the lake's tainted memories, the joy, the commonplace, dressed in loss.

Mary's head is hammering, she can feel the blood trickling over her lips, and all these trees seem to tunnel away from her. To her right, a steep drop-off into the lake. Her body, for years just a collection of hurts barely tethered together, carries her farther than it ought to be able.

As relentlessly as she's been pulled inside each of these girls, still she thought she was apart from them. But they are running just ahead of her now.

The girls are running, and they part slightly to make a place for her, and the world falls away. Where they go, she will go.

The clop of hooves and the distant dinner bell calls them home, and she thinks: We are witness. We are exaltation. When is a girl no longer a girl—when we are notes that together make a song. *Legato*.

There is no boundary between them. Her sight had always been too small.

She is on fire, and the rain sizzles as it hits her skin. She is scalding the ground with her footsteps, and she is Jack Washington, she is Polly Starking, she is Evie Lawrence, she is Marjorie Ann Wise, she is Paula Jean Welden (she is she is she is), breathing so loud her own skull becomes a country, a cave, and her outer bounds don't matter now, for there is only here. The forest is girls, the trees are girls, the mountains are girls, bowing, sheltering. Not burrowed but soaring. A horizon. A shared idea, a collective gesture of grace. A row of news-print paper dolls, singeing, curling, the blue flames giving them speed and rise.

She stretches her arms outward instead of around herself, open-ing to all of them, no longer keeping herself in one piece, and finally finally she breaks apart into a hundred thousand cinders winging upward into the violet sky.

Everything is laughter and the sound of water moving between fin-gers and feet.

It's just a hair colder than a witch's titty out here, and the thrill of the jump warms them all, their goose bumps a blanket on their bare arms and legs.

Jack treads the tea-colored water near the big rock on the shallow side. Her sweetheart holds her forearm across her chest, mostly cov-ering her large, pointed nipples pressing through the wet pale yellow of her undershirt. Mostly. Jack winks at her, feeling hot and big.

Each time Jack climbs out of the water to make another jump: Jack's wrinkled fingertips caressing the inside of her sweetheart's arm, so breathlessly close to the side of her breast, the both of them swooning with the *almost* of it.

The slick danger of Jack's feet on the mossy rocks, the cold nickel smell of the leaves and the water and the stone, the owls and crows beating wings in the trees,

the tight-nose height from the top of the jump,

the euphoria of the moment before—

the breath-hold of *almost*—

and then:

flight.

ILLUSTRATION CREDITS

2 Newspaper excerpt, "Paula Welden Missing Since Sunday From College Campus; Search Is Made Over Wide Area," *Bennington Evening Banner*, 12/3/46, Bennington, Vermont, courtesy of Vermont News & Media, LLC.

2 Newspaper excerpt, "$500 Reward Offered For Information Leading To Location Of Missing Paula Welden; Halt Intensive Hunt On Trail," *Bennington Banner*, 12/6/46, Bennington, Vermont, courtesy of Vermont News & Media, LLC.

6 Newspaper excerpt, "Clairvoyant's Tip Leads Father of Paula Welden to Parka Frozen in Walloomsac," *Bennington Evening Banner*, 1/14/47, Bennington, Vermont, courtesy of Vermont News & Media, LLC.

6 Newspaper excerpt, "She's 'Not My Daughter,' Mrs. Welden Says, After Talk Over Telephone," *Bennington Banner,* 12/29/47, Bennington, Vermont, courtesy of Vermont News & Media, LLC.

38 Newspaper excerpts, "Sneaker Footprints in Snow Speeding Mountain Search For Paula Welden" and "Foul Play Suspected," *Bennington Evening Banner,* 12/5/46, Bennington, Vermont, courtesy of Vermont News & Media, LLC.

38 "Missing Person" poster, on or about 12/3/1946.

72 Newspaper excerpt, "U.S. Detectives Come to Montreal In Search of Missing Welden Girl," *The Gazette,* 1/25/47, Montreal, QC, Canada, republished with the express permission of *Montreal Gazette,* a division of Postmedia Network, Inc.

96 Newspaper excerpt, "File of Missing Persons," *Bennington Banner,* 6/5/47, Bennington, Vermont, courtesy of Vermont News & Media, LLC.

130 Stamford High School yearbook, 1945, Stamford, Connecticut, courtesy of Stamford Public Library.

130 Newspaper excerpt, "Boston Police Clue Peters Out," *Bennington Evening Banner,* 12/4/46, Bennington, Vermont, courtesy of Vermont News & Media, LLC.

162 Newspaper excerpt, "Paula Double Identified," *Bennington Evening Banner,* 3/1/47, Bennington, Vermont, courtesy of Vermont News & Media, LLC.

162 Newspaper excerpt, "Welden vanished 30 years ago," *Bennington Banner,* 12/76, Bennington, Vermont, and Bennington Town Museum files, courtesy of Vermont News & Media, LLC.

194 Newspaper excerpt, "Western Union Messenger Claims Paula Welden Signed for Package in New York City," *Bennington Banner,* 12/6/1950, Bennington, Vermont, courtesy of Vermont News & Media, LLC.

194 Newspaper excerpt, "Grill Youth in Disappearance Of College Girl," *New York Daily News,* 12/25/48, New York, NY, republished with the express permission of UPI/Newscom.

194 Newspaper excerpt, "Lead Still Sought in Disappearance," *Bennington Banner,* 5/28/47, Bennington, Vermont, courtesy of Vermont News & Media, LLC.

194 Newspaper excerpt, "2 Waitresses Not Missing College Girl," 2/13/47, courtesy of *The Daily Gazette,* Schenectady, NY.

194 Partial inventory listing from exhibit, "Useful Objects of Fine Design 1947," Museum of Modern Art, New York.

ACKNOWLEDGMENTS

All the thanks and ice cream go to Dorian Karchmar, for the brainstorming sessions and the two-hour phone calls, and being my rudder in this labyrinthine process. And to name Kate Medina, editor of myth, possessor of all patience and grace.

At William Morris Endeavor, so much gratitude to Alex Kane, Jessica Spitz, Caitlin Mahony, Tracy Fisher, and Matilda Forbes Watson. At Random House, tremendous thanks to Noa Shapiro, Gina Centrello, Andy Ward, Robin Desser, Avideh Bashirrad, Susan Corcoran, Maria Braeckel, Barbara Fillon, Madison Dettlinger, Paolo Pepe, Michael Harney, Sandra Sjursen, and Susan Turner.

Thank you to Susanna Ralli at *Provincetown Arts* for publishing an earlier version of "Where Thou Goest" (under the title "Ghosthunter") and to Brad Morrow at *Conjunctions* for publishing a version of the prologue (under the title "The Many Deaths of Paula Jean Welden"). Thank you to Amy Hempel for encouraging me to submit that piece.

Gratitude to the following art grants and the committed folks who administer them, for providing essential and often just-in-the-nick-of-time support: the Minnesota State Arts Board's Artist Initiative Grant, the Loft Literary Center Emerging Writers Grant (funded by the Jerome Foundation), the McKnight Artist Fellowship, and the James Jones First Novel Fellowship.

Much of this novel was composed and revised at artist residencies, where I met incredible artists who filled the otherwise solitary work of writing with fellowship and cross-pollination. I'm deeply thankful to these residencies and their staffs, and I recognize the particular humility, labor, and sacrifices required in order to support art, community, and individual artists: the Hambidge Center, the Edward Albee Foundation, the Millay Colony, Dickinson House, Vermont Studio Center, Hinge Residency at Springboard for the Arts, Wildacres Retreat, EastOverArt, and Arteles. This book would not have been possible without your space, your grace, and the invitation to try and fail and try again.

I'm indebted to Shirley Jackson for her complex and wicked mind and for writing her short story "Missing Girl," which led me to Paula Jean Welden for the first time; to Sallie Powell, for her immersive reminiscences about Jones Lake; to Anne Moody, for her stunning memoir; to Marijane Meaker, for both her fiction and the memoir of her relationship with Patricia Highsmith; to Ann Bannon; to Brett Harvey for her oral history of women's lives in the 1950s; to the Burlesque Hall of Fame in Las Vegas; and to the people of Bennington, Vermont, who have kept the mystery and memory of Paula Jean alive for seventy-five years. Libraries and librarians have been key to my research for this novel and often were the sole source for newspaper archives and local historical information—including the generous staff of the Bennington Free Library, the Stamford Public Library, and the Bladen County Public Library in Elizabethtown, as well as the Bennington College's Crossett Library. The Bladen County and Bladenboro Historical Societies were eager sources of information, as was the Bennington Museum. Thank you also to Kevin Moran at New England Newspapers, Inc., and Jordan Brechenser at Vermont News & Media, LLC, for allowing me to borrow so heavily from the historical record.

It appears to me an insurmountable task to truly pay my debt to the many artists, makers, thinkers, and writers whose work shaped my own thinking and my curiosity over the past seven years. I will note that I've been deeply influenced by the writings of Ruth Ozeki, Franny Choi, Jess Row, Ruby Hamad, Danez Smith, Jia Tolentino, Tressie McMillan Cottom, Dola de Jong, Dorothy West, Ann Petry, Luigi Pirandello, Italo Calvino, Marion Meade, and Lee Israel. The Roger Raveel Museum, Hamburger Bahnhof—Museum für Gegenwart—Berlin, the National Gallery of Prague, the Walker Art Center, the Minneapolis Institute of Art, MASS MoCA, and performances by Minneapolis's Dykes Do Drag troupe all offered inspiration and objects of contemplation. The grounds at Olana in Hudson, New York, became a version of the Vermont woods when I needed them.

This project had a bounty of early supporters, including Éireann Lorsung, whose practice of being an artist and a human is a model of joy and patience, and Kiese Laymon, who is redefining American letters. I am grateful for the interest and trust of Bao Phi, Victoria Clausi and Sven Birkerts, Megan Culhane Galbraith, the Bennington Writing Seminars, Valerie Borchardt, Helena Maria Viramontes, the late Randall Kenan, Margot Livesey, Hester Kaplan, and my 2014 Bennington Writing Seminars MFA cohort. You are all dreamboats. I'm appreciative also for the close attention and investment of my Bennington instructors Alice Mattison, Amy Hempel, Bret Anthony Johnston, and Martha Cooley. Thank you to VSC bud Darien Hsu Gee for recommending that I query Dorian. Thanks to Walter Robinson for the line about twins. Thank you to Minneapolis poet powerhouse Su Hwang for doing so much dog sitting, and to Erin Aldrich and Kyle Meerkins for making our home a place where art could happen.

Thank you to the BreadLoaf Writing Conference, the Sewanee Writers' Conference, Helen and Starr at Quiethouse Editing, and the Northeast Tuesday Night Pie Group of 2016. Thank you to Grub Street of Boston and the Loft Literary Center of Minneapolis. Thank you to the regular attendees of Out2Brunch in 2010 and 2011 in Roslindale, Massachusetts, for being incredible humans and elders and sharing so many personal and community stories, and thank you to Mel Larson for asking me to volunteer over and over. Thank you to the person who gifted me the IBM Selectric II typewriter on Freecycle and launched the "ghostwriter" chapter. Thank you to the manuscript's early readers: the vivacious Joanne Proulx, the insatiable Samantha Johns, and the singular Maria Teresa Accardi, pal and confidante of thirty years (*et multos plus*).

Thank you to my therapist.

An artwork, even a piece that takes place in the past, is necessarily a product of its time. Much of the final revision for this novel happened in South Minneapolis during the spring and summer of 2020, less than ten blocks from George Floyd Square. The National Guard was staging on our street. The police were shooting "less-lethals" at our neighbors. Cops from neighboring suburbs were launching so much pepper spray into the air that our streets and parks were often still uninhabitable deep into the following days. The righteous, necessary, courageous, and deeply caring, placemaking work done daily, then and now, by youth, Black leaders, community organizers, artists, and the stewards of George Floyd Square, is part of this book's DNA, is embedded in its questions and problems and challenges and fumbles—and any and all shortcomings or failure of imagination there are mine, and mine alone.

Much of this novel is a love letter to the idea of community, and I treasure mine beyond measure. Anna Kunz, Kimberly Dark, Judith G. Levy: I'm so glad art brought us together. To Nikki LaSorella, the 15th Avenue prom queen. Kathryn Savage, Roseanne Pereira, Susan Pagani, and Allison Wyss of the Minneapolis Writing Coven, and Virginia Borges, Ron MacLean, and William Moore of Story Lab— two of my artistic homes, and writers who deserve much credit for the better parts of this book. My family, my found family, and my queer family, custodians of my heart. Thank you to my parents for teaching me to read, and to my brother for being an early critical conversationalist; to Steph & Jess Gauchel, for essential ballasting and ongoing mutual admiration; to the Gotterjees—Erik, Ayesha, and Tara—for love and joy and future commune living; to my Moby Dicks, for making our Wednesday nights a new kind of home; to Jamison and Lexi and Maxie for being family; to Wen and Jessica, my ride-or-dies. You all knew I could do this long before I believed it, and that made all the difference.

The home we are making within this world is the home I was writing toward.

And to my main squeeze Rye Gentleman, first of his name, unparalleled French tutor, critical thinker, world imaginer, dogged cheerleader, tireless chair-pusher-in-er, skilled gaycationer, weird-life-co-maker, and best group project partner ever. Large mammals in footwear. If you know, you know.

ERIN KATE RYAN's fiction has been published in *VQR, Glimmer Train, The Normal School,* and elsewhere. She is a James Jones First Novel Fellow and a McKnight Artist Fellow. She holds an MFA in fiction from the Bennington Writing Seminars, where she was an Alumni Fiction Fellow. She lives in the Hudson Valley with her partner and found family.